A TONY FLANER MYSTERY

THE FINGER TRAP

First paperback edition: November 2015

For information on subsidiary rights, please contact the publisher at rights@jollyfishpress.com. For information, write the publisher at Jolly Fish Press, PO Box 1773, Provo, UT 84603-1773, or visit the publisher's website at www.jollyfishpress.com.

Printed in the United States of America

THIS TITLE IS ALSO AVAILABLE AS AN EBOOK.

Library of Congress Cataloging-in-Publication Data

Worthen, Johnny, 1966- The finger trap / Johnny Worthen. -- First paperback edition.
    pages ; cm. -- (A Tony Flaner mystery)
  ISBN 978-1-63163-038-5 (softcover : acid-free paper)
1. Murder--Investigation--Fiction. I. Title.
PS3623.O778F56 2015
813'.6--dc23
                                                    2015022154

10 9 8 7 6 5 4 3 2 1

For animus

ALSO BY JOHNNY WORTHEN

Eleanor

Celeste

A TONY FLANER MYSTERY

THE FINGER TRAP

JOHNNY WORTHEN

JOLLY
FISH
PRESS
Provo, Utah

Flâneur | flä'n'r, - 'nœr | (also flaneur), ORIGIN French, from flâner 'saunter, lounge.'
Noun—an idler or lounger.

CHAPTER ONE

I sat down beside her on the little bed. I stole a glance at her shapely thighs and stroked her hair over her ear, preparing to plant the tenderest of kisses there.

She was cold. Low body fat had its drawbacks, I thought. I reached to pull the bedspread over her and brushed against her neck. It was cold. I put my hand on her thigh. It was cold too.

I rolled her over. She flopped like a stringless marionette. Half her face was pale as the nearby lace curtains, the other was a bruised plum.

I caught my breath like I'd stepped in an ice bath. I told myself not to jump to conclusions. Don't jump. Don't conclude. You're jumpy Tony, I said to myself. I often call myself Tony when I talk to myself. It's my name, so it works out.

I took a deep breath and returned to the room from my scattered brain.

Her eyes were open, her mouth agape. I touched her neck feeling for a pulse like I'd seen in the movies, but didn't know how or where to do it. I grabbed her wrist and felt nothing but more deathly chill. Finally, I pushed my aching head against her chest and listened. Hearing nothing, I pulled up her sweatshirt and saw a pink bra over her bruised body. I pushed my ear against her ribcage and listened for a long time—a long, dark time. She was still and lifeless and the cold crept out of her body and into my cheek.

The throbbing in my skull beat fast and sharp, hangover and heart-stopping stress, but with each beat came a healthy dose of adrenaline, which sobered me up fast. I sat on the floor collecting my wits, driving them into order from the nooks and corners of my mind where they'd gone to hide.

"Oh no. No. No no no no. This is trouble," I murmured. I often say the most obvious things in such low tones. "Yeah. Trouble."

In my underwear, on the floor of a dead girl's apartment, I traced this moment back to a group of Kubrickian widescreen Technicolor monkeys throwing bones at a black monolith. It was an inspiring and thought-provoking image but did little to help place me in my current situation. I fast-forwarded to a more recent moment, one I'd actually been a part of, one that hadn't won an Oscar. One that could serve as a starting point of my current misfortune. It had to do with marine life and luggage. Doesn't it always?

CHAPTER TWO

S he looked like a fish.

"Thirty dollars is too much," she said.

I said, "I agree."

People don't usually look like fish. It takes a certain kind of physiognomy to pull it off. Very unique. In Mrs. Hall's case, she needed to have parents with recessive face-pinching genes, a touch of jaundice, collagen-engorged lips caked in burgundy lipstick, wild, enraged eyes—which my company, Fly Away, could take credit for—and a hair dresser with a sense of humor to perfectly flare the dyed blond hair bob to mimic fins. Plant that handsome head over a seafoam business suit and you'll find few wage slaves willing to take her seriously.

"But I have six bags," she said, trying to impress me with her math skills.

In fact, she had eight bags.

"That's why the extra charge is one hundred ninety-five dollars," I said, dazzling her with my math.

She stared at me, made to make a sound, but only opened and closed her mouth in sync to some unseen current. She clutched a purse the size of U-Haul trailer, occupied by a bug-eyed, panting mascot rat-dog surely burdened with some name like "Fluffy," "Little Darling," or "Kill Me Please." It shook and lunged at me from its depths. She also had the obligatory carry-on makeup case, which I knew had more industrial strength chemicals than a shoe bomb. I'd let the folks at security deal with those.

"But shouldn't it be one hundred-sixty dollars?" she said. It was a regular algebra quiz today.

"There're tax and fees associated with the transaction," I said, glancing at the line behind her. It snaked around crotch-high chrome pillars between nylon strap lanes, like the queue to the Matterhorn at Disneyland. Wait time from this point, forty-five minutes and growing. Pregnant women and people with a heart condition are advised to step away.

"This is outrageous," she said.

"Yes, I agree," I said, but Mrs. Hall thought I was patronizing her. I was, but not as much as she thought. I really thought the bag fee was a cheap move by Corporate, a bad idea stolen from a bigger bad airline that could afford to lose customers because bankruptcies and bailouts were part of their business plan. When the last Mrs. Hall refused to bend over and pay the ticket counter ransom, their shares would soar like the silver pencils in their commercials. And so, by the schoolyard business rules of follow-the-leader, dodgeball, and kick the can, bad service had become standard industry practice, naturally adopted by forward-thinking Fly Away Airlines—"Fly away with Fly Away." I didn't have to like the policy to get paid to dole it out. And, as far as I'd found, I didn't even have to keep my dislike of it to myself.

"Tony," she read my name from my badge, squinting down her nose in the antique gesture of condescension and nearsightedness oft abandoned today in favor of outright rudeness and hostility. Oh, the good ol' days.

"I'm a frequent flyer—over a hundred thousand miles—this is ridiculous."

I searched the blue computer monitor recessed in my desk. That thing had to be older than me. Did they even make monochrome displays anymore?

"I don't show any miles with Fly Away, Mrs. Hall," I said.

She stared at me with dull aquatic eyes, her lower lip quivering to either frame another objection or strain krill. I knew what she was going to say, and if the denizens of the line hadn't been looking around for the Angry Mob Outfitters kiosk, I would have let her bring the conversation around herself. As it was, I knew that a third of the line would miss their flight just because that's how things didn't work around here. If I really tried, and got lucky with the complaints, I might be able to get that down to a fourth.

"Mrs. Hall," I said. "If you'd read your mail, watched TV, or left your aquarium for more than an hour in the last year, you'd know that Escape Travel went belly-up like a dynamited trout. Your miles were with them. That company was bought out by Fly Away during bankruptcy. I'm afraid your miles didn't transfer, but your credit card number did. Your options are to either check your bags with me, leave them, or try your luck at the UPS kiosk in terminal four. They're cheaper but it could take a couple of days to get your bags. Also, that tribble there in your bag will need special treatment." I spoke softly in caring tones and hoped the speech didn't sound too rehearsed, too familiar. I punctuated it with my warmest, most understanding, most sympathetic face I'd perfected in my latest acting class.

"Fuck you," she said.

She produced a checkbook from beneath the rat and scribbled out the payment. She was so angry, she shook. Her hair flares bobbed and twitched in station-keeping oscillations. Her big, blank eyes stared death into the paper and her mouth moved in its soothing rhythm as she silently mouthed each word she wrote. She slapped the check on the counter and then put away her checkbook before I could ask for a check-guarantee card. But I did anyway.

"Are you serious?"

"Not usually," I said, but she wasn't listening. She could feel the pitchforks and torches massing behind her. After another minute of seething silence, I wished her a good flight and watched her swim away into the flow of humanity along the concourse.

I'd worked for Fly Away for six months. I applied for a job with Escape Travel, was interviewed during its bankruptcy and hired by

Fly Away. My first day, they fingerprinted me, gave me an eighty-page manual on company policy and a sky-blue tie, and fitted me for a yellow sports coat. I never read the manual, I spilled curry on the tie three days in, but the sports coat was magic and I treasured it. It got me past security with a wave, allowed me access to the employee cafeteria and bar (a wonderful throwback to the Dean Martin days of travel), and couldn't be stained by tar or wrinkled with an iron. I'd had it dry-cleaned once and they'd starched it. For a week I felt like the tin man while I reworked the joints, calling for an oil can out of the corner of my mouth every hour or so, much to the irritation of my coworkers. Now when I need it cleaned, I just throw it in with my socks and wash it at home. I once tried to translate the Chinese label to divine what type of polycarbonate super plastic my jacket was forged from, but gave up after figuring the first three characters meant "fondling frogs to much joy." I suspect my translation was faulty.

I sympathize with modern travelers. People like me vex them, frustrate them, and humiliate them. We search them, screen them, rob them, and then, if they didn't complain, we'll identify them as suspicious and bring out the guys with the big fingers and blue rubber gloves just to see how far we can take it. There is a good reason weapons aren't allowed in airports; any sane person would use them after going through the post-9/11 hell of American air travel.

Mrs. Hall reminded me that I was coming up on my seven months. Seven months is the average time I stay at a job. Nancy, my wife, calculated it after five years of marriage. She went through my pay stubs and laid out a spreadsheet. She even had graphs, income variances, and some other statistical jargon I could only nod at. She was right. I didn't know it was seven months, but I knew my tolerances and suspected I displayed some biannual biorhythmic need for change. Seven months sounded good. I like seven. Most people like seven. It's the most common lucky number; the roulette number never left bare; the number of chakras, dwarves, and sins. And besides, it's prime. Wonderful. It measured me and my ability to tolerate what once I wanted.

I've had lots of jobs. Seldom has money been the reason for taking a job or leaving it. I just get disinterested in what I'm doing and build up a new interest somewhere else. I leap from job to job as my moods take me, fondling frogs to much joy. Before manning the complaint desk/ticketing counter at Fly Away, I carved headstones with a sandblaster. Before that, I drove deliveries for a consortium of businesses too small to warrant their own truck. Before that, I learned all I could about coffee and was a barista at a drive-through kiosk on Highland Drive. Each job was fun for a while. The barista was about four months. The headstone carver was about five. I drove for over a year though. I liked the time alone in the truck. I got through a huge backlog of books by listening to them while I drove. All in all, according to Nancy, I'd averaged seven months a job, while my marriage to her is fourteen years four months exactly, tomorrow. And scheduled for divorce.

I took the Fly Away job for a purpose: I wanted travel perks. Faced with my pending life-changing event, I figured a little trip would be just the thing when it happened. So, planning ahead—a rare and untried behavior in my life—I applied to every airline I could and, for my sins, I made it here.

"Hey, Tony, you ready for a break?" Mittens was speaking to me. He was a strong, short, stocky man of unplaceable origin. He could have been Cajun or a tanned Irishman, a Cherokee or an Italian, depending on the light and the phase of the moon. He was the baggage swinger. He rose through the ranks of baggage handlers to be a "swinger," which meant he got to stay up in the terminal where it was warm and deal with bags there, but he kept the nickname he earned on the frozen tarmacs. He liked me because he knew me from the time he was run over by a conveyer belt truck and was laid up in Western Peaks Hospital where I was stretching my seven months into nine as an orderly/CNA. Mostly I scrubbed up vomit.

"Look at this line, Mittens," I said. "I can't." The line was hellishly long with sad, suffering commuters.

"Rhonda's got them covered," Mittens said. "You've been on your feet since you got here."

"After this rush," I said. I felt for the poor slobs out there. Before working for Fly Away, I had once flown on Escape Travel and the lines were the same. Their blazers had been green, though.

I tried to explain to a family of six that there were no assigned seats on the plane. Since they'd be lucky to make the flight as it was, chances were they would not be sitting together.

"You can ask when you get on the plane. Nice people are not unheard of, even here. Look for the halos. Someone might change seats for you."

Crestfallen, the father wracked his mind and searched the counter for something to say. He was close to finding something when he was pushed aside.

"What am I supposed to do with Rags?" The fish had forced her way back to me. I looked at the family and pointed to my watch indicating that they better get moving.

"What rag are you on about?" I said.

She plucked the rat-dog out of her purse and thrust it in my face. A pink tongue darted for my eyes with an inbred urgency that went beyond desperation. It lunged and squirmed and twisted to get closer. That dog had to lick me or it would explode. I cringed, bracing myself against incoming Pomeranian shrapnel.

"They won't let me take my dog past security," she said.

"That's because they're not going to let you bring it on the plane either," I said.

"But other people have dogs." The angry crowd had gone silent, all eyes on us.

"Show me a dog," I said.

She pointed down the concourse. The whole line turned to look. They saw about a thousand people rushing along the white tiled hall but no dog.

"Those are people," I said.

"There was one. I saw it."

"Could have been a service animal, Seeing Eye dog, or folks traveling by charter. If not, security will send the phantom dog and its mythical owner back the way they came."

"Why didn't you tell me they wouldn't let me bring my dog?" she said.

"He did!" said a chorus of people behind her.

She ignored them. "What am I supposed to do now?"

"Fuck me," I said. The crowd laughed. Callbacks are always so satisfying. She burned beet red. For an instant, I thought of telling her to go to the back of the line and I'd deal with her later; she needed to be taught some manners. But I didn't. I'm not a total jerk, just mostly, as my friends tell me.

"Mittens?" I called. "Can you take care of Mrs. Fish's animal?"

"Mrs. Hall," she corrected.

"Come over here, Ma'am," he said.

"Will I miss my flight?" she asked.

I was about to say yes, when the flight board shuddered. "Delayed" flashed next to her flight and the one under it and the one under that. In a moment, every flight that could be listed on the board was "delayed."

"Looks like you'll make it," I said.

Later, I learned that one of the Tetris crew had driven a baggage cart into a United Airlines landing gear. The delay was only four hours, ten times longer than it should have taken, but a respectable time for these days. And so, for once, I got through my entire line confident that no one would miss their flight because of me. Then, of course, all morning flights were ultimately cancelled.

After lunch, I saw the same tired, angry faces as I had that morning, and I knew it was time to go. I should have walked out then and there, but I was determined to hold on a while longer. I had those travel plans coming up, and though I felt the familiar push to leave, there was no accompanying pull. I hadn't fallen into another interest yet. That was strange.

"You going to be at the Cellar this week?" Mittens asked, kicking a duffel onto the conveyer belt. The Cellar was the Comedy Cellar, a dive bar entertainment establishment for the hip and unshaved.

"Probably Friday," I said. "Wayne Matticks is performing. I'd like to see him."

"But not Wednesday?" Wednesday was open mic night. I sometimes did a set then.

"Nah. I got family stuff."

"Oh, yeah, I keep forgetting you're married," he said.

I almost corrected him, but I didn't feel like going into it. I could see the afternoon lines thickening, and I braced myself to see all the nice people from the morning again.

"God, not her again," I said as she swam up to my counter.

"Hello, Mrs. Hall," I said. "Good to see you again." Big smile.

"I hope you die," she said.

CHAPTER THREE

I was in my den trying to open a MasterLock padlock I'd lost the combination to. There was a video on the Internet that showed how. I'm a sucker for stuff like that. If it worked, I'd go around town looking for padlocks just to open them. I once found an article that showed how to cheat a cigarette machine into dropping a pack of cigarettes with a free book of matches. I searched everywhere for a machine to test it. Finally, I had to leave the state to find one. It was in a strip club outside of Elko, Nevada. I tried it and it worked. Of course, it didn't dispense cigarettes anymore. They made that illegal shortly after the article was written, but I appreciated the free condom nonetheless.

I heard Nancy come in. The sound of the garage door closing carried through our Oaks Estate home along the mauve walls, over the bazillion thread-count beige carpet, past the mahogany banisters that led to the bedrooms upstairs and into my converted nanny's apartment/ hobby den. The sound cut off when she closed the door. I heard her keys jingle as she hung them on the tole-painted key rack in the hall. I imagined her checking herself in the mirror there, fixing a smudge of lipstick, poking at her hair, lifting up her breasts, and turning to examine her backside. It was a routine whenever she was alone and in front of a mirror. She liked to keep herself "in order." It was her thing. It defined her.

Nancy had bought this house two years earlier. If I had a seven-month average for jobs, she had a three-year schedule for homes. She was a realtor and a good one. Even when things went sour in the industry, she still kept up her numbers. She was very good at what she did. It was part of the plan. She had a plan.

"Tony, I'm home," she called.

"Hi, honey," I replied. I heard her go upstairs to change. I had half an hour before Nancy's plan.

I met Nancy at a college party. I was in my fifth year of a four-year undergraduate degree taking unrelated classes year round and not planning on ever graduating. Nancy was in her third year of psychology with a pre-business law minor. We fell in love because love is good and then, after she graduated the next year, we had a baby—Randy. A year after that, I graduated. I didn't want to. Nancy made me.

I opened the lock. Using the method on the Internet, I was able to figure out the combination in half an hour. If I could cut that down by a third, I'd be able to steal bikes, break into storage sheds, and rule the world. I watched the video again to memorize the procedure.

You never know when knowledge like that will come in handy. For instance, I know that you can remove bubblegum from a drunk friend's hair with dry ice and a hammer. That's how I met Nancy. She was impressed. It was her friend. And my gum.

Randy, our son, turned fourteen exactly four months ago. According to Nancy's psychology reading, he should be able to handle his parents' divorce now without undue mental scarring. Fourteen was what the book said, but Nancy thought we should add a couple of months so he wouldn't associate his birthday with his parents' divorce. I forgot how we exactly got to four months, but that's what it became. Nancy took timing issues very seriously and often very literally. Today was the day we were going to announce to Randy that we were getting a divorce.

I loved Nancy and she loved me. We were just too different to live together, and Nancy's plan did not include spending her life with a roommate. She wanted a husband with similar interests and all that. I couldn't blame her. I didn't blame her.

She decided we would divorce six years ago. We were in our second home then, just after our third move. Randy was eight. There was no screaming. No one threw anything, though I did pace a lot and throw my hands around as if trying to mold a different relationship out of the air. I can get pretty animated when I'm upset, like I'm speaking in stereo between English and body language. If you speak either, you should be able to understand me.

We are so different, Nancy and I, but we understand each other and even like each other. She is more organized than I am, able to curb her emotions better. When there was yelling in our relationship, I did it. I'm not as emotionally developed as she, I suppose. I never had a plan. I still don't. Any plans I had for my life or my relationships did not extend beyond that night.

So, for all intents and purposes, we divorced that night six years ago when Randy was eight and asleep in his room in the blue-doored Rambler on Seneca. Nancy declared that, for the good of Randy, we had to maintain a facade of a happy family and loving couple. She'd consulted her books and found the magic age to avoid damaging Randy's childhood. And so, with a mark on a calendar and the setting of a stopwatch, we shifted from man and wife to roommates.

In our next house we had separate bedrooms. We told Randy that it was because I snored. Nancy snores, too, but I took the hit. Randy could think of me as a chronic snorer if that's what it takes to keep his childhood unscarred. I'd set him straight about that when he was older. I considered asking Nancy when would be a good age to reveal the snoring deceit to him. Deathbed confession?

It was okay if we had others on the side. We figured out the rules for it, or rather, Nancy set them. First, it had to be totally out of the home. Second, it could be with no one we both knew. Never ever. Third, it could in no way affect the nuclear family facade we maintained. In short, it had to be discreet. Fourth, and this was my rule, the other person must in no way ever even suspect anything is going on. I'm prone to jealousy. Intellectually, I know it's all good, but emotionally, I turn into quivering jelly whenever I think of Nancy with anyone else.

Surprisingly, things worked out pretty well. If Nancy played around,

I didn't know about it. And I had looked. I know I shouldn't have. It was in bad taste and against the rules—rule number five, to be precise: "don't go looking for it." But I did anyway. I suspected Nancy knew I would.

I had a one night stand a few years ago with a black girl because I always wanted to sleep with a black girl, but that was it. I've been content with porno and the "friends with benefits" encounters Nancy and I still have occasionally. I know I kidded myself into thinking that Nancy had been equally satisfied, but who knows? She might have been. She stuck to plans and avoided complication whenever possible. She'd make allowances but wouldn't go out trying to mess things up. Her plan was to have a nuclear family until Randy was fourteen-and-a-third years old and then we'd go our separate ways.

It'd been a good six years. We hardly ever fought after the de-facto separation. Before, we used to fight all the time. Nancy really hated my flippant attitude toward life, serial jobs, and ever-changing interests. Every time we moved, we had to get a bigger place just to house all the crap I'd collected for my latest hobbies. I once had an entire room dedicated to a model railroad depicting Mt. Shasta honeycombed with train tunnels and anachronistic buildings and people. It took me about seven months to finish. It broke in a move and got tossed. I beat against Nancy's structured habits and uncluttered plans. It never got us anywhere, all that fighting. We were struggling against the very definitions that made us who we were. In this case opposites attracted, made a baby, and lived out a plan to separate after fourteen years.

In the years since the plan went online, Nancy became a double millionaire with her successful real estate work, and I skipped from job to job, hobby to hobby, sometimes making above minimum wage. We found we could tolerate each other better once the relationship was on a countdown, and she was as generous to me financially as if I'd been her husband, which, actually, I still was. At least until she came downstairs.

We hadn't spoken about that day for over a year, maybe two, but I knew it was here, and if I knew what day it was, you can bet your spleen with bile sauce that she did, too. Randy was up in his room on his computer, and I was home for the night. It was coming. A pair of pinking shears angling toward the thread holding the sword above me.

It's not that I hadn't had time to think about the day. I've had thousands of days to think about it. I just hadn't. Unless a problem stares me right in the face with poison-dripping fangs, reaching for my unprotected throat, laughing hysterically at my impending doom, I don't usually give it much worry. Most things people worry about never happen. They just sort themselves out. Of course, in the rare event that the thing actually happens, folks who've spent time thinking about it are actually prepared for it. That's not me.

Shit, I was in for it and I knew it.

At least I could open a padlock. That was something.

"Hey, Tony, got a minute?" She stood in the doorway behind me. My first impulse was to say "No." My second was to dive under my desk and hide there. I went with the second.

"Tony," she said. I couldn't see her. She was a presence in the door-way, a shadow glimpsed out of the corner of my eye before I snapped them shut. A menace, a monster, a doom.

"Dammit, Tony, we have to talk."

"I know. Why do you think I'm hiding under my desk?"

"Do you know what day it is?"

"I refer you to my previous answer."

The shadow moved closer, cast its shade across the desk, blocking the light into my little cave. A cold, clammy claw of doom touched me on my shoulder. "Sweetie, come out from under the desk," she said.

Slowly, I backed out of my space, clutching my open padlock, the open hasp flopping around limply.

"Before we begin. I just want to say one thing," I said.

"Yes?"

"I get the house."

"No."

"Okay."

I just wanted to say something. I really didn't expect the house. I didn't really want it. I just wanted to see if I could alter her plans.

She sat down on a box of boomerangs I'd made. I was into boomerangs a couple of summers ago. I got pretty good with them. I could make them and throw them, and when they came back, I could sometimes catch them.

Nancy looked at me hard. Nancy had straight brown hair that went to her shoulders. There was a red tint to it she'd paid a hairdresser for. It accentuated her pale skin and bright eyes. She had light brown, hazelnut eyes, with plenty of squiggles in which to lose yourself. She'd kept herself in great shape these many years of marriage, unlike me. After Randy was born, she worked off the baby fat with the determination and drive behind all her plans. She kept it off and stayed trim. She ate healthy and saw to it that we did, too. When I got into jogging once, she joined me on my first and only marathon. I beat her, but only because she kept waiting for me to catch up, and then I sprinted past her the last six feet to the finish line. Cheap, I know, but it was my idea, the marathon.

"Tony. Do we need to see a counselor about this?"

She meant a divorce counselor. She'd brought it up before. What kind of world has divorce counselors? I knew about marriage counselors, but before our arrangement, I never knew there were actual "divorce counselors"—social workers specializing in the clean breakup of a family; counselors to ease the passing of a marriage. Damn disposable society.

"Are you okay?" she asked.

I sat on the desk and faced her.

"I love you, Nancy," I said.

"And I love you," she said.

"Then why are we doing this?"

"You know why." She said it with a certainty that would have hurt me if it hadn't been dead on. I was afraid of the change because I didn't see my next step. For a guy who flitted from one thing to another, I was terrified of this change because I didn't have a place to go, just one to leave. Who was I to be now?

"Yeah, I do," I said.

She smiled.

"Let's go tell Randy," I said.

"Not so fast there. Let's talk a bit; plan out how all this is going to happen."

"Okay, talk."

She did. Naturally, she had a plan. It was a good plan. We'd announce our love for each other to Randy, but explain that it was time to separate. We'd stress it was in no way his fault while keeping from him that it was, in fact, his fault that we'd stayed together this long. She said something about comparing our divorce to the changing seasons, rolling tides, freak epidemic or something, but to be honest, I was kind of in shock then and wasn't listening as well as I should have. Marriage was one of the few things in my life that hadn't grown old after seven months or even seven years. I liked the safe, comfortable life it gave me. A stable home is a great nest to perch from, to explore from, and to return to. Considering my ever-changing interests, it was strange for me to mourn reordering of my home life, but there it was. Push; no pull.

"I've found you a lovely place in town. A neighborhood in Sugarhouse. I picked it up for a steal. It'll appreciate like mad. You could sell it for twice what I paid just by putting in a lawn and replacing the windows. It's wonderful. You'll love it."

"You bought me a house?"

"No, you did. I'll debit the money out of the settlement figures."

Some reptilian node stirred in my skull, my manhood challenged by Nancy's accounting. It stirred, blinked at the light, and retreated.

"Hot tub?" I said.

"Of course."

"Space for my stuff?"

"If you put in shelves," she added. "And maybe a shed. Storage units are cheap."

"What about you?"

"I'll stay here with Randy. It'll be the least disruptive for him."

I nodded. I wouldn't fight for custody. I didn't need a divorce counselor to tell me that I am unreliable. That went without saying.

"So, Randy's staying with you because I'm unreliable?" I said anyway.

"Yes."

"Big house for just the two of you," I said, just to say something. I've always found awkward silences awkward.

She didn't respond. Her eyes fell on my framed scuba license and third-place dominos trophy. There was an awkward silence.

"Ah, fuck," I said. "Who?"

"Not now, Tony."

I looked at her.

"No one you know," she said.

I kept looking.

"Doctor Mudge," she said. "My yoga instructor."

"I thought his name was "Leafcaller?"''

"That's his spiritual name. His real name is Hank Mudge."

"I can see why he goes by Leafcaller."

"He's very nice. You'll meet him soon."

Again the reptile in me spoke, told me to ball up my fists and pound on something. Visions of chipping flint into knives and sticks into spears burst like meteors into my mind. It took longer to subdue the lizard brain this time. All I could manage was a nod and forced grin. I felt scales forming on my back and fought an urge to taste the air with my flickering tongue.

"You can't be jealous," she said. "We haven't made love in over a year."

"Yes, I can, and it hasn't been that long."

"Yes, it's been thirteen and a half months," she said. She must have written it down, had a great memory, or was bluffing.

I was about to call her bluff when she said, "The night after mother left. Remember the pillow?"

I'd torn a pillow in our snuggling struggles. She wanted to stop and clean it up but I wouldn't let her. We made love in feathers for what seemed like hours, but was probably more like four minutes if we're to believe *Cosmopolitan*. We were covered in down. It was in our hair, our noses, and possibly other places. It clogged the drain when we showered. Another four minutes there. I couldn't remember a time after that. I guess she was right. Thirteen months. Damn.

"It hurts my feelings," I said.

"It's okay, sweetie. It'll all be fine. Better than fine."

"What about money?" I had to ask.

"Half, as calculated by Moneybank." Moneybank was our accountant. Is that a great name for an accountant or what?

"What about the equity here?"

"I get that," she said. "For Randy."

"Oh," I said. "Is there anything for me to read or sign?"

"Yes, but that can wait. Are you ready to talk to our son?"

"Sure," I said.

"I think I should do the talking with Randy," she said. "I have a degree in this kind of thing, you know. I'll break the ice, ask how he's doing, learn something of his day and his life, talk about goals, short- and long-term, and then carefully ease into the question of happiness and the pursuit thereof."

She explained her plan in greater detail. She had the whole thing mapped out and scripted. All I had to do was nod and be supportive, display only positive emotions. At least I think that's all I was supposed to do. My mind was distracted, wondering if yoga makes one tough or only limber.

Finally, she took me by the hand and led me out of the room. She slid her arm around my waist, and I did the same. I felt her warm midsection through her blouse and had the urge to slide my hand southward, but refrained.

We got to the stairs and, hand in hand, walked up to Randy's room.

Music was thumping through the door. I knocked. No answer. I knocked again. Nothing. I tried the knob. It was locked. I knocked louder. Nothing. I shouted, "Randy." He must not have heard me. I shook the doorknob and pounded on the door while calling. The three together seemed to do the trick and the music faded.

"Hello?" he said.

"Hey, Randy, your mother and I want to talk to you. Can you open the door?" I said.

There was a squeak of a chair, and what I imagined to be a crashing tower of magazines sliding from some mid-level height into a chain reaction of toppling CDs, pens, lozenge boxes, and maybe a live chicken. A little while later the door opened, and my son, Randy Flaner, stood in the doorway.

My boy would be taller than me. His feet were already a size bigger than mine and still growing. He'd be heavy if the mass wasn't being stretched like adolescent Silly Putty by his growth spurts. He had his mother's mild nose and fine fingers, but my dark brown eyes, heavy brows, and upturned lips that made it look like he was always smiling.

Randy waited for someone to speak. I thought I heard someone call his name over a tinny computer speaker. I could see over his shoulder and around his body that the room was a mess. I saw several cardboard boxes stacked in the corner. Video game magazines were spread out in a clean line where they'd spilled from the desk. No chicken. Probably hiding.

"Can we come in?" Nancy asked. Randy moved aside.

On the computer screen, brightly-colored characters trotted along an idyllic medieval-forest path, red-eyed cartoon wolves stared at the group from behind pixelated trees.

"What are you playing?" asked Nancy to open the conversation.

"Knightly Rampage," he said.

Randy loved video games. Nancy once tried to make a plan to limit his gaming, but I reminded her that we'd spent as much time in front of a TV growing up and we did all right. Besides, it was actually very social with live connections to his friends. I won that discussion. It wasn't a fight—fighting was so "pre-arrangement."

"Hey, Randy," came a voice from the computer. "Let's blow this shit and play Colonies. Randy?"

I saw Nancy swallow a rebuke about the cussing and then focus on Randy. He stood impatiently by his computer chair. We stood awkwardly to the side. No one sat down. There was another awkward silence.

Nancy started to speak, then halted, put on a warm salesman smile and tried again. Her mouth opened and then closed. Randy looked from his mother to me.

"Your mom and I are splitting up," I said.

"'Bout time," said Randy.

Nancy's mouth opened again and didn't close. It just hung open for a while.

"Why do you say that?" I asked.

"Because you two have been living together like freakin' roommates for years. It can't be an enriching relationship."

Drool pooled in Nancy's lower jaw.

"Yep, that's about the size of it," I said. "I'll be moving to a house in town. You stay here with Mom until you finish school, then we'll see what's what."

"Okay."

"Okay," I said. "Is your homework done?"

He gave me a look that clearly said it was a stupid question. Randy was an Honor Student, hadn't seen a "B" since third grade. He was self-motivated, self-aware, and more mature than most people I've worked with.

"Well, okay then," I said.

"Yeah, okay," said Randy twitching his head to his computer. "Game on."

I took Nancy by the hand and led her out. In the hall, I carefully ran my fingers through her hair, tickled her ear, and traced the outline of her jaw. When I got to her chin, I gently pushed it closed.

CHAPTER FOUR

"So that's when I gave up drinking." Big laugh. "For a while."
Bigger laugh.

Wayne Matticks was funny; his timing was good, his material practiced and polished. A good act all around. I'd heard his name mentioned by other comics at the Comedy Cellar, mostly those who travelled the circuit. The circuit being a series of paying dives, bars, and comedy clubs stretching from your hometown to your dreams. Some had tried it. Few ever saw the end of it.

"Did you hear that? He stole that joke." It was Standard Flox speaking from across the booth. Standard was his real name, but he liked to be called Stan, so I called him Standard. He tried the circuit once, but gave it up so he could eat. Now he just did the occasional open mic at the Comedy Cellar like me. His shtick was relationships and eating dog-food tacos, but his real passion was plagiarism. A night never went by without him going batshit over something he swore was stolen from someone else. God help you if you touched upon a subject in your set he'd once seen in Asswipe, Tennessee. God help you.

"Chill out, Stan," said Critter. "It's a trope. Everyone does drunk jokes."

"I heard the exact same bit in Albuquerque," insisted Standard.

"Again about Albuquerque. You played six shows there and heard every joke there was. Well, gooooolllly," teased Critter, shaking his head to emphasize his disgust. His nylon fangs swayed morosely.

Standard stared daggers at Critter, his body tensing for a fight, but Critter stared right back and didn't blink. He couldn't. Critter was a puppet. He was Garret Corta's prop. Garret had been the opener and hadn't put Critter away when he came into the audience. Unless he was specifically ordered by Barry, the owner, to put it away, the puppet usually accompanied Garret. At first I thought it was a cheap ploy to keep his act going, some attempt to steal energy from the next performer with his shag-carpet, saber-toothed hand puppet, but after he kept doing it, I began to suspect I was witnessing true psychological dysfunction and came to peace with it.

Garret wasn't funny, but Critter was. Their personalities were so different that it was impossible to remember that they were the same person. I'd given up trying, and based on the ire in Standard's expression, he didn't associate the carpet-baiting him with the man sitting beside him sipping a beer.

"Can you guys shut the fuck up and listen? You might learn something about how professionals perform," said Dara Sutter, a.k.a. Dare-a-Slutter. She was a cute, petite, short-haired dirty blonde. In our comedian group, she was the youngest of us, just out of college, and by far the shortest. She claimed to be five foot four but exaggerated at least an inch, if not two. She was a Sarah Silverman kind of comedian, a foul-mouthed girl who made men, women, animals, and puppets uncomfortable with the sailor rap pouring out of her virginal visage. She looked like the girl next door, but after the third joke, when her show really started, the blue language came out hard and escalated like crap from a pressured sewer main, growing ever deeper, ever more disturbing. They say moans are as good as laughs, but I think Dara could induce vomiting if left to her own devices.

Matticks was killing.

"He stole all his material. I saw Carlin do that."

"You never saw Carlin," said Critter. Garret wasn't paying attention.

"On a record, stupid," said Standard. "He made, like, fifty of them."

"Well, if you saw it on a record," said Critter. "It must be true."

"Will you shut your stinking pie holes so I can hear," said Dara. Even then the words didn't match her floral-patterned, high-neck dress and girlish curls. It was unsettling. Mission accomplished.

We were on our third pitcher of beer. Critter was the only one nursing his. The rest of us, I was sure, were trying to drown our envy at being in the same room as a comedian who actually made a living at it.

I tried it once. I stuck with it for almost a year. I thought up a bit, then a set, and then begged for stage time all over the state. I tried every open mic until I thought I was ready to be paid for it. Barry gave me a show with door percentage that didn't pay for my drinks. Later he turned me on to a guy he knew in Pocatello, Idaho, who actually had posters made for me. I ran up there for a couple of weeks. I made enough to pay for my hotel and food, but that was about it. I got another offer for Boise, but I balked. They wanted an hour show and I had thirty-five minutes, forty if I stuttered, twenty if I couldn't swear, which turns out to be a lot of places in Utah and Idaho. Go figure.

I came home to work on the other twenty-five minutes and got pulled away into acting. I did a local commercial for a convenience store and followed the acting bug for a couple of months. By the time I came back to the Cellar, I'd gotten over the comedian career thing and just enjoyed the occasional set. I still kid myself that I'll be discovered someday, but if I'm not, at least I'm surrounded by people like me; people struggling with debilitating mental illnesses in non-violent ways. I had a T-shirt made that said as much.

"So just like that, she dumped you? Damn," said Perry White-house. Perry had been quietly watching the show and listening to us. Unlike the rest of us, Perry had actually seen Wayne perform before. Of all us denizens of the Comedy Cellar dungeon, Perry was the most talented. If any of us were going to make it big, it would be him. He would either get his break or go totally off the crazy rails. Like the rest of us, he had psychological issues that drove his narcissistic desire to stand up exposed and alone on a stage and try to sway an audience of strangers into loving him. But Perry also had deeper, more traditional personality quirks, which a hundred years ago would have taken him off the circuit and into a tight white coat. I once found him in the parking lot after a show, stone-cold sober, in the middle of a red-faced screaming quarrel with someone called Flint. He was alone. The fight had something to do with olives and was about to get violent. If I'd been Flint, I'd have run. Maybe he did. I don't know. When Perry saw me, he demanded that I side with him about black olives and kale. When I wouldn't commit, he yelled some choice profanities and threw his wristwatch far into the parking lot before getting into his car and driving away. We never spoke of it again.

Critter turned to Perry and nodded in agreement. "Women can be so mean, Tony," the puppet said. "It doesn't surprise me she'd spring a divorce on you just like that."

"No, it was all arranged," I said. "I told you about it. I even did a bit on it, remember?"

Critter hadn't heard me. He turned his big plastic eyes to me in sympathetic sadness.

"No. It's been coming for a while," I said. "No surprise at all."

"You're in denial dude," said Standard. "You were blindsided."

"No, actually, I wasn't," I said. "We'd talked about it before. It was planned."

"Our whole lives are preordained," said Critter. "God knows every grain of sand, every drop in the sea, and yet it surprises us when a hurricane levels a village in India."

I could only stare mutely at the puppet.

"I never thought of you as a spiritual man, Tony," said Standard. "I guess trauma can really bring a person closer to the source."

"No. We planned it. Not God. It was an agreement. It was time."

"To all things there is a season," quoted Critter.

"If you don't shut the fuck up right now, I'm going to call Luke over here to throw your limp, cankerous dicks out onto the street," said Dara, loud enough that people from nearby tables turned to look at us.

Luke was the bouncer. He was usually very nice, but he could throw all our dicks out into the street if he wanted to, cankerous or not. He was a male model, a body builder, and hung like a god. I'd seen him in the bathroom. It was very impressive. Though he never bragged about it, or otherwise showed any unnatural interest in it, his member was a common topic of conversation around the bar. I knew some of his modeling was of the adult variety. I also knew that at that moment, Luke was staring right at our table from the door. Dara had gotten his attention. We shut the fuck up.

The Comedy Cellar was first and foremost a bar. It was open six days a week, had paid acts three nights a week, open mic two, but every day had a happy hour and regulars to fill the tables. I guess I was a regular. So were my friends. We had our favorite table that the other regulars respected, a special place we could carry on a conversation and not bother the performer. Much. It was Dara we were bothering, not Wayne on the stage.

Barry was good to us. We didn't have to pay the cover since we performed now and again, but we had to pay for our drinks, so I guess he wasn't that good. We had fans. Barry gave us our own shows when we had enough new material or someone better cancelled. Critter and Garret had a group of animal rights people who watched the marquee for his name. Dara had a weird, hard-core lesbian biker gang show up whenever her name was up, and I had a mixed group of people who liked me for reasons I couldn't imagine. I do autobiographical comedy, observational and smart-ass bits, sometimes taken verbatim from my day's events. More than my friends, I am myself on stage and some people seemed to like it. People who hear me get the sense that they know me. Most performers face that, but in my case, there's a lot of truth to it. It makes me more approachable than the puppet or Dara Dirtymouth, but just barely. Sometimes a fan approaches me and actually connects. It's rare. But it does happen.

"I saw you last week," she said. "Your Marxism was showing."

I was at the bar. Wayne Matticks had finished his first set and the early crowd had turned over to the evening crowd. They were still filing in, milling about and spending money, to Barry's delight. The stage was bare and the club settled into drinks and fried jalapeño poppers. Light jazz played over the hanging speakers, barely perceptible beneath the hum of conversations, come-ons, and rejections. I waited at the bar for Barry to see me and bring me another pitcher of ice-cold Forget Nancy, when she spoke to me.

I'd seen her before, noticed her laughing at my jokes, which is an easy way to endear oneself to someone trying to make you do just that. She was in her mid-twenties, slender, but with shapely hips. Her hair was auburn brown and shoulder length. She wore it pulled around in a fashion that I hadn't seen before, but seemed classic. She wore a knee-high, sleeveless dress that had echoes of a Depression-era feed sack, but was fitted in a way to accentuate her curving figure. It was light blue with purple zigzag sound waves across the bosom. I like sound waves and purple. And bosoms. She had a red leather purse resting on her right hip and a Barry's best disposable plastic wine glass in her hand with bubbling pink wine. I like pink too.

"Marxism is due for a comeback," I said.

"You go to politics when you don't want to talk about yourself. Am I right?"

"Couldn't I have just wanted to wail against the corporate state? Did they send you to censor me? Are you one of Them?"

"I'm right, aren't I?"

She was.

"I'm Tony," I said.

"I'm Rose. Are you going to answer my question?"

"Nope."

She smiled. "You still working at that airline?"

"For now. I figure it'll last another year."

"No, it won't," she said.

"No. It won't."

"Come meet my friends and drink with us." She gestured across the room, but I didn't look away from her. My mind put events into familiar patterns. A nudge in my brain and a twitch in my jeans made me wonder if Rose wasn't the pull to counter Nancy's push. Like most things in my life, I just went with it.

"Okay, let me drop this off first." I hefted the beer pitcher and splashed some on the floor via my shoe and pant leg.

She followed me back to the booth. Every eye was on Rose. I'm sure they were trying to figure out what the sound wave was saying and not sizing up her breasts. Yeah, that's what they were doing.

I put the pitcher down, and Garret slid over to make room for us.

"Guys, this is Rose," I said. "I'm going to drink with her for a while. You guys suck. Critter, shut your mouth before a spider moves in."

"Hey, Dara," Rose said and winked. Dara shot her a half-smile dripping with disbelief.

I was about to ask what it all meant, when Perry spoke. "There's Matticks," he said, craning his neck to look.

"Hey, Wayne!" He waved over the paid comedian.

"Great set," said Standard. "We're comedians too."

He looked at each of us in turn, lingering his gaze on Critter who finally had to turn away, unable to keep eye contact.

"No, you're not," Matticks said. "You're wannabes, nobodies, and losers. I've already talked to the club owner, Barney. I won't go on stage if any of you idiots go up before me and stink it up again. Save your wit for YouTube and your stupid friends. Stay away from real talent. These people paid money to see me, not you."

There was a moment of shock and silence. Then Standard giggled, testing to see if it was a joke. Matticks's sharp glare shut that down quick. He wheeled around to go.

"Excuse me," I said.

He turned to face me.

"I just want to say that although I found your comedy amusing and your timing excellent, you are, in fact, a complete waste of human cells, a tactless, classless, fucktard nobody, hurrying to be a has-been. May you die soiled and alone after wolves take your penis."

"Screw you," he said.

"Behold, the wit of the talented on display." I made a carnival barker gesture. "Witness the unscripted comeback of a true professional."

He was about to say something, but thought better of it and strolled away.

Critter yelled "Tony Flaner, one; Wayne Matticks, zero, as in owned!"

The table applauded. Matticks held up his middle finger and disappeared backstage.

* * *

Rose's group had two tables close up front. She introduced me to her friends.

There was Tonya. She had screaming bright-red hair. She told me she dyed it with Jell-O.

"What flavor?" I asked.

"Red," she said. That was Tonya.

Melissa was a heavy girl with black hair precisely cut into straight bangs and worn like a helmet. She was crying. Her eyes were bloodshot and her makeup had long since washed away.

"Melissa is why we're here tonight," said Rose into my ear. "She lost her pet today. We're trying to cheer her up."

"Oh, that's too bad. Hit by a car?"

"No, she lost it. It's a chameleon and it got out of its cage."

Melissa stared at her hands and stifled sobs with a wadded-up, neon green Comedy Cellar napkin.

"You're kidding?" I said.

Rose shook her head. "She has a lot of pets, including a cat, so it's more serious than it appears."

"Oh. Okay. I see," I said.

"The cat's blind."

Calvin was a lip-pierced hipster hitting on Tonya. I didn't get much of a story about him beyond his name and that he sold DVDs through vending machines. He reeked of attitude and careful nonchalance. He had a leopard tattoo on his neck, partially concealed by his hair—partially.

Patricia was a bartender and a raging atheist. I was warned not to even speak to her unless I was ready to be converted.

Everyone waved and said they loved my act, except Melissa who just cried. I'd seen them all before, but now I liked them.

I sipped beer and talked to Rose. The noise necessitated intimate conversations. I liked the smell of her hair and I breathed it all night.

"I've got to ask," she said. "Are you still married?"

"For another week or so," I said. "Officially."

"So can you date."

Something stirred between my legs. "Yeah. In fact, sad as it sounds, she wants me to. And you?"

"Unattached right now," she said into my ear and then nipped my earlobe. My underwear shrunk two sizes, and I groaned involuntarily.

"Hey Rose, there's Justin," said Patricia, pointing across the club to the door.

A thin man, also in his mid-twenties, stood next to Luke and squinted into the crowd. He had a lot of hair, which made me a little jealous. It was thick and mussed up, and would probably break a comb. His pale features and narrow glasses made me think "geek," but that was a stereotype, so I dismissed the label out of consideration for my new friends, and the easy knee-jerk shortcut definition such leaps offered. It's an unfair way to judge people. The crowd shifted and I glimpsed his T-shirt. It said, "There's no place like 127.0.0.1." Geek it is, then.

"I'll be right back," Rose said, getting up.

I watched her weave through the crowd and meet the stranger at the door. He glanced sideways at Luke, who saw something suspicious in the glance and brought his attention. That moved the newcomer. He followed Rose to the bar. They talked in each other's ears for a few minutes. He was trying to tell her something, but she kept shaking her head as if not hearing it over the crowd noise. He spoke deliberately then, and I saw her write something on a napkin. She showed it to him. He examined it, nodded, said what I assumed to be curt goodbye, and then left. She disappeared into the restroom, and I felt someone tugging on my sleeve.

"There's no god you know," said Patricia. "Are you Mormon?"

"Nope," I said, smelling the sulfur of an unseen burning fuse.

"What are you?"

"I'm a flighty wanderer whose life is unraveling. I don't know where I'll be living in a week." That stopped her. At least for a minute.

"And now, ladies and gentlemen, turn on your funny bones for Wayne Matticks!"

The house lights dimmed, the stage lights came up, and Wayne, the funny, but now total asshole as far as I was concerned, Matticks walked on.

"Hey, Salt Lake City," he said. "I'm glad I could stop off on my way to saner places." Moderate laugh. The crowd was pretty drunk.

Rose appeared at my side and I stood up to let her get to her chair. Matticks paused, prepared to unleash some anti-heckler/distracter tirade at the stage-side table, but hesitated when he saw me.

"What do you have to do to get a drink in this city," he said, re-turning to script.

The show was the same as the earlier one with minor tweaks, changing his act to better suit the city's temperament. I laughed out of professional courtesyw but secretly imagined a storm of tomatoes and rotten cabbages raining into his smug face. I was polite and didn't heckle once, though the urge was nearly overwhelming.

Sometime during the show, probably around the parrot story, Melissa lost all control and took her sorrowing-self away to the bathroom. When Matticks was gone and the clapping over, her rising sobs announced her return. The entire table—minus me—huddled around the distraught woman and tried to comfort her. There was nothing for it, however. She insisted on going home, and, though I could see her friends would rather drive nails into their foreheads than go with her, they all agreed to help her look for Mr. Spotty, the two-week-old chameleon who'd slipped its cage.

"Hey," said Rose. "I gotta do this."

"I understand," I said, but didn't. The lizard was two weeks old. How attached could someone be to a two-week-old reptile?

Before leaving, Rose produced a fat blue pen from her small red bag and scribbled a number on a flat green napkin. She gave it to me. It said, "Rose," and had a phone number. The "O" in Rose was a heart.

"Call me," she said, and kissed me. On the lips.

Yes, there was definitely a pull there.

CHAPTER FIVE

"You're no help at all," said Nancy from the top of the stairs. She stormed away in disgust at my lack of progress boxing things up in the basement. What really made her mad was not that I was packing slowly, but that I kept unpacking old boxes to see what was in them.

The basement was unfinished—cold concrete floors and spider nests. The only walls enclosed a corner space behind the stairs where the furnace, water heater, and fuse box were housed. They were visible through the lattice frame. I hadn't gotten around to putting up the sheet rock yet. The rest of the basement was a labyrinth of discarded hobbies, collections, and assorted junk I'd never had to part with. There was a moped under a torn quilt without an engine—the moped, not the quilt. I'd intended to get the bike running and give it to Randy, but lost interest when he did. There was a respectable stack of Star Trek action figures under a dense layer of dust. One day they'd be worth serious money as long as I didn't remove them from their original packaging and the mice didn't gnaw the edges.

A suit of Renaissance armor I'd made from plastic sheets stood majestically against a wall of exposed pink insulation. It took three months to piece together. But I'd finished it. It was exquisite and won the office costume contest hands down back when I worked at the bookstore. It wouldn't fit me now. I could sell it on eBay, if I could part with it. But, of course, I couldn't. I couldn't part with anything. Nancy called me a pack rat, and we had many "discussions" over my inability to let go of anything. After our divorce arrangement, she found an elegant solution that fit her plan of social ascension and my penchant for clutter: bigger houses with bigger basements.

Every box, every stack of magazines, every ball, bat, and glove was a landmark on the map of my life I was unwilling to forget. Years could go by and I'd not think of the trip to Hawaii, and then I'd descend into the basement and I'd find dried flowers on a wooden surfer statue and slide into reverie.

Everyone has moments like that. Everyone has an attic full of memories, but my problem is I create new ones at an alarming rate. My vacillating interests produce a crate of detritus with each change. Good, bad, or indifferent, I cling to them all. Up until then, Nancy had given me space to house it, but now I didn't know. I'd been warned there might not be enough storage room in my new house. Nancy mentioned it twice. No, three times.

I had one week to pack, and then movers would carry it all to the new digs. I hadn't even seen it yet, but it was nice; I'd like it. Nancy mentioned that six times. Nancy offered to drive me over Wednesday, but I declined. Offered again Thursday and Friday, but I had too much to do. That morning she thought would be a perfect time to see it, but again, there was just too much on my plate. Someone had to organize the Babylon 5 videotape collection. I thought Nancy suspected I was resisting the move. My coy strategy of pretending none of it was really happening so she'd forget about it might not have been working.

I could have been wrong, but I think Nancy was actively and progressively making me more unwelcome. I almost didn't notice when she didn't buy any half and half. But when she cancelled the adult channels on the cable receiver, I began to suspect she wanted me to leave. That morning, I found out not only that "Leafcaller" Mudge was coming over for dinner, but that she put in a change of address request for me at the post office. So, while I was getting cuckolded, I was not getting mail. As another subtle gesture, she bought a palette of cardboard boxes and a new tape gun and dumped them all in my study. There was a message there somewhere, if only I could have deciphered it.

Mudge was coming to dinner. Nancy thought we should all get together to show Randy how adult we all are. A helluva way to spend a Saturday, storing your past and meeting your marital replacement. I'd seen a stack of official-looking papers in Nancy's briefcase, plastic post-it labels indicating signing pages. She didn't give them to me. I'm sure she didn't want to sour my mood before meeting her new guy, the doctor, the guy who's done something with his life. I think she was worried I wouldn't behave, that my reptilian brain would creep out of its cage like Melissa's chameleon to hide against the polite domestic background, waiting to pounce. Do chameleons pounce? No, they strike with their tongues. So much the better.

Rose was on my mind. I'd known her only a couple of hours, but she'd burst into my thoughts every time I saw the end of my life in this house, which was about every fifteen minutes. Like the sight of a distant island from the bow of a sinking ship, I took her bearing and readied myself for an uncertain swim.

"Dammit, Tony. Did you just un-box those?" Nancy was on the bottom step. I hadn't heard her come down. I was sitting amid a pile of my self-published tome of poetry *Words Best Spoken on Paper*. My agent had done nothing with them, so I still had about five hundred copies.

"Maybe," I replied as defiantly as the ambiguous word would allow.

"Tony, we agreed, you'll be out in a week. I have a plan."

I returned the books to the box.

"What's for dinner?" I asked.

"Arugula quiche with watercress salad."

I didn't know what watercress was, but I was pretty sure arugula was a kind of insect found in the Amazon. Sounded expensive, imported meat and all.

"Sounds great," I said—pretty convincingly, I thought. "Mudge's idea?"

"Leafcaller," she corrected.

"Sorry."

"Are you inviting anyone to dinner?"

I hadn't thought of it. I didn't know I was allowed. It made sense. Nancy was a fair person. If she was going to dump her boyfriend on me, she wouldn't have blinked if I brought a girlfriend to return the favor. But I didn't have one. I only had an idea.

If I were a squirrel, I'd be dead by now. Not just because squirrels don't live to be thirty-seven, but because I wouldn't have saved any nuts. I might have found a nice niche to secret my stash, but when the snow fell, there wouldn't be an acorn or grub to be found. My niche would be full of feathers, shiny bottle caps, and used chewing gum. Planning wasn't my strongpoint. Here I was at the end of my fourteen-year relationship, the planned conclusion, the foreshadowed definite final act of my marriage, and I hadn't as much as made a date. I stared stupidly at my soon-to-be ex-wife, as ill prepared for dinner as I was for the rest of my life.

"Eh, let me make a call," I said.

"Okay," she said. "And Tony, if this stuff isn't out of here by Friday, it'll be out by Saturday."

Nancy could turn a threatening phrase like no one else. She had a gift. She retreated up the stairs and I found the green napkin. I dialed the number like I was signaling from the 2:00 a.m. Titanic. She answered on the second ring.

"Hello, Rose," I said. "This is Tony. Tony Flaner?"

"Tony. You called."

"What makes you say that?" I said defensively. She laughed. "Rose, are you busy for dinner? I'm facing the worst meal of my life in about three hours, and I'd be able to handle it better if a beautiful, young, sexy woman like you were sitting beside me. Do you know anyone?"

She laughed. "Sounds terrific."

"Yep. So can I count on you?"

"I've had that dinner before, and believe me, I'd help if I could. But I've got unbreakable plans."

"That's okay," I said. "Say, do you happen to know if suicide by rat poison is painless?"

"I don't think so. Go with a gun. That way you can take a few down with you."

"You're very wise," I said.

"I'll tell you what, Tony. There's a rave tonight at the hangar. Why don't you meet me at the Sailor at ten o'clock, and I'll take you?"

The Sailor was a bar downtown. They didn't have acts like the Comedy Cellar, but I'd been there before to sample their Kentucky bourbon for quality and nutritional value.

"What's the hangar?" I asked.

"It's a warehouse by the airport. Someone rents it and throws a rave there. You know, a big dance party, about once a month. It's all word of mouth, underground stuff, but it's great. Love to take you. If you've never been, it's an experience to be had."

That settled it. I was there.

"See you at ten," I said. "Should I bring something? A corsage, maybe?"

"Don't be old-fashioned," she said.

"Don't be ungrateful."

It was the best conversation I'd had all day.

After unloading six boxes and loading seven, I figured my work was done and went upstairs. I expected to smell succulent, acrid scents of broiling Amazonian bug, but smelled nothing. Dinner would be soon if Nancy kept to schedule. I heard chopping and smashing and clanking from the kitchen, so I snuck up the stairs to Randy's room to bond with my son while I was still the man of the house. I had about an hour.

There was once a time, as near as when I was a child, when being sent to your room was a punishment and playing outside a reward. How things had changed. Everything that my son valued was in his room. He had his own TV, which he hardly used; his bed, which I assumed he used; and his chest of drawers, the use of which I doubted. His clothes were stacked in neat Nancy-folded piles on the floor. But the center of his world was his computer.

When it got too cold to fish, I found a multiplayer game that promised to suck away more time than an imploding TARDIS. My son and I played for weeks and explored other games, some online with more players than Kansas, and some LAN games where we'd invite friends to link up on a Friday night for a frag fest. After a time, I moved on to something else, but Randy stayed with the magic box with all the answers, all the connections.

Nancy bought him his own computer two years ago. Since then, Randy has upgraded it countless times. The last two he paid for himself out of funds he got by using his computer, consulting or something. He once told me the specifics of the upgraded machine but my eyes glazed over with a waxy sheen I'm sure he took for gross ignorance. Randy's smart.

His door was closed, as usual. The sounds of a battle issued from beneath it: distant screams, explosions, and what I imagined to be Martian heat rays. I rapped on the door.

"Who is it?"

"Ozymandias," I said.

"Come in, Dad."

He didn't look at me. His attention was glued to the monitor where a frenetic battle of colors, movement, and sounds flickered in some relationship to his mouse clicks and keyboard taps.

"This is GG, Dad," he said. "I'll be with you in a second."

"What's GG?" I asked.

"It means 'good game.' Net etiquette, you know. The game's over, he's about to surrender. He's a noob."

Trumpets sounded and "Victory" flashed on the screen. It was a big screen. Really big. Bigger than the TV I had in my study. Randy dismissed the alert with a click of his mouse and swiveled in his chair.

"What's a noob?" I asked.

"It's short for newbie," he said. Then, seeing no light of understanding added, "Newcomer. Novice. An Inexperienced player."

"Oh," I said.

"What do you want, Dad?"

"Just wanted to say hi," I said.

"Hi."

A surge of sadness churned in my belly and threatened to erupt like vodka and Oreos. I took aim at my son, readied my tear ducts for an emotional expulsion, but then swallowed hard, dropped my testes, and said, "So what were you playing?"

"Colonies," he said. "It's a great game. Practically a sport."

"Who makes it? Microsoft?"

"Stormcraft. It's their signature game. Made them billionaires."

"Why haven't I heard of them?" I asked.

For an answer, my son focused his "you're so lame" gaze on my defenseless body. The chill raised goose bumps.

"Is it hard?" I asked.

"Challenging. Fun on single player, but the real game is the multiplayer."

"Do you still play Unreal or Quake?"

"Nah, they're pretty old now. The engines are still around, but the games are called different things."

"But you still play them?"

"Sometimes."

"We should play," I said.

"Sure," he said, but I could see a look of pity in his eyes. I'd never be competitive with him in video games again. My glory days ended when he left elementary school.

"We should talk about the birds and the bees," I said.

"Why?"

"Because it's probably time," I said.

"Dad, I've had uncensored Internet for years. I probably know more than you do."

What father hadn't heard that before?

"Well, there's more than just sex. There's caring and respect and relationships and all that."

"Can you teach me that?"

That gave me pause. I told you he was smart.

"No, I guess not. Not with words," I said. "But I can tell you it's more important than sex."

"Makes sense."

"And use protection."

"Dad, I'm not sexually active. I don't plan to be for quite some time."

That was a relief. I really hadn't come up to have *The Talk* with my son. I floundered into it because I didn't want to melt into a crying blob of insecurity seeking sympathy from a fourteen-year-old boy.

"Will you tell me when you are?"

"Yeah, okay," he said.

"Before you start? When you're thinking about it and things are beginning to happen?"

"Yes."

"Promise?"

"Yes, Dad. I promise." He smiled an embarrassed grin and turned away.

"Good. Cool. That's fine. I'm parenting. It's all good," I said.

"Tony," came Nancy's voice from below. I think she was yelling for me in the basement. "Come clean up. It's time to get ready."

My upper and lower intestines rose into my stomach, did a little jig, and wound around each other into a knot the size of a bread loaf.

"Well, I better go," I said.

"Okay," Randy said. I noticed an open cardboard box filled with what appeared to be external hard drives—dozens of them. I was about to ask him about them, when I heard his game start and saw him clicking away on a map of some alien world.

I went to my bedroom to clean up. My hair was dusty, my hands dirty, and my clothes too comfortable for a dinner with my wife's new man. I tossed my clothes onto the floor and showered. I stood under the water until it ran tepid and then dried off slowly. I found a pair of slacks and a dress shirt laid out for me on the bed when I came out. At least there wasn't a tie.

Okay, I knew Nancy had a plan and my costuming was part of it.

She wanted a smooth transition, a mature adult evolution. But I've seldom been called mature or adult.

I ignored the slacks and put on a comfortable pair of jeans. I left the shirt right where it sat and found the most colorful Hawaiian atrocity I owned. It had parrots and pineapples, hibiscus leaves and even some cannabis designs around the hem, which I did not tuck in. It was red and green with glowing yellow blossoms fighting for attention between fluorescent leaves and stems. The shirt was loud and obnoxious and fit me like a second skin.

CHAPTER SIX

Doctor Hank Mudge, aka "Leafcaller," was punctual. The bell rang at 5:15 precisely. I don't know if that was when Nancy asked him to come, but I bet it was. I stood in front of the mirror contemplating whether to have a button open. I went with two.

I heard muffled "hello's" from the entryway. When I got to the top of the stairs, Nancy and Mudge were chatting. Nancy took his coat, or sweater, or hide, or something. It looked like a poncho with sleeves and hung on him like a horse blanket. I don't think it was wool. Alpaca nose hair, probably. That would explain the Andean pattern and native colors. Where would someone buy such a thing as that above the equator?

I'd met Leafcaller about eight months earlier. Nancy had talked me into trying yoga. She'd gone to a few instructors but stuck with Leafcaller's class because he was "in tune with all his chakras."

My chakras had been a little flat lately, so I'd agreed to try it. I don't remember if I was between hobbies then, but I bet I was.

The class was held at the local athletics center. It was like a real athletics club with pools, basketball courts and such, but it was run by the city. The dues were low, and you could buy a day pass if you just wanted to swim, lift weights, or work on your chakras. Nancy had a pass. Mine had expired from my short-lived weight-lifting hobby. There was no sauna or steam room, and the pool was shut down regularly to clean up toddler puke and baby poo. The walls were light gray concrete, and there was always a pack of Cub Scouts getting some badge or other somewhere in the building. A chess club met there, and a knitting circle, and several aerobic teachers rented space on alternative days, pocketing a percentage of class fees. I suspect Mudge did the same with his yoga class.

There were about twenty people in his class the day I went. Eighteen were women. The other man, besides myself and Mudge, kept looking at me with challenging eyes, as if I were another stallion wandering too close to his herd. None of the women glanced at me. They all had eyes for Leafcaller, alias Doctor Hank Mudge.

It was a miserable experience. I was as limber as a railroad tie and every move made me feel like split kindling. I pulled every muscle I knew and several I'd never been acquainted with before. The high point was when I tried to make the "rotting stump" position or something, bent over and blasted a fart loud enough to silence the cheerleader practice in the next room. I finished the class, but didn't linger afterwards. Nancy agreed, not for the first time, to carry on without me.

Now the yoga guru stood in my foyer, holding my wife's hands. He had to be ten years older than me with a body ten years younger. He didn't have a hint of a bald spot. I knew then I would hate him forever.

"Tony. Come meet our guest," said Nancy, seeing me on the stairs. She must have felt the waves of animosity surging from above. I smiled a tight smile and waved.

They didn't release each other's hands until I was on the floor staring at them. That's when my wife's lover offered me his hand to shake.

"Tony, you remember Leafcaller, don't you?" Nancy said.

"I thought it was Mudge, Hank Mudge," I said, sliding my hands into my pockets.

"Yes, that's the name my parents gave me," he said, nonplussed. Yes, I was going to hate him forever. "I am now called Leafcaller."

"And who gave you that name?" I asked. "Legolas?"

He laughed. I hated. Nancy shot me a look that would have knocked over a vase. Luckily I'm not a vase. So, I had that going for me.

"I think a man should choose his own name," Mudge said. "He should define himself by his own terms, make his own way, seize his own destiny. Be his own man, so to speak."

I nodded. "I've been toying with calling myself Slappy McStiffrod."

"Memorable," he said.

"Let's have a drink before dinner," said Nancy, taking my arm like an eagle takes a salmon and leading me into the family room, which a hundred years ago would have been called a parlor. I said as much, and buzzed like a fly. If anyone got it, they ignored me.

Nancy brought Hank a glass of red wine and asked me what I wanted. She knew what Mudge drank, but not me? I asked for a Fuzzy Navel, with two umbrellas. The crockery crushing look swung at me again.

"Whisky and water," I said. Mudge and I stood in silence until she returned. The highball glass was nearly full. If there was water in it, it had evaporated on the way from the kitchen. It tasted like battery acid, just the way I needed it.

"So," I said, not liking awkward silences, which Leafcaller seemed to enjoy, "are you still teaching yoga at the Y?"

"I'm opening a studio on Lambert Street," he said. "I'll offer two yoga classes a day and two of aerobics. I'll have five instructors."

"Where on Lambert Street?"

"Back behind the bank, by the knife shop."

"Didn't that used to be a karate studio?"

"I'm not sure," he said.

"Yes, I think it was. And a homeless shelter before the cops found a meth lab in the back."

He sipped his wine.

I went on, "They finally closed it down after the murders. I'm glad it's got a new tenant; that neighborhood needs all the help it can get."

"Dinner," said Nancy. I drank the rest of my Kentucky grog and loped upstairs to get Randy. He was not pleased to be called away from his game. I saw clothes laid out on his bed as they'd been on mine. He didn't even glance at them, but followed me downstairs in his black sweat pants and stained Disney T-shirt. A close examination of the shirt showed Mickey extending the middle of his three fingers in a timeless gesture. Out of the mouths of babes, I thought.

The table was a fairyland of candles, ferns, and flowers. We all sat down in our accustomed places; Nancy and I on opposite ends, Randy to my right, interloper to the left. When we were all seated but Nancy, she made a big show of taking all the foliage off the table to make room for the meal. Of course Mudge showered her in compliments about the arrangements, which Nancy said she'd done herself, having learned how at a class. I didn't know she knew how to arrange flowers, nor did I know you needed a class to do it.

After the plants were removed, Nancy brought out a big wooden bowl piled high with more plants. I didn't know we had a big wooden bowl.

"Watercress salad with balsamic peppermint dressing," she bragged.

"Is this new?" I asked, gesturing to the bowl.

"We got it for our wedding from Barbara and Nick," she said warily.

"Oh yeah," I lied. "We don't use it much. I forgot." Who the hell were Barbara and Nick?

Next, Nancy brought out a baking dish. "Arugula quiche," she declared.

Whatever it held was mostly orange and yellow, but there were green clumps—which I took to be the insect parts, dotting the surface like craters in no man's land.

Nancy refilled Mudge's glass and poured water for Randy. I was on my own I guess.

"Randy, this is Leafcaller," she said to our son.

Randy was texting on his phone and didn't look up. "Hey," he said.

"Will you say grace?" she said to Mudge.

I should note that we never say grace. Not even at Thanksgiving. We're not religious and we're not atheists. We just don't give a damn. Apparently, Nancy did now. Randy kept texting.

"Shall we join hands?" inquired Mudge.

"No," I said.

Nancy moved to looks that could chip marble outright. One came my way, but I dodged. Mudge closed his eyes and spoke.

"May this food strengthen our bodies as our friendship for each other strengthens our spirits," he said in a voice straight from a pulpit.

Then instead of saying "Amen," or "God Bless," or "I'm going to do your wife if I already haven't," he sounded a Nepalese nasal hum that lasted for at least a minute. If there was a word in it, it might have been Aum, or Yum, or Dumb. I can't be sure.

That endured, Nancy dished up the food. She cut a big piece of bug for our guest, then one for me, Randy, and herself. She let us get our own salad.

"What's this?" Randy said, stabbing his food with his fork as if it were still alive and squirming.

"It's dinner, Randy," said his mother. "Organic and wholesome."

"By organic, you mean it doesn't contain rocks and metal?" I said.

"I mean, no preservatives or artificial chemicals."

"Excellent," said my new worst enemy. "Absolutely superb. I've never had this prepared so well."

"You've had this before?" I asked.

"Oh, yes. It's one of my favorites."

Randy and I exchanged looks.

I tried the salad. It was sharp and bitter.

"The salad's perfect," I said.

We ate in silence. Randy poked his food, moved it around, crushed an exoskeleton with his fork, and then asked to be excused. He left before anyone could answer, taking his dish into the kitchen to perfect his escape.

I tasted the food. It was like an omelet, I guess, but I didn't recognize the green flavor. I was beginning to suspect it might have been vegetable, but I wasn't convinced.

I took a long look at Mudge during dinner. I tried to keep chewing so as not to be tempted to talk. Mudge was probably forty-eight or so. He had gray temples and a strong chin. If he had any body fat he kept it in a storage shed in Barstow. He had bright blue eyes that shone with a confidence that made the reptile in me wish for meat cleavers. He was about the same height as me, but I knew I could take him, if only for the thirty-pound weight advantage and reptilian assisted caveman hormones pulsing in my veins.

"Most illness is from the soul and can be cured by positive energy to the right power centers," he told me. I realized then that he'd been speaking for a while. "Crystals can help harmonize the cosmic vibrations, to drive out the negative energy and replace it with light."

I put down my fork and nodded in agreement.

"When I worked at Stoneworks, making headstones," I said, "I had a buddy who had a six hundred pound block of granite fall on his leg and crush it. There I was, surrounded by crystal and, like an idiot, I called an ambulance. Wish you'd have been there—he might be able to walk now. Hey, maybe it's not too late? I'll give you his number and you can meet up with him tomorrow at therapy and enlighten his femur back to life. You'll have to ask him what they did with it though. Maybe he still has it in a jar."

"Tony!" said Nancy, dispensing with looks and going for volume.

"I take it you don't believe in the unseen forces of the universe," Mudge said, taking more quiche. He was welcome to it.

"Oh, I know there are unseen forces in the universe. Like how you forced your way into my wife unseen to me."

"Tony!" Not as loud, but sharper and more venomous.

"Nancy explained your arrangement to me," he said. "It's most enlightened."

"Man, I can't tell you how happy I am that you like it," I said. "I think I just came in my pants."

That caught Nancy speechless, but her stare could cut glass.

"In times of crisis, weak souls sometimes regress in maturity," Mudge said.

"Was that an insult?" I said gleefully. I'd gotten to him.

"It is from the teachings of Master Xio, Fifteenth Guru of Qusum."

"So you're quoting insults? Not man enough to come up with your own?"

"I am secure in my manhood and all things. I am at peace with all," he said with a smile that begged to be caved in.

"That's good. Maybe your security will shield you while I act out my insecurities on your gonad chakra."

"Tony!" Nancy stood. I think Mudge was worried, but I wasn't sure. We both looked at her.

"Even for you, you've been extraordinarily rude," she said. "That's saying something, Tony Flaner." She used my full name. Never good. "We're all going to have to get along. You might as well be civil."

"Why do I have to entertain your lover, in my house, under my roof, with my favorite wooden bowl?"

"For Randy," she said.

"He's gone now."

"Then for me," she said and moved behind Mudge. She put her hand on his shoulder, and he reached up and held it, pity and sympathy in his eyes.

"And for me," added Mudge.

I catapulted a spoonful of dinner at his face.

I missed of course. The goop splashed against the window behind the pair. Though unmarked, the gesture wasn't wasted. A look of horror, disbelief, and rage bubbled over Nancy's face like boiling gumbo.

Mudge hadn't even flinched, but I could see his patient façade slide away like the goop on the glass behind him. I watched his pale ears turn crimson. And I tried, not very hard, to suppress a grin.

"Tony, I think you should leave now," said Nancy. That brought me out of it. Some prehistoric part of me thought I was winning her affection with my brilliant use of cafeteria warfare, but Nancy was a modern woman and beyond my ability to charm with tantrums.

Mudge spoke before I could protest.

"You two are going through a tough time now. I can see that. Nancy was too optimistic as to your level of understanding. This was premature. I'll go."

He stood up. For the first time in my life, I saw hate in my wife's face. It sobered me. I didn't mind hurting Mudge—wanted to really—but Nancy, I liked.

"Wait," I said, pretending to be civil. "You're right. I've been a jerk. I am a jerk, so I was just being myself. But that's not your fault."

Nancy's look softened, and I went on.

"I'm still in denial about this. Nancy's put up with me much longer than any other woman in the country would have."

"World," she corrected.

"Yeah," I said. "You guys have dessert. I have plans tonight, anyway. I'll go." Losing with aggression, pouting seemed like an obvious alternative.

I'd like to think Nancy had new respect for me, but I think the expression on her face was relief.

"See ya, Nance," I said. She gave me a peck on the cheek and pushed me to the door.

"Nice meeting you, Tony," Mudge called.

"Die in a fire, fuck-face," seemed the appropriate response.

CHAPTER SEVEN

I drove around for an hour after dinner, digesting insects and the current state of my life's collapse. It wasn't as if anything was a surprise. It wasn't as if I was really hurt that Nancy had moved on to the fit yoga teacher. My possessiveness was instinctive. As I drove counting potholes and speed traps, I realized nothing of any importance, and that seemed kind of strange because driving around after a blowup is supposed to clear your mind. That's when epiphanies come up, right? Not for me. All I could think about was when it'd be ten o'clock.

I'd avoided relationships even when I suspected Nancy was in one. I always thought that it would be trouble. Trouble was something Nancy could handle, plan for, and cope with. Whereas for me, trouble was something I usually caused in small, amusing increments. Nothing that'd leave a mark. Never anything that would jeopardize the comfortable life I had with my papier mâché family. As I drove the lonely streets, burning time until our meeting, I kept thinking that Rose was trouble. But I also said to myself that I was ready for it and, better still, eager for it, and lastly, pushed to it.

I found an open florist and bought a corsage of pink roses and white chrysanthemums. At quarter to ten, I drove past The Sailor.

The Sailor is a gay bar, but gay isn't what it used to be. The open-minded and ignorant frequent it as much as the regulars. I'd gone there a few times with friends. The drinks were cheaper than some places and it always made me feel good to have someone hit on me. That never happened in straight bars. Maybe it's my clothes.

I'm not an ugly man. Sometimes, I think I'm quite dashing. But I'm past my physical prime. I know I'm about twenty pounds heavy, though my doctor has some trumped up bullshit number like thirty-five. What does he know? My hair, once a magnificent mane worthy of an eighties pop band, has migrated in tribes to warmer climes in my drain and hairbrush. I'm not bald, but the term "thinning" applies more to my head than my belly. The wrinkles I'd summon on demand for worry or laughter in years past, have found it more convenient to linger. So I wear them with ever deepening permanence. In short, I was approaching middle age, unless I only lived to be seventy-four, then I'd reached it; seventy-three and I was downhill. Fuck.

Luckily, I'm more sensitive to my physical shortcomings than the public at large. No one throws their forearm over their eyes when I pass, mothers don't clutch their children to their breasts to protect them from my horrible visage. However, as I drove to The Sailor in my sensible four-door hybrid-electric sedan wondering if I should take my wedding ring off or not, I couldn't help but wonder what Rose saw in me. I decided that if there was an opportune moment, a time in our "date" where I might subtly bring it up, I would try to divine her motives. Maybe she trafficked in stolen organs and I was her next mark. That wouldn't have turned me off, but it would be interesting to know.

I paid a child in a blue vest five dollars to park my car. I handed him the keys and he gave me a pink raffle ticket. I walked to the bar, watching the time so that I wouldn't arrive at exactly ten. At 10:01, like the rebel I was, I entered The Sailor.

Rose was at the bar. I saw her immediately. She was wearing a tight, blue-sequined dress that reminded me of the roaring twenties. She was flanked by two hard-bodied men bulging out of T-shirts two sizes too small. A third man was reaching for a napkin, his bicep nearly bursting from the strain of lifting the paper. She saw me at the door. She smiled. At that moment I grew about a foot, returned to my college weight, and lost ten years. I smiled back. The threesome turned to look at me, disbelief on their disappointed faces.

Rose led me to a table on the wall. I pinned the corsage on her dress just above her left breast. She shook her head as I did it, but let me, and smirked a little, too. Score one for old-fashioned.

Before she could sit down, I said, "So what do you see in me?" I am nothing if not subtle and patient.

She laughed. "Are you kidding?"

"Yeah. No, well kinda. No," I said suavely.

"You're an idiot."

"And you find that attractive? I'm in love."

"I've had a crush on you for years," she said. "I love your honesty on stage. You're funny and you're not bad looking. Don't sell yourself short."

I guess she saw confusion on my face, which made sense, since I'd put it there.

"I'd have had you a long time ago if you hadn't been married. Most of the girls at the club would have."

I recognized syllables and words, but the meanings arrived slowly, like a cocktail waitress at the nickel slots. Then it hit me like a stroke.

"Wait. What? Who? They would?" I stammered.

She grinned.

"So what changed?" I said. "You knew my marriage was over the other night?"

"You have mentioned it on stage. Plus Dara told me the details in the bathroom. She said you were available or soon would be."

Dara was a foul-mouthed gossip. I needed to send her a thank you note.

"Who were your friends?" I asked, pointing to the three suitors at the bar.

"Straight guys who don't know where they are."

"They might get lucky yet." I gestured to a group of men at the other end of the bar watching the trio with some interest. "Tonight might change lives."

A thin man with a thin mustache in a blue-and-white sailor suit took our order and sauntered back to the bar.

I was glad then that I'd worn my Hawaiian shirt. It fit in well here.

It was Rose that looked out of place. The sequins were fine; it was the breasts that were all wrong.

"So how was your dinner party?" she asked.

"I chucked food at the guest."

"What kind of food?"

"Quiche."

"Did you hit him?"

"No. That's the kind of night it was. I couldn't hit the fucker with a spoonful of goop."

"Was there pie?"

"I don't know. I left before dessert," I said. "Pie would have been good though. Damn. I should have waited for dessert. Throwing a pie—now that would have been classic."

"Next time."

Our drinks arrived. I was staying with whisky and water. She had a Mai Tai. Hers looked better.

"So what was it all about?" she asked after a sip.

"It's why I'm available," I said, and for the next fifteen minutes I told Rose, who I'd known all of three and a half hours, the story of my shifting interests, disconnected son, serial jobs, and preordained divorce to my roommate wife. To my credit or my shame, I didn't get emotional. It was just a story. I told it like it happened to someone else.

"My life has always been about following the path of least resistance. It's all about pushes and pulls," I said. "I'm not like Nancy. I don't have a plan. I wait for life to push me in one direction and find it pulls me along to a new place. You know that hackneyed phrase 'God never closes a door without opening a window'? Well that's my life plan right there. Wait for doors to close and windows to open. Push and pull. Only problem is it happens with frequent regularity. I can't stay put. Before I know it, the pull becomes a push and I'm off to a new thing. I'm like a lazy bullet in a gauss gun."

"I like it," she said. "Though I don't know what a gauss gun is. It's really living. It's *carpe diem*."

"It's worked up until now. But now? Now, I don't know. I've grown accustomed to the security of a home and a wealthy spouse. I've been spoiled. Now, there's a push and I don't feel a pull. Now I just don't know."

"You'll be fine," she said with a grin. "I've never met anybody who liked seeing an old lover with someone else. You wouldn't be a human animal if you didn't feel something. Your wife was cruel to put you through that."

"She did it on purpose to push me out," I said. "She's making things clear. She's practical."

"Practical has its place."

"It can be a real buzzkill," I said. "Once, years ago, when Randy was maybe three years old, Nancy was gone to an open house, and I was in charge of him. I was laying out plans for a glider I wanted to build. Never finished it, by the way. Anyway, it was a hot summer, and the air conditioner wasn't up to snuff. Randy came in and saw me sweating.

"'Do you want a nice cold one?' he asked.

"'Sure,' I said.

"He trotted away and came back with a cup of cold water. It was the sweetest thing. I drank it and gave him a big hug.

"When Nancy came home, I had Randy go get me another 'cold one.' Again he trotted away and returned with a glass of water that I drank like it was a cold, crisp beer. It was so sweet."

"And Nancy didn't like it?" Rose asked. "Was it about drinking alcohol?"

"No. Nancy stared at me and shook her head. 'You do realize,' she said to me, 'that the only water source Randy can reach is the toilet?'"

Rose burst out laughing. I had to as well.

"Kinda sucked the magic out of the moment," I said. "She was right, but it was still cute."

"That's a great story," she said.

"Yeah, I used it in a bit. Randy changed it up and put it on the Internet. It went viral, he told me. I think that's a good thing."

I remembered then that Randy would be living with Nancy and

not me. I had to change the subject. I could feel my emotional maturity teetering toward a nostalgic free fall.

"So what did you have to do tonight, if you don't mind me asking?" It would have been so great to have had Rose with me at dinner. Maybe Nancy would have felt primitive jealousy like I had. Rose might have calmed me down, or at least steadied my aim.

"I was supposed to meet someone," she said. "But it didn't work out."

"You had two dates tonight?" the primate in me articulated.

"Not a date, just a meeting. A business thing. He didn't show up. Weird."

"You were going to meet him here?"

She nodded.

"So what happened?" I asked. "Afraid of the gay?"

"Don't know. We used to come here all the time," she said, and I thought I saw a hint of worry cross her beautiful face. "Anyway," she said and then downed her drink in a single gulp. She gestured for me to do the same, like it was a dare.

I did and coughed.

"Good thing I didn't want to taste it," I said.

She winked.

"Another?" I asked.

"No." She took a twenty-dollar bill out of her purse and slapped it on the table.

"So you take all your dates here?" I said.

"Some of them."

"But not all?"

"Hell no," she said. "Only those I like. Like there's this artist jerk I met on a cruise. I dumped his sorry ass last year before he got in here. It's an old hangout with good memories, mostly."

"Mostly?"

"A friend of mine died. We used to come here."

"Love of your life?"

"Friend. He was gay. Now he's dead."

"Sorry," I said, feeling the life sucked out of the conversation.

"Don't be," she said. "It was his choice."

"Yikes."

"Life is for living," she said and stood up. "Let's go get some."

Something told me I was getting into trouble. I'm sure it was "married man guilt," which had no business worrying me at that point, but still I hesitated.

She grabbed my hand and pulled me to my feet. She pushed her mouth into mine and kissed me.

I swooned. My knees turned to rubber and my brain swam in floral perfume. Something short-circuited, something else pulsed. Everything tingled. Magnets drew my blood in throbs and thrums.

She pulled me out the door.

CHAPTER EIGHT

I redeemed my raffle ticket for my car. The change in my ashtray was gone, replaced with a cigar butt. The air in the cab was gone, replaced with a blue cloud of cheap tobacco. I'd survive the valet's assault, but I felt sorry for all the asthmatics who used coin operated laundries and couldn't find parking. They were goners. I tipped the murderer five dollars, got in, and Rose directed me toward the rave.

I told Rose I knew where the airport was; I worked there after all. But I was wrong. Six months working for an airline and I didn't know there were two airports in Salt Lake. I guess stuff like that is dispensed on a need-to-know basis. The one we wanted was called, cleverly enough, Airport Number Two because it was the second airfield in the valley and it was shitty.

We drove through housing developments that hadn't existed a week before, past fields that would be housing developments next week, along a highway I didn't know existed, to a place right in the middle of my city that's been as near and unknown to me as a mole on my back.

As we approached, I passed cars parked on the secret highway, saw groups of young tight-bodied people in tighter clothes walking toward an aluminum-domed hangar. Rose told me to drive on. A man with a yellow reflective vest and lightsaber directed me onto a runway and I parked there. I hesitated, but then thought that if someone in a yellow vest told me it was okay to park my small foreign car in the middle of a runway at an operational airport, it must be fine.

To be classy, I ran around the car to open the door for Rose. She didn't see me and flung it open just as I arrived, cracking me across the knees and throwing me to the ground.

"Are you all right?"

"Just admiring the stars," I said, lying on the tarmac. I rolled over and got to my feet. Suddenly the air was a gush of engine roar and I ducked from the plane landing on top of us. The jet passed a hundred feet above, gear down on final approach to the real airport. I forgot about my kneecaps and concentrated on regaining my hearing.

"Let's get inside," I yelled. Rose nodded.

Hand in hand, we walked to the hangar where all the activity was. As my hearing returned, I could sense deep base thumps. Then I could feel them. Then I could see them in the throbbing aluminum roof. Through an open door, I saw bright, colorful changing lights leak out and dance to the music. I saw hordes of people standing and swaying outside the door, smoking, talking, drinking from red plastic cups and clear plastic wine glasses. I smelled perfume and cloves and pot, and felt Rose's hand in mine. I looked at Rose and realized then that my face was twisted up in a wide, toothy grin.

"This looks like fun," I said.

Raves are outlaw parties that might have existed when I was younger, but I didn't know about them if they did. I remember house parties and frat parties, some even with a designated person to mind the CDs and speakers lest someone steal something, break something, or play something country. If we had a name for parties like that, it was "keggers," so called for the silver totem smuggled across the border from Wyoming where, unlike the local fare, the beer was strong enough to get you drunk. Keggers were a wonderful thing growing up in Utah.

Raves, I learned, are a different thing entirely. They are as spontaneous as a strip mall, and nearly as commercial. Someone figured out that parties could be profitable. Whereas in my day, it was customary to chip in to pay for the holy keg and plastic cups so the host wasn't totally bankrupted, now the people behind raves were putting their kids through college and buying second homes with the profits.

After hocking a femur and taking a second loan out on my car, I paid the cover charge with a Visa. We were directed to a table where we received armbands and an invisible hand stamp before going inside.

The space was huge and filled with people. The moment I stepped through the door I had the sense of being on an acid trip. There was mist issuing from a half dozen smoke machines that mingled with cigarettes and sulfur from sporadic pyrotechnics. The lights of the fireworks were set to the music, and glowing bulbs illuminated a stage where three bouncing people in headphones stood behind technological tables. Furiously, but gracefully, they adjusted knobs and dials to make lights move, smoke billow, and music rise and fade to synthesized primitive rhythms. Green lasers drew shapes on the walls and ceiling. Red ones dashed like fireflies on every visible surface, leaving tracers in the mist. The music was nothing I recognized. There was no band, it was all from computers and had vibrant rhythms and throbbing choruses that made me sway and swagger just to keep on my feet.

Rose drew me into the thick of the crowd. I felt out of place. Self-consciously, I measured my years against the crowd around me, my weight against the shirtless Adonises who danced on their hands as much as their feet. Rose must have seen my trepidation. She looked at me, pulled my face down to hers and kissed me. My body jolted as if by high tension, and my confidence surged to the voltage.

As her tongue parted my lips, I felt a tablet pass from her mouth into mine. She pulled back and smiled. I swallowed the pill. It came on in fifteen minutes.

* * *

"A rave is a traveling speakeasy," I explained to the table. I'd been sharing my thoughts about the event as a first-time participant. Rose was there, and Tonya and Calvin whom I'd met at the club. Melissa, I wasn't sorry to hear, was still in mourning for her missing pet, who had yet to appear. Patricia, the atheist, was there with a man named Paul, who chain-smoked spliffs he pulled out of a Ziplock plastic baggie he kept in his shirt. The other member of our table was a man named Donovan. He wore a velvet cape, had unnaturally dark jet-black hair, pale skin, eyeliner, and sharpened fingernails. He looked like a vampire.

"You look like a vampire," I said.

"That's because I am one."

"Oh. Okay. That makes sense." And surprisingly, it did at the time.

We'd been at the rave for about five hours by my best calculation. We'd arrived before eleven and it was just past four. The party showed no signs of slowing down, but luckily the ecstasy Rose had given me had.

We'd met up with Rose's friends and made a base at a table not far from the stage and away from the speakers where we could talk. One of us made regular trips to the concession stand, for beer, wine, toys, and bottled water.

There were a lot of toys. I couldn't help but buy five neon light sticks when I'd gone up. I spun them around and admired the tracers in my retinas and the brilliance of their cold chemical light. I finally made necklaces out of them and handed them out to people I thought deserved them. That made me popular. They sold other toys too. They sold tops and fake tattoos, pens that only showed up in black light, which there were many of in the hangar, and assorted oddities only the stoned would want to own. They were selling out.

"So what's with the pacifiers?" I asked the table, seeing if anyone was still talkative. Paul replied.

"They're to suck on," he said.

"No shit? Really? Well that explains why everyone has them in their mouths."

"Yeah," he said. Paul was stoned. I wished Rose would come back. She was getting us some water and mentioned something about using the bathroom. I'd seen the line to the girls' lavatory and hoped she'd brought a lawn chair.

"So they're for sucking?" I looked at Donovan. "You know something about that, don't you?"

He gave me a look that he thought was menacing, but I found merely theatrical.

"It's for the ecstasy," Donovan said, revealing his long incisors. "The drug can make you grind your teeth. The pacifiers are for that."

"Did you sharpen your teeth?" I asked.

"Don't need to," he said.

"Want some?" Paul passed me a fresh joint. I took a toke. It took the edge off the fading hallucinogenic.

"Thanks," I said.

"No problem, dude." I was happy to see that even in these times, smoking pot together made you "dudes."

Calvin was on second base with Tonya. The two made out like drowning divers sharing a last gasp of oxygen. He tried to steal third, got slapped away, but made it safely back to second.

"Tony, it's all just chemistry," Patricia said, picking up where she left off an hour earlier.

She was talking about the euphoria of the rave. Earlier, I'd said something like, "There is a God, and his name is Now." I was very proud of it when I said it, but it opened the floodgates of Patricia's atheism and she'd been on me about it ever since.

"You can't even say God," she said. "You might as well say Santa Claus, or elves."

"Or vampires," I said, baiting Donovan into the argument. He ignored me.

"You have to save yourself from the delusion the zealots are selling," she said. Her eyes were big and wild, dilated from drugs and eager to proselytize.

"You need to come to my AA group."

"You're in AA?" I said. "What is that? Your eighth drink? Shouldn't you be calling a sponsor right now?"

"Hell no, I'm not in AA. That's just another church selling lies about reality. Higher being and all; steps to salvation. Bah! No, I'm in AA," she said.

I didn't pretend to understand.

Then she seemed to. "AA means Atheist Alliance. We meet at the city library on alternating Mondays."

"They're kinda bummer meetings, dude," said Paul. "Better to watch baseball."

I glanced back at Calvin and Tonya.

"That's because you don't care enough to fight," said Patricia, turning on her date. "If someone doesn't put up resistance to the fundamentalists, we'll all be enslaved and sacrificing babies before you know it."

"Vive la revolution!" I declared.

"What was that?" said Tonya, coming up for air and sensing a surprising number of blouse buttons undone without her knowledge. She glared at Calvin and did them up.

"What's taking Rose so long?" she asked.

"I don't know," I said. "I think I'll go look for her."

Tonya grabbed my arm when I got up. "When you find her, ask her if she found any Percs, okay?"

"Okay," I said.

The music was throbbing, and my ears would be ringing for days. My eyes were wide and sharp and easily distracted by the colors and shapes dancing in the fog, or flickering in the laser lines, or glowing under black lights, or just imagined, but I moved through the crowd as if I belonged there.

Tonya's request for "Percs" was not the only time someone had approached my date that night asking for some kind of drug. People she didn't introduce to me asked her for X and she sold a couple on the dance floor. Another guy asked her for blow, but she didn't have any and said to look for Carlos. She offered X for free to the table if anyone needed any and then tucked the orange bottle into her red purse and didn't speak of it again.

Suddenly, I found myself next to the stage. If this had been a rock concert, I'd have been crushed by eager fans rushing to see their heroes, hoping to touch one, feel the splattered sweat splash from their clothes. Here, it was just another place to stand and dance, sway and shake.

The man closest to me on stage smiled and held one hand to his headphone and adjusted something on his board. He was illuminated in neon-blue computer light. He looked older than me, had sharp stubble on his chin, a Mohawk haircut, three earrings and a loose, black sleeveless T-shirt that read "The Clash" in red and white letters. Perhaps out of deference to me, the music transitioned into the Thompson Twins, heavily altered and electronically enhanced, but still recognizable. I wanted Rose badly then. I wanted to dance.

I moshed my way through the crowd toward the woman's bathroom. The line extended onto the dance floor. The men's room also had a line. Unlike the women's line, however, there were men standing in that one, but it was still mostly women. Gender inhibitions, meet bodily needs.

I didn't see Rose.

The colorful parade of apparitions I'd seen dancing in the lights now stood in united ignominy waiting for an empty stall. The planners of this rave should have invested more into porta-potties. With measurable regularity, I watched men peel out of the line and head for an exit only to return a few minutes later and a few pints lighter. The women were more patient or more modest, but not all.

"Hold Me Now" echoed off the rounded ceiling and I grinned, remembering some far off, happy, sunny day when that song played on the radio and I was at peace with the universe. That day never actually happened, but it should have. So I bobbed my way through people, looking for my date to share my Hallmark delusions.

"Hey, bro. You here with Rose?" A light-skinned Latino man held my right bicep in a firm, but non-hostile way. He pulled me off my groove and nearly off my feet. He was a little shorter than me, younger, stronger, and more fragrant. I could see a cloud of cologne hovering around him as a hazier shade of smog against the white-fog machine smoke. He spoke with a trace Spanish accent, well worn but detectable in the vowels. He wore a knowing lecherous smile that made me uncomfortable.

"I'm sorry, I don't remember being introduced," I said. "Or possibly we were, and I just blocked it out because you make me feel uncomfortable."

"We haven't been introduced," he said.

"That explains it."

"Hey, bro, I'm Carlos. I saw you with Rose. Just wanted to see what the new flavor was."

I probably should have slapped him across his face with my fencing gloves, but I didn't have any. The best I could do was squint my eyes in disapproval.

"No, bro, it's not like that," he said. "I know Rose. We go way back. We're friends."

My eyes widened a little. Carlos measured my pupils.

"You're high, bro," he said. "You need some blues?"

"Are you planning on breaking my heart?" I said. He laughed and slapped me on the back like we were old friends from the hood.

"Have you seen her?" I said, stepping away. He pointed across the hangar. Through the masses of people. I spied Rose's shimmering sequined dress and moved toward it. I put Carlos behind me and let the music work its way back in.

It was hard to move. Dancers and dreamers and sweaty bodies of all shapes and sizes bounced and rubbed against me. I dripped from spilled water and sweat, homegrown and borrowed. Raves are moist. In the spaces between the pulsating humanity, I caught glimpses of glittering Rose.

She was by the concession stand. She wasn't in line, just standing in the glow of black lights that lit up hand stamps and outlined bras beneath women's clothing. A man was with her. He stood in the shadows, out of the light, but the panning spots caught him in flashes. He wore a dark, buttoned shirt and sunglasses. He had to be tripping hard, I thought, to need sunglasses in this murk. In the flashing light, he had silvery hair and a shifty face. He didn't look at Rose, but watched the crowd instead, and kept his back against the corrugated wall. Rose dug in her purse, and he waited.

She produced a slip of paper, brilliant green in the purple light, and handed it to the man. He tucked in his front pocket and smiled. Rose saw me then and must have said something to the man because he looked up at me and then shrank away into the shadows. Rose picked up a sack from the floor and headed my way. When we met up, I glanced back to where she'd been. The man was gone. The drug deal complete.

"Who was that? An ex-lover?" I joked.

"Yes," she said, taking me by the arm and leading us back to our table.

"Surprised to see him here," she said. "At least I got that done."

"Got what done?" I asked. We were passing a wall of speakers then that shook my fillings. If she heard me or answered me, it was lost in the sound. She covered her ears, and we loped back to the table.

Tonya looked up, beseeching Rose with an expectant expression.

"Oh," I said into Rose's ear. "Yeah, Tonya wants to know if you found any Percocets."

"I didn't," said Rose, shaking her head. Tonya looked pouty and disappointed for a moment and then went back to tongue wrestling Calvin, who waited on second.

"There're couches on the other side," Rose yelled across the table to the kissing couple. They didn't hear her.

Paul puffed on another joint, and Donovan, I noticed, had disappeared.

"Must be close to dawn," I said.

Rose nodded and dug in her purse. She brought out a pint of spiced rum in a brown paper bag and put it on the table.

"You had this all the time?" Glass was forbidden at the rave. I'd seen a dumpster full of confiscated bottles on the way in. At first I assumed it was for safety, but having bought a couple of drinks, I figured the ban was economic.

"Just got it," she said, still rummaging in her purse.

"Here," she said. "I got you a present."

She handed me a blue and red braided tube. Like everything else in the place seen through my eyes, the colors were vibrant and intoxicating.

"What is it?" I asked.

"It's a finger trap," she said, sliding the tube over my right index finger. She then put her left one in the other side.

"Push," she said. We did.

"Now pull," she said. We did, but not very far. It locked. We were connected then.

"This, my new friend," she said with an emphasis on friend that made me quiver, "is kind of like your life. It's push and pull. It brought us together."

Her smile was arousing. I was aroused.

"But it's a trap," said Paul.

I would have told Admiral Akbar Buzzkill to shut his filthy mouth if mine hadn't been so pleasantly engaged at the moment. I pulled Rose closer to me. She didn't push away.

CHAPTER NINE

Half-past eleven in the morning, the sun shot lasers into my face, fusing my retinas through my eyelids. I rolled over and felt dried drool crack on my cheek. Someone had planted a Chia Pet in my mouth, and it wasn't house broken.

I rubbed my eyes, blinked, and squinted. My arms were heavy and stiff. One had been pinned beneath my hip and celebrated the long-awaited return of blood circulation with a fireworks show of a million pins and needles, sharp, deep, and long. I moaned through the grass in my mouth.

Someone had replaced my wallpaper with a window—an eastern-facing, eye-stabbing, dick window from hell. My thousand thread count duvet had been replaced with a cotton quilt, my pillow with a pair of wadded-up jeans and a loud Hawaiian shirt.

I sat up and instantly regretted it. I took in a chipped rosewood armoire, a faded silver mirror, a colonial hat rack, embroidered pillows, none of which were mine. There was a scent of pine polish and old things, sweat and lavender. I scraped my tongue on my teeth and wished I hadn't.

My heart beat in my forehead, and then the back of my skull, and then raced down my neck where I was introduced to a whole new kind of hangover.

"Oh, God," I mumbled and dropped my pounding head into my hands. Maybe I could siphon the pain away with my palms. It didn't work, but it was worth a try.

I sat that way for a while, eyes closed against the cruel light, head cradled like a broken melon, and remembered I was in Rose's apartment.

"Classic," I said to myself. I'd passed out moments before the most exciting sexual experience of my life. My rebirth as a man had been forestalled by spiced rum.

Judging from my arm pain and hip displacement, I'd fallen asleep on the couch and rolled onto the floor without rousing me enough to move my pinched arm. I wasn't usually such a lightweight, or maybe I was and nobody had bothered to tell me.

Nancy flashed through my mind. Would she notice I hadn't come home? Did she care? Did I?

"Rose," I said louder than I could stand, but not loud enough to be heard. No answer came back.

I stood up. That hurt. I was wedged between the couch and the table pretty tight. The rum glasses were gone. Great, I thought, she cleaned up around me. I sure know how to show a lady a good time.

I wondered if my face was covered in black Magic Marker, painted while I was passed out. Even now, photos of my stupid mug could be going viral across Facebook—"Look, thirty-seven-year-old can't handle rum!" It was all the rage to do to drunks, according to the Internet, and I deserved it if anyone did.

"Hey, Rose," I said, staggering into the doorway of the bedroom. "I don't know what happened to me." I usually say that after sex. It felt weird saying it before or, in this case, in place of it. Maybe I should get used to it. This was a new low.

I caught my reflection in a glass vase and was happy to see the Sharpie fairy hadn't visited.

The bedroom door was open, and I leaned against the jam. Rose was face down on her bed asleep, still in her panties and sweatshirt. The room was another exquisite display of tasteful antiques. The bed had to be older than the state, the wood heavier than my car. An intricate scene of domestic country bliss was carved in relief in the headboard. The scene was of two little girls in wide-sweeping skirts prancing around a sheltering tree with a lamb. It would have been heinous if painted, but stained it was classy. Four identical lathed posts stood firm and erect, as I hadn't. In similar Victorian style, there was a chest of drawers and vanity table opposite a white-laced curtained window. A closet set in a sidewall was ajar, and I glimpsed last night's blue sequined dress and white corsage hanging within.

With relief, I realized Rose had passed out, too. By the looks of it, she'd gone out about the same time I had. My manhood was saved. Instead of a limp loser, I was a consummate gentleman, sleeping on the couch while sleepyhead girl got the bedroom. I was still in play.

I sat down beside her on the little bed. I stole a glance at her shapely thighs and then stroked her hair over her ear, preparing to plant the tenderest of kisses there.

She was cold. I reached to pull the bedspread over her and brushed against her neck. It was cold. I put my hand on her thigh. It was cold.

I rolled her over. She flopped like a stringless marionette. Half her face was pale as the curtains; the other was a bruised plum. I touched her neck, feeling for a pulse, and felt nothing but a deathly chill.

* * *

This is where you came in.

* * *

She was dead. The liveliest girl I'd ever known was dead.

I pulled her sweatshirt back over her cold exposed body and slid off the bed onto the floor in a heap. I sat there looking at her, but not seeing her. Looking through her as I tried to piece together the night before.

I remembered leaving the hangar with Rose. We drove side streets and through questionable neighborhoods to avoid police traps. Rose directed me to her apartment in the alphabet streets of northern Salt Lake City.

I remembered parking on the street, one wheel on the curb so as not to draw attention for being too well parked. The pinned tricycle under the bumper had completed the illusion.

I remembered a streetlamp illuminating a beautiful, old brick building. A carved stone by the entrance and a little comparative history told me the building was older than two world wars and one tussle with Spain. We'd ascended a wide flight of stairs to the third floor, the top one, and went to the right side apartment. Number six. The last one.

Rose had unlocked the deadbolt and then the doorknob lock with a single key she had in her red purse. Forgetting my age and gracelessness, I made to carry her through the threshold because it suddenly seemed like a good idea. I missed my scoop and managed only to goose my hostess with a misaimed hand. Rose shrieked and said, "Wait a minute."

She threw open the door and gestured for me to go in. My penis entered the room six inches ahead of me. Rose closed the door, threw the deadbolt, and turned the knob to lock it. "Let's have some privacy," she said, fluttering her eyes. "Sit," she told me and disappeared through a doorway that led to a bedroom.

The couch was something my parents would have thought modern when they'd married, boxy and green, and stylish in a Matt Helm kind of way. It made you nostalgic and uncomfortable at the same time. A kidney-shaped coffee table squatted in front of it, almost to ankle level. A copy of *Life Magazine* September 1968 lay on it as if it had just arrived. The Beatles stood grouped on the cover. Only Paul McCartney could make a pink suit look good.

Rose returned in a gray sweatshirt and pink panties. She looked warm, comfy, and sexy all at the same time. She carried two tall glasses adorned with faded Flintstone characters. I recognized them instantly. I'd broken a set just like them when I was a kid at my grandma's. She poured each glass three-quarters full with the spiced rum she'd showed me at the Rave. I took Dino; she had Wilma.

"These are cool," I said.

"And very valuable," she said. "I have the whole set."

"To eccentric friends," I said.

"To adventure."

She gulped the entire drink down in one pull. She liked to drink her liquor all at once. I didn't know what to make of that. I decided it was a good thing.

"Drink it or you'll never sleep," she said. "You'll need rest in a little while." She smiled.

I drank it in one gulp. We put our glasses on the table next to the bottle. I was careful to avoid the magazine, and used the vintage Copacabana coasters.

She unbuttoned my shirt and ran her hands through my chest hair. I had plenty. I purred.

I took in the eclectic collection of furniture and decor. "This place is great."

"Thanks. I'll show you around."

She took me to the kitchen. There wasn't a modern machine in sight. A percolating coffee pot stood on an electric heating coil on a white enamel stove. The fridge was round and bulky, the kind of thing kids used to get trapped in by the millions if you believed the after-school PSAs. The freezer was caked with ice and held two frosted, steel ice trays that'd pull the tip of your tongue off if you dared lick it. She showed me where she hid her blender, electric coffee grinder, and mini-microwave, but admitted that she hated to have them. "I'll get rid of them when I find classic replacements."

"Good luck finding an antique microwave."

"I'm going to have one modified to look like a breadbox," she said. "I know a place that'll do it. It's expensive, but money is coming."

She showed me the bathroom, for which I was grateful at the time. She let me admire it alone in my own bladder-bursting way. The white enamel tub had bright brass legs that ended in eagle claws grasping spheres.

The medicine cabinet was behind an etched glass mirror and contained dozens of orange pill bottles. It was probably a jerk move to look, but that's me. Most were without labels, marked in codes with a Sharpie; some had pharmacy labels with printed names. None were recent. None said Rose.

When I came out, she showed me her library. It was a second bedroom converted in the classical style of the Victorian Age. It was walled in dark wood bookshelves equipped with rails to roll a ladder along so you could reach the upper tomes. Classic books—antiques in their own right—occupied the shelves. She showed me a leather-bound copy of French poetry by Baudelaire she was very proud of, and a hundred-year-old copy of *Huckleberry Finn* she kept on a shelf devoted to Twain's books published before his death.

Then there was the computer. It looked as out of place as a Tesla coil in a tiki hut. It was the newest model by Apple, the one Randy drooled over whenever he saw an ad for it. It stood on a worn leather desk blotter, beside a green hooded desk lamp and crystal inkwell on a rolltop desk. The machine obscured the back of the rolltop, completely blocking access to the cubbies and drawers behind it. The keyboard and mouse fought for space on the remaining surfaces and were losing. In a small stack of computer discs, I recognized system programs, Internet setup discs, and a couple of game titles—Colonies, Tetris, and a World of Warcraft thirty-day trial.

"I didn't figure you for a computer gamer," I said.

"It's temporary," she said.

Then she took me by the hand and led me out. We stumbled together as we walked. My feet were heavy. I wanted to lie down. She put me on the couch and told me to undress. I took off my shirt and pants. Rose went back to her bedroom and I saw the flicker of candlelight. "Just a minute," she said.

The booze hit me hard, and my head swam. I wadded up my clothes and lay down for a just a second.

Then the fucking light woke me up.

Then I dragged my hungover body through the apartment to the bedroom.

Then I saw Rose in her sweatshirt and undies lying on the bed, and I bent down to kiss her.

But she was cold and still. And dead. And the carpet welcomed me because I couldn't melt through the floor.

Beside a wind-up clock the size of a Frisbee on the end table, a red candle had burned out. It sat on a chipped china plate. The wax had poured out and over the saucer and had dripped onto a hand-laced doily covering the table. On the floor beneath the table, a bottle of lavender-scented massage oil had tipped and lay in a thick purple pool. I picked up the bottle and capped it, but left it on the floor. I couldn't tell you why.

I stood up and took a deep breath. I closed Rose's eyes gently with my fingers, but they wouldn't close. I needed some pennies. Not the American tiny copper things, but big Victorian disks heavy enough to close her lids and valuable enough to pay Charon for his services. I bet I could even find some in this house if I searched.

I tried to think, but it was like a concrete fog had settled around me and seeped into my head. I was numb beyond shock, as cold and lifeless as the young girl on the bed.

"I didn't even know her last name," I said to no one.

I returned to the front room, acutely aware that I was wandering through a dead woman's apartment in nothing but my day old underwear. I dressed and sat down on the couch, still trying to catch a memory that explained this or, better yet, directed me to some action.

Naturally, I thought of leaving. Then I thought of wiping down all the surfaces with a towel and then leaving. But I'm not a total jerk, and I only entertained these thoughts for a few minutes, fifteen maybe, thirty at the outside, while I watched my hands shake.

Finally, I gathered myself together, stilled my hands, and found my feet. I crept to the corner of the living room where a beige princess phone sat next to a writing pad and a gold pencil. I'd had a phone just like this growing up. Even the color was the same. I made the call.

"I'd like to report a death," I said. "She was sweet and beautiful, and I think she overdosed."

Luckily I didn't have to give them the address. I didn't know it. They traced it to the phone and asked me if I wanted to stay on the line. I said I didn't, but they told me not to leave: people were coming.

I sat back down on the couch and thumbed through the *Life Magazine* not seeing a thing.

I got up and closed Rose's door. I found my way into the bathroom and took a leak. My head was bursting. I opened the medicine cabinet to get an aspirin and found it bare except for a single glass thermometer and a box of feminine products I didn't need at the moment.

I searched the bathroom for the bottles I'd seen the night before but found no sign of them. Maybe I was questioning my drugged and drunken memory, maybe I needed something to do, or maybe I just wanted some goddamn aspirin, but I looked in every cabinet, under every towel, and behind every piece of plumbing a pill might have rolled behind. I found nothing.

In the kitchen, I found a clean sink and some vitamins in a cabinet. I took one of those. I could find nothing else to dull the developing adrenaline headache that was then actively competing with my others. Zinc would have to do.

In my pocket, I found the finger trap Rose had given me the night before. I stared at it for a long while sitting at her little kitchen table, sipping water out of a Fred Flintstone collector cup. When I'd drunk enough water, my eyes filled with it, and I let some drop onto the floor.

CHAPTER TEN

I waited for the police in silence, feeling the creeping weight of shock and grief spread over me like a frost. It was quiet in Rose's kitchen, and white, and clean, and cold. So it was there I sat and waited.

Suddenly, I heard hard pounding on the door. It sounded like someone trying to chip wood samples from the paneling with the edge of a metal flashlight: the policemen's calling card. I imagined splinters in the hall and divots in the door as the hammering roused me out of my chair.

I'd just turned the knob past the latch when the door burst open and knocked me square in the forehead. I tumbled back into the room and fell over a chair. The room erupted in thunder. Three loud gunshots rang out before I had time to realize I was no longer on my feet. The room filled with cordite smoke. A flashlight beam danced through haze in a grotesque mockery of the previous night's dance party light show. Hidden in the smoke, a nine-year-old squeaked "Halt! Police! Don't move, or I'll shoot!" The final exclamation point was another gunshot.

I didn't move. I moaned.

A man in a black uniform, shiny badge, and new acne ran up beside me and hit me upside the head with a nightstick. As my consciousness decided it had better places to be, I thought I heard an adult somewhere in the distance shouting, "God damn it, Devon! Stand down!"

* * *

When I came to, I was lying on Rose's couch again. Two paramedics were winding gauze around my head and right foot. The head I remembered; I asked about the foot.

"Bullet grazed you," a gloved EMT said.

A tall policeman appeared behind him. I cringed when he approached, but relaxed when I saw he was black, had three stripes on his shoulder, a holstered gun, no nightstick, a mustache, and no acne.

"Mr. Flaner?" he said.

The paramedic must have taken mercy on me while I was out, because I felt the soothing effects of his chemical kindness. For a moment at least, I no longer wanted to wrench my skull off with a shovel. The room slid into soft focus, and I was grateful for it. The sun had moved out of the window—another mercy. I wondered what time it was, but didn't care enough to find out.

I noticed my wallet on the coffee table, the contents arranged in neat columns beside the Fab Four. "Yeah, that's me," I said to the policeman.

"I'm Sergeant Barkley, Salt Lake City Police, Internal Affairs. I was called in after the shooting was reported," he said.

He waited for me to say something. "And?" I said.

"I'd like to apologize for Officer Devon," he said. "He thought this was a hostage situation. He regrets shooting you."

"And clubbing me?"

"Yes, that too."

"Why didn't he just say 'hello'?"

"He thought there was a hostage situation," the cop said to the wall behind me.

"Why did he think there was a hostage situation?"

"He was confused. The codes for hostage situation and dead body are pretty close."

"No, they're not," I said. Of course I didn't know, but he was lying. I knew that.

The cop hesitated and then faltered. "No, they're not," he admitted. "But he was still confused."

"Well, it's good to know that if there had been hostages here, Devon would have gotten them all."

"He did knock," the sergeant said.

"Right. So the kidnappers had time to line them up for Devon the Destroyer. Snazzy," I said.

"Officer Devon is a rookie. You have to expect things like this."

"Do I? My mistake then for not wearing my Kevlar socks."

The paramedics packed their tackle boxes and promised to take me to the hospital in a little bit. I watched them go past the chipped door, past a pimple-faced cadet who ducked back in the hall when he saw me looking.

"Are you the man who called about the dead body?" It was another young cop. Maybe twenty-five, maybe twenty-two. Though his age suggested Wendy's night manager, I figured he was a detective because he had the same narrow mustache as the sergeant, but wore a trench coat instead of a uniform. I didn't know they still made trench coats, nor did I think they were still in fashion. And I definitely missed the memo about wearing them indoors in the summertime. His badge hung on his belt and he stabbed at a sixty-five-cent notebook with a pencil stub. When he spoke he made slow, drawling syllables as if imitating Humphrey Bogart without being too obvious.

"Yes, I'm the guy who called about the dead body," I said slowly.

That interested him enough to make a note in his pad.

"I understand you were shot resisting arrest," he said.

"No," I said. "I was shot answering the door."

"Then you were bludgeoned for resisting arrest."

"No, I was bludgeoned for moaning."

These answers confused him. He looked at the sergeant who studied the wall. I glanced back and saw three neat holes about chest level drilled through a framed Van Gogh print.

The detective shifted gears then. "You don't live here?"

"No, I'm just visiting."

"But you knew the deceased, Rose Griff?" he said, reading from his notebook.

"Griff? That's her last name," I said. "I didn't know it."

"But you knew her?"

"Yeah. We met a few days ago. We went out last night to a party and then came here."

"Where was the party?"

"At the airport."

"Oh, yeah, you're a pilot or something?"

"Something," I said. "But it wasn't there."

"Wasn't where?"

"At the airport."

"Then why did you say it was?"

"It wasn't that airport. It was the other one."

"What other one?"

"The other airport."

"What other airport?"

"The other one," I said.

He gave me a look that said he knew I was lying. He started a new page in his notebook and went on.

"Do you know what they do to people who break the law in other countries?" he asked.

"Make them king?"

"No, they're very harsh. In Arab countries, they cut off thieves' hands."

"I've heard that."

"And not just their own people. There was a Canadian caught cheating in a marathon in Thailand. Know what they did to him? Sentenced him to twenty years hard labor, no parole, for using a bike. See where I'm going with this?"

"Uhm," I said. "You're going to deport me to Thailand for riding a bike?"

"I saw no bike here." He looked around.

"My bad. You're deporting me for reporting a death. I've already been shot and clubbed for answering the door."

"No. Neither. That's not what I meant." He was flustered. His face turned red.

"Don't tell me you're actually trying to intimidate me with what happens in other countries? I'm the victim here, in case you didn't notice the bandages or my dead friend in the next room." My patience was running out. Luckily the painkillers weren't, and I settled back after an uncharacteristically short outburst.

"I just wanted to make a point," he said, thinking he'd made one.

"Then, no. I have no idea where you're going with this. What's your point?"

"Crime doesn't pay."

"Is there a grown-up I can talk to?" I searched the faces in the room, silently beseeching Sergeant Barkley for help. He responded with a pained look and a shift in his weight. I was on my own.

"Mr. Flaner," the little detective went on, "you said on the 9-1-1 call that she overdosed?"

"Yes, I think so."

"You think you said that or you think she overdosed?"

"Yes."

Again he paused, confused, but shook it off after scribbling a note.

"What makes you think she overdosed?"

"There were drugs at the party." He recorded this revelation.

"But she was alive when you arrived here, correct?"

"We both were," I said. He made another note.

"So she died after you were both here in the apartment?"

"As far as I know," I said. This interested him very much, and he underlined something.

"Did you have intercourse with the deceased?"

"No. Not even when she was alive." He looked up from his notepad, confused and wary. He didn't want to be tricked.

"No," I said. "We didn't have sex."

"But you were planning to?"

"Would have been nice, but we passed out. She didn't wake up." He nodded as if I'd proved his complicated theory and he'd solved the case.

"I couldn't help noticing a wedding ring on your finger, Mr. Flaner. Does that mean you're married?"

I didn't feel like explaining to this bozo, so I just said, "Yes."

That made him smirk.

"And who the hell are you?" I asked.

His face became a picture of horror. He looked around like he'd misplaced his keys and was late for a live liver transplant for his favorite child.

"Didn't I introduce myself?" he stammered. "Didn't I read you your rights?"

"No," I said.

"Sergeant, you heard me identify myself to Mr. Flaner, didn't you?"

"I'm not sure," he said. "You might have, detective . . . detective . . . ?"

"McGraw," he said.

"Yes, Detective McGraw, you definitely, probably, introduced yourself to Mr. Flaner prior to taking his statement."

"Good."

"Probably," added Barkley.

"And his rights? Did you hear me read him his rights?"

I turned and looked squarely at the Sergeant, daring him to lie again. He balked.

"No, sir, actually, you didn't. But you don't have to unless he's a suspect and being charged."

"Oh, good. Then everything's okay." He closed his notebook with a cardboard snap.

"Detective?" called a man from Rose's bedroom. McGraw got up and shambled over.

The young gunner still hovered in the doorway but ducked when he caught me looking at him again.

"Devon's a menace," I said to Barkley.

The policeman looked around to see if anyone was close enough to hear him. "Yes, he is," he said quietly.

"McGraw, any relation to Lt. Governor McGraw?"

"Cousin."

"He's an idiot."

"Yes, he is."

McGraw skipped out of the bedroom and down the stairs. In a

few minutes he loped back up as excited as a kid at Christmas. Behind him came three people wearing blue rubber gloves. One began to take pictures. Another dropped a stack of cardboard on the floor and set about folding them into boxes, while the third went with McGraw into the bedroom.

"I suspect you'll want to issue a complaint against the Rookie Devon?" said Barkley, apparently just for something to say.

"I don't know," I said. "Ask me later."

"There'll be an inquiry, anyway," he said, just passing the time.

"Uh-huh."

"Sure is a lot of paperwork in a shooting case," he said, just making conversation. "Maybe you have some parking tickets we could help you with? You know, if you let bygones be bygones?"

"You do realize I was shot and clubbed and possibly sodomized while unconscious?"

Barkley's implacable expression waxed over in new dread.

"I had not heard about the latter incident," he said.

"I don't know for sure he's a rapist," I said. "I'll have it checked out at the hospital and let you know. I'm sure we'll need a semen sample from Devon for comparison. You might get him started on that."

Somehow, the volume of my voice had risen during the last part of our conversation and the other officers in the room hushed to listen.

"I better talk to the captain," Barkley said, reaching for his shoulder radio and making to leave. I caught him before he did.

"Just how long has Devon been a policeman?" I asked.

"Six and a half hours," he said with a glance at his watch. I waited for the punch line. It didn't come. He was serious. He was worried. He was at the scene for damage control, and I wasn't being controlled.

I felt a scene coming on, an outraged tirade about police brutality and excessive force worthy of a *60 Minutes* segment, but I couldn't quite get it primed. I was hungover, shot, and beaten. I'm sure I was in shock too. The paramedics had put a blanket around me; that usually meant shock, right? Either that or I had no clothes on. I was still dressed. I checked. I was not having a good day. The physical pain was dulled by the magic medic injection, but I hurt more than that. I suddenly really missed Rose Griff, the stranger who'd become my new interest, my island, my salvation, my pull. Now where was I?

McGraw trotted out of the bedroom and presented himself directly in front of me with a little hop. I looked up and leaned back because his crotch was in my face, and I didn't like him in that way. He smiled at me. I smiled back. It was all very smiley. He reached into his front pants pocket and took out a dog-eared, laminated card. "You have the right to remain silent," he read with giddy enthusiasm. "Anything you say can and will be used . . ."

I knew the lines. Every TV watcher in America knew their rights thanks to TJ Hooker, the CSI teams, and a cavalcade of giggling patrolmen trying to wedge a screaming, naked meth-addict into the back of a police cruiser every Saturday on *Cops*. I was very glad I'd gotten dressed.

When he finished, he twitched his head at the sergeant in some kind of code that was as lost on him as it was on me. He tried it again and got the same result. Finally McGraw said, "Book him."

One of the policemen snickered.

McGraw's face reddened. "Cuff him," he said. "I'm arresting him for murder."

"Why?" I said. "What's happened? What's going on?"

"I've been informed that Miss Griff was strangled to death, Mr. Flaner."

"*Possibly*," came a loud voice from the bedroom.

"Excuse me," he said. "I've *possibly* been informed that Miss Griff was murdered."

There were more titters among the ranks, but none from me or from Barkley, who helped me to my feet and cuffed my wrists before sitting me back down.

"Is false arrest serious?" I asked Barkley.

"Can be," he said.

From the doorway, I saw a look of joyous redemption beam across Officer Devon's pimpled baby face.

CHAPTER ELEVEN

McGraw was so excited to have an actual murder case, I expected to receive a thank-you card from his wife, girlfriend, or tissue supplier. He was the most junior detective in the city, possibly in the history of the city, possibly in the history of the history of cities. He was the favored cousin of the man who was an obese heartbeat away from being governor of the state. He nearly cried when I refused to talk to him anymore at Rose's apartment.

"I won't say another word without a lawyer present," I said.

"Please," he begged.

"No."

"Come on." His powers of persuasion were formidable, but I resisted.

I never got my ride to the hospital. They took me to jail instead. The painkillers had worn off by the time we rolled into the underground parking structure and boarded a steel elevator only cargo could love.

I was fingerprinted, photographed, felt up and felt down, de-shoe-laced, stripped, costumed in a dashing creamsicle sack they called a jumpsuit, and accessorized with chains before being marched in baby steps to a cement closet. There, they were nice enough to take off the chains, so I had to say the day was getting better. However, I was very hungry and asked the locked eye-level door slit when I'd be fed. It didn't answer.

I tried to remember prison songs, but went as far as "swing low sweet chariot" before realizing I didn't know the rest of the words to that one. I sang them again anyway. I then chanted "Brubaker!" for a while, then switched to "Attica!" and then tried to explain that what we had here was a failure to communicate. Nothing drew the attention of a guard, let alone a taco vendor, so I laid back and tried to think away the bumps on my head and magically knit new skin to cover my leg wound. Mudge would be proud. After a while, I forgot my pain, but I couldn't forget Rose.

"What a waste," I said to the light bulb behind a steel cage in the ceiling. I think it understood and felt the same.

I must have fallen asleep because when I woke up, the room looked exactly the same as before, but my breath was worse.

"Flaner, time for your phone call," said a uniformed guard dangling silver chains and handcuffs.

I was tied up like a fly lure and perp walked to a room with a phone old enough to interest Rose. There was no dial and no buttons. I picked up the receiver and heard, "What number please?"

I gave my home number, and waited. I heard it connect, heard it ring. I knew the answering machine would kick over at the sixth ring and panicked when the fifth came and went. Someone picked up.

"How was I supposed to know you were in the bathroom?" yelled Randy across the receiver. "Hello?"

"Randy, it's me, Dad."

"Hi, Dad." I could hear computer games in the background.

"Can you get your mom for me?" I asked.

For an answer I heard a loud crash, a rattle, and a thump.

"Sorry," he said, "dropped the phone." I could hear the telltale sounds of the phone being pinched between neck and shoulder, scrunch and squeak.

"I need to talk to Mom," I said, holding the phone to my ear with my two cuffed hands.

"She's in the bathroom. She'll be done in a minute. Why don't you call back and she'll pick up." I heard the phone move off his shoulder and screamed.

"Randy, get your mother on the line right now." I used my "I'll take away your computer" voice. That got his attention.

"Okay."

"Mom! It's Dad!"

Another extension picked up. Randy hung up before Nancy said a word.

"Are you done running away?" she asked. "Have you finished with your little tantrum now? Have you, Tony? Are you ready to be an adult now?"

"No. No. Yes, and never," I said.

"What?"

"Nancy. I've been arrested."

"I should have known," she said. "Well, I'm glad you spent the night in a drunk tank. Teach you a valuable lesson. You wrecked the car, I assume, and need a ride?"

"I think the car's all right," I said. "I didn't get arrested for drunk driving."

"You got lucky then."

"Well, no. Not really. You see I've been arrested for murder."

She sighed. "You're not really at the jail are you? This is just a pathetic cry for attention. I expected it. Leafcaller said you'd try something like this. He's met you just the once and already reads you like a book. He is so wise."

"Twice," I corrected her. "He's met me twice. And he's an idiot."

"I'm not playing this game with you, Tony. Come get your stuff, or I'll throw it all out on the lawn."

"Nancy, I'm really in jail."

"The caller ID says pay phone. Get your lies straight."

"Nancy," I begged.

"Nice try, Tony. I'm hanging up."

"Nancy, I'm really in jail, you've got to—" She hung up.

You'd think after fourteen years she'd know when I wasn't joking. Then again, maybe it was because she'd known me so long that she thought I was.

I hung up the phone and raised it again. There was no voice on the other end this time. The guard escorted me back to my cement room.

McGraw was in the hall when I turned a corner. He had his foot against the wall and his hands in the pockets of the same worn trench coat he'd worn earlier. He looked like Columbo, the streetwalker.

"So when is your lawyer getting here, killer?" he said in Bogart.

"Alleged killer," I corrected him.

Panic flashed in his eyes, and he looked to see if anyone else had noticed the faux pas. Then he realized I was messing with him. I don't know how he figured it out so fast. I think I was witnessing evolution in action.

"Oh, you did it," he said. "And I'm going to send you to the chair."

"Utah doesn't have the chair," I said.

"Nice try, Tony," he said. That line was a refrain today.

"He's right, detective. Utah has a lethal injection now for capital crimes," said the guard, who struck me as young, but still twice as old as McGraw. "Before that we had the firing squad. Never had the electric chair."

Then it hit me where I'd seen McGraw's expression before. He had that stay-up-all-night-studying-and-still-fail-the-quiz look seldom seen this side of fifteen. I bet his coworkers saw it a lot, though.

"Yeah, but they sit you in a chair when they shoot you full of poison," he said menacingly.

"No, it's a gurney," corrected the guard. "Like a hospital bed."

"Maybe there's a chair involved at the last meal," I offered. "At breakfast maybe, unless it's buffet style. Then you might as well eat in line standing up." I urged my guard to take me away from the silly man.

Since all my rights had been properly observed, I was released into the general population. My new cell was no larger than my earlier one, but I got to share this one with five other men who didn't like bathing, and spoke in monosyllabic profanities and grunts. If only I had smuggled in a lighter or a book, they'd have worshipped me as a god. As it was, they left me alone.

It wasn't prison. It was jail. The accused and the guilty mixed together like dancers at a cotillion. Killers and jaywalkers played dominos together while rapists and embezzlers talked sports under a seventy-year-old six-inch TV hanging in the common room.

There were serious hard cases, but they had their own cliques, some would call them gangs. I certainly did. The hard cases messed with other hard cases and the hard case guards messed with them. I was no hard case. I was soft and squishy. Even when I told my cellmates I was in for murder, they didn't believe me. They thought I was joking. "Nice try, Tony," they said.

The next day I met my lawyer, Morris Mollif. We had ten minutes of quality time in a beige concrete room with two plastic chairs and a steel table bolted to the floor. Mollif was a court-appointed public defender. I couldn't judge how old he was. From a distance, I'd put him in his forties, but up close, he looked like an unwrapped mummy. He'd either spent years of his life under a blazing tropical sun, or fallen asleep in a food dehydrator. His suit was as worn as my orange sack, and his tie didn't match his shirt, which didn't match his pants, and none of it matched his gray penny loafers. The most striking feature of my champion were his eyes. When seen through the clear dinner plates he used for glasses they made him look like a starving child I'd seen painted on black velvet at an I-80 truck stop. It was magnified despair. When he took the glasses off once to clean them on his shirt, I saw that the despair wasn't being magnified by his glasses, only televised.

"Today's only a hearing," he told me. He had a folder with my picture clipped to a form. "You should stand mute for now. We'll figure a plea after I've talked to the DA. Maybe we can get this over with this month."

"I'm not guilty."

"Innocence proves nothing," he said. "They want you on murder one, but that's always hard to prove even if they have you on film and caught you with the bloody knife." He looked up at me then. "They don't, do they?"

"No."

"Okay, no witnesses. We'll go for manslaughter. They may wave around the murder word for a while until the DA decides if there's traction in the case, then they'll settle up. Is there any?"

"Is there any what?"

"Traction. Is there something about this case, you, or the girl that will get the DA on the front of a newspaper or talked about? It's nearly sweeps week."

"I won the Nobel Peace Prize in 2003," I said. "And the victim was Obama's secret love child."

"I don't see any of that here," he said, glancing down at his file. "Background is always sketchy this early on."

"I was joking," I said.

"About what?"

"About there being traction."

"You didn't win the Peace Prize?"

"No."

"And the girl?"

"Not Obama's love child."

"Are you sure?"

"Pretty sure, but I didn't know her that well."

"So she could be?"

"I guess."

"Best keep that under our hat. No need giving them ammunition."

There was a knock on the door, and Mollif stood up.

"Let's go," he said. "Try and look innocent."

"I am innocent," I said.

"Good. Go with that."

The hearing was brief. At one table, there was Mollif and me. In the middle, on a dais behind a bench, sat Judge Steiner, a man so bald, light reflected off his head like a disco ball. At the other table, McGraw sat next to a woman in a slate gray business suit beneath a severely short, primer gray haircut. She looked like a granite block. A granite block with pink lipstick. She introduced herself as Ms. Penelope Sweet from the District Attorney's office.

Judge Steiner asked what I'd been charged with.

McGraw sprang up from his chair so fast I think his feet left the ground.

"First-Degree-Homicide-with-malice-aforethought-exhibiting-deviant-behavior." The sentence came out as a single word.

"I don't know who you are," Judge Steiner said, "but the question was directed to Ms. Sweet. If you speak out of turn again, I'll give you a time out. Now sit down and shut up."

I suppressed a smile behind my innocent face.

"The charge is murder, Your Honor," said Sweet.

"What are the recommendations for bail?"

"No bail," said the not-so-sweet Penelope Sweet.

Mollif spoke then and said that since I was such an upstanding, gainfully employed citizen, I should be released on my own recognizance. The speech would have been more moving if he hadn't said it in a tone of such pathetic resignation that I think everyone in the court wondered why he'd bothered speaking at all. I wanted to put my arm around him and comfort him. He needed a hug.

Steiner looked at my enemies again and asked for an actual bail suggestion. Sweet asked that bail be set at 17.5 million dollars, claiming that I was a flight risk since I worked for an airline, had a history of committing crimes out of state, and was obviously hiding something since I'd refused to make a statement. When the judge asked what other crimes I'd done, the woman DA had to admit that I'd been arrested for disorderly conduct in New Orleans during Mardi Gras.

Mollif said I hadn't been given a chance to provide a statement since I'd asked for counsel, and he'd received the case only forty-five minutes earlier. The judge asked if I intended to make a statement, and I said I already had, but would again if that pleased the court. I thought saying "pleased the court" would make him my buddy.

"Bail is set at five-hundred thousand dollars," he said.

What a pal.

"And counselor," he said to Sweet, "the accused has the right to remain silent."

"Yes, Your Honor," she said. She was unflappable. Unchippable.

Back in the shrinking concrete room with the heat-sucking steel table, Mollif smiled a forlorn grimace of surrender, which was as expressive of true happiness as he was able.

"That went well," he said. "Sweet is the most junior Assistant DA in the building."

"She looks hard," I said, thinking that the word was exactly right.

"She's inexperienced. She'll be zealous, but will make mistakes. Zealous is bad, but mistakes are good. If she's smart, she'll deal."

"What about the plea?" I said.

"That's later."

"Then what was that all about earlier?"

"Making sure you don't plead on accident, so I can go to Sweet and make a deal."

"But we haven't seen the evidence," I said. "And I'm innocent, remember?"

"Eh-huh," he said, looking at me but seeing something else, probably my poisoned, bullet-ridden body slouched in a lounge chair.

"You got someone on the outside working for you?" he asked.

"You," I offered.

"Someone else? Family? A lodge brother? Anybody?"

I told him about my phone call to Nancy and mentioned the divorce. He shook his head in resigned sympathy and passed me a card. It read: "Nephi's Freedom Bail Bonds and Pawn."

"Ask for Ganesh Lahkpa," he said, standing up.

"That's it? You're leaving?"

"I've got three more hearings this morning," he said. "I'll get with Sweet and see what's what. Call Lahkpa, he'll get you out in a couple of hours, if you have the money. Don't lose my card."

And he left, without giving me his card.

They gave me another call, or rather they charged my prison account for it, and I called Ganesh Lahkpa. I told him my problems. He told me to "forget about it" in the worst Nepalese New Jersey accent I'd ever heard, which, to be fair, I didn't have a lot to compare to.

Lunch was chili. Dinner was burgers. Breakfast was scrambled eggs. Then lunch was PB&J and dinner was stew. And then we had oatmeal, and soup for lunch.

I guess Ganesh Lahkpa had forgotten about it. So had Morris Mollif.

Then Nancy came to visit.

We faced each other across a small table separated by glass so thick it made everything look green. Black plastic phones with three inches of cord carried our voices to each other.

"Well, Tony, I never suspected the depths of your inability to cope," was how she said hello.

"How's Randy?"

"Leafcaller is balancing his grief centers. He'll pull through, but I don't think he'll ever look at the you same."

"I didn't do it."

"Denial is the first phase."

"Nancy," I said, trying to remain calm, "I didn't kill anyone."

She was about to reply, but I fixed her with my gaze and she paused. "I didn't do it Nancy," I said again. "I'm innocent. I'm Tony, the slacker, not Jack the Ripper."

I could see rehearsed lines drain away like pee down a flushed toilet.

She said, "I know you didn't do it, Tony. In my heart I know this is all some kind of mix-up. I promise I'll do all I can to help."

"Good. Did Ganesh Lahkpa call you about bail?"

She hesitated, looked over my right shoulder and prepared to tell me something bad. I knew her body language. She took a deep breath and spoke.

"Maybe this is a good thing you're in jail," she said.

"Ehhhh! Oh, God!" I blurted out. The guards turned my way.

"Mr. Lahkpa says we need half a million dollars in collateral," explained Nancy.

"We've got that in the house and more in savings," I said.

"Yes, but since we're in divorce limbo, it's not clear how all this will be divided up."

"Okay, put my half up as collateral," I said.

"You're not taking the divorce very well, Tony," she said. "You showed that at dinner with Leafcaller."

"So?"

"I know you've been in denial about all this. I couldn't help noticing you did absolutely nothing to prepare. You had six years to put things in place and haven't done a thing."

"There's still time," I offered.

"And you didn't box up a single thing on Saturday. And you weren't even curious about your new house."

"I boxed stuff up. I'm curious."

"What I'm saying, Tony, is that I think this whole divorce will go a lot smoother with you out of the picture for a while. I could put together a plan to get you out, arrange an attorney, and handle this mess for you, but, as Leafcaller said, it's time for you to spread your own wings and fly."

"What? He's involved?"

"I'm told that the final papers will be done in a week or so. There were some changes because of this situation. When they're done, we can sign them and put this behind us."

My jaw twitched to frame words that slid off my teeth, unspeakable and blurred, surreal and profane.

I swallowed hard and said, "Didn't you just say that you'd do anything to help me?"

"I am helping you, Tony. Sometimes you don't realize what's best for you."

"And you do? Mudge does? Here? Now?"

"Tony, this is for the best. One day you'll see it and thank me."

I didn't know what to say, then it came to me. "Ahhhhh!" I shrieked.

She smiled soothingly. My molars ground my fillings flat.

"So," Nancy continued, "after the papers are done and the assets are clear, you can bail yourself out, see?"

"No, I don't fucking see," I said. "What about my stuff and my job?"

"Oh, yeah. You were fired yesterday for not showing up. Leafcaller and I can box your things up and move them into your wonderful new home. Everything will be happy and waiting for you when you get out."

"Nancy, you know that bail is just the beginning, right? I have to fight this thing. I'm in trouble. I gotta get out of here and figure out what's what."

"And you'll have your own assets and your whole life ahead of you to deal with those challenges. Leafcaller is right. This is the first step to your new life. Leafcaller told me to tell you not to let the first step be damage."

"Damage?"

"Emotional damage," she said.

"I think he meant the financial damage of a trial."

"You need to accept this change, the divorce, and your new challenges."

"So you and Mudge are going to leave me in here to rot until after the divorce is final." I wanted it to be a question, but it was fact and came out as fact. I was fucked.

"It's a good thing, Tony. Time for you to get in touch with yourself. A blessing, really. Use this time to meditate, undistracted on life's little surprises."

"You've got to be kidding."

"No, Tony. I'm not kidding."

"What about a lawyer? I've got an overworked, defeatist mummy on my case now. Can you at least get me a good lawyer?"

"I've met with Morris. He's a good man. He'll do until the assets are cleaned up, and then you can pick the very best lawyer you can afford. Leafcaller knows a Shoshone tribal lawyer who's very good. I'll get his name, but we're not sure if he can practice off of the reservation."

"This isn't happening," I muttered into space. Some of it spilled into the phone.

"Don't worry, Tony. I believe in you." She blew me a kiss, waved like she was off to the hairdresser's, and left me holding the black plastic phone against my ear like it was a pistol.

CHAPTER TWELVE

The judge had made it a stipulation that I make some kind of official statement for bail release, if only to officially say I wouldn't be making an official statement. I think he was trying to help Sweet save face. Ever the optimist, I wanted to make the statement without delay so I could be bailed out immediately when Nancy came to her senses. Three days later I was called away from my Hearts game with "Steel Shank Raul," "Drive-by Massacre Menendez," and "Trevor, the condom shoplifter" to make my official statement.

Morris Mollif and I were seated at a wooden table in a small, stuffy room with a mirror on one wall and cameras in two corners of the ceiling. A silver microphone as big as my fist stood in the middle of the table, the wire snaking through a hole and connecting to a socket in the floor. Many someones had etched graffiti into the table, obscenities mostly. The words "Take the 5th" were written three times in three different hands. Oddly, each had exactly five exclamation points and five heavy underlines. It was a theme. There was also a column of "No's" eleven inches long written recently in blue ballpoint over a succinct piece of advice directed to the police.

Opposite us sat McGraw, Sweet, and Sergeant Barkley: an eager child, a stone pillar, and an irritated cop. McGraw tried to look tough, but looked petulant, young and jumpy. Sweet tried and succeeded at looking serious. Barkley tried to look interested but looked put out. I looked innocent. I'd been practicing my innocent face ever since my hearing. I'd spent hours staring at myself in the polished metal mirror in my cell, perfecting the ultimate expression of confidence and purity.

"Why'd you kill the girl?" said McGraw as Bogart to break the ice.

Penelope Sweet put her pale gray hand on McGraw's sleeve to silence him and spoke into the microphone.

"Interview statement with Tony Flaner concerning the wrongful death investigation of Rose Griff." She added the date and time down to the second. She had to look at her watch. There were no clocks in the room. It was a devious psychological ploy, not letting me see a clock, a cruel form of torture so terrible the Geneva Convention hadn't the heart to even bring it up. I feared that at any moment my nerves would crack and I'd collapse into an emotional heap, confessing everything from Roswell to the War of 1812. Luckily, for the moment, at least, I held strong.

Morris spoke then. "Are we to understand that we're not going to discuss the police brutality complaint at this time?"

Barkley flinched. McGraw shifted his eyes. Sweet spoke.

"That was Morris Mollif speaking before. Now Penelope Sweet speaking. I wasn't aware of any complaint being filed," she said.

"It was filed yesterday," Morris said. I'd had half an hour with my mummy the day before and filled him in as best I could about the fateful night. I told him I wanted to file a complaint. He said I'd just make things worse. I reminded him I was charged with murder and asked how things could get worse. He'd said, and I quote, "Things can always get worse." I told him to file it anyway, just so my story held together.

"Penelope Sweet speaking again," she said. "Then, no. That'll have to wait until later."

Mollif made a half nod, half shrug that meant he didn't really care.

"Let the record show that Mr. Mollif nodded in agreement," said Sweet into the steel mesh microphone.

"You don't need to do that," whispered Barkley.

"That was Sergeant Barkley speaking," said Sweet.

"No, you don't need to do that," he said louder. "It's all on video."

"That was Sergeant Barkley speaking again," said the junior assistant DA.

We all stared for a while. After a moment a wave of understanding moved across her face like a passing truck tremor in a teacup. If you weren't looking for it, you'd have missed it.

She was in gray again. It was a lighter gray than before but still grave and mineral. When she sat up straight, I thought I was addressing a weathered obelisk.

"My client is prepared to make an official statement," my attorney said. "And wishes to remind everyone that he already spoke to police at the time of the incident before his arrest."

"But not afterwards," said McGraw. "Why? What are you hiding, Flaner? The truth?" He slipped out of Bogart for a second and into Nicholson. It's hard to say "the truth" dramatically without channeling Jack.

When no one said anything, he went on. "I've seen a thousand guys like you, Flaner. You think you're tough; you think you can do the crime and not do the time. You think you can handle the pressure, but let me tell you, you can't. I'll get to the bottom of this if I have to break things to get there."

In the silence that followed, McGraw shot Barkley a cueing glance. Barkley stared back, then realized he'd missed his line. He said, "Now, detective, there's no need to get hostile with Mr. Flaner. We're all friends here. I'm sure Tony will cooperate if given a chance."

Barkley's monotone recitation was lost on McGraw, who squinted at me with barely concealed, manufactured malice. The sergeant attempted a lifeless, unconvincing smile meant to put me at ease, but it set my teeth on edge.

Sweet scanned her papers and missed the whole good cop, bad cop routine, or maybe she hadn't, and just chose to ignore it, which was the sensible thing to do.

"When can I tell what happened?" I asked.

McGraw drew a deep breath, about to emote again, but was stayed by the monolith beside him when she put a hand on his sleeve.

"Any time is good, Mr. Flaner," said Ms. Penelope Sweet, expressionless and detached. I smiled through my innocent face and waited for a reaction. Of course, there was none.

"I met Rose at the Comedy Cellar at the beginning of the month," I began.

In the brief moments I'd had with Mollif before the meeting, I'd hurriedly told him the whole story. When I'd finished, I'd asked him directly if there was anything I should add or leave out when I spoke to the prosecutors. He'd said only, "Probably."

Some ignorant moron once said "the truth will set you free." I never believed that for a second, but I couldn't think of a better course, so I told them the whole thing: The Sailor, the rave, drugs, friends, dancing, music, lights, car ride, locks, privacy, rum, glasses, tour, and the missed sexual liaison. I told them about the missing pill bottles in the medicine cabinet and the burned candle on the nightstand. I even told them that my wife wouldn't bail me out because she was divorcing me on schedule and was shacking up with a wannabe-dryad named Mudge. The last comment brought Mollif's hand onto my sleeve. A magical gesture, that. I stopped and returned to Rose.

I told them about calling the police and turning the doorknob only to be shot and beaten. Penelope Marble Sweet reacted to my story at that point, but Mollif said it needed to be in the record with the ferocity of a deceased snail and Sweet let me continue. I finished by mentioning handcuffs, jumpsuits, and McGraw threatening me with a lounge chair, though I admitted I didn't know what he meant by that.

It took a while to recite the events that had fucked my life up so completely. The bad cop kept his steely eyes on me, looking for the chink in my armor. The good cop kept stealing glances at his watch, and the assistant DA moved only enough to breathe. Her stillness unsettled me. Once I stopped and waited for her to blink, just to make sure she wasn't dead or a statue.

When I was finished, we got a short break.

I was escorted to a restroom, where I learned how hard it is to pee in handcuffs and a creamsicle jumpsuit.

I hoped no one noticed my crotch spot as I re-entered and took my seat. The three government people sat suspiciously still and quiet. Mollif came in after a minute looking tired and beaten, so no change there.

"Resuming interview with Mr. Flaner concerning the wrongful death of Rose Griff," Sweet said into the microphone. This time, as she spoke, she turned three-quarters profile into one of the ceiling cameras.

"Flaner, your story doesn't line up," said McGraw. I waited for the sleeve touch, but it didn't come.

"To what do you refer?" said Mollif.

"There was no rum bottle in the apartment," he said, as if that settled the entire thing. When I didn't immediately confess, he added, "We searched the garbage and the dumpsters, and took an exhaustive inventory. The boys in blue were thorough. No rum bottle at all, and the only pills we found were in your car."

"Can you explain the pills in your car?" Sweet asked when I still didn't break down.

"I get headaches, thus the aspirin. The hay fever pills in the glove box are in case I ever meet Elvis. I heard he had a thing for ragweed."

"Don't be a smart-ass, Flaner," McGraw said, smashing his hand on the table for emphasis. It startled me.

"Now, detective," said Barkley on cue, "Tony didn't mean any disrespect." Using my first name meant we were buds, I guess.

"We're referring to the sedatives," Sweet said. Then reading from a paper she added, "Flunitrazepam, also known as 'Rohypnol' or 'Roofies.' The date rape drug."

My innocent face changed to surprise.

"What?" I said. "Where?"

"In your car," said McGraw with authority. "In your glove box, you sick bastard."

I don't remember Bogart ever calling anyone a sick bastard, so that, too, unnerved me.

"Not mine," I said, real fear sinking in. "I don't know what you're talking about."

"Miss Griff had a huge amount of the drug in her system at the time of her death. Enough to possibly kill her," said Sweet, reading. "But cause of death was strangulation."

"You drugged her and then tried to rape her," said McGraw. "When she refused to be raped, you strangled her. She was passed out and defenseless, and you killed her."

Mollif moved to say something, but I put my hand on his sleeve. Wow, the power of that gesture is awe-inspiring.

"First point," I said to McGraw, "you're an idiot. A total knuckle-dragging, spit-drooling idiot. If she was passed out and defenseless, how can she refuse anything? Refuse to be raped? You mean if she was awake and armed she could consent to be raped? Do you even know what the word means?"

"So you admit you raped her?"

"I was unaware of any proof of intercourse," said Mollif.

"There isn't any," said Sweet.

"A knuckle-dragging, spit-drooling idiot," I said.

"What's your second point," asked Sweet.

"My second point?" I said, still caught up in my first. "I'm innocent. I passed out. I don't know what happened to the pill bottles or the rum, or how the roofies got in my car. But it's pretty clear there was someone else in the apartment."

"That's not at all clear," said Sweet.

"Have you ever paid for sex before?" asked McGraw.

"What are you talking about?" I said.

"Before your trick with Rose, had you ever employed a call girl before?"

"You're calling Rose a prostitute?"

The lack of a clock had finally gotten to me. I was freaking out.

"Do you deny she was a prostitute?" McGraw said.

My head swam. Damn, if only I knew what time it was.

"Why are you defaming the deceased, Detective?" alliterated Mollif.

"Just putting the pieces together," he said. "I talked to the neighbors. Assembled a profile and came to an obvious conclusion."

"Had Miss Griff ever been arrested for prostitution?" Mollif asked.

Penelope didn't have to look at her papers. "Yes," she said.

To everyone's surprise, Barkley spoke then. "When you opened the door for the officers, did you unbolt the lock?" he asked.

"Sergeant, we're not discussing that incident right now," said Sweet. Ignoring the prosecutor, he looked at me and waited for an answer.

"No," I said. "I got to the door, turned the knob just past the strike plate and boom; I was on my ass."

"You didn't touch the deadbolt?" Barkley said.

"No," I said, realizing the good cop was a good cop. "No, the deadbolt wasn't latched."

"So what? It's still your story against the evidence," said McGraw. "If I were you, I'd get a good lawyer. No offense, Mr. Mollif."

Mollif wasn't offended, which offended me.

"If you have nothing else to add, Mr. Flaner, we'll wrap this up," said the Stone.

But McGraw was not finished. He screwed up his best bad cop face and leaned over the table, index finger waving an inch from my face.

"We got you, Flaner," he said. "There are three elements that convict killers like you." He held up three fingers. "Opportunity," he said, folding down his first finger. "You were the only one there, Flaner, all night long with a drugged girl." He folded down his ring finger. "Means. Your murderous hands to strangle a defenseless girl."

He waved the last finger in my face, the middle one. I think he was trying to communicate something with the gesture, but it was lost on me, and my innocent face became all confusion and anger.

"And motive," he said. "You're a sick killer going through an ugly divorce and needed some easy love. When you didn't get it, you snapped."

He held the middle digit right in my face. "Motive, means, and opportunity," he said. "The three pieces. We got them all. You're going down murder one—genocide."

I held up three fingers of my own.

"One," I said, folding my fingers back the same way the detective had. "Genocide is the extinction of an entire race, not a single person. Learn the language, you ignorant dipshit."

"Two," I said, folding my ring finger down and leaving only the middle digit. "I didn't do it."

"Three," I said, waving my middle finger in his face. "You're a stupid, lazy idiot who gives other idiots a bad name. Get off your nepotistic ass, you fuck, and do your job. Catch the real killer." My cool was lost by then. The shit was real.

There was a touch on my sleeve. McGraw made a grab for my finger. I pulled it away before he could reach it. "Too slow, gotta go," I said, remembering the line from middle school.

The interview over, Morris took me into a private consultation room.

"I'll get this down to manslaughter, don't worry," he said.

"But I didn't do it."

"Doesn't matter," he said. "It looks like you did. They have evidence; we have a story. I'll get with Sweet later and work something out."

"Can't we just wait for the police to finish their work? I'm sure new clues will turn up and prove me innocent."

If he'd been a more cheerful man, he'd have laughed at my ignorance. Instead he said simply, "There is no investigation. You're it."

It was then that my stack came in. My armor of sarcasm was pierced, my cruel sword of truth had failed me, and my personal charm aura was useless. I'd put up a good front for days, but when I was taken back to my cell, I waited until I was alone, and then counted my misfortunes on two hands and a foot before I fell back into my cot, buried my face in my pillow, and screamed until I had no more voice. The little tantrum did wonders for my chakras.

When my voice returned, I called Ganesh Lahkpa, sure that Nancy had changed her mind, or at least hoping she had.

He told me he'd talked to Nancy, her lawyer, my lawyer, and that things should be ready in a couple of days. Or maybe weeks. Months at the outside. For sure. Maybe.

In fact, I had two and half weeks of terrified contemplation. One thing I'll say about Nancy's plan, she was right—by the time I finally made bail, I was ready to accept the divorce.

She didn't come herself. She sent a lawyer named Nosferatu with papers. I might have heard the name wrong, but I didn't miss the intention. I was to sign as instructed and then I'd be a free man, in more ways than one.

I didn't read a stinking word of anything. Mollif hadn't been able to move Sweet off of a murder charge, and McGraw was collecting evidence proving my unstable nature. Mollif was toying with an insanity plea and talked about throwing me on the mercy of the court. "It's your first murder after all," he said.

I signed, trusting fourteen years of cohabitation that I wasn't getting screwed too badly. I had to get out.

Six hours later, Lahkpa came through, and I was fitted with a GPS ankle bracelet. They gave me a shoebox containing my clothes, wallet, shoelaces, jewelry, keys, rave wristband, and finger trap. My clothes hadn't been cleaned, and still smelled of sweat, cloves, lavender, and Rose.

CHAPTER THIRTEEN

"Thanks for the lift, Perry. I'd have called Nancy, but one murder charge is enough."

"No problem, Tony," he said.

I'd healed in jail. My head wounds were memories, and my bullet graze a big scab. I craved pizza and closing the door when I pooped. The little things. I wasn't very talkative on the drive, and Perry was distracted trying to lose a black SUV he swore was following him. I didn't even look. He pulled into the driveway of the house Nancy had said was my new place.

"Nice," he said. "Does it have a pool?"

"I'm seeing it for the first time right now," I said. "But Nancy said there was a hot tub."

"Wow."

The key was under a terracotta planter next to the door that might as well have had the words "key under here" written on it in reflective tape.

"How're things at the club?" I said to fill the awkward silence.

"Fine," said Perry. "My agent got me an audition for Last Comic Standing and a few gigs in Nevada. I'm still banned from that place in Denver because of the biting incident, but things are good."

I opened the door, revealing a dark hardwood floor and stacks of cardboard boxes.

"Everyone's good. We'd have visited, but we're all flakes," said Perry. He surveyed the boxes. "You should unpack."

"You think?"

The house was nice, but hard to see because of the boxes. Some had contents labeled in black Magic Marker, like "paint," "clay," "porno," "hard porno," and "Tony you need help." Many just had question marks on them.

The kitchen didn't have brown boxes. Nancy had sent me nothing of our old kitchen. Everything was new. Clean, white Bed Bath & Beyond boxes showed me my new dinner plates in bright colors printed on the side. A butcher block table and chairs, still with the "On Sale" price tag dangling from a leg, made the room look like a homey scratch and dent showroom.

"I know a guy who can get you a used fridge and stove for cheap," Perry said, always the optimist. "Might want to air them out first, though."

A note on the counter explained the garage codes and garbage pickup schedule. It was in Nancy's handwriting. A neat stack of installation notices stood on the counter. They detailed my phone lines, gas company obligation, electric company obligation, and yard service obligation.

A bank statement with a signature card waiting for my autograph told me that I had a sizable chunk of cash with which to redecorate and start my life over. The house, which was paid for three weeks ago, was now hocked for a half-million dollars for my bail.

My old bedroom had been reconstructed in the new master bedroom, down to my unwashed laundry and hanging love beads. I saw Nancy in that. As cold and heartless as she was leaving me in jail at the mercy of bullies, cutthroats, and dine-and-dashers, she strove to make my first night "home" as familiar and easy as possible.

The rest of my things lay concealed in cardboard. The house was decorated in soothing earth tones—corrugated butcher-brown boxes.

"You want to get drunk?" asked Perry. "I could call the guys over. I'm sure they'll all come and welcome you back. Well, all but Dara. She hates your fucking guts. She thinks you should fry in the electric chair for killing her friend. After being tortured with spiders, that is."

"Utah doesn't have the electric chair," I said. "It's lethal injection. Before that, firing squad."

"Oh," he said. "I'll tell her. Spiders still work though."

"Does everyone just assume I did it? Do all my friends think I'm a murderer?"

"No," said Perry. "Not everyone. And besides, those of us who think you might have done it understand how it could happen. I mean, who hasn't wanted to kill someone before? Really, who hasn't tried?"

"But Dara's really bad? I thought she knew me better than that."

"I don't know," said Perry. "Dara and the dead girl were friends. They went way back. She needs a target for her sadness."

"Yeah, I understand that. I guess."

"Yeah, I bet it'll blow over after the trial."

"And execution," I said.

"Exactly," said Perry. "So how about that drink?"

"I'm not in the mood to socialize right now. I think I'll just unpack a few boxes and maybe get a fridge delivered."

"You want that fridge guy's name?"

"No, I have a guy, too."

"Probably the same guy."

"Yeah."

Perry left me waving goodbye in the doorway like an unkissed prom date.

I watched the sun set from my new back patio before ordering a pizza. I found my car in the garage wedged between a box leaking fragrant oil I couldn't identify and a set of homemade bamboo golf clubs I never finished.

In the main room, under a nest of garbage bags marked "quilting supplies and kite string," I saw the shape of new living room furniture.

With tooth and nail, I ripped shrink-wrap off a new, plush, tan easy chair and flopped into it. I put my feet up on a box marked "knickknacks #34," ate pizza, and fell asleep.

I woke to pepperoni slices spilled on the floor, face down. It was half a thin-crust mandala, a broken Italian dreamcatcher with extra cheese welcoming me to my new life. I peeled a slice off the carpet and had breakfast—lots of fiber; synthetic, but fiber nonetheless.

I was in trouble. I remembered the premonition that I'd find my-self here, but my mind went to the auburn-haired girl who'd died in a room while I slept in the next. The cops were sure it was me, and even though I wrestled with some doubt because I had no memory of those hours, I knew someone else had murdered Rose Griff. And no one was even looking for the killer.

I held the finger trap Rose had given me like a holy icon. I knew somehow that it was the key to everything. I pushed my fingers into the ends and studied the lesson: it's easier to get into trouble than out. Yep, that was it. The lesson I was to learn. But then there was escape and the lesson was more profound. With a shudder I realized that to escape the trap, you must first go deeper into it.

I saw then my life's familiar pattern and smiled. Push, I had to find who killed Rose to keep myself out of a bullet-ridden lawn chair. Pull, I had to find Rose's killer because no one else would. Push and pull to the same thing. My life was in shambles, but back in order.

Nancy had done right by me in her own way. My arrest and murder charges didn't fit into her plan, so she worked around them, albeit with a little help from her new boyfriend. But she hadn't stiffed me. I had money, new furniture, and a home. It could have been worse.

There was a ring at the door.

Three men with knuckle hair installed a set of stainless-steel kitchen appliances. Before they were done, a fruit basket from Nancy's real estate agency arrived by special carrier. "Hope you enjoy your new home!" read the card, not in Nancy's handwriting.

I tipped the installers a pineapple each.

"Nice house, dude," said the one with the furriest hands. "What do you do?"

"I'm a detective," I said, trying it on.

"For how long?" he asked, admiring the marble countertops, mea-suring his career against mine.

"I give it about seven months," I said.

They left.

I examined the suspects: me.

I considered grilling myself under a hot lamp to sweat the truth out of me, but I didn't think I'd get more than the police had. Besides, my heat lamp was packed away with my lizard tank. Poor Scaley. He went too soon.

My seventeen days of contemplative terror in a crotch-binding jumpsuit had reaffirmed my belief that I was not guilty, but I was in the minority. The cops, the good guys, the taxpayers' champions, had already judged and condemned me, and now only waited on formalities before locking me away for a very long time or mixing me the big hemlock cocktail. Their interest in the pretty girl in the blue dress went no further than a crime statistic. But she was a complex human being, a nice girl with eccentric friends and superb taste in furnishings, if not in dance partners. She was also the crux of the mystery.

I heard ghostly applause as I imagined Marlowe and Poirot, and Spade and Holmes standing over my shoulder encouraging me to go forward. With their approval, I plunged into my detective career with precious few leads and fewer clues.

Rose and I had one friend in common: Dara. But Perry had warned me away from her, and knowing Dara and Perry, it was good advice. Many people at the rave had known Rose, but I'd lived in this city my whole life and never heard of a rave before that night. Chances of me getting another invitation to the traveling drug dance were slim. I settled on a hopeful plan of looking for familiar faces at the Comedy Cellar.

My GPS ankle bracelet and locator beacon was already chafing. The rules were that I could go about my business between the hours of 6:00 a.m. to 9:00 p.m. But if my radio babysitter signaled that I wasn't in my house at night, they'd send someone like Officer Devon to get me. Of course, it couldn't be removed by normal humans, and any tampering would mean immediate jail.

But, like I said, it was already chafing.

I plugged in my computer and found an underground video in three and a half minutes. Rather than search my boxes, I made a quick trip to the hardware store for a new soldering iron, cabling, and a sheet of reflective insulation. I already had the microwave oven.

I was feeling pretty good when I put the anklet in my nightstand. I sang, "I fought the law and the law won," before realizing it wasn't the sentiment I was looking for.

The phone rang. I jumped like I'd sat on a baby—a baby with a cattle prod. My freedom would be short lived. I was singing the right song after all. Oh, and people really shouldn't give babies cattle prods.

I found a phone in the kitchen. "Hello?"

"Hello, Mr. Flaner," came the lifeless voice of Morris Mollif. "I just called to see that you made it home all right."

"Yes, you were very helpful," I said. "Oh, wait a minute. No, you weren't."

"I'm sorry I couldn't be there for your release," he said. "Public defenders are busy."

"Why are you calling?"

"I have a list of lawyers that do capital cases. I'll circle the ones that have won some and get it to you," he said.

"That'd be swell."

"I'll be the counsel of record until you change over," he droned. "You should do it right away."

"Because you're busy."

"Yes," he said.

"What can I expect, by the way?"

"Manslaughter is your best chance," he said.

"You know, I really wish innocence mattered in cases like this."

"Yes, that would be good."

I said, "I'm going to investigate the case myself. I'll find the killer and bring him to justice."

Silence on the line.

I went on. "The police aren't looking for the real killer and I don't have much time."

"It's a crap idea," Morris said. "Tell me you're joking. You'll make things worse."

"How can I make things worse?"

"Things can always get worse," he said, repeating his family motto.

"I've got to try," I said. "I believe in my innocence. And I hate seeing innocent people punished."

"Especially if it's you," he said.

"Was that a joke? Mollif have you found a sense of humor?"

"No, just gas. It'll pass," he said. "But you're right. The police aren't doing anything with the case that doesn't prove you guilty."

"I'm innocent."

"Yeah, sorry, presumed guilty."

"Presumed only until they prove it in court."

"Exactly."

"Even if it's totally wrong?"

"That's how things work."

"I'm on the case," I said.

"I have to advise against it. Hire it done if you must. You don't want to be accused of tampering with evidence."

"Couldn't I be accused of paying someone to tamper with evidence?"

"Yes, that can happen."

"So it really doesn't matter."

"I guess not, when you put it that way," he admitted. "Except professionals are good at what they do. You'll make things worse."

"No I won't."

"Yes you will."

"Betcha I won't."

He took in a long loud breath and said, "I'll send over a list of recommended attorneys tomorrow."

"What if I want to keep you?" I asked.

"You'd be a fool."

"But you'd still represent me?"

"I would unless I petitioned the court to be removed."

"What would cause you to do that?"

"I'll let you know," he said.

"Okay, pretend I'm going to keep you. What does it look like?"

"Looks like you're going to jail for a long time."

"How would you defend me?"

"I'd try to bargain down to manslaughter while intoxicated, and get a first offense reduced sentence and counseling."

"And if you couldn't, or your client refused to accept it?"

"Insanity defense," he said without hesitation.

"Another joke?" I said. "I'll look for the list tomorrow."

"It'll be there," he said, starting his goodbye.

"Oh, wait, Morris," I said. "While I still have you, is it possible for me to see what evidence they have against me?"

Morris Mollif was practically a fixture in the halls of justice. Half the guys I met in the stir had him as their lawyer. I figured his position had some unseen perks. Mollif might have access to a secret underground information network where he could bribe somebody, who'd blackmail another, to sneak a peak into the opposition's playbook.

"Oh, yes, of course," he said. "I'll send you copies of everything. Your new attorney will need them anyway. Give me a little time to pull it together."

"Don't get caught," I said.

"What?"

"Don't get caught taking the files," I said.

"You have a right to see all the evidence against you," he said. "It's the law."

"Oh, yeah, I knew that," I said. "Just don't get so caught up in making copies that you make too many or forget something."

"Eh-huh," he said. "You need a good lawyer, Tony."

"I'll look at your list," I said and hung up.

A professional detective, or anyone who'd seen *My Cousin Vinny* might have known that little detail about the American legal system, but I was undeterred. What I lacked in knowledge I made up for in enthusiasm, vengeance, and self-interest. I was on the case.

CHAPTER FOURTEEN

"Hey, Killer!" yelled Standard Flox as greeting. The entire club turned to see me enter. It wasn't open yet, so only the special regulars were there. I scanned their faces, and they gauged my threat. There were some smiles, some frowns, some glares, and some who couldn't look at me, but nobody ran away screaming. So, that was something.

"Tony." It was Barry. In one word the club owner said, "Hello," "How've you been?" and "Get out."

"Barry," I replied, conveying in one word "Hello back," "Life sucks right now," and "No, I'd rather stay, please."

With that cleared up, I slid into the usual booth beside Standard, Garret, and Critter.

"Well, I'll say it since the others are too polite," said Critter. Garret looked uncomfortable. "We're not sure we want to be seen with you, sport."

"I didn't kill anyone," I said.

"Accidental killing is still homicide and frowned upon in certain circles," said the shaggy Muppet.

I said, "I'm being framed."

"I knew it," said Standard. "I told you he was set up."

"No, you didn't," said Critter. "You said you always knew he would snap, and we were lucky he hadn't gone postal on us long ago."

"I was joking, you stupid plush toy. Don't you know a joke when you hear it?"

"I guess not when you say it," the puppet replied. Garret snickered at the comeback. If he weren't schizophrenic, I'd think it was self-serving, but since he was, it was an earned laugh.

Barry sent a pitcher of beer over to the table. He didn't bring it himself, but the waitress said it was on the house, a "welcome back" toast. I poured drinks for everyone, giving Critter half a glass, I doubt he'd even drink that much. I raised my cup in the time-honored gesture of celebration and camaraderie. Standard sipped his beer directly. Garret left his on the table and found something to interest him on the empty stage. Critter just watched me with googly stink-eyes.

"Cheers," I said and drank the whole drink before putting down the glass. I didn't slam it all in one shot, but I held it up to my lips until it was gone in homage to Rose.

"*Tequila Mockingbird* is not even a real book." Perry's voice boomed at no one in particular. He'd entered the club through the back door from the kitchen. "Super classic book every kid is supposed to read, and it's not even a real book."

Several of the wait staff laughed, thinking he was working out a new bit. The glare he shot back said he wasn't. He saw me at the booth and brightened.

"Tony," he said. "Tony, free at last, dear God almighty, free at last." He slid into the booth, pushing Standard over with a hard hip check that shoved him next to me.

"That's an old joke, Perry," Standard said. "*Tequila Mockingbird*'s been done. I saw it in Fresno. If you do it, a thousand comics could say you stole it."

"Stan, if a thousand comics could say he stole it, doesn't that mean that at least nine hundred ninety-nine others did the same?" said Critter.

"Stealing is no way to build your career," he replied. "It's criminal. No one likes a criminal." He glanced at me. "Oh, sorry, Tony," he said, "I didn't mean anything by that."

Perry looked confused at the whole discussion. I looked at each of my friends in turn and then purposefully placed both hands on the table and spoke.

"Let's get this out of the way right now. I am not a killer. I did not kill that girl. And screw you for even thinking I did. Haven't we known each other, sober and drunk, for years? In that time have any of you even seen me try to murder anyone?" They all shook their heads.

"There. You know me. Don't believe the crap you've heard. I'm an innocent man."

"Dara says you got high and your evil side came out, like Kirk in that *Star Trek* episode," said Garret.

"I don't remember seeing her there," I said. "How can she be so sure?"

"Maybe she can't be sure," said Perry, "but she sure can be mad. Steer clear of her."

"Yes, steer clear," the others echoed in chorus, heads nodding, buttons bouncing.

"Guys, I need you to believe me," I said.

"We've all wanted to kill someone," Perry said. "We've all made plans, bought the necessary supplies and stalked our victims. It happens to everyone. It's understandable that one might just forget not to go through with it. We've all been there."

The table fell silent. Everyone stared blankly at Perry. Standard shifted a little closer to me.

"Be that as it may," I said, "I did not kill that girl. I liked her. We had a date. Someone else killed her, and I was framed. The police don't want to find out what really happened since they think they can pin it on me."

"Can they?" asked Critter. "An innocent man?"

"This is America," said Perry. "Of course they can."

"So what happened?" said Critter. "The papers said it was some drug-crazed-homicide-sex-accident-rape-ritual-slaying."

"He's making that up," said Standard. "He doesn't know how to read."

"I went home with Rose after a big party. We got comfortable, had a shot of rum, and then passed out. When I woke up, she was dead, and I was in a world of trouble."

"And someone set you up?" Perry said. "Why do you say that?"

"Because I didn't kill her," I said.

"Why else?"

"Because there were signs that someone else had been there. Because things were missing, unlocked, and planted."

"Surely the police —" began Standard.

"The police busted into the apartment, shot, and clubbed me before I could say good morning. They're worthless."

"They shot you? Where?" said Garret, suddenly joining in the conversation.

"My heel."

"Fuckers," said Perry. "Trust no one. What do you need from us?" His eyes squinted conspiratorially.

"I need you guys to believe me." I donned my innocent face and looked at each in turn.

"I believe you," said Perry.

"I guess I do, too," said Garret, while Critter nodded assent.

"Better story if you're guilty, but yeah, I guess you're not the killer kind," said Standard.

"Thanks, guys." I signaled for another pitcher.

"So what are you going to do?" asked Garret.

"I need to know more about Rose Griff."

"The victim," said Standard, in case someone didn't know.

"Thank you, Standard," I said.

"I prefer to be called Stan," he said.

"I know."

"Well, Dara would be the one to talk to," said Perry, "but . . . you know."

"You guys must know something about her and her friends. Aren't they regulars?"

"No, not really," said Perry. "They are and they aren't. I never talk to them. They come every day for a month and then not again for a year. Usually we see them at that front table on nights Dara has a set."

"Which isn't very often," added Standard.

"Have you seen them since Rose died?"

"I don't know. I'm not really sure who we're talking about," said Standard.

Perry said, "They've been here."

"I need to talk to them. I need information."

"What makes you think they'll talk to you when Dara—your friend Dara—wants to see you dead?" said Garret.

"Dead?"

"That's just what she said. I wouldn't put too much into that," said Standard.

"She bought a gun," said Critter.

"Shut up," said Garret to his right hand.

"I gotta try," I said. "Dead, huh? A gun? Really?"

The Friday crowd trickled in, then surged through the door. Luke patted down a couple of tan-skinned fellows in a blatant display of racial profiling and came up with a knife, a set of brass knuckles and a glass pipe. He confiscated everything and sent them out the way they came. Luke caught my eye, smiled, and winked sympathetically. At least the well-hung bouncer didn't have it in for me.

We sipped beers, talking about the acts I'd missed while away. Wayne Matticks, the traveling comedian who'd insulted us, played for the rest of the week and did very well for Barry. He even did a new bit about a comedian who had to literally kill to get a laugh. He called the bit, "Tony the douchebag." He ended it by saying, "This bit really killed, like Tony, the douchebag" to a big laugh. The gang giggled, remembering the performance. Since I hadn't been there, I couldn't appreciate the humor.

The first act took the stage. It was a musical group, a flute and guitar jazz thing that played instrumental show-tune covers. Since the crowd didn't know many show tunes, most thought they were geniuses and applauded wildly to "Cabaret" and "Luck be a Lady Tonight."

I watched the door for Rose's friends, but came up empty. Before the second act, I saw Dara walk in, see me, and walk right back out again.

The second act was a juggling comedian who'd been drinking. He dropped his balls and most consonants.

Occasionally, a patron would wander by our booth and give me a long, hard look, trying to place me. Sometimes I saw recognition dawn and watched them scurry away, but mostly they just scratched their heads and went to find a more sober friend with which to confer. Eventually, everyone who had noticed me had figured out who I was and knew what I'd been accused of doing. Then everyone in their groups knew, and then their groups told neighboring groups until more people were looking into our booth than at the stage. This was particularly true after the juggler exited. I watched Barry weighing my appeal as an attraction versus my distraction to his paid performers. When a couple pointed, got up and left, it swayed the scales, and Barry signaled for Luke.

Perry got up. He was next to perform. I followed him backstage before Luke could get me. Barry followed me with his eyes but didn't leave the bar. I heard whispers as I walked. Most were "Is that really him?" Some said, "Sick fucker" and "Why'd they let him out?" One girl pouring out of the top of her dress caught my arm, leaned close, and said, "I'll let you do anything you want to me," and licked my ear. Now, why couldn't more people be like that? I blushed and followed Perry behind the curtain.

I'd drunk water since the second act, foregoing conviviality for a clear clue-gathering head. I wanted to leave, get away from all these people who knew me just enough to judge me, but I had nowhere else to go. My detective plans didn't extend beyond these familiar walls.

I thought about going to Dara's, but if there was one of my friends who was capable of killing, besides Perry, who I was sure was capable of anything, it was Dara who had it in for people who'd wronged her in their sleep.

I found a wooden stool and sat down in the wings to watch Perry make his entrance.

Applause.

"Hello, Cellar Dwellers!" he called. "How're you feeling tonight?"

Cheers and applause.

"That's cool. That's great. I'm going to tell you a story that'll change your fucking lives, but first I gotta do something." With that, he replaced the microphone on the stand and walked off stage. Confused murmurs and awkward laughs issued from the floor, but off he went.

Perry came to me on the chair and leaned in close to my ear.

"In table two, front row," he whispered. "Two girls, two guys, and a dude who couldn't make it through a metal detector naked without an hour's notice. Same gang you were with the other night." He concluded with the conspiracy wink, and I replied with a knowing nod. Just for punctuation, he touched the side of his nose and winked again.

He returned to the mic.

I peeked out the stage door. I'd missed their entrance. Tonya was there, Calvin, too. His lip piercings twinkled in reflected light and his leopard tattoo was more visible than before. The large lizard-losing girl, Melissa, was there also, along with two boys I didn't know. I might have seen them at the rave, maybe even at our table before, but I couldn't recollect seeing them. They watched Perry's show and laughed. Perry had a way of retelling his old jokes with new flares that made them fresh on retelling. He had three sets and would rotate some jokes through each and see how they played. And, of course, he had new material and ad-libbed when the mood hit him. He was Barry's favorite for a reason. He was the best of us.

"Will steal for food. It was on the sign," said Perry. "Truth in advertising got me an acquittal." Big laugh.

I hadn't recognized Tonya because she'd changed her hair color. It was yellow-blonde now. It glowed in the light cast from off the stage. It might have been her natural color with added highlights. It might have been a wig. It might have been tapioca-lemon jello.

Melissa wore the same black helmet hair over her puffy eye sockets. She was crying again. I saw her dab tissues to her face through the entire set. She didn't laugh once, and I could tell that it was getting on Perry's nerves. More and more he targeted her directly with his jokes, waiting for her before dropping the punch line. Again and again he missed. He tried a couple of softball heckler comebacks to stop her crying, but she ignored him as effectively as if he were in another building. To his credit, Perry gave up on entertaining her before his last show-stopping bit about road kill cafés. Then, with his last joke about a dead schnauzer, he hit a nerve. Melissa bawled out loud when the crowd cheered and clapped. Something about scraping Mr. Bootsie off a hubcap didn't sit well with her. Go figure.

The group gathered up their things and readied to leave. I slid out from behind the curtain and down the stairs to the bar. Barry was filling orders and didn't notice me.

I arrived just as Tonya finished writing out a check for the bar tab. Barry didn't accept checks. No bar did. This would be bad. My showing up would make things worse.

"Tonya, Melissa, Calvin," I said energetically through my innocent face. "How're you guys doing?"

They stared. The two I didn't know looked to the others and waited. Surprise turned to loathing faster than it took the spotlight to fade.

"Go to hell, you fucker," said Calvin, shifting behind Tonya. "I'd fuck you up right now if we were alone."

He had me in weight, height, age, body illustration and conductivity, but still he used his girlfriend as a human shield. I wasn't worried. I amped up the innocent face. The waitress looked disapprovingly at the check. Sensing the tension, she scooped it up and scurried away to the bar. People at nearby tables hushed and watched us.

"Guys, I didn't kill Rose," I said. "I was framed."

Did that line ever go down on the first telling? I think not. Even I didn't like the sound of it.

"I need to talk to you guys so I can find the real killer," I said.

"Didn't O.J. say that?" said one of the strangers, a kid in a ragged denim jacket, with carefully placed tears. His buddy had the same rips, but his jacket was a shade lighter.

"Are you Dee or Dum?" I asked.

"What?" said the first stranger.

"You're the Tweedle brothers right?"

Tonya shot me a look and turned her back with a toss of her hair and a flick of her chin. It was good.

Melissa stopped crying long enough to collect her thoughts and then bawled louder than ever, adding a few hyperventilating screams into the mix.

"Guys, I just want to talk," I begged. "Just for a second."

Melissa burped out a shriek that alerted security.

"Shut the fuck up you stupid, humorless cow!" Perry appeared at my side. "Shut the goddamn fuck up!"

That shut her the goddamn fuck up. She looked at the blond surfer who'd just tried to make her laugh and now wanted to crush her.

"You don't go to a comedy club to cry, you dimwitted, unloved, future bag lady!" Big laugh and a smattering of applause. Perry still had the crowd.

Tonya was halfway to the door. Calvin followed her closely at a trot while watching me over his shoulder.

Clutching her suitcase-sized handbag, Melissa ran after them, bowling over two chairs and three bystanders in the rush. The ripped-jacket boys shuffled away.

Luke, the bouncer, grabbed my arm and whispered in my ear, "I think you're done for the night."

"Et tu, Luké?" I said.

"Dude," he said in explanation.

He had a point.

"Okay," I said. "Let me go apologize to Barry first."

Perry followed us to the bar. The crowd who hadn't seen the altercation begged those who had to explain what they'd missed. We crossed the shrinking border separating the two factions and were at the bar in a moment.

"Tony—" began Barry.

I cut him off. "I didn't do it," I said. Innocent face.

He nodded, but then looked around at all the people and shrugged, making the same point Luke had.

"They paid by check," I said.

Barry could make a pained look I could only envy. If my innocent face could display the pathos his pained face could, I'd be out of trouble already.

"I'll show you," I said, shoving my way around the bar and reaching into the till. I lifted the change tray where the big bills were kept, and lifted out a rainbow unicorn check and showed it to him.

"Who took this?" he demanded, looking for the waitress who was nowhere to be seen. "If it bounces, I'm coming to you, Tony." He snatched the check away from me, put it back in the register, and stood in front of it so I couldn't open it again.

"Sure thing," I said, making to leave.

Barry pointed to the back/service/murderer exit.

I said goodbye to Perry, who still had another set to do, and left through the back door.

I wasn't worried about the check bouncing. It was only for forty-six dollars, but thanks to my speed-reading hobby of two years ago, I knew where Tonya lived.

CHAPTER FIFTEEN

I fell asleep reading Morris's list of lawyers. I think he just printed it from the National Attorney Databases (NADS) and circled random names. A handwritten note accompanied the list, reminding me to get a new attorney right away. While I transitioned, he would petition for delays.

I didn't take Morris's obsession with dropping me as a client personally, or at least I tried not to. I'm sure he tried to drop every client he got. He really didn't like *me* because I wasn't interested in a plea bargain. But that was all right; the opposition wasn't interested in one either. Mollif's specialty was plea bargaining, the easiest way through the legal system short of a shoelace suicide. When no one wanted to deal, he was lost.

The morning was bright and cheerful. It pissed me off. I was divorced, living out of boxes, fighting for my life, and I'd been thrown out of my favorite bar. I pulled on my robe, went out to the garage, and rummaged through several boxes before finding what I wanted. I returned to my bedroom, put the stuffed elephant on the floor by the bed, and kicked it. That accomplished, I cleaned up and prepared to travel across town to visit the chromatic Tonya.

* * *

Tonya lived in a stucco condo built in the early eighties along with its fifty-three copies. These fifty-four domiciles comprised eight actual structures behind narrow, chipping concrete driveways and plenty of stairs. They were the modern equivalent of the shotgun shack; "narrow" was the key word, but you wouldn't find that listed on any real estate flyer. What you'd find was "spacey," "quaint," and "affordable."

Window wells spoke of basements. Some had upper stories. For the time and price point, they were wonderful; they all had front facings for a one-car garage and a back patio that would hold a single grill or two chairs if you were content with setting your drinks on the ground. The front entries were raised in split-level fashion. Green AstroTurf stairs led to a platform shared by two units. Apparently the residents had decided that neon green permanence was preferable to biannual wood staining; laziness, meet kitsch.

Pillars of white-painted bricks marked the entrance into the complex. A painted sign declared I was entering "Sandy Cove." The common areas were clean but unused. Most of the cars I passed while looking at addresses had blue handicapped parking permits on the mirrors and a manufacture date that was old when I learned to drive.

Tonya's place was unremarkable from its unremarkable neighbors, save the car in the driveway was newer. It was a little blue sports car—Japanese, but I didn't recognize the symbol. It could have been Korean. I'm not up on my car insignia. I didn't think it was Tonya's car. I figured her for something more girlish. This was the kind of vehicle a guy would buy when he didn't have the money or confidence to buy an American muscle car. It screamed Calvin.

I wasn't in the mood for Calvin and his testosterone-fueled pseudo-heroics. I was planning a charm offensive on Tonya and decided to bide my time.

I parked in a narrow visitor lot across the street from Tonya's building, next to a row of mailboxes a quarter mile long. My first stakeout.

I'd come prepared. I'd brought a thermos full of coffee and a sack of sunflower seeds to pass the time. I adjusted the rearview mirror to take in the front of Tonya's condo and waited. I noted the time, 10:14 a.m.

At 11:32 a.m., my bladder was to capacity, and my gums were bleeding freely from misaligned seed husks. I squirmed and squeezed my thighs, and eyed my thermos with malicious urinary intent, wondering how much a new one would cost. Then Calvin came through the door.

He wore the same clothes from the night before: jeans and T-shirt with silver stripes and circles that either meant something cool or would confuse you into thinking it did. He skipped down the green stairs, unlocked his car, slid in, and started it in one motion. Four cylinders of Asian fury hiccoughed into life. He tuned the radio to something loud enough to shake his windows and drove away, his facial piercings beaming in the morning light.

I was out of my car and up the green plastic stairs before the screeches from Calvin's speakers had faded in the distance. I rang the bell and knocked on the door without let up. Tonya opened it.

"What did you forget, Calv—?" she said before recognizing me.

I looked her straight in the eye and while hopping on one leg, my other crossed in front of me, demanded to know where her bathroom was.

In shock, she pointed down a narrow hall. I brushed past her and bounded into the lavatory.

I took in the pink towels, shaped soaps, and designer tissue dispensers while I relieved myself of fiber and fluid. In a copy of *Elle,* I discovered the hidden power of black undergarments for raising self-esteem.

I washed my hands to resurrect my charm offensive with Tonya; how could she deny me anything after I'd charged into her house with a bursting bladder. Even *Elle* couldn't argue with these tactics.

I turned on the fan, opened a window, and lit a match before opening the door. Tonya stood in the hallway. She held a phone in her left hand while her right index finger hovered over the buttons as if it were a plunger on a dynamite spark box.

"I'm calling the police," she said, but she didn't press anything.

"Tonya," I said. "I didn't kill Rose."

"You came all the way to my place and stunk up my bathroom to tell me that?"

"Yes. I mean, no. The second part was an accident. I'm not used to so much coffee."

My explanation didn't move her, which was good—she didn't move her hand to the phone.

"I need to talk to you," I said. "Rose said you were very perceptive, and if anyone could help me figure out who killed her, I figure it would be you."

The lie stalled the finger. I wasn't close enough to see the wheels turning in her head, but I heard them creak. She was thinking.

I donned my innocent face and emoted earnestness.

Creak, clunk, sputter.

"Let's sit down and talk. You can keep the phone, and we'll just talk, okay?"

Grind.

"Nice place," I said. "Is it yours?"

"Yes. It was my grandmother's, but she died and left it to me," she said.

I nodded appreciatively.

She went on. "I'm going to fix it up a bit, put a hot tub in back and surround sound, but the Homeowners Association is afraid I'll throw wild parties or something so they blocked it. But, I mean, it's my right to throw parties, isn't it? I pay the damn fees like everyone else. They don't need to call the cops every time I have people over to swim."

"Two worst words in the English language," I said. "Homeowners Association."

"So true," she said. I waited.

Finally, she closed the phone.

"I guess I can talk to you," she said. "You're not dangerous or anything, are you?"

"No. Not at all."

She waved me into the last room down the hall, the living room. It opened to the width of the condo, maybe twenty feet. A sliding glass door overlooked a green carpeted back porch with a yellow plastic lawn chair and blue plastic lounger. I sat on a beige couch with daffodil patterns woven into the cushions. By the smell and style, I knew Tonya had inherited it with the house. She sat in a matching loveseat set at a right angle to the sofa. A whitewashed, florally-detailed coffee table was littered with empty beer cans and scattered Cheetos. The house smelled of beer, bacon, and nursing-home musk.

She was made up for the day. I don't know what this girl did on Saturdays, but full makeup and a tight dress was the costume for it.

"Why should I believe that you didn't kill Rose," she said. "You were arrested for it. All the TVs said so."

It was hard to argue with all the TVs, but I had an idea.

"They let me out," I said, framing my innocent face with my hands.

She couldn't argue the logic of my being free. It must mean I was innocent. The nuances of the bail system were lost on her.

"So who did it?" she asked, leaning forward.

"I don't know, but I'm going to find out and you're going to help me."

"How?"

"Tell me about Rose," I said.

"Whatcha wanna know?" From her purse, she found a pack of gum, tore a piece in half, peeled it, and popped it in her mouth.

"What did Rose do for living?" I asked.

"Rose didn't have a job. She never had a job. She was lucky that way. When she needed money, she just got it. She was like that. Really lucky that way."

"She had a rich family?"

"I don't think so. I don't think she had any family. Her parents were killed in a car crash coming back from Wendover when she was in college. The insurance wasn't much, but it got her through school, I guess."

"Is that where you met her?"

"Yeah, kinda. I didn't finish school. Too many rules and stupid politics. I got a job at Maxi's Beauty Salon, and now I'm assistant manager."

I bet the rules she disliked had to do with grades, but I didn't say that.

"So, how did she just get money do you think?" I didn't want to come out and ask if she was a prostitute, so I chipped around the issue.

"Never asked and she never said. I remember once she was worried about making rent, or was it she needed money to buy a book? She liked books. She read them even when she didn't have to. She was weird that way."

"What happened when she needed money that one time?" I asked, steering her back.

"Oh, well that one time she did a deal with a guy, and they made some money with some deal they did with a travel agency in St. George. It had to do with coupons for a hotel in Cozumel. That's in Mexico. I asked her if I could have one, but she said I didn't want them. She was usually right about stuff like that, so I didn't ask again, but I've always wanted to go to Mexico, even though it's really dangerous, but I heard that some places are still safe. Maybe in the spring."

"Who was the guy she did the deal with?" I asked.

"I don't remember his name. It was a long time ago. Last year, for sure."

"Did Rose have a lot of boyfriends?"

Tonya smirked. "You can't get jealous now," she said.

"I am just curious."

"She called herself a 'serious monogamist,' which meant that she never stepped out on any guy, but kept getting new ones when the old ones wore out."

"Serial," I corrected her.

"I'm sorry. Haven't you had breakfast?"

I let it go. It was hard, but I did. "Can you remember the names of any of the guys she dated?"

"You think one of them killed her?" Her eyes grew large.

"Maybe."

"I got a picture of one of the guys. I'll go get it." She sprang off the couch and hurried down the narrow hall, turned, and ascended unseen stairs.

I waited, smelling the deep old musk of the room, thinking that

Tonya should paint, carpet, and refurnish before she did any other remodeling. Maybe take up smoking to mask the underlying smell.

I heard her moving upstairs and got up to pace the room. My insides were still a little queasy from all the nuts and coffee. I walked to the end of the stairs, turned around, and was back at the couch when I heard something crunch under my foot.

I lifted my shoe and saw a dead rat under it.

Is there anything that screams decay more than a rat in a house? I couldn't even imagine the embarrassment Tonya would go through if she knew that I knew she lived in a literal rat's nest.

I heard her upstairs—shuffling along aged, squeaking floor, opening and closing drawers—and moved fast to save our interview.

I went to the kitchen, pulled a paper towel from an under-cabinet dispenser, and used it to scoop up the mess by the couch. It had bled only a little, a couple of pinpoints of red on the light carpet. I dropped the mess into a garbage can under the sink and was sitting down when Tonya came back. I carefully kept my foot over the stain in the carpet.

She marched straight up to me and dropped a photo of Rose and Luke on my lap.

"That's Luke," I said in surprise. "From the club."

"Yeah, I think that's where they met. Didn't we see him last night? Wasn't that him? Well, she and him went out for a while. I think it was after the deal in St. George, but I can't be sure. I mean, it's hard enough to keep track of my own life, let alone everyone else's."

"Thanks," I said, looking at the picture. I handed it back. "Who was the guy she met the night we were all together? What was his name? Jason or James?"

"Justin," she said. "Yeah, she had a thing with him for a while, but it was over before she was with you. Serious monogamist. One guy at a time."

"What do you know about Justin?"

"Nothing. He's smart and hard to talk to."

"Can you think of any other boyfriends?"

"Lots of guys, but they never lasted long. Rose and I didn't see each other all that often. Maybe once a month or so. Sometimes more, sometimes less. It changed."

"And she had different guys each time?"

"Pretty much," she said, smacking her gum. "We usually got together when Melissa was having one of her dramas. Rose would bring the gang together to cheer her up. It never worked. Melissa is always having drama. You know *she* might know more about Rose and her boyfriends. They knew each other since high school. That was the only reason she was ever around. She was Rose's friend. I mean, Melissa is so un-fun it's unfunny."

"How can I get in touch with Melissa?" I asked.

"I have her number and address here on my phone." She fished it out of her purse. "She works at Mountain Dell Hospital as a CNA. That's some kind of nurse."

She punched up the information.

"Thanks," I said, writing it down.

Tonya smacked her gum. "I'm avoiding her right now. So don't mention me, 'kay?"

"Over last night?" I asked.

"No," she said. "She asked me to babysit Nuzzles, her stupid gerbil. The dumb thing escaped from its cage this morning."

CHAPTER SIXTEEN

Needless to say, I couldn't bring myself to visit Melissa just then. Luke would be a better lead to follow. Even though he threw me out of the Comedy Cellar—my second home, a place of safety and love, and now public humiliation—I still thought of him as a friend. Acquaintance, at any rate. Okay. I knew him. He'd been nice before he'd escorted me out. This was doubly significant after learning that he and Rose once had a thing.

He'd be at the Comedy Cellar that night, and I could get to him without actually entering the bar, since I was no longer welcome there. It would have to wait though. Stupidly enough, I had agreed via text messages to return to my erstwhile home for dinner that night in order to counsel my son on how it is bad to kill people. Nancy thought I should emphasize to Randy that killing was wrong, lest his unbounded admiration of me lead him to copy my murderous acts and land him on death row beside me. That is, if he still knew who I was. Nancy made no promises.

I stopped at a store to pick something up. It was no longer my home. I would be a guest, and a guest should never arrive empty-handed. I wandered the aisles looking for something fitting to bring.

With a round button on a wall, I summoned the butcher. He was a ragged man in a dirty white apron. The blood on it had dried to a nice, brown hue, like much of the meat under the curved glass.

"How can I help you?" he said. He was skinny, but had Popeye arms, thicker at the bottom than the top. He had bushy, comb-able eyebrows under a disposable white paper hat. He smiled and showed a gold-crowned incisor. "What do you feel like eating tonight?" he asked.

"I think I'll have to eat crow," I said.

He looked thoughtful, scanned the display and then said, "Let me check in the back." He was gone before I could stop him.

"I'm afraid we're out of crow," he said. "I can order it for you."

"How long will it take?" I asked.

"Let me find out."

While he was gone, I wandered up and down the meat aisle, wondering what kind of meat would most offend a vegetarian.

When he returned, he said apologetically, "Uhm, I've just been informed that we can't actually get crow. Our supplier doesn't carry it. Something about it not being legal. I'm so sorry."

"It's okay," I said. "It was just a—"

"I'm not supposed to say anything," he said quietly. "I know a place that has a guy I can hook you up with. He can get most anything. He carries elk and moose, sometimes bear. I've heard he can even get baby seal and pygmy." The last sentence was said so low, I'm not sure it counted as human speech, but he'd said it. It sucked my eyes back into my skull.

"It's cool," I said. "Give me some pig's feet."

"Fresh or frozen."

"Oh, fresh, of course," I said.

He scooped up a set and laid them out on a Styrofoam tray, wrapped it in plastic, weighed it, and slapped a label on it. He winked when he handed it to me. I made for the checkout lanes with my pink hooves and a six-pack of pale ale.

The lines were long with obnoxious kids hanging on haggard housewives and sports fanatics with carts full of chips and pizza bites.

I walked the row looking down each aisle gauging time by cartload. With my two items, I made the unfortunate, but common, mistake of entering the "ten items or less" lane. I entered the line a step ahead of a guy with a basket of bologna and gourmet rye bread. It was a clean race; I'd won it fair and square.

Triumphant, I turned my back to him to face forward only to have my heart fall. The woman ahead of me had a cart full of groceries. It was an actual cart-full. It overflowed with feminine products, TV dinners, soup cans, cat litter, wooden spoons, assorted vegetables—fresh, canned, and frozen—hamburger meat, buns, ketchup, salad dressing, shoe inserts, diarrhea medicine, fabric softener, lemon pepper, air freshener, cookies, and three types of SpaghettiOs. And that was just what I could see on top. I glanced up at the "ten items or less" sign and then down the row to the other long lines and decided to stay.

Delores, the checker, was a middle-aged woman with light brown hair cut back off her face. Her cheeks were red with exertion, but she was cheerful sliding items across the scanner. She smiled and made eye contact. I liked her.

Then there was the woman with the cart. She was obese and wore a skirt that could have been called a muumuu or a tent, depending on your disposition. She rolled up to Delores and began unloading onto the conveyer belt.

Delores looked at the cart, smiled friendly into the muumuu's face and said, "Which ten of these items would you like to buy?"

I fell in love.

If indignity had a smell, it would be the unshaven underarm funk of an unwashed muumuu woman. Her face popped crimson like an expanding balloon. She was speechless. Delores grinned.

I applauded. The man behind me joined in. The woman behind him, too. Muumuu woman pushed her cart through the aisle and stormed out the door empty-handed.

"My name is Tony," I said, handing Delores my hooves. "I think I love you."

She winked.

I returned to my new home with some good beer, some bad meat, and Delores's phone number.

What does one wear to a humiliation? My hair shirt was at the cleaners; my leather leash and ball gag were packed away with my baby photos. I stared at the pile of clothes on the floor I'd dumped out of three boxes. Well, two had clothes and one had felt swatches, which had sounded like clothes when I'd shaken it.

I went with comfortable. I arrived at my old front door in a pair of shorts with a torn pocket where my spring-knife had cut through it one day, and a tie-dye concert T-shirt. I tried my key in the lock. It slid in, but didn't turn. The door opened and Nancy stood in the threshold. I was bent over, my key erect.

"I changed the locks, Tony," she said.

"I was just making sure you had," I said. "I didn't want to have to bring it up at dinner, so I thought I'd just try my key and settle the issue without having to face the ugliness of explaining to you why you needed to change them."

She stood stern and unmoving. There was an awkward silence.

"So why did you change them?"

She stood aside and gestured me in.

I smelled something nutty from the kitchen and heard synthesized harp music from the living room.

Hank Mudge sat in my recliner reading a book. I saw his eyes flash on me. His eyebrows furrowed.

My old study had been turned into a real study. A new desk stood where my old one had. New bookshelves lined two of the walls. On the other were framed diplomas and pictures. I stepped in to look.

"You don't want to go in there," Nancy said, pulling my arm. "How about a drink?"

"Sure," I said, but not before I saw Mudge's name on a diploma from "Xanadu Enlightenment College of True Sight and Healing" proclaiming him a "Doctor of Spiritual Development." I also saw a photo of him, short-haired and tanned, posing with five strangers on the deck of a cruise ship. He held up a drink the size of a fishbowl in salutation.

"Where's Randy?" I asked when we were in the kitchen. She poured me a glass of white wine and refilled her own.

"He's upstairs. I wanted to make sure you'd behave before seeing him. What did you bring us?"

I handed her the bag. "What are you talking about? You don't honestly think I killed anyone, do you?"

"Leafcaller says we all have inner demons. The man I married would never do such a thing, but if some other Tony, from a previous life perhaps, slipped out, who knows who that man might be and what he might be capable of doing?"

"I have memories of my previous life," I said. "I remember a distinct lack of assholes sitting in my easy chair and a sane wife who trusted me."

"What I really meant is that I don't want you behaving badly toward Leafcaller. I want you to be mature and non-confrontational."

"Nancy," I said disgustedly, "remember who you're talking to."

She pulled the hogs feet out of the bag and gave me a dirty look.

"What? Is Hank still a vegetarian? How was I supposed to know that?"

The look didn't clean up at all.

"Why am I here?" I asked.

She put the beer in the fridge. It looked like a terrarium in there with all the foliage packed inside. She pushed cabbages and moved a bushel of carrots to make room for a few bottles. The rest of the kitchen looked like a rainforest nursery. Plants hung from the ceiling in macramé nets, which, incidentally, I knew how to make. A Pygmy palm in the corner made me remember the butcher. Potpourri baskets littered every surface that didn't have a hand-thrown teacup or bowl of river pebbles on it.

"I want to normalize relations," she said. "We need to be adult about things. Acceptance is paramount to healing, and you must accept Leafcaller."

"Fuck the druid," I said. "You said something about Randy?"

"Randy is still young and impressionable. He looks up to you. You're his biological father, and I don't want him getting the wrong ideas about how to behave in the world."

I swallowed the entire glass of wine in one gulp.

"Biological father?" I said.

"Yes, you knew that."

"Yes, I knew that," I said. I felt my face flushing muumuu crimson with rage and white wine. "I'm just stunned that you'd refer to me that way. I thought I was his father. Father—no adjective."

"Leafcaller will bond with Randy and probably supplant you as his primary male role model. You have to be ready for it."

I hadn't been Randy's role model since he met Master Chief. I was good with that. He was his own boy. Nancy hadn't caught on to it.

"So have Hank 'Figleaf' Mudge go talk to him," I said.

"The bonding isn't complete yet. He still relates to your energies."

"Did you say 'my energies?'"

"Yes."

"Do you know how dumb you sound?"

Dirty look again. She was good at dirty looks.

"Nancy, my dear ex-wife, who left me to be gang-raped in jail for two and a half weeks, I want you to know that there's nothing I wouldn't do for you, but you must know that you are absolutely not acting like yourself. Where in your plans do energies figure?"

She looked horrified. "Did they really rape you?"

"It's only rape if you resist," I said. "What about your plan and the energies?"

"I'm learning to open my horizons to the universe."

"So you've become suddenly adventurous and spontaneous?"

"No," she said. "Just attuned."

Brainwashed, I thought. Still it was interesting.

"I'll go talk to Randy," I said.

"After dinner."

"Now," I said.

She shrugged. "Make sure you tell him that killing people is wrong."

"There are some lessons he has to learn for himself, dear."

Dirty look from her. Grin from me. I went upstairs.

Randy was in his room. I could hear the clatter of keystrokes and video game sound. I knocked.

"Come in, Dad."

I went in. Someone had made him clean his room—I had to speak to the warden about such affronts to liberty and individuality.

The computer screen was a familiar battlefield. Tanks and soldiers marched around shooting at already burning buildings. Suddenly, the word "Victory" appeared, and then a flash screen announcing that my son had reached "Platinum" level.

"Yes!" he cried.

"That's cool. What does it mean?"

"It means I'm now qualified to join select online competitions and can brag my guts out at school. Now I can really make a name for myself in Colonies. Fame and fortune, you know."

"Yeah," I said. "Fame and fortune. Good things."

"How ya' doin', Dad?"

A bubble of desperate paternal emotion moved up my throat, a cry of anguish, rejection and terror. I swallowed it.

"Son, your mom wants me to encourage you not to kill people in real life," I said.

"Hadn't planned to."

"Good."

We sat there a moment.

"Is there anything else?" he said, glancing at his computer where a countdown for the next match flickered ever lower.

"Yeah," I said. "I want you to know I didn't kill anyone."

"I didn't think you had," he said, and I believed him.

"Thanks, son."

"No sweat."

"You coming down to dinner?"

"Nope."

"Do you like Hank?"

"Who?"

"Hank Mudge. Leafcaller?"

"Is that his real name?" he asked.

"Yep."

"Nope."

"Good."

"Yep."

"Love you."

"Love you, too, Dad."

I got up to go.

"Hey, Randy," I said. "What's left after Platinum?"

"Diamond."

"After that?"

"That's it. That's professional level. Like the NFL, NBA, or NASCAR."

"But on a computer?"

"Yeah."

My son, the athlete.

I said, "Make me proud."

"You, too," he said, beginning his game. I'm sure it was just a reflex response, but as I walked down the hall that used to be mine to have dinner with a wife who used to be mine with a man I'd like to mine with claymores and such, I thought my son had spoken a true challenge to me, a call to greatness, a directive to solve the finger trap and capture a killer.

* * *

Mudge said a prayer to an earth deity he called "Gaia Enshrined."

"Oh, God," I said.

Nancy shushed me, and Mudge hummed through his eyelids at the end. Nancy retreated to the kitchen. I sat quietly. Mudge stared pagan daggers at me across woven straw placemats.

"Where're the hogs knuckles?" I protested when Nancy placed a blended green salad in front of me. It had actually been blended. In a blender. Pureed, at least. It smelled like cilantro and looked like moss gruel. It flowed over the plate like it wanted to absorb it. "This must be the appetizer," I said.

"I see you dressed for the occasion," said Mudge. He sat at the head of the table now, but out of deference to me, no doubt, it was Nancy's end. She took my old seat. I was on the side where guests sat.

"How would you have me dress?"

"Do I have to take this, Honey Blossom?" he said to Nancy angrily.

"Honey Blossom?" I said. "Please tell me you haven't been visited by dryads and renamed, too."

"We're just trying it on," she said.

"Hank, Hankster, the Mudge-Man," I said. "You need to relax. Balance a chakra, smoke some grass, rub one out."

He crashed his fork on the table. I was thinking spoons would be more appropriate for this salad. Maybe straws. "The only reason I let you in this house is because Honey Blossom seeks a spiritual balance with the past that I think is unnecessary with one such as you."

"And what 'one' would I be, exactly?"

"One murdering bastard," he said.

"Leaf!" said Nancy. I never thought of calling him Leaf. It had kind of a cool Viking feel to it, or 70s heartthrob vibe. I'd stick with Mudge.

He calmed down under Nancy's piercing gaze. She had a talent. I, however, felt absolutely no need to proclaim my innocence, justify myself, or even put on my innocent face for this philandering, alpaca-loving, nouveau-hippie.

"Tony says he's innocent," Nancy said noncommittally. "We're not here to discuss his problems. We're here to realign our energies."

Mudge stared more daggers. He hadn't been this mad when I'd missed with the quiche. He was really mad, I realized. Violently, or nearly so. Something had him going. Trouble in paradise?

"Let's close our eyes and reopen them to a new awareness," Nancy said with practiced diction.

Daggers from Mudge. Squints from Nancy. I closed my eyes.

When I opened them, Mudge was controlling his breathing in long, deep, nasally breaths. His eyes were still shut and he was evidently concentrating very hard because his forehead had more lines in it than an open blind. I glanced at Nancy; she smiled and gave me a reassuring nod. She refilled my glass, and I drained it in a gulp.

"Why do you do that?" demanded a calmer Mudge in a voice whose calmness eroded with every syllable.

"Do what?"

"Drink all your wine at once like that?"

I looked at Nancy. She smiled reassuringly.

"I was thirsty," I said. Hell if I'd tell him about my drinking tribute to Rose.

There was a loaf of bread, round as a tire and nearly the same color. I tore off a piece and felt it crack like bone china in my hand. I asked for butter. No butter. No animal products. Would I like some homemade dandelion jam? Sure.

We ate our gruel. I found that if I dumped the dandelion jam into it and scooped it up with the dark bread, I could swallow it without throwing up. Nancy was pleased.

"So, Tony," Nancy said. "Do you like your new place?"

"Nance, it's wonderful. Your house-sense is super, like usual. Thanks. It makes things easier."

"I knew you would need help with the furniture," she said. "While you were away."

"Again, fine choices. Thanks."

Mudge put his fork down and said, "Why don't you two just go upstairs and fuck, then he can murder you, too!"

Nancy's jaw dropped onto her lap. Mine did, too, but I picked it up before she did.

"Works for me," I said, "but not the murder part."

"You bastard!" yelled the chakra-balanced yoga maniac at the end of the table. "You're scum. I hope you fry."

"Utah doesn't have the electric chair," I said and flicked a forkful of gruel right into Mudge's left eye.

"That's it!" He pushed the table aside to get at me, real rage in his eye. The other was green and slimy with a dollop of dandelion jam. I ran around the table behind Nancy's chair.

Nancy screamed. Mudge kept after me. I ducked into the kitchen.

He followed me. Something broke over my head. I hoped it wasn't my favorite wooden bowl.

I heard a drawer open, followed by the rattle of silverware—sharp silverware. I ducked in the hall and ran for the exit.

"Thanks for the delicious moss," I yelled, opening the door. "And remember, Randy, violence is for losers!" I pulled the door shut as Mudge ran into it. He crashed into it at full speed, totally taken in by my clever "closing the door ploy," or so enraged as to not slow himself for the impact.

I was in my car and speeding away before it came open again. Nancy and Mudge were framed in the doorway, yelling into each other's faces like they'd hated each other for years.

CHAPTER SEVENTEEN

"Is Luke there?"

"No." Click.

I called back.

"Hey, Sheryl," I said. "I'm looking for Luke."

"Not here." Click.

It was Sheryl Waterman, Barry's secretary, known affectionately among the regulars of the Comedy Cellar as "The Bitch." She was the laziest, most ill-tempered woman I'd ever met. Her sour demeanor was matched by a crooked nose, fallen chin, and a haircut that would have gotten her stoned to death as a goblin just thirty years earlier. She had the torso of a barrel, legs like croquet posts, and arms furrier than a shedding malamute. She worked part-time at the Comedy Cellar, and it was a mystery why Barry kept her on. I suspected it had something to do with a deep-seated self-hatred he'd developed during childhood. Dara had said she was the perfect guard against creditors and salesmen. I once asked Luke about her. He just shook his head.

"Sheryl. It's Tony," I said quickly.

Click.

I called back.

Deepening my voice, "Is Luke there?"

Click.

I called the back line. Sheryl picked up.

"Sheryl, where can I find Luke?"

"He's not here."

"Do you know where—" Click.

I called back.

"Where is he?" I knew I had caught her in a good mood; she kept answering the phone.

"Gone now. Photo shoot later," she said. "You kill someone, Tony?"

"No," I said emphatically.

"Pity. At least then you'd be interesting." Click.

Luke was a model. His hewn good looks, muscular frame, and huge penis brought him steady work. He had a favorite director I'd met one year at Sundance, a beach ball of a man appropriately named Rollo. I found a listing for his agency, "Skin Flixxx," on the Internet. Remembering I was a detective, I channeled Jim Rockford, Easy Rawlins, and Baretta. I readied my story: I was a talent agent from Dawkins, Texas, and Luke was late for an appointment.

A silken voice answered, "Skin Flixxx, how would you like to get off?"

The affectionate greeting threw me.

"I'm looking for Rollo," I said. "I had—"

Click. Music. *You really got a hold on me.*

My Texas drawl was very convincing. Too bad I'd forgotten to use it.

The music stopped. "This is Rollo."

"Hello, Rollo. My name is . . ." I'd forgotten my cover name.

"Yes?"

"I'm looking for Luke," I said. "Do you know how to get ahold of him?"

"What did you say your name was?"

"I'm a friend," I said. "From Dawkins, Texas."

"Uh-huh."

I'd forgotten my drawl again. I sounded more Des Moines than Dawkins.

"Really, I know him from the club." I said.

"Uh-huh."

"From the Comedy Cellar."

Silence.

"Okay, Rollo," I sighed. "We met a couple of years ago at Sundance.

Luke said you were his favorite director, and I need to find him. I'm in a bit of trouble."

"What kind of trouble?"

"Murder," I said. Play-acting hadn't worked.

"Tony Flaner. I thought that was you."

"You did?"

"I've been waiting for your call. I want to shoot you. Didn't Luke mention it?"

"No, we haven't talked. I've already been shot by the police. What do you have against me?"

"Nah, Tony. I'm always looking for celebrities for short films."

"Porn?"

"Art house," came his easy reply. "Soft focus, no close ups. Unless you want to. Then, we can do that."

"That's not why I called," I said. "I need to find Luke."

"I left a message with your brother, Leafcraver, last week. Didn't he tell you I called?"

"Nope."

"So whatcha think? A big tittied blond cornered on the bed, but eager in every way? You come in, tear your shirt off—that's my trademark you know, the shirt tearing—and you fuck. Real art stuff, with a social message because you're a killer and everything. Could help your case. Show you in a tender light for the jury. Or we could do spankings. That really sells."

"Do you have Luke's cell phone number or know where I can find him now?"

"You want to do a group scene with Luke?" he said. "I like it, but I wouldn't recommend it. He'll make you look small no matter how massive you are. He can shame horses. You don't want to go there, trust me. So how are you hung?"

"Utah uses lethal injection," I said.

"What?"

He wasn't getting it. I was trying to save my life. He was trying to see my junk.

"I need to talk this over with Luke," I said, changing tactics. "I've never done a movie before. If I talk to him, he can advise me. Put me at ease. And then, maybe, I'll call you back."

"Yeah, okay," Rollo said. "First time jitters. Don't worry. I have girls to help with that."

"Let me talk to Luke and I'll get back with you," I said, as if weighing his offer with serious intent, while in fact I was only half considering it.

"Yeah, okay," he said. "But let's get this done before the trial. We want to ride the publicity." He gave me Luke's home and cell phone numbers. I thanked him and hung up before I caught something.

A machine answered at Luke's home. I didn't leave a message. I tried his cell. It went to message, too.

I considered my options, evaluated my position. Scratched myself.

* * *

I was at my kitchen table in my underwear with a cup of coffee. Visions of Mudge's fury the night before had lulled me to sleep like sugar-plums. I'd call Nancy later and get the recipe for the green slime and dandelion jam just for a keepsake.

Mollif had dropped off a box of papers sometime in the night. I guess all lawyers work best away from sunlight. I found it on my doorstep when I got my paper, only to find I didn't get the paper and that my neighbors have a five-year-old girl who isn't used to seeing strange grown men in their underwear on Sunday mornings. How screaming and pointing improved the already uncomfortable situation was beyond me, but that was her plan, and she went with it. I waved and retreated inside.

My interview with Tonya had me uneasy. I'd assumed the crap from McGraw and Sweet about Rose being a prostitute was bullshit, but Tonya made me think otherwise.

I remembered another thing McGraw had said. I listed the three elements of a murder: motive, means, and opportunity. He was right. I had all three, though the facts would need to be supposed, stretched, and contorted to fit me into motive, I had little doubt the American justice system could do just that. I didn't think I could wriggle out of any of the three pieces to save my life—literally. But there was someone else that fit, too. Fit better than me. My salvation was in finding that someone.

Means. Okay, the killer used hands to kill. Two hands. My theory of a one-armed man had to go. It could have been a woman, I thought. A forensic team might have determined that, but none had bothered, according to the meager box of papers Mollif had sent over.

Opportunity was key because whoever killed Rose had had both: opportunity and a key. I'd seen Rose lock the door and found it unlocked the next morning. There was no sign of break-in, and the timing was perfect. We were drugged but not out before the rum. Rum can make you slur your words in a bad Keith Richards impersonation, but it doesn't flatten you like a plank after one shot. The rum was spiked to give the killer opportunity. Eat your heart out, Ms. Marple.

Motive. This was the hard one. I dismissed a random act of violence, theft, and jihad in turn, but not time-travel assassination. I'd need to know more about Rose to rule that one out, but I liked it better than the obvious one.

I'd liked Rose. She was lively. She was a gift of hope when I needed it. Thinking ill of her made me nauseous, but there were bad things in her life that couldn't be overlooked. I took a deep breath, straightened my invisible fedora, and considered prostitution, jealousy, and drugs.

Mixing my gut hunch with my diaphragmatic nausea, I mixed prostitute with jealousy and envisioned a drugged man so infatuated with the lovely Rose as to lose his sanity and kill her rather than share her with the likes of me. Maybe he was from the future.

I called Luke's cell phone again. It went to voicemail. I hung up and called it again. I repeated the incessant calling five more times, then he picked up.

"Who the hell is this?" he said, not angry but annoyed. "I'm in the middle of something."

"Luke, it's me, Tony. Can I talk to you?"

"You seem capable."

"It's about Rose," I said.

"Oh," he said. "Yeah, I guess we should talk."

"Where are you now? I'll come over."

"Now's not good, but I'm meeting some people for a shoot in a bit. I can talk to you then. Why don't you meet me there?"

I'd have packed my snub-nosed thirty-eight in my shoulder holster and planted a backup twenty-five in my sock if I'd had either. Instead, I cleaned up and ran out the door with a bagel in my teeth. I saw the neighbor girl pointing to my house beside a concerned man. I waved and sped away in my car.

Luke had given me the address of a house on the high east bench. Houses were pricey in that area, and often bigger than Superman's Ice Fortress. My phone rang on the way.

"Hello," I answered, unable to think of anything cleverer to say.

"Tony! It's me, Mittens. What's up, dog?"

"They fired me," I said. I could hear a jet engine idling far off in the background. Even far off, it sounded like a rift to an extra-dimensional reality, sucking hapless baggage handlers to their *Twilight Zone* deaths.

"We got your job back, man," he said. "The Union has a rule that you can't be fired if you're only accused of a felony. You have to be convicted and extinguish all your appeals before they are allowed to fire you. It's the 'Hatchet Henderson clause.'"

"Didn't Hatchet Henderson kill like a dozen people in a trailer park?"

"Yeah. The rule's named after him."

"Didn't he kill some coworkers, too?"

"Uh-huh. Lots."

"Wasn't he finally executed?"

"Yeah, but he sued the airline for unfair termination and won."

"Glad it worked out for him."

"Anyway, the foreman got you reinstated and on paid furlough."

"Cool."

"No problem," said Mittens. "We gotta stick together."

"Thanks," I said and meant it.

I pulled up to a black-hatted guard in a stone gatehouse. He put down his third-period trigonometry book long enough to ask me where I was going. I told him the street Luke had told me. He nodded and lifted the gate with a button. Today's secret password was "Evans Way."

The house was made of green stone, which could not have come from this state. The roof was copper, which could have come from the state, but wasn't used for roofing much because it was really expensive and lately there'd been a rash of thefts as copper prices skyrocketed. Lucky for these homeowners, there was a minimum-wage teenage guard in a stone booth and a plywood gate to protect their shiny roofs.

I parked on the street and hiked to the house. The front door rivaled my garage door in size. I rang a bell and heard Beethoven's *Ode to Joy* through three inches of oak.

The door swung open, and I beheld two glorious, bare breasts hovering before me. They were unnaturally plump and pert, the size of volleyballs. One had a tattoo of a unicorn, the other a heart. A faraway voice asked who I was and what I wanted. The dazzling breasts swayed and jiggled with each syllable. I pinched my eyes shut, angled my head fifteen degrees upward and opened them again. Chestnut-brown eyes with six-inch lashes surrounded by blue eye shadow stared back at me.

"Boob nipple, breast titties," I said.

She understood and let me in. The door swung closed with a low thud. "You're here to see Luke, right?" she said through fire-engine red lips. "He said to expect you."

She led the way. I followed her tan, naked bum from a carefully calculated distance to take in the surroundings. I think I was indoors, beyond that, I can't be sure.

We came to a bright room. Hot lights shone on a chaise lounge set under a wall-sized window that overlooked the entire valley. A naked man hung from the ceiling in leather straps, spread eagle and spinning like a mobile. He nodded hello when I came in.

"Hi," I said, as if I'd seen countless erect male leather-clad chandeliers before.

"Hey, Tony. Over here," Luke said from a side door.

The woman I'd followed in sat down in a plush chair beside the door and picked up a paperback copy of *Eleanor, the Unseen* with interest.

"That's Felicia," Luke said. "We're next after them."

Luke sat behind a desk reading Facebook posts. He wore a blue robe with an embroidered gold shield on the left breast.

"What is this place?"

"Someone's home. Sergio rented it for the shoot."

"Does the owner know what you're doing here?"

"He's the guy hanging from the ceiling."

"Oh. Okay, then."

Luke pointed me to the couch.

"First, dude," said Luke. "It was Barry who booted you the other night. I was cool with you there."

"Yeah, I know. That's kind of why I'm here. That and another thing."

He waited. I admired his chiseled chin and bright eyes.

"You don't think I killed Rose, do you?" I asked.

"Hell no."

"Why?"

He looked thoughtful for a moment, a perfect depiction of the emotion, worthy of sculpture. "I thought about it," he said. "You're not the type, and I know types. Plus, if you were the kind of guy who could fool me, you'd be smart enough not to get caught so easily."

"Did you do it?"

I'd expected a blush or a pall, a telltale twitch broadcasting his guilt and tormented inner thoughts. Instead, he raised an eyebrow.

"Why would you ask that?" he said.

"You knew her," I said. "You dated her. You're big and strong and maybe the jealous type. Then again, you might even have been her pimp."

"Tony, what the fuck are you talking about?"

"The police said she was a prostitute? Was she?"

"Not with me," he said. "Rose was Rose. We fell in love for a week or two, and then she moved on. She heard about me and wanted to try. We were friends."

"You didn't sleep with her?"

"Of course I did. She liked sex. She was good at it, and I should know."

My face must have betrayed me because Luke said, "Oh. I'm sorry, man. I'm just telling you like it was."

"Yeah, okay," I said. "I didn't know her very well. Not well at all. But they think I killed her, and no one but me is looking for the real killer."

"That's what I thought," he said. "How can I help you?"

"Could she have been a prostitute?"

"She could have been anything she wanted to be, but I don't think turning tricks was her thing. She liked men. Liked trying anything new, be it men, women, oysters, or skydiving. She had a lot of boyfriends. I think she just grew bored easily."

I knew the feeling. "How did she get money?" I asked. "Family?"

"Nah, she had no family." He was holding something back. I could tell. We heard a slap and a muffled shriek from the next room.

"They've started again," he said.

"You were going to say something, just now. What was it?"

He bit his lip and looked at me.

"If Barry knew I knew, I'd lose my job. Not that it would be a big deal, but it could ripple onto others and, well, you know."

"What?"

"Well, when I first met Rose, she was selling drugs. She sold out of the Cellar and a couple of other clubs I worked at. I turned a blind eye because I figure adults have a right to be adults, even if the law doesn't agree. Most club owners think the same, and turn their own blind eyes. But if they know about it, if they can't turn that blind eye, then they gotta step in and stop it or lose their license. Rose was good and low key, but she was a seller, no doubt about it."

"What did she sell?"

"When I first met her, she was still in college. She sold only prescription stuff then. After a while, she stopped. Her clientele went elsewhere. Recently, she'd been selling again, but it was more sporadic, and she changed her inventory. She sold shrooms and dope and ecstasy, the stuff you can't get except from private growers and home laboratories. If I had to say what Rose did to make the rent, I'd say it might have been selling drugs."

"But she didn't do it much?"

"No, not much," he said. Whipping noises, groans, and screams filtered through the door. "She had other things. I think she only went back to drugs when she was short."

"What other things? Jobs?"

"I don't know."

"Where'd she get the drugs?"

"I don't know that either. But I do know she had a loyal clientele. If she had it, she could move it. People trusted her. Whoever was behind her must have been bummed when she wasn't selling for them."

"Bummed enough to kill her?"

"If I knew who it was, I could answer that," he said.

"Yeah, right. Just thinking out loud. So do you know any of her other boyfriends?"

"You," he said. "She told me that you were on the list."

"She said that? When?"

"She mentioned it months ago, after you did the bit about your planned divorce. But she said your time had come that night you massacred Matticks at the Cellar."

"Wow," I said.

"As for others, I didn't know many names. I saw a few of them when she came to my clubs. There was a banker way back when, and a gymnast she flaunted for two months, but again, that was a while ago. Her friends would be the ones to ask."

"They're not being overly helpful," I said.

Slap, screech, moan, muffled commands.

"I know there was a guy named Harris, Harris Tamlen. She really hated him. Something with him didn't end well. Said he sent the cops after her."

I wrote the name down and showed it to Luke for spelling confirmation. He shrugged. Half-hearted cries for mercy came from the windowed room. "No," came the cold, sought-after response.

"There was a guy called Justin. I don't know his last name. He didn't last long. You might have seen him. He came to the club the other night. Actually, it was the night you and Rose hooked up."

"The geek?"

"That was him." No more description necessary.

"We broke up when she went to Europe for a while. It was months before I saw her again. She told me about some guy she met on a cruise. Some kind of trainer or something. She had a lot of men, but Rose never had multiple guys at once."

"Serial monogamist," I said.

"Yes. She'd love them and leave them. I'm sure she broke a lot of hearts. She was not the marrying type."

"You think a jealous ex-lover could have killed her?"

"That'd be a guess. Rose went through men and dumped them all eventually. None of them ever dumped her, if you know what I mean."

I did. I'd known her a few hours, and my whole life had changed. Imagine if it had changed for the better, how little I'd want to give her up.

"What do you know about Justin?"

"Computer geek," Luke said. Wagner's "Ride of the Valkyries" boomed through the wall. "He's a programmer for some start-up at the point of the mountain. Chronoboost, Inc."

"And the trainer?"

"Never saw him."

There was a slow, but growing, female moan of passion and the rumbling lower moan of a male orgasm, both rising to crescendo with Wagner.

"They're almost done," Luke said.

"Thanks, Luke. I'll take these leads and see what I can find."

Luke nodded. "If you find the son of a bitch who did this, I'd be interested to know." He stood up and walked me to the door. His powerful, muscular frame every bit the bouncer.

I nodded at the brunette who let me in; she smiled and winked. I blushed. I skirted the flashing cameras and tripod lights along the back wall to make for the exit.

On the chaise lounge, the hanging victim was now being happily smothered between the thighs of a barrel-chested, stick-legged, furry-armed woman known affectionately among the regulars at the Comedy Cellar as "The Bitch." A man with a thousand-dollar camera orbited them snapping close-ups.

Click.

Click.

Click.

CHAPTER EIGHTEEN

My meeting with Luke had given me an indelible vision that my analyst and I would work through for years. I'd also netted me Justin's work and a new name: Harris Tamlen. I found Harris and Susan Tamlen in the phone book and found an address for Chronoboost, Inc.

I called Melissa. No answer. I left no message.

I called Harris.

"Hello?" answered a woman.

"I'm looking for Harris Tamlen," I said. "Is he home?"

"May I ask who's calling?"

"Charlie from the club," I said. Everyone has a club, even if everyone didn't have a Charlie.

"Charlie!" she said. "I didn't recognize your voice. How's Cynthia?"

"Oh, she's fine," I said. "Fit as a fiddle."

"So the chemo is working? That's good," she said.

"Like a charm. She'll be up and around in no time."

"She's already been fitted for her prosthetic legs?"

"Yep, it's all taken care of."

"Did you get your mortgage squared away?"

"Uhm, yes?"

"That's good."

"Sure is," I said.

"Because I thought I saw a foreclosure sign on your front lawn and a moving van there yesterday."

"Yeah, uhm, that's what I wanted to talk to Harris about," I said, drowning fast. "Is he there?"

"No. He's at the club."

"And where's that?"

"You card!" she said. "Give our love to Cynthia. Tell her losing her hair is nothing after losing both legs."

"I think she knows that," I said.

"Bye."

"Bye."

I decided to follow another lead.

I arrived at 10:15 a.m. the next day. Break time. A group of kids with Chronoboost employee badges huddled together outside on the sidewalk and talked in low tones while keeping their burning cigarettes as hidden as possible. It reminded me of the dumpster behind my high school gymnasium after fifth period.

If the building had been more domed than boxy, I'd have thought it was an industrial igloo. It looked like it had been built out of inky-blue glass blocks. A cosmetically-dilapidated rusting sign proclaimed the name "Chronoboost, Inc." in tarnished iron letters on a chrome plate. It was written in a computer font that went out of style before most of the smoking employees had been born. It had a rustic technological look that I'm sure cost a fortune. The building hadn't been there last year, and I'd bet money the sign would change before the next. Such was the world of technology start-ups. The only people guaranteed to get rich were the makers of square igloos and trendy signs.

I presented myself to the receptionist. The foyer was done in the same rust and chrome motif as the sign. It fought with the blue tint of the windows and made the entire room seem like the inside of a sunken submarine. A blonde with big eyes and six-inch fingernails greeted me.

"Can I help you?"

"I'm looking for Justin," I said.

"Justin who?"

"I don't know," I said. "That's where you can help me."

Her eyebrows met in strained concentration and then stoic determination. She turned to her computer screen, shrunk the Solitaire game down to an icon, and began stabbing keys with her fingernails. Plastic chipped as each tentative finger found its mark and speared a letter.

"We only have one Justin," she said.

"Just one Justin? Not another, just in case?" I smiled at my clever pun.

"No, just the one," she said, missing my rib-tickling wit.

"What's his last name? Case?" I tried again.

"No. Bertone."

"That's him," I said. "Where can I find him?"

"Oh, well since you know him, go through the doors there. He's in one of the cubicles."

"Works for me." I walked through double doors marked "Authorized Personnel Only" and stepped into Dilbert's nightmare—a maze of three-quarter-height cubicles and copy machines. There was a wall of doors marked "Mainframe, Authorized Personnel Only," "Records, Authorized Personnel Only," "Support, Authorized Personnel Only," and "R&D, Authorized Personnel Only." Another wall with windows had offices. Full-height glass walls partitioned the more important people from the lowlings who labored behind beige carpeted ones. Most of the glass was blocked by nifty vertical blinds that were tacky before they were hung and now dated the office badly.

"Stormfront needs the damn code by Thursday," someone shouted from the back of the maze. "Overtime is allowed, but clear it first."

I wove my way through the matrix of walls toward the sound of authority. I passed a door on my right that said "Men, Authorized Personnel Only." Beside it was another that said only "Women." I guess anyone could go in there.

I leaned over a wall and found a young black man squinting at his computer screen like it was the fine print of a loan document.

"I'm looking for Justin," I said.

"Do I look like goddamned Justin?" he said, waving his hands in desperation, wheeling on me like I'd just insulted his mother, girlfriend, and haircut.

"Uhm, no," I said.

He gazed at me with wild, stress-filled eyes. "Justin is a thin slice of Wonder Bread with mayo for brains. Do I look like I have mayo for brains?"

I paused to measure the cholesterol in his cranium.

"It's a simple goddamn question," he demanded.

"Without a cat scan, I can't be sure. But I'll go with no, you don't have mayo for brains."

"Damn right I don't. Now leave me the fuck alone."

Either I was talking to a senior member of the company, or I was witnessing a caffeine-deprived, stress-driven deadline meltdown. I glanced at his nameplate. It said "Mallory."

"Hey, Mallory, where can I find Justin?"

"Do I look like a goddamn road map?" This time he kept his hands on his keyboard and his bloodshot eyes on the screen. Realizing I wasn't going away, he waved his arm behind him and pointed to the right.

"Thanks," I said.

"Ahhh! Leave me the fuck alone!"

Scanning brown plastic name plates hung with black plastic clips on the beige plastic partition walls, I found Justin playing a computer game in his cube.

I startled him. His face flushed when he saw me, mistaking me for his boss, I supposed, or a schoolyard bully ready to pull his underwear over his head.

"What?" he said.

It was the same guy I'd seen at the club. His narrow glasses, albino complexion, and bad haircut were not one-of-a-kind, but if there'd been any question, his shirt—"There's no place like 127.0.0.1"—put that to bed. I hoped he hadn't been wearing it since that night.

"Got a second?" I asked.

"What?"

I moved a pile of plastic bound reports, plastic discs, and plastic soda cups from a lime-green plastic chair like they have in second-grade classrooms and sat down.

His cubicle was as individual and homey as the management would allow. His computer screen was the size of a middle-class TV. His walls had pictures of the Starship Enterprise in each of its five iterations, a close up of Tolkien's Ring of Power, runes glowing its operating instructions, and a swimsuit calendar showing barely legal girls with brass braziers.

"Interesting style," I said, noting the metallically clad vixen on his wall.

"Steampunk."

"Ah," I said. "Is that Colonies you're playing?"

He flushed. I'd busted him playing. "Yeah. So?"

"So nothing. My son plays it. Says it's really good."

He stared at me. An awkward silence.

My eyes darted around the room looking for more small-talk fodder to soften him up. My charming appearance wasn't doing it. I tidied up the stack of papers I'd moved off the chair, hoping my good housekeeping skills would melt his heart.

I picked up a book. It was a thick, glossy brochure, magazine size. The paper was crisp, the ink vibrant, the layout breathtaking. It was the nicest sales brochure in the history of the world. Just holding it made me want to own whatever it was selling. According to the price tag, the brochure alone had cost ninety dollars. It was a deal. The Egyptian paper and perfumed ink had to cost more than that. It was hard bound. On the cover, above a picture of the coolest sports car I'd ever seen, was the word "Tesla." A business card for a dealer in California bookmarked an electric-blue, two-seater convertible.

"Tesla?" I said, flipping through the pages of automotive pornography. "Isn't this that electric supercar?"

"Yeah," he said warily. "Totally boss."

Someone had penciled in prices on a back page, breaking down different options like high-speed Internet, custom rims, and cloaking device.

"Makes my hybrid car look like an old shoe," I said. "This costs over a hundred thousand dollars. I thought electric cars were supposed to save money."

"They save the environment," he corrected me, taking the book out of my hands. "Can I help you?"

Finally, my opening. Who needed charm school?

"I saw you the other night at The Comedy Cellar with Rose Griff a few days before she was killed," I said in a matter-of-fact voice meant to instill fear that he was a suspect and awe him with my uncanny powers of perception. "I want to ask you a few questions," I said, practically accusing him of the murder. "Do you want to talk to me here or . . . ?" I trailed off, letting him fill in the rest of the threat himself.

"You're not a cop. Don't pretend," he said nervously. "You're the guy who killed her."

He'd made me.

"Are you here to kill me, too?"

"What?" Get accused of killing one person, and the world thinks you're a killer.

He coughed and reached for an orange bottle behind a speaker. He opened it and washed down a horse pill with the dregs of a Mountain Dew.

"No. I'm not here to kill you." I didn't think he believed me, so I put on my innocent face. "I didn't kill Rose." I felt like I'd been saying that nonstop for weeks, and I probably had. I thought I should get a T-shirt made to save time. At least a business card.

"Police said you did," he said. "TV, papers, and the Internet."

"The police are wrong. TV and papers are wrong. The Internet? Well, it seems to know more than most, but I'm leaning toward it's wrong too. I didn't kill Rose. I'm trying to find out who did. I'm hoping, since you knew her, you might be able to help me."

"Why should I help you?" he spat the words out.

He hadn't heard me. T-shirt. Definitely.

"I'm looking for the killer," I said. "Someone killed our friend and it wasn't me. I'd like to know who it was, and why, and all that. You know, to get out of jail and do justice for Rose."

He stared at me, icy apprehension in his eyes, but thawing at the edges.

"What happened?" he said.

"I went to a party with Rose. We danced. We dosed. We drank. We went to her place. We passed out. When I came to, she was dead and I was framed."

He looked scared.

"Yeah, the police didn't buy it either," I said. "Can I just ask you a couple of questions? I won't move from this chair. Okay?" I took his frightened blank silence as an enthusiastic yes.

"How long did you know Rose?" I asked.

"A couple of years."

"How'd you meet?"

"Sci-fi convention."

"How long did you date?"

"About a month. A little less. Maybe a week and a half. Two weekends, really."

"But you remained friends? After the break up?"

"Yes."

"How often did you see her after that?"

"Hardly never."

"You mean very little?"

"That's what I said." It wasn't, but I wanted to make sure that's what he meant.

"Assuming I didn't kill Rose," I said, all innocent face, "who else do you think might have done it?"

He stared again. I took that for a yes, but didn't know how to apply it.

"Did you know she dealt drugs?" I asked.

Light in his eyes. "Yes," he said cautiously. "She knew a Mexican guy named Carlos. He was from Guatemala, I think."

"That would make him Guatemalan, not Mexican."

"Yeah, right. But he looks Mexican."

I remembered the rave. "I saw him," I said. "Could he have killed her?" I was thinking out loud, but Justin took it as a legitimate question.

"Maybe," he said.

"How well do you know Carlos?"

"By name and reputation?"

"What's his reputation?"

"He's a drug dealer."

"Yeah, I got that. Anything else?"

"He's Mexican."

My programmer was in a loop. I changed tactics. "Why would he kill her?"

"Maybe she owed him money. When she needed money, sometimes she'd go to Carlos and get drugs. He wouldn't make her pay for it up front. She'd pay him back after she sold them and had the money."

"Pretty nice drug dealer," I said.

"No, not really. Rose was just nice enough for everyone."

"But she sold drugs."

"That didn't make her a bad person," he said defensively. "People do things to get along. Sometimes people have to cut corners and grab an opportunity when they see it. It's survival in the U.S.A. You do what you have to do to make it."

He made Utah sound like the Warsaw Ghetto.

"Rose was sweet," I said softly. I waited a moment then said, "Did you know she was once arrested for prostitution?"

"She wasn't a hooker," he said bitterly. "It was that guy Harris. A deal went bad, and he did that to her in revenge."

"What deal?"

"I don't know."

"How do you know about this?"

"Rose told me."

"Why?"

He paused for a moment and thought. He hid his eyes from me behind the thin rims of his glasses. Since he was naturally squinty, it was an effective blind.

"Nothing I tell you can be held against me, right?" he said.

"I'm not a cop," I said soothingly, but knowing that if he told me anything useful, damn right, I'd use it. If I thought he was involved in Rose's murder, I would personally drag him by his pale, elven ears down to McGraw and Sweet and kick him in the balls for fun.

"You can trust me," I said with a warm smile.

"She wanted my help to get into his computer and get her money back."

"Did you help her?"

Justin found an interesting stain on the rust-colored carpet and studied it for fungal growth. "Yes," he said quietly to the fungus.

"Was that what you were doing at the Cellar?"

He flinched.

"What is it?" I asked.

He brought his face up and looked at me hard for the first time. He was nervous, a Chihuahua in Chinatown. His forehead furrowed in anger, rage, determination, or gastrointestinal distress. My detective senses weren't honed enough to differentiate.

He started to say something, then stuttered, and stopped. Something shifted inside his mind, something set aside, another thing picked up. It was like watching a railhead at a roundabout.

"It could have been Harris who killed her," he said finally. "He's a total asshole. He ripped her off and got her arrested. But Rose got her money back, and I bet he was mad. Really mad."

A man peeked into Justin's cubicle over the partition, then stepped into the opening. He wore a pink, short-sleeved dress shirt with a pastel-green tie. His mustache was little more than a shadow, but he carried himself like Napoleon.

"We have a deadline, Justin," he said. "Have you forgotten?" He stared menacingly at Justin and made a show of ignoring me.

"Right," said Justin, turning to face his computer, the Colonies splash screen still on it.

I stood up, turned, and faced the dictator. I was a foot taller than him, and he shrank when I stepped closer, giving me eighteen inches on him. I didn't say a word, just loomed in the doorless doorway. Detectives don't get pushed around by little men in pink and green outfits, I thought—WWMD (What Would Marlowe Do)? Another

T-shirt? The pastel Napoleon found something pressing to do down the hall and walked briskly away.

"I gotta get back to work," Justin said.

"Here's my name and number," I said, writing it on a scrap of paper, making a mental note to get some cards printed up for my new detective persona. "If you think of anything else, contact me."

I tipped an invisible hat with my thumb and forefinger and left Justin holding the paper, wondering what the gesture had meant. Noob, I thought.

CHAPTER NINETEEN

I'd once had a job with Ace Printing and Binding. When I applied, I had visions of setting type, applying ink with a paint roller, loading an eighty-ton roll of newsprint with a forklift, and watching newspapers spring to life as the cornerstone of the fourth estate. Either that, or learning how to put paperbacks together, vowing to always use enough glue so pages wouldn't drop out. That's not what happened. I learned how to change toner cartridges and reboot crashed computers. I memorized the number of the Xerox repairman and moved boxes of paper around like a bricklayer. As far as retail went, I'd had worse. With corporate copy places popping up all over the place, that little shop survived on repeat business that stretched back before the Great Depression when someone surely had to glue spines and set type. Originally a family business for fifty years, it changed hands every two years after they sold it for reasons as mysterious but as certain as the tides. I went there for business cards and didn't recognize a soul.

Bill Achmad Nu Zahor Izadohawni Smith was pleased to take my order. Despite his common Utah name, I didn't think he was from here. His accent was as thick as a ream of twenty-pound paper, and his cologne had been applied with a hookah. Still, sixty-three dollars and seven hours later, I had a box of stiff white business cards. Between a magnifying glass icon on one side and a sad face on the other, in upright block letters, it read: "Tony Flaner, Private Detective. I did not kill Rose Griff." My cell phone number was at the bottom. There was no address since I didn't have an office yet.

I wasn't sure if I'd get in trouble for saying I was a detective. A bit of research showed me that there was an actual private detective license available. It mostly came down to three hundred dollars and a bunch of hours detecting already. I had the money, but not the hours, and definitely not the time to wait for the government to issue me a certificate. I began a log of hours detecting, and strategically kept the word "licensed" off the card. They were temporary cards anyway. I'd either prove my innocence or go to prison. In either case, I'd need new cards: "Tony Flaner, Licensed Private Detective" or "Tony Flaner, Please don't make me your bitch."

I'd met three of Rose's lovers—Justin, Luke, and myself, though the last was arguable. The only thing we all had in common was a Y chromosome. Rose's taste in men was eclectic. Everyone who'd known her agreed she liked many men one at a time. She went through men faster than I did jobs, hobbies, and underwear.

I could hear Nancy, the psychology major, lecturing me about Rose, speculating about father figure issues, possible childhood sexual abuse, and levels of insecurity so deep as to offer a shrink an entire career. But I didn't buy it. She danced like a happy woman. Her home was specific and tailored. The Rose I knew wasn't shackled by repressed trauma, but liberated as no one else I'd ever known. Rose went through life like it was a splendid buffet to be sampled and savored. When I thought of timid Justin, sexy Luke, and obnoxious me, I saw us as an assortment of flavors for Rose's curious and lively pallet. No one said she was a call girl except the same legal machine that said I was a killer of lovely women. I suspected the machine was wrong on both counts.

The court records suggested Rose never held a regular job in her life. Ever. Even in college, she didn't work. It was brought up in her prostitution hearing. Since she couldn't produce a pay stub, the judge assumed she lived by "illicit means." She was found guilty and sat in jail for a week before someone paid her fine and she was let go, but now with a record. She refused to answer the judge's direct question as to how she made her living. She took the fifth to avoid both the question and a contempt of court charge.

Rose's court documents were part of the discovery the prosecutors had put together against me that Mollif had dropped on my doorstep.

The name of the "John" in Rose's case had been kept confidential. It was the county that prosecuted her, and her "client" agreed to testify against her for immunity. Word on the street, and out of Justin's mouth, was that the client was Harris Tamlen, royal asshole and friend of Cynthia and Charlie, legless cancer victim and club member.

I couldn't see how there had been enough evidence to convict Rose. It was her word against his, but still she went away. Evidence had been irrelevant.

Fuck.

Her fine had been paid by a Mr. Carlos Serrano. There was my connection. There was an address. I filled my pocket with new business cards and set out to detect.

* * *

The address was a restaurant called Hot Tamale's, occupying a slice of a stucco strip mall built about the time Columbus was chewing on crayons. Someone had repainted it recently, and someone else had tried to cover that up with weak white latex paint that didn't conceal the graffiti half as well as it should. The other storefronts, the ones that didn't have blue "For Lease" signs in them, had signs in Spanish. Most didn't even have an English translation. The check-cashing store logo was familiar from a TV commercial, but the words on the door were all foreign. The tobacco shop said tobacco, but I think it was just the same word in both languages. Hot Tamale's was the exception. Its sign had some English, so they obviously welcomed indigenous white folks. Since it was lunchtime and I liked food, I went in.

When I opened the door, the smells hit me like a board and singed the corners of my eyes. Raucous voices in Latino accents with Spanish verbs rode on the scents. I took my place in line and listened, never hearing a word of English.

It was a small place. A sign on the wall, autographed by the fire marshal himself, suggested no more than thirty-two patrons should be there at once. There were at least twice that number.

There were no waiters. You ordered your food at the counter, paid, got a number, and waited. Seating was at a premium, tabletops more so. Many stood and ate out of white Styrofoam boxes, chatting with friends who, through seniority or punctuality, had secured a table or a chair, but not necessarily both.

The menu was hung on the wall above the counter. It was in Spanish, but there were some faded pictures to help navigation. The prices were reasonable and the portions hearty. This was a working man's diner. I liked it.

By the time I got to the counter, lunch hours were ending and people were filtering out, walking sideways to get through the throng. I was optimistic about a table.

The man ahead of me in oil-stained jeans flirted with the woman behind the counter, making her blush demurely before taking his order. I liked that reaction. I wish I knew what he'd said and wondered if it would translate into English. Then it was my turn.

She was a raven-haired beauty. Her long shining hair was braided in a complex weave behind her back, brightening her fresh, tan face. Her big, dark eyes made me sigh. She looked at me, took in my European features, my brown hair, my T-shirt and jeans, and said in clear English, "What would you like?"

"Is Tamale here?" I said, kidding about the name.

Her smile told me she hadn't heard that one in a couple of minutes.

"I'll have a pork burrito," I said, hoping I'd translated the entry properly, but pointing just in case. Then, just to be on the safe side, I added, "The number three."

She gave me a waxed paper cup and a number torn off the bottom of an order pad. I gave her some money.

"Is Carlos here?" I asked casually.

"Which Carlos?" she replied.

"Carlos Serrano."

Her bright expression darkened with suspicion.

"Carlos Serrano?" she shrugged. Her perfect English failing her.

"That's okay," I said offhandedly.

I found a table by the window. I felt the woman's stare follow me as I wiped off some spilled lettuce and sat down.

I'd seen Carlos only once, but knew I would recognize him if I saw him again. I had to account for the vivid aura glow and morphing features the ecstasy had imparted to his features, but I'd seen his face transfigure into enough different forms that night to give me a pretty good idea what he actually looked like.

My number was called in English. I collected a red plastic tray with my white Styrofoamed lunch and sat down. There was a collection of hot sauce bottles scattered among the tables. I took a green one and an orange one. I couldn't read the labels, but bright pictures of peppers on one suggested spice, while the smiling señorita on the other suggested happy contentment.

The señorita lied. I downed half my coke from a single splash of it on my lettuce. The green was kinder, and brought out the spice in a way that wouldn't cripple me the next day.

I took my time enjoying the authentic ethnic food and giving the woman at the counter time to do something if she was going to do anything.

She didn't do anything.

I finished and bussed my table. I even asked for a moist cloth to wipe away a spill, when, in fact, I hadn't spilled anything. Such little deceptions are the daily trade of a private eye. I wiped the table conscientiously and returned the cloth with a smile.

"If you see Carlos," I said, giving her my card and a twenty dollar bill, "please have him call me."

She took the money and looked at the card. Then she looked up at me angrily.

"You," she said, her English returning. "You're the one who killed Rose."

"No, I'm not," I said. "Read the card."

She glanced down again.

"See?" I said.

She wasn't convinced.

"I need to talk to Carlos," I said. "If you see him, just give him my card. Okay?"

I could tell she was choosing between spitting in my face, keeping the money, and tearing up the card, or some combination of the three.

I donned my innocent face and said in parting, "The food here is excellent, by the way."

"I know," she said.

I left and went to the parking lot.

I had my hand on the car door before I knew they were there. Three large men appeared in my peripheral vision like glaucoma. I turned, putting my back against the car. Two looked Spanish, one had the unmistakable features of a South American Indian—Aztec or Mayan. They crowded into my personal space.

"Whatchu' doin' here, gringo?" said the native in thick, accented thug.

"It would appear that I'm getting into my car," I said. "From your perspective it might appear that I'm trying to hump your leg, since you're standing so fucking close to me."

"What the fuck does that mean?" said the one on my right.

"It means you're sucking up all my oxygen. You all need to take a step back so I can shift my weight to my other hip." Smart-ass comedian translated well into hard-nosed detective.

"You the one needs to step back, homie," said one on the left.

"You don't look like a pig," said one on the right.

"There's probably a genetic reason for that," I said. "Let me get to a computer and I can answer that better."

"Hey, smart ass," said the Mayan. "You some kind of narc?"

"Is this where I tell you your mother is so fat she's got her own zip code, or do you start?"

I felt a hand slide down my butt, into my back pocket, and remove my wallet. I turned on Righty who was already rifling through the bills and cards.

"Buy me flowers before you do that again," I said. I grabbed at my wallet, but he pulled it back out of my reach. Visions of lost third-grade lunch money made me yearn for paste and blunted scissors.

The Mayan reached out a hand, and Righty tossed him the wallet. He pulled out all my money, allowing it all to fall to the ground like confetti. He read the credit cards and let them drop, too. He withdrew my driver's license and a business card. He read the card, looked back at the license, and mouthed my name, then looked back at the card.

"You the one killed Rose," he said.

I leaned forward and pointed to my card, underlining my denial with my index finger. He dropped the card, license, and wallet onto the pile at his feet. He stared at me.

"You ain't no cop," said the big Indian.

"Good, Captain Obvious. I'll buy you a cookie," I said. "I'm a private detective."

"Who you working for?" he asked.

"That's confidential," I said, recalling the line from a thousand detective movies.

He stared at me. I heard knuckles crack.

I stared back, raising my eyebrows in anticipation.

"You're working for yourself?" he said.

"I can't confirm or deny that," I said. "But, duh, dumbshit. Can you wipe yourself yet?"

I suppose my inflection was disrespectful, but I felt no danger in the parking lot of a Salt Lake City strip mall in the middle of the day. I knew they were just playing tough, hassling the white guy in a Spanish-speaking neighborhood. That's why the punch in my side made me scream. It was the surprise of it. And the pain. There was pain. Then there was the second punch that knocked the air out of me. That one hurt, too, but I didn't scream. I couldn't. I doubled over to get a better look at my credit cards and find the breath that'd been slammed out of me. Surely, it was there on the ground somewhere.

"I should cut you now for what you did to Rose," said Lefty. I heard the snick of a switchblade opening. Old school. I liked that. I'd have complimented him on his choice of weapons if I could have breathed.

"Mind your manners," said the Indian. I don't know if he said that to me or one of his cohorts. I was too busy examining shoes.

They turned on their heels and walked away. I took a little rest against my car, air finding its way back into my abdomen in small increments.

My first beating as a private detective left me feeling empty. On the one hand, I'd made the rite of passage, joined the honored ranks of Rockford, Spade, and McGill. On the other hand, my side hurt so much my eyes teared.

Detectives don't cry, I told myself collecting oxygen for ten more minutes. Several people saw me sitting on the asphalt and walked right by me into the restaurant. One even pointed. That was as much help as I was going to get in that parking lot.

I collected my things, crawled into my car, and drove away, trying not to let the beating I'd endured taint my impression of Hot Tamale's "authentic ethnic flavor."

CHAPTER TWENTY

One look at Perry's jerky steps, twitching eye, and ducking gait told me that he was off his medication. I'd never seen him this bad before in the daylight, and it alarmed me.

"You alarm me," I said.

"I'm good. I'm good. I'm good," he repeated. "I got news. News for you. I know something."

He was waiting for me in the bushes when I pulled into the garage. He followed me into the house.

"What have you been doing?" he asked. "Obviously not decorating, or are you going with brown?"

"I've been doing the detective thing," I said.

"I thought so," he said, bursting with energy. "So have I."

We sat down at the kitchen table where I'd left the list of lawyers and Rose's court records.

"Are you going to tell me, or do I have to beat it out of you?" I said.

"Remember that prick at my show who tried to act tough with you?"

"Calvin. Yes."

"You know his name?" He was disappointed. "Well, anyway, I was driving yesterday, and I saw him in this blue sports car. The kind of thing most people grow out of by seventeen."

I nodded. I knew the car.

"I recognized him. I followed him thinking maybe I'd get a clue. And guess what?"

"You found out he lives with his mother?" I offered.

"Does he live with his mother?"

"I don't know," I said. "It's just a hypothesis. Tell me what you found."

"I discovered his hangout. He went to a cybercafé on Pine Street in the Midvale old town. He was met by two other guys and they all went in together like a gang. They were in there for five hours and fifty-two minutes, until the place shut down and kicked them out."

"You watched them for five hours?"

"No, I watched the building. I didn't go in; I didn't want to be recognized."

"For five hours?"

"Uh-huh."

"Where'd he go after that?"

"I lost him on the freeway. Southbound. He speeds like he's got something to hide."

"What could he be hiding?"

"Something weird and illegal, I'm sure. I didn't see anyone else enter or leave the café the whole time. It would be the perfect place to launch a cyber attack or upload porn, or download porn, or some other porn stuff. I don't know what exactly, but I'm sure it's immoral."

"Is that it?"

"He's there now. He arrived right after noon and hasn't left. I figured it was time to make our move and shake him down. If he's into cyberterrorism, it's the perfect motive for killing that girl. She was probably about to turn him in to the cops or something."

"Uh-huh," I said. "That's one theory. Wait. How do you know he hasn't left? How long have you been here?"

"A couple of hours, but I left Garret and Stan there. They'll call if anything changes."

"Where's Critter?"

"Home. This isn't the kind of thing for a puppet."

"Absolutely not," I said, exhaling a heavy sigh. My friends. At least they were trying to help.

"So, are we going?" said Perry.

"Sure, why not? Let's go."

"You drive. I left my car at home to throw them off."

"How'd you get here?"

"Cab. I had them drop me off at that 7-Eleven by the middle school." He pointed.

"That's two miles away."

"I cut through backyards. No one saw me." His left eye twitched a moment after the right one winked.

"Are you off your meds?" I asked casually as we got in my car.

"Hell yeah," he said. "Can't think clearly when I'm on them."

"Have you slept much?"

"Some. Mostly I've been trying to figure out how to help you, Tony. You've always been a stand-up guy for me."

"That's an old joke," I said. "Standard would rail on you for that one."

"True, but he's a prick and you're not. Remember when I told you that I was being followed? It was after I posted my theory about government vapor trails and UFOs?"

"Yeah, it was in a show-business chat room. I remember warning you that someone would steal your idea and you'd get no credit. Hollywood is bankrupt of ideas."

"I didn't care if anyone stole it," he said, eyes wide, but winking. "It's the truth. I wanted the truth out there. If they made a movie out of it, so much the better."

"So what about it?"

"You were the only one who believed me when I said I was being followed. That really meant something. You believed me when no one else would."

I didn't remember saying I believed him. He'd been off his meds then, too. He'd surfed the Internet for sixty nonstop hours, collecting proof for his conspiracy theory before posting it online as an eight thousand word punctuation-less manifesto. I told him to come to my place and sleep where no one would look for him. I never said I believed his story, but neither had I said I didn't. He just needed rest. I even got him to start taking his medication again so he'd "blend in better. Just until the heat was off."

"What ever happened with that?" I asked.

"I'm still being watched. There's been a surveillance van parked in front of my house for months, but they haven't moved on me yet. I've acted normal and kept my head down. But this thing with you, Tony—I have to help. Don't you see that it's payback for you helping me?"

"That's a theory."

"Think about it. I post from a library computer. Calvin's gang are computer terrorists. Or pornographers. Or maybe spooks. They're trying to set you up to cover their asses."

"I don't understand," I admitted.

"I don't either," he said. "That's the genius of it."

Perry's arguments aside, I figured I had to talk to Calvin eventually. He wasn't a suspect any more than Tonya or Melissa were, and I frankly hadn't any direct questions to ask him. Nevertheless, I thought I'd pick his tiny brain and hope something useful spilled out. I was out of hot leads until I found Carlos or cornered Harris, and I didn't know how to do either yet, so Calvin would have to do. At least with Perry and the boys, jokes that they were, I stood less chance of being beaten up again.

The cybercafé was in another strip mall, probably older than the one I visited that morning, but recently renovated with new asphalt and trees.

The place itself was called simply Midvale Cyber Café. It had a roadside retro look that I found charming—lightning bolts and red blinking letters. It was the last of a dying breed of public computer spaces. If the rent had been anything greater than a daily cheeseburger, I'm sure it would shut down.

Standard and Garret were in a Camry next to an Arby's.

"Hey, Killer," said Standard.

"Stan and I have been watching the place for hours," said Garret, stretching when he got out of the car. Arby's sauce stained his shirt in three places. One spot was still wet. "What took so long?"

"He wasn't home," said Perry. "I had to wait."

"Tell me again why you couldn't have just called him?" asked Standard.

Perry reeled on him, wild, twitching eyes ablaze. "Dude, the phones aren't safe. They never have been. Not for this. Not for anything. Remember that."

"He's off his medication," said Garret to me under his breath.

"Yeah, I know," I said. "Why are you guys here?"

"Guilt," said Garret.

"We felt bad about thinking you were a murderer," said Standard. "You aren't, are you?"

"No." I handed them cards.

"So, what's the plan?" said Standard.

"What's happening?"

"A bunch of guys are in there now," said Garret. "Six went in while we were watching. None have left. That would mean at least ten in there now, plus employees."

"What does it look like inside?" I asked.

"Hell if we know," said Standard. "This is as close as Mastermind there would let us get."

Perry glared at him.

"Okay, I see. Here's the plan," I said. "I'm going to go in there. You guys give me about sixty seconds and then come in after me. If I'm getting my ass kicked, save me. If I'm not, just chill and see what happens. Come on," I said and marched across the parking lot.

The retro look extended inside. Neon lights stretched along the inside walls like electric doodles. Glass light fixtures hung from an exposed frame ceiling fifteen feet up, and ended in plumb-sized LED bulbs. The walls were lined with steel and plexiglass tables with computers set between glass privacy barriers that reminded me of the prison visiting room. Down the center was a similar table that ended in a ring with a neon sculpture depicting a yellow lightning bolt shooting out of a neon green electrical plug. The smell of coffee and onion rings filled the air. A man read a magazine at the far counter, a paper food-handler's hat tilted on his forehead. No one looked up when I came in.

I scanned the room for familiar faces and found Calvin on the middle left. His tough guy bravado was completely absent, lost in the rattle of mouse clicks and frenetic keyboard chords.

I came up behind him and peeked over his shoulder. He was playing a game I recognized: Colonies. Glancing at the other computer screens, I saw that this was the game of choice for the room. The banter suggested a tournament in progress.

"You're going to be powned once the new patch comes out," said someone to the right.

"Your whole guild will be garbage," said the left. "They've upgraded the neutron cannons and tweaked the build times on all biologicals. The reign of cheese is over."

"How many more patches before nationals?" asked someone in the middle.

"At least one," someone said. "Probably two before world."

Suddenly Calvin yelled, "Shit!" and violently pushed his chair back. Simultaneously, a man on the opposite wall yelled, "Noob!"

"Defeat" flashed on Calvin's screen. The mouse skidded off the desk and hung swinging by its cord. Then he saw me. "What the fuck!"

"Got a minute?" I said.

Calvin's alarmed tone drew a few faces from their games to see what was up.

"Remember me?" I handed him my card.

"Arghhhhh!" The scream came from the back. No one moved. No one seemed interested in the terrible cry of anguish. Then my posse burst in.

Three panting part-time comedians took up a phalanx position blocking the door. Perry was in the middle, knees bent, eyes searching for danger. Standard was on his right, his hands in his pockets, but his stare serious enough. Garret was on the left, his hands held in front of him as if to push away an oncoming shopping cart.

"Arrrgghh!" came the cry again. As before, no one looked to see what the screaming was about.

"Aaaaaaahhggah!"

Calvin looked terrified. I pushed his chair back into the desk.

"Excuse me," I said and walked to the circular center table.

A young man with headphones and a flushed purple face jumped in spasms and shrieked under his breath. Then his whole body jolted and he screamed. "Aaaahhhhh!" It chilled the blood.

He took no notice of me, but kept playing. I traced wires from his computer down the table, along the floor, disappearing up his pants leg.

I tapped the shoulder of the guy next to him, a man in his late twenties with a full head of silver hair. He glanced at me, but didn't move. I tapped his shoulder again. I was a detective, and detectives got answers. He paused his game and pulled off his headphones. "What do you want?"

He looked familiar. I wondered if he'd flown recently and crossed my ticket counter.

"What's his story?" I asked gesturing to the wired boy.

"You don't have to tell him anything, Rex," shouted Calvin. "He's not a cop."

"Leave the man alone, dude," said a teenager to me from across the round table. "Can't you see we're in training?"

"I just want to know why this guy keeps screaming and none of you care."

Rex, the one with gray hair, said, "He's got wires attached to his testicles. He wrote a program that shocks him whenever he makes a mistake in the game."

"You're kidding."

"No, I'm not," he said. "Now leave me the hell alone, jerkoff." He put his headphones back on and re-entered Colonies.

"Just wanted to know," I said, returning to Calvin. "Friend of yours?" I asked.

"They belong to another guild, the Wreckers. We're the Arsonists. Friendly competition. Training for nationals."

"So you're in diamond league?" My knowledge surprised him.

"Platinum," he admitted. "But rank doesn't mean anything for this. You just gotta win."

"I need to talk to you about Rose," I said.

The other players had grown bored with me and my friends, and were all back to their games.

"Arrrgghh!"

"Tonya said the police let you go," he said. "That doesn't mean I have to like you."

Another person who didn't understand bail. I went with it. I pulled a chair over and crowded into his cyber space.

"How well did you know her?"

"Rose? Hardly at all. She was Tonya's friend."

"How'd you meet Tonya?"

"Comedy Club. You were there."

"That night? That was the first time you met Rose?"

"Yeah."

"So why all the hostility?"

"Gotta represent," he said.

"Aaahhhhhh!" I ignored the sounds of agony, a little surprised at how quickly I'd become desensitized to them.

"Do you know a guy named Carlos? Harris? Justin? Luke? Kissinger?" He shook his head to each name. It didn't surprise me that he didn't know any of them.

"Uhhhhhgggghaaa!"

Perry watched me, bouncing on his heels, eager for the signal to rush in and drag Calvin out with a bag over his head to our waiting Camry. I shook my head. Dead end. The acrid smell of burning human hair reached my face, and I knew it was time to go.

"You guys are hard core," I said.

"You know it."

"Keep my card. If you think of anything that might help me catch this killer, call me." It was an order, not a request.

He put my card in his pocket, and I walked back to my friends. The gray-haired man watched me as far as the door and then returned to his game.

Outside, Perry said, "So what now?"

"It was a good lead," I said encouragingly.

"No, it wasn't," said Standard. "I said it wasn't."

"No, it wasn't." I agreed. "But thanks for trying. Garret and Stan, you're stand-up guys."

"That old chestnut?" said Standard. "Wait. You called me Stan."

"No, I didn't," I said.

"I think you did," said Garret.

"Nope," I said. Stan smirked, and slid into the car.

"We had your back," said Garret, taking the driver's side.

"That you did. I'll take Perry home."

Perry was crestfallen that more hadn't happened, but cheered up quickly on the drive.

"I'll keep my eyes open," he said.

I gave him my card. He laughed. "Best card ever."

"Thanks," I said. "And I'll call you if I need backup."

"We need a code word because my phones are tapped," he said. "Use 'Jell-O' in a sentence and I'll know we're on."

"Works for me."

When I got to Perry's neighborhood, it was dark. He told me to drive past his door and then go around the block. He got out in front of an adjacent house and snuck across their yard to his backdoor and went inside without turning on a light.

On the way home, I saw an unmarked van sitting under a telephone pole, kitty-corner but facing the front of Perry's house. Two men sat in the front seats. One smoked a cigarette, the other's face was illuminated by the green glow of an electronic display.

Just because you're paranoid doesn't mean people aren't watching you.

CHAPTER TWENTY-ONE

The next morning found me sitting in my car across the street from the Tamlen residence. I was alone on another stake out. I'd left the coffee and sunflower seeds at home, and brought my camera with a zoom lens.

Tamlen's lights came on at 6:00 a.m. sharp, then moved to the front of the house half an hour later.

It was an expensive house in an expensive neighborhood. No home-owner cared for their own lawn or trimmed their own shrubs here. They were professionally done by minimum-wage foreign artists, stealing jobs the homeowner couldn't be bothered to do.

At 7:15 the garage door opened, revealing an immaculate three-car warehouse. Two silver Mercedes—one a sedan, the other an SUV—were in the main garage. I could see a sports car under a khaki dust cover on the side. A man of about forty-five slid into the sedan and started it. My Nikon rattled off a fusillade of shots as fast as the memory chip could save. He was lean, athletic, trim for his age. He had a dark mustache that was a tad too light for his hair. I could almost smell the dye and maybe the scent of Rogaine wafting over the manicured yard.

I followed him through the elite neighborhood, past homes that cost more than an airplane and cars that cost more than my house, all owned by people who moved and shook while I sauntered and strolled.

I followed him to a brick and glass office building where he inserted a magic keycard that opened a gate. I parked on the street and followed as quickly as I could.

I sprinted through a brass and glass revolving door and caught up with Harris Tamlen in front of a coffee kiosk in the building's lobby. White and pink marble tile made an abstract mosaic centered around a shallow, bubbling fountain in the middle. A single spout spurted too-blue water three feet into the air before lapping back into the pool.

There was an etched brass building directory by the door and several pink and white benches. The kiosk looked out of place, a wooden cart with exaggerated wheels that harkened back to the turn of the century. I couldn't imagine that there was enough business just in that five-story building to justify that little coffee cart, but there it was. To its credit, they also had pastries and sandwiches. The prices were premium, like their coffee, as advertised on a blackboard in hand-drawn, pastel chalk lettering.

I stepped in line for a latte behind Harris. One woman was ahead of him.

Harris's suit was tailored, and his white shirt was so clean it glowed beneath the gray pinstriped jacket. There was enough starch in it to slow a bullet. I couldn't guess at the brand or expense of his shoes. Their style was European and had pointy toes no working-class American this side of the Keebler tree would ever wear.

"Hello, Mr. Tamlen. The usual?" said a fresh-faced boy in a brown apron.

"Try not to burn it this time, you idiot," was Harris's pleasant reply. "I like it hot, not ruined."

The fresh face wilted before turning to the espresso machine.

"No need to be rude," said the woman ahead of him waiting for her coffee.

"No reason for you to be so ugly, but I can't do anything about that, can I?"

It wasn't even a good comeback. The woman wasn't ugly; she could lose a pound, but she didn't deserve that kind of attack. She stood her ground.

"Do you work in this building? I'm calling security."

"Fifth floor, ugly," he said, not even looking at her. "We own the building. Which office is yours? Maybe your lease is coming up?"

"What a complete asshole," she said.

"Bitch," he replied.

A female barista presented her with coffee and a complimentary Danish, and the woman stormed away to the elevator.

"Hurry up, Jack. I don't have all day," Harris said.

"My name's Bryan."

"Your name is 'shut the fuck up and give me my damn coffee,' you moron."

"Here you go, Mr. Tamlen," he said and slid a paper cup across the counter.

He lifted it to his lips to taste it. My right arm involuntarily shot up like a spring and caught the bottom of the cup, smashing the hot, but not burned, triple-espresso latte, no foam, right into his face. As the cardboard crumpled between his head and my palm, coffee shot up his nose, over his forehead, and around his eyes, and then down his cheeks and onto his impossibly bright shirt and thousand-dollar suit.

He staggered backward, blind and burned. He dropped his briefcase and screamed. As if to retreat from the burns, he took another step back, and then another, until his legs were against the fountain. Another attempted step toppled him over and onto his ass into the fountain. Blue liquid—it couldn't be water, more like ink or, possibly, washer fluid—splashed into his face and dyed his clothes. His whole head went under, which was good for his burns, but bad for his breathing. He bobbed up, gasped, and screamed. His lungs didn't know which way to flex.

The coffee clerk looked at me with amazement. His coworker stared, too; no one said a word. Tamlen splashed and screamed. The elevator announced itself with a bright bell. A grinning woman vanished inside it.

I laid a twenty-dollar bill on the kiosk counter.

"You didn't see me," I said.

Bryan slid the money back and passed me a complimentary Danish. I jogged out the revolving door just as Tamlen filled the lobby with enough curses to bring down Pharaoh. I'd talk to him another time, I decided. Glancing at the directory as I ran, I knew where he worked.

I fled to my car and went looking for another coffee shop. I had a real craving now. I passed two police cruisers speeding toward Tamlen's building, but they didn't have their lights on. I passed eighteen Starbucks shops before I found a locally owned place called Grounds for a Cup. With a suppressed grin and a coffee, I sat down at a table to think.

Tamlen worked for a real estate investment firm, Mortgage Buyers, Inc. They specialized in foreclosures and preyed upon desperate people. They'd been in the news a couple of times, and their late-night commercial ran incessantly, like a recurring nightmare where your pants are still in the closet and you're late for fifth-period history. It showed a house spinning out of control and then down a computer-generated drain while a voiceover promised a lifeboat to save equity. The business was sleazy, but legal.

Had Harris just been another flavor for Rose? I cringed at the thought. Rose was high on the pedestal I'd built for her; I couldn't imagine her with that jerk. Besides, he was married. Based on my encounter with her, she had a rule against that.

Then what? Was her house in foreclosure? Did they have mutual friends? Enemies? I couldn't wait to ask him, but I had no idea how to approach such a prick.

My phone rang.

"Hello."

"Is this Tony Flaner, Private Investigator?"

"Yes," I said.

"And you didn't kill Rose Griff?"

I thought I recognized the voice, but without earsplitting base feedback, I couldn't be sure. "No, I didn't."

"How do I know that?"

"Because it's the truth. And it's written on my card." Don't people read anymore?

"Yeah, I got your card, and your message. You're looking for me?"

"Carlos Serrano. I need some answers, and you might have them."

"First, I don't know you. Second, they say you killed Rose and I liked Rose. Third, you're in trouble with the cops and might be setting me up to save your own skin."

"First," I answered, "how will you ever get to know me if we don't spend time together? Plus, we met at the rave. I was the stoned guy in the loud shirt. Oh, wait, that describes about everybody there, doesn't it? Well, I was that guy. Second, everyone liked Rose, including me. Third, I hadn't thought of setting anyone up. Do you think it would work?"

"Just make things worse for you if you tried," he said.

"Then I won't. Will you come see me? I'm in a coffee shop on Foothill. I'd come to your neck of the woods, but some rough boys roughed me up. Roughly."

"Boys will be boys."

"Your boys?" I asked.

"Where on Foothill?" He ducked the question or just didn't care enough to answer it.

I told him the address and said I'd wait an hour. If I had to wait longer than that, I was going to call him back and ask what the holdup was. My terms were harsh, but he agreed to them.

In twenty minutes, a boxy Chrysler LeBaron with thin wheels and spinning rims pulled up. A man stepped out and scanned the street. He wore a wifebeater T-shirt under a translucent white guayabera, a thing I hadn't seen outside of Miami. I imagined his face contorting to the Thompson Twins and then, when his cologne met me ten yards before he did, I was sure it was Carlos.

"That is one stupid ugly car," I said.

He was offended. "Why you say that?"

"It's a ghetto stereotype."

"It's boss," he said, sliding into a chair opposite me. "Where I work and live, this is better than a Rolls Royce. Those rims are gold plated; the spinners will go for half an hour after the car's stopped. It's got speakers that can start a party in a Walmart parking lot and annoy the shoppers way in the back buying guns. It's a party machine and can walk as well as cruise."

"It's a stereotype," I said.

"Don't care. I like it. It's real and it's boss. You should try it. What you drive?"

"A Prius."

"Stupid, ugly stereotype, bro."

"What?"

"White, liberal, yuppie, midlife-guilt car," he said.

I was offended. "It's boss," I said.

He smiled.

"You want a coffee?" I said.

"What you're having."

I signaled for a barista. They don't usually come out from behind the counter, but my winning smile and yuppie midlife-guilt must have attracted her.

"Could you bring us two caramel lattes?" I said, giving her the twenty that'd been refused at the day's earlier coffee stand. She took the money and fired up the steamer.

"So you spent some time in lockup," Carlos said. "How was that?"

"Super," I said. "And I did so well there, they want to bring me back for a longer engagement. Life."

"And you say it's all a misunderstanding?" I couldn't tell if Carlos was accusing me of lying or asking for details. Optimistically, I gave him the details.

"I was set up," I said, and outlined the night I'd spent with Rose and the terrible morning after. I told him about the missing Flintstone glasses, the missing rum bottle, and the missing pill bottles. I told him about the unlocked door and my shooting. I told him about the roofies they found in Rose's system and in my car, and the strangle marks on her neck.

When I'd finished, he was halfway through his coffee, unaware of the foam mustache over his thin, real one.

"Was she face up or face down?" he asked when I'd finished.

The question surprised me. "Face down," I said. "Why?"

"She was drugged and killed by a cold-hearted, sleazy motherfucker, but someone who knew her, bro," he said. "Couldn't look at her when he did it. Strangled her from the back. Low-life, coward motherfucker."

"Does that mean you believe me?"

"Are you saying I don't think you're a cold-hearted, coward, sleazy motherfucker?"

"I bought you coffee."

"Yeah," he had to admit. "I can't see you doing that."

"The cops think it's me and aren't lifting a finger to check other possibilities. I'm screwed if I don't do something myself."

"Get a good lawyer," he said.

"That may save me, but it won't avenge Rose."

"So you want vengeance?" He raised an eyebrow in surprise, not in disapproval.

I thought for just a second and considered my motives. "Damn right, I do."

"Okay," he said, finally wiping the foam off his lip. "What do you need from me?"

"I'm trying to find who killed her."

"Any suspects?"

"Two," I said.

"Who?"

"A guy named Harris Tamlen and you."

"Me? Are you joking again? Because I don't see it in your eyes this time."

"You're on the top on my list," I said.

He looked at me hard.

"First, bro, let me say that you have some coconuts on you." A small, silver automatic pistol appeared in his hand as if by magic. He put it on the table in front of him. "You think I'm a killer and you invite me to coffee to tell it to my face? That's some coconuts."

"Why, thank you," I said, blushing.

"Some coconuts, particularly since I was thinking of offing you myself."

"But you won't," I said, "because you like my coconuts."

"Because I believe your card, bro. I don't think you killed Rose." He palmed the gun, and it vanished into the ether from where it came. "But why do you think I killed her?"

"Drugs, money, police. Something like that," I said. "I told you about the pill bottles disappearing from her house. Someone got rid of those. You're into drugs. You deal. You supplied Rose. She was a pusher for you."

"Take a step back, bro," said Carlos. "She was no pusher. Not for me. Not for anyone. Do you understand, bro?"

He was serious. I was scared. I pressed on.

"She didn't sell drugs? She didn't sell drugs for you?" I glanced at the barista I'd tipped so well, hoping for a rescue or at least a witness to my imminent murder.

"A pusher pushes drugs," he said, tapping the table for emphasis. "They push drugs wherever. Rose was no pusher. I don't know any pushers. Pushers are motherfuckers. The kind of trash that sells to little kids. Pushers don't last long, bro. I move them out or take them out."

"Did you take Rose out?"

"You got a hearing problem, bro? Rose was no pusher."

"So you didn't kill her? You're denying it? It wasn't you?" I figured I was so deep into the accusations, no reason to stop now.

"You wearing some kind of wire? Need everything spelled out in little words?"

"I just want to hear it."

"I didn't kill Rose," he said. "There? You satisfied?"

"But she sold drugs?"

"That's different. That's filling a need. That's capitalism—supply and demand. That ain't pushin.'"

"She sold drugs for you?"

"No," he said, and then seeing my objection, immediately added, "she sold drugs for herself. I just supplied them. She'd buy some weed from me or some shrooms or some of that fun ecstasy you liked at the rave. She'd keep some to get high and some she'd sell at a markup."

"Did she buy from you on credit?"

"Who you been talking to?"

"I'm a detective now," I said.

The answer didn't satisfy him, but his question was more rhetorical than not.

"Yeah, I'd let her have some on the come. She always paid me back."

"That's real nice," I said sarcastically. "Do you give all your friends that kinda credit?"

"Hell no," he said. "Rose was different. Rose was Rose."

"Were you lovers?"

He sipped coffee. "Ah, that's it, then," he said. "You don't strike me as the jealous type."

"I am," I admitted. "You should see me with a spoon of green slime and jam, but I'm still asking you. Were you sleeping with her?"

"I did once, a long time ago. We hooked up when she was just out of college, if that helps," he said.

I didn't know whether to feel lucky to have had a chance with Rose or horrified at the competition I'd have faced.

"You thinking someone killed her out of jealousy?" said Carlos.

"It crossed my mind. The cops say she was a prostitute."

"Fucking Harris set her up with his lawyer friends as payback."

"Tell me about that. I know you paid her fine."

"Yeah." He leaned back in his chair. "No bond, all cash. With my name all over it on purpose to scare that motherfucker Harris."

I waited. I could sense anger, and I wanted him to share his feelings. I interlaced my fingers and slowly nodded in understanding. I arched my eyebrows in sympathetic Freudian concern.

"You're a trip," Carlos said.

"Tell me about Harris."

"I don't get into others' business unless someone makes it mine," he said. "What I do know, what Rose told me, and what I believe, is that she and Harris did a hustle together and he got her arrested to cover his own ass."

"What kind of hustle?"

"Don't know. She seldom pulled the same one twice."

"I'm not following, Carlos. Do you mind if I call you Carlos?" He shook his head. "You're telling me that Rose was a conman-woman."

"A good one," he said. "She saw angles on everything. But she was careful. She wouldn't scam if there was a chance she'd get in trouble, no matter how big the take. Sometimes, if a deal was good, but too hot, she'd tell me, and I'd try. So Rose was all right with me, bro."

We sat for a while—me pondering the new image of Rose the conman, and Carlos watching me do it with some amusement.

"She wasn't rich," I said.

"She wasn't greedy. She just worked when she was light, like selling my weed when she had no deals to run. She liked to be the middleman, bro. Stay safe from both ends, making connections in the middle for profit."

"Was I a mark?"

"Look at Mr. Insecurity, here," he laughed. "Cool it, bro. You wouldn't have seen it coming if you were. But, nah, I think you were just the new thing. The last thing." He trailed off.

"No thing," I admitted.

"Pity," he said.

We sat in more silence. Several times my mouth opened to say something, to stop the silence, but each time I just smacked my lips, fell back into thought, and shut it. Carlos had given me a whole new motive to consider: payback for a con.

"So have you met with Harris yet? Like this?" Carlos finally said.

"I followed him this morning. I was going to have a nice chat with him, give him the third degree like I am you now." Carlos raised an eyebrow. "But he's not as friendly as you. I never said a word, just blindsided him with a right hand."

"What? You hit him?"

"I hit the coffee he was drinking. While he was drinking it. Crushed the cup. And maybe his nose. Burned him pretty bad for sure. Nearly drowned him in paint besides."

"What did he do?" Carlos was amazed, but guarded, unsure if I was kidding or not.

"He was being an asshole, and I snapped."

"For real?"

"Yeah," I said with a shrug. "Out of the blue, I just smashed a hot coffee into his arrogant face. I got a free pastry for it."

"Why?"

"I think it was your fault."

"What? How?"

"Your friends at Hot Tamale's," I said. "They challenged my manhood and my detectiveness, if that's a word. I acted out on Tamlen."

"You got issues, bro. But I like you hit him. I sure wanted to."

"Why?"

"Because he fucked with Rose."

"Why didn't you hit him?"

"Because Rose said to let it be, and Rose was Rose."

"Yeah," I said. "Is there anyone she didn't sleep with?"

Carlos gave me a look. "She was emancipated, not a whore, bro," he said. "But, yeah. I don't think she slept with Harris. He was just business."

"What business?"

"Don't know. Some deal down south."

"Saint George?"

"Think so."

"You know anything about a club he belongs to?"

"Beehive Athletic Club on fourth. Exclusive membership. Dark parking garage. He goes Monday morning, Tuesday, and Wednesday afternoons. Thursday, if he misses one of the others. Friday for lunch, always."

I stared at him.

He shrugged and said, "I had some time to kill back when I was mad at him."

"Don't think it was time you wanted to kill," I said.

He smiled.

CHAPTER TWENTY-TWO

After my meeting with Carlos and the revelation about Rose, the conman, I went home with my head swimming.

A message on my phone from Mollif suggested I find a new lawyer. Soon.

I went through the list and circled names that had the right feng shui before logging on to my computer to research Mortgage Buyers, Inc. and The Beehive Athletic Club, then I went to bed.

The next morning I went out for breakfast and a carton of half and half. Delores was working. I only had a couple of items, and she was in a regular lane, so I waited behind a family of six buying the store out of Hot Pockets. Delores's smile made it worth the wait, and the screaming kids, and the poopy diaper, and the spilled apple juice on my shoe, and the six-inch stack of coupons, and the drawn-out argument with the manager about expiration dates and mail-in rebates.

When I got home, someone had vandalized my house.

I liked my house. Though I still had feelings for my old place—Nancy's place now—I was warming up to my new digs. My cluttered boxes, bay window, and hot tub were my castle and some lowlife had messed it with eggs. Apparently, the neighborhood wasn't as good as Nancy had promised.

I grabbed the hose and went straight to work on the bay window.

The first one cracked me on the back of my head so unexpectedly that I shouted and stumbled forward. The second one hit me in the small of the back like a sniper round. I reeled around and took the next one square in the chest. My hand went to the spot and came away wet and dripping. The next one, in my crotch, really hurt.

I came to my senses and dodged to the right. An egg flew by my ear and smashed on the window with a squishy bang. I saw my attacker beside her scooter, a pink sticker-covered helmet on her head and a cardboard carton of eighteen farm fresh eggs on the seat, two just like it empty on the ground.

I ducked as another one whistled past my right ear.

"Goddammit, Dara! What the hell are you doing?"

I took one to the shoulder. It stung. I thought girls weren't supposed to be able to throw hard. She could throw hard. Very hard.

"Just stand there, you fucker," she said. "And take it!"

"But—" Crotch again. I doubled over.

"You better pray I work this out of my system now," she panted, pelting the top of my head with a split-finger, grade-A fastball. "This or bullets!"

"Thrown or shot?" I grunted.

I rolled on the ground to make a smaller target. I caught one on the shin but three missed me and broke on the lawn.

"I'll shoot you, you fucker! Goddamn sex addict and your fucked-up sex games!"

"It wasn't like that."

"Then you're worse than a worthless murderer. I'm getting my gun."

"No, don't!" I rolled over to see, my arms protecting my face.

No more eggs. She was rifling through her purse.

"Dara," I yelled, realizing I was about to see the business end of her new gun, "has it occurred to you that I didn't do it?"

"No!"

"Why not?"

"Why should it?"

"Could be fun, you know? For a change of pace."

She spilled the contents of her purse on the ground and searched the debris for her side arm.

"Dara. I didn't do it. It wasn't me. You gotta believe me."

"I don't have to do shit."

"But you should anyway."

She bent down and came up holding a blue steel pistol in both hands.

"Dara, just think about it, okay? You don't want to kill me. I'm the only one trying to catch the guy who did kill your friend—our friend."

She took aim, but waited. I felt gooey, cold egg-white slime drip down my forehead and into my ear.

"I've been working up a damn good mad against you, Flaner," she said.

"Damn good one," I agreed. "I can see that. Lotsa eggs. Good aim. High impact. You have talent. No doubt about it."

"I'm still pretty pissed."

"Yeah, I get that, too," I said. "But it's misguided."

"How do I know that?"

"Look in your heart," I said.

She raised the gun.

"No, wait! I have a card." I ducked under my arms.

She didn't shoot.

"Okay. I'll think about it, Flaner, and get back to you."

"Works for me," I said into the lawn.

She hurled the rest of her eggs. I heard them explode on my door, window, and siding, but no more at me. I kept my head down and waited. I lay there until the sound of her scooter had faded away in the distance.

I had raised red lumps all over my body, migrating to yellow and blue. I hadn't felt this way since I'd tried paintball. At least then I'd had a helmet. And a cup.

Mostly from my knees, I hosed off the eggs for an hour before staggering into the house. I took four Advil and fell on the couch. The day was shaping up spectacularly.

The phone rang. If it had been farther away than my pocket, I'd have ignored it.

"Tony," said the monotone drawl of my court-appointed attorney, "do you have a new lawyer yet?"

"No, not yet," I said.

"Get on that," he said.

"Is that why you called me, Morris?" I asked.

"Yes. And to tell you that you're facing new charges if you don't stop."

"What?"

"Witness tampering. Detective McGraw met with some bubble-head named Tonya who said you'd been to see her. She told McGraw that you told her you were cleared of all charges."

"I never said that."

"Doesn't matter. She's a witness. You can't have any contact with a witness."

"How was I to know that?"

"Real detectives know that," he said. If I'd have said that, I would have said it sarcastically, but Mollif was deadpan earnest. A missed opportunity, I thought.

"Can I get a list of witnesses?"

"No," he said.

"Why?"

"Because they haven't made it yet."

"Am I missing something here?"

"They're making it now."

"Are they broadcasting the list telepathically in the meantime? Do you have a frequency or a medium I might consult?"

"This isn't a kidding matter."

"Yes it is. It's ridiculous."

"It's the legal system," he said.

"Exactly."

Mollif sighed. "You're probably right. They can't stop you talking to anyone until they have given me a list, or better yet, your new lawyer a list. But they can still get mad and get a judge to lock you up again."

"How?"

"It's the legal system."

"Ridiculous," I said.

"We've already done this one," Mollif said, deadpan.

"I'll go over the list of lawyers again and make some calls, okay?"

"Okay," he said. "I'd love to chat, but I've got to be in court."

"No you wouldn't."

"No, I wouldn't."

* * *

I'd seen two guns in two days and neither was mine. And I called myself a detective. I'd had a gun way back when, but got rid of it like a Chernobyl brick when Randy was born. He was no longer in my house. It was time to rearm.

"All American Sports means guns," according to their commercial, and their store proved it. A bright backlit billboard-sized sign over the door showed a Tommy gun facing off against a Kalashnikov in sparking orange flames. The building had once been a supermarket, then a Christian college, karate studio, farmers market, and then turned into a gun store. It was vast. Rows upon rows of targets, scopes, holsters, videos, survival equipment, and guns. Lots and lots of guns.

The employees were all packing. They were having a sale on hollow-points. It was my lucky day.

I approached the closest counter. A large man called Art, according to his blue plastic nameplate, met me there. He greeted me with a broad smile. He was as wide as he was tall, and standing over six feet meant that he was huge. Upon closer inspection, I saw that he was wearing a bulletproof vest under his stretched shirt. I could see the outlines of plating and the snaps at the shoulders. He was heaving under its weight and sweating under its warmth; still, he was friendly and eager. He had a black automatic in a nylon holster on his belt. The snap was undone—just in case.

"How can I help you?" he asked.

"I'm a private detective, unlicensed, but I still want a gun," I told him.

"What do you have now?"

"I don't own a gun."

"You don't already own one?" His eyes widened in surprise. "How old are you?"

"Thirty-seven," I said.

His eyes widened more, this time in horror. "And you don't have any guns at all? No pistol? No shotgun? Not even a twenty-two for rabbits?"

"I've been lucky so far," I said. "The rabbits have left me alone."

"Well, you've come to right place and not a minute too soon. Anarchy is coming, and you better be prepared."

"Anarchy in the UK," I agreed. "Best defense is Sexpistols." It was wasted on him.

"We have a nice starter package here. It comes with a 9mm Baretta automatic, with quick release leather holster, M1 Carbine with camo shoulder strap, two shot derringer for the car and a Kevlar windbreaker to stop small-arms fire," he said. "Oh, and six thousand rounds of ammunition."

"Do you gift wrap?"

"Sure do."

"I was thinking just a pistol. You know, something to wave around if someone else has one, too."

"I understand. You want to start small. Learn to love your first gun and you'll come back for the rest later. Happens all the time." He dropped several guns on the counter and waited for me to say something.

"These look nice," I said.

"Since this is your first gun, and you look timid, I figured we'd go with the smaller calibers—cut down on recoil. Don't want your gun flying out of your hand the first time you kill someone."

"No," I said. "How could I kill again?"

"Exactly," he agreed. "This first one is a .38 snub nose. The same gun Al Pacino wasted the cop and gangster with in the *Godfather*. Noisy and brutal. A great gun." He let me hold it.

"So I just let it fall out of my hand when I'm done?"

"No way. More crimes are committed with stolen guns than purchased ones. That's why you're in the right place."

I stared.

"This one is a 9mm. It's like the Baretta I told you about, but made of plastic. It's a Glock. German made. Those krauts know how to make guns."

"I know this gun. I've used it before," I said.

"I thought you said you didn't own a gun?"

"I used this one in an X-Box game."

"Oh," he sneered. Virtual killing didn't merit respect. I wanted to ask him how many real people he'd killed and compare it to how many computer-generated ones I'd murdered. Even though I was no expert, I'd bet my tally was higher. "Glocks are nice," I said instead.

"Not really. Huge clip. The gun of choice of the Columbine School killers. Shoot and shoot and shoot. Still crappy, though. I wouldn't recommend it."

"Why?"

"Columbine aside, they got a bad reputation these days. Old and blocky," he said. "But still, everyone owns one. Go to a gun show and they'll give one away as a door prize. This one is new, so it's pricey."

"They're not usually?"

"Not if you get one in a giveaway."

His logic was incontrovertible.

"And the .45?" I said, trying to impress him with my recognition of the most famous pistol in the world.

"The classic side arm of the American Army since 1911. They're issuing 9mm Barettas now, but real soldiers still prefer this."

"And this one?" I pointed to small, elegant pistol.

"Walther PPK. The new version anyway. Really shitty gun."

"Why are you showing it to me?"

"Everyone wants to see one. James Bond used it until recently. Best-seller."

"Do you tell everyone it sucks?"

"No."

"Why'd you tell me?"

"I don't know."

"Is it cheap?"

"No."

I held the gun and fought back an urge to do a James Bond quick draw. I hummed the Bond theme instead.

"Sometimes you can get better deals on them used at a gun show," Art said.

"Are you telling me to go to a gun show to buy a gun? Don't you want to sell me one?"

"Gun show's over. There isn't another one for a month. Besides, guns are like razors; we make more money on the ammo than the gun."

"But you still make money on the gun sale?"

"Oh, yeah. Lots."

"Okay, Art. I think I want something that doesn't jam and isn't bulky and won't pull my pants down if I have it in my pocket. What do you recommend?"

"This Beretta Storm holds thirteen rounds, which isn't a lot for a modern 9mm. It has a plastic stock and concealable. Not the most accurate, but no pistol is, unless it's a .22 target pistol, which won't kill shit."

"It looks complicated."

"It's a pistol."

"I think it would be better if I had something with fewer moving parts."

"Then you want a revolver. What you lose in ammo, you make up for in charm."

"Sounds like me."

He put a Smith and Wesson short-nosed magnum on the counter. It looked like a gun.

"With a revolver you have fewer shots, so you want them to count. This one is a .357 magnum. I'd rather have a .44 magnum, but you're a wimp, so this'll do for you."

I picked it up. It felt like a gun. The handle was short, the weight impressive, the bullets long.

"Good stopping power," Art said encouragingly.

"I'll take it," I said, feeling the shape of the gun in my hand. A surge of testosterone squirted from my egged groin, and I felt manly and powerful. Caveman and reptile joined hands and danced a rite of passage around a primordial fire in my midbrain.

"No problem," he said, pulling out a pile of papers. "Fill these out."

"Oh, I might have a problem," I said. "I've been accused of a felony."

"Convicted?"

"No."

"Not a problem."

"I've been indicted for murder. Murder one, to be precise."

"Convicted?"

"Not yet, but it's not looking good."

"Not a problem."

"Oh. Okay," I filled in the squares with block letters. "So, I'll come back in three days after the background check?"

"Nope."

"How long then?"

"You can walk out with it now."

"Now?"

"After you fill in the form," he corrected himself.

"Will you sell me ammo, too?"

"Sale on hollow-points."

"Okay," I said. "But I'm really angry right now. Look at my face. I was just attacked at my home, and I'm really pissed off about it. And I know where the person lives who did this to me."

"I wondered about those goose eggs," he said.

"Chicken," I corrected.

"What?"

"Nothing. It's just that I'm in a murderous rage," I said calmly.

"Don't blame you," he agreed. "That would piss me off for sure."

"And I can still have the gun?"

He nodded.

"Now?"

He nodded again.

"With hollow points?"

"On sale."

"Do you take Visa?"

"Of course."

Before leaving, he signed me up for a concealed-weapon permit class and an hour on the shooting range, which just happened to be in the back of the store behind the taxidermy exhibit. A nice lady with fashionable ankle holsters showed me how to load and shoot my new gun. She brushed her breasts up against me on purpose several times. I began to understand the allure of guns. I went through a box of bullets and, before leaving, bought two more, a cleaning kit, and a molded leather waist holster. I waved goodbye to my new gun friends and got in my car, where I was told I could legally keep my gun loaded at all times.

I put the gun in my glove box and started the Prius. I found an on-ramp and merged into rush-hour freeway traffic, daring someone to cut me off.

CHAPTER TWENTY-THREE

I looked at my pre-burn photos of Harris Tamlen as I waited in the dimly lit parking garage of the Beehive Athletic Club. If Carlos was right and Harris kept to his routine, I should be seeing his pompous silver Mercedes any time.

At 11:20 a.m., Harris's silver sedan rolled down the ramp and past my parked Prius. He drove straight to a handicapped space next to the elevator and got out. His car key-chirped in recognition of his superiority as he boarded the elevator. I followed him in the next one.

The club occupied the entire three-story building. During my bodybuilding hobby phase, I'd thought of joining the Beehive Athletic Club. I was told I'd need someone to sponsor me and after a background check, credit check, and an affirmative vote by the secretive selection committee, I'd be fitted for a stick up my ass and social climbing boots. That sent me to the city Rec Center, vomity pool and all, where I muscled up with the "po-folks" for five months until I fell off my diet and exercise routine, overcome by a debilitating passion for homemade pizza and cheesecake.

There were two places to eat in the club: a quick snack bar-café place on the main floor and an expensive sit-down joint on the third floor called "The Top View" for important people.

I headed in, knowing where to look.

The elevator opened on the third floor to a hostess desk. A perky brunette with wide eyes and abs of steel greeted me with a smile bright enough to signal a satellite from a life raft.

I winked and walked by her without a word. She blinded me with her teeth and watched with weary eyes that didn't match her eager grin.

The Top View was a dinner place; black tie after six o'clock, coming-out parties for the members' nose-jobbed daughters on Saturdays. Weddings on Sundays for members finding eternal love for the sixth time, presents optional.

Harris sat at a table with two other men, photoshopped copies of himself—sports coats over white shirts, gaudy ties, and designer belts matching their swarthy Italian shoes. A smug air of superiority hung over the table like a fart.

Harris's face was red and shiny with topical burn cream. The group sensed my approach, aware of the subtle difference in class and classiness I represented.

"Mr. Harris Tamlen?" I said as authoritatively as I could.

"Yes?"

"I'd like to ask you a few questions." I held him in my best steely gaze. "In private."

"What's this about?" he said. "Is this about the assault on me the other day?"

"No, Mr. Tamlen. I don't do petty crimes," I lied on several levels. "Would you like to have the conversation here or is there someplace we can go?"

He glanced at his friends, and turned his burned face to me, saying, "I guess we can find a conference room. Are you a detective?" Harris asked.

"Yes."

There was a God in heaven: he'd said "detective," not "police officer." I'd have answered yes to whatever the question was, but this way I had wiggle room if McGraw tried to pin some impersonation thing on me. I am so clever.

Harris led me out and down a hallway, past velvet signs with white plastic letters announcing room reservations and times. We went in one scheduled for a "Confidence Power Luncheon" in an hour. We sat down at a table, and I poured us each a glass of water from the sweating decanter set in the middle.

My adrenalin pulsed. I was playing a total bluff in enemy territory. Sitting across from me at that moment was probably a murderer, a low-life creep who'd strangled an unconscious girl while I slept in the next room.

"Wait a minute," I accidentally said out loud.

"What?"

My mind spun. I looked at Harris's burned face and bloodshot eyes, and wheels locked into place.

He didn't recognize me. He thought I was a cop. He hadn't recognized me from the coffee assault, and worse for my theory, he hadn't recognized me from Rose's apartment.

"Shit," I said.

"What is it?"

I reached behind me and pulled my gun out of my waistband, slapping it on the table, making an impressive argument for my pretended position.

"This thing is killing my back," I said, emphasizing "killing" on accident.

"What's this about?" Harris said to the gun.

"Rose Griff," I said. His eyes widened. I let it sink in.

"You strike me as a real dick," I said, sliding into gumshoe. "Several of my associates have you pegged as the button man. But I'm not sure. I'd like to hear a story from you before I report back to District Attorney, Penelope "The Hammer" Sweet. She likes her cases cut and dried so she can get the death penalty on the first go around. Before The Hammer falls on you, I thought I'd give you a chance to save me some digging. I have a box of evidence and it fits one way. If you can show me how it fits different, well that might save us all some embarrassment."

"What evidence?" he said.

I looked at him hard for a whole minute, waiting for telltale beads of sweat to appear on his scalded cheeks and forehead.

"Tamlen, I shouldn't be here. I should just let The Hammer drop, but you see, I'm involved in this, and if we get the wrong man it might be bad on my record. A little. However, it would be very bad on whoever was arrested, innocent or guilty. That man would spend years trying to clear his name of accusations, and his bowels of prison spunk. His whole life would be scrutinized, publicly, under a microscope. Every detail dragged up and shown around like a twenty-pound catfish. His friends would run like rats. His wife would leave him. He'd be bankrupted by legal fees, fines, and alimony payments. Besides, Sweet wants a conviction on this one. Innocence proves nothing if we can fit the pieces together convincingly enough. Pick twelve people at random, sport, and behold the average IQ of a jury. Once in court, you're as good as gone."

I thought I did a good job scaring Harris. I scared myself. Everything I said would happen to him was already happening to me. If McGraw had given that speech in the interrogation room, not only would I have more respect for the man, but I think I'd have shit myself.

"What do you want to know?"

"Tell me about your relationship with Miss Griff," I said. "And be quick. There's a Confidence Power Luncheon here in less than an hour. I don't want to miss it."

He looked pained. A terrible storm raged inside his conceited head. I could hear the waves of ego crashing against the rocks of facts and fear.

"Maybe I should get my lawyer involved."

"Okay. If you want to play it that way, we can," I said and stood up. "We'll see how it all lands."

"Wait," he said, grabbing my sleeve. Per the request, I kept silent.

"You mean, I can't talk to you with my lawyer?" he said.

"You can do whatever the hell you want, sport. For now," I said. "It's just that if you have a lawyer, then I should have one, too. Then it's at a whole different thing."

He didn't let go of my sleeve, so I sat down.

"We were involved in some business," he said.

"Some illegal business," I said. It wasn't a question.

"I don't know what you've heard, but I knew nothing about anything illegal," he lied.

"I'm looking into a murder, not a scam. Keep talking."

"I did nothing wrong. You can't prove I knew anything or did anything illegal. If anything wrong was done, that is. Besides, there are a dozen corporations between me and anything you think I might have done. Allegedly."

He spoke slimeball fluently.

"Were you sleeping with her?" I said. The question was burning my caveman brain centers. It had to come out eventually.

"No, not at all," he said. "She hit on me, but I wasn't interested." I believed the answer but not the explanation. The lie was so apparent, it made me feel better about Rose and me.

"So how did you meet?"

"A friend of a friend. I did some mortgage work in Saint George. The housing market tanked down there, and there're great deals if you can strike when the seller is weak."

"So your business with Griff involved real estate?"

"No, not with Rose," he said. "She had some valuable vacation coupon books. They had discounts to places in Mexico; free lodging, meals, and tours. Great deals. I knew people in Saint George who could sell them, travel agents and the like. It was a perfect outlet."

Tonya had mentioned something about Mexican coupons.

"So what was the scam?" I said.

Harris tried to look shocked, but looked stupid instead. It was easy for him to look stupid, a God-given gift.

"Nothing I know about," he said.

"But you heard rumors about something. Rumors that had nothing to do with you, but had something to do with the deal?"

"Yes," he agreed. "Someone may have mentioned something about them being forgeries."

"Why not sell them closer to home?" I asked, more to myself, but aloud nonetheless.

"They were designed for retirees," said Harris. "There were

'grandchildren free' deals and all-inclusive resorts with a doctor on call. Even thirty percent coupons on medications bought at a local pharmacy. Golden Years travel."

"But forged?"

"I don't know anything about that beyond the rumors," he said.

"A smart guy like you keeps his ear to the ground. What else did the rumors say?"

"Allegedly," he began, "there was supposed to be a run of only twenty books, but, I think, Rose had a hundred of them."

Harris leaned back in his chair, secure in his obfuscation. "I never actually saw them, but supposedly they all had numbers on them, one through twenty. The numbers repeated a few times."

"Where'd she get them?"

"I don't know," he said smugly, begging for a fist in his face or a hot beverage. "I never asked. I guess I'm just the trusting sort."

"So you innocently arranged to sell these coupon books to pensioners in the retirement paradise of Saint George through a travel agency, and made lots of money."

"There and Mesquite. Oh, and we wholesaled some to a Phoenix agency and some in Tucson. I assumed they were legit."

"How much you make?"

"We netted a thousand per book."

I did the math in my head. "So you got a million dollars," I said, impressed.

"One-hundred thousand."

Oops. "Oh, yeah. Right," I said. "Then what?"

"I had taken a lot of risks. It was my connections that moved the books out fast," he explained.

"So you thought you deserved a bigger cut of the pie?"

"Yes, I did," he said.

"So how much did Rose get?"

"She got twenty-five thousand."

"How'd she take being cut out?"

"Not well. She expected half, but didn't understand business. But what could she do? We had no contract. And there were those rumors. I told her she was lucky to get what she got."

"But it didn't end there, did it?" Harris's smug little pinched, pink, punchable face knitted in thought as he wondered how much I knew.

"No," he said finally. "The bitch got access to my credit cards on the net. Over the course of a week, she funneled forty-thousand dollars into a dummy checking account before I caught on and stopped it."

"I bet that made you mad," I said. "I bet that made you really mad."

He was about to say something nasty, but remembered the gun and why I was there.

"Not mad enough to murder her," he said. "I'm no killer."

"So, how mad did it make you?"

"She underestimated me," he said. "I got even."

"How?"

"On each of the five-thousand dollar credit card billings, she'd put 'Love from Rose' as the transaction description. I figured that the statements would make good evidence. She'd screwed me out of my money, so I went with her play. With a little help from an attorney friend of mine here at the club, I got her arrested for prostitution."

"Did you get your money back?"

"No," he said. "I let it go. She sent some Mexican to intimidate me, but I was done with her. I figured I'd made thirty-five thousand dollars for a couple of phone calls and a weekend golf trip to the desert. Good enough."

"Was Rose's friend a Latin American fellow who wears too much cologne, calls you 'bro,' and has a disappearing silver pistol?" I asked.

He nodded. "That's the guy. He caught me in the parking garage here at the club with two others. I didn't see a gun, but I knew it was there."

A waiter came in with a tray of porcelain coffee mugs. He left when he saw the gun.

"Your story works as far as it goes," I said, "but it still doesn't clear you of Rose's murder. You've given me motive. You're obviously a man of means; that just leaves opportunity. Do you have an alibi?"

"The night she was killed, I was here at the club. My wife and I attended a dinner."

"Was Charlie there?" I asked for fun.

"You know Charlie? No, he was home. His wife's sick."

"So, are there other people who can corroborate your story?"

"I'm sure there are."

"How long did the dinner go?"

"Midnight."

"Ms. Griff was murdered in the early morning. You could have still done it." I said.

He was silent for a while. The long pause from my short statement was suspicious. I wondered how to make a citizen's arrest.

"Harris Tamlen," I said finally with as much menacing authority as I could muster, "you are a suspect in a capital murder investigation. If you cannot provide me with an alibi for that night, you will become the primary suspect. Do you understand?"

He shifted butt cheeks and swallowed.

"After the dinner," he said, "the wife and I swung by a friend's place."

"Who?"

"Is that necessary?" he asked.

For the first time since he began talking, he looked nervous. He said, "How do I know that what I tell you won't come back and bite me?"

"Can't say that, sport. Things with teeth will always bite eventually."

He glanced around. The wait staff had all exited. We were alone in the room.

"But I can guarantee you one thing," I said. "Nothing bites harder than murder. They kill people in this state. No do-over for the needle."

"I thought we had the electric chair."

"Nope, lethal injection," I said, being the expert I was. "I'm only looking into the murder. That's it. Unless you were meeting with Al Qaida or poisoning the city's water supply, I doubt it can be worse than what's facing you now. Fess up. You're going to have to anyway. With me now, off the record, or in front of a judge, jury, stenographer, and journalists on the record. With your power and prestige, it'll probably be on the six-o'clock news for a month."

I played on his sense of self-importance like a kazoo.

"We swung by the McConnels," he said quietly.

"How long were you there?"

He looked behind him again. Seeing the room was empty, he leaned forward. As he did I saw a waiter enter the room with an armful of napkins.

"All night," Harris said quietly.

"All night?"

"I said we *swung* by the McConnels." He winked.

I shook my head.

"Swung," he said again, waiting for me to catch on. His arrogance melted a bit and I saw a trace of embarrassment. I broadened my mind and upset my stomach.

"You swapped wives? You had a sex orgy with the McConnels?" I said.

The waiter froze.

"Yes," Harris said. "We stayed all night and had breakfast with them in the morning."

"Would they testify to that?"

"Not willingly. Jim McConnel is a bishop," he said. "And his son is on a mission in Holland."

"He's probably seen it all then," I said.

"Not this."

"Then let's hope it never gets that far."

He nodded sullenly. The waiter scurried out of the room on tiptoes and disappeared around a corner. Harris surveyed the room again after the waiter was gone. He relaxed. I smiled. I liked my new job.

Harris waited for me to say something, but I stared at him, lost in a jigsaw puzzle of new information.

He was an unsubtle stuck-up prick, a social climber. He was the kind of guy who'd spend ten thousand dollars a year removing key scratches from his car. He was a loathsome member among the other vapid vipers of the smug class, but I didn't peg him as the killer.

He could have been playing me. He might have recognized me and was just feeling me out. But why? I'd given him nothing. He'd as much as confessed to false accusation, fraud, and moral turpitude. This was Utah. This was the Beehive Athletic Club. If any of his confession even floated in whispers, his life here would be over. They could forgive him picking the bones of upside-down, bank-raped mortgage holders, but maybe not ripping off wealthy WASP pensioners in Saint George. And swapping wives with a bishop was off-the-scale pariah behavior.

"So are we done?" Harris said when he could stand my silence no longer.

"For now," I said because it sounded more threatening than "yes." Then I had a thought. "You know a slick jerk like you could have hired someone to kill Rose," I said.

"Over forty thousand dollars?" he said. "You must not think much of me."

I didn't, but even I couldn't see him killing anyone over so paltry an amount. Not in his world. I shook my head, and Harris mistook my disappointment for disbelief.

"Listen, before seeing her name in the paper," he said, "I hadn't even thought of Rose in a year. And I hadn't seen her in longer than that."

"Who do you think killed her?" I asked.

"I don't know. Didn't you already catch the guy?"

"Not yet, but I'm working on it."

A crowd of white-clad workers entered the room. They placed coffee carafes, arranged sweeteners and cream, plugged in microphones, and arranged chairs for the upcoming Confidence Power Luncheon.

Harris and I walked out together. The workers all got very quiet when we passed. Several wore knowing smirks on their faces. I smiled. Harris looked worried and hurried past me on his way out of the club. I didn't give the McConnels long either.

CHAPTER TWENTY-FOUR

I slept like shit that night. I lay in my bed staring at the ceiling the entire night. I tossed and turned and bounced and rolled. I worked a worn trench into my new mattress. When the sheep walked off the job—demanding better working conditions, overtime pay, and a dental plan—I counted shadows until their foreman threatened a strike. I twisted my sheets into sailors' knots and fluffed my pillow so many times, I felt like Ron Jeremy's personal assistant. I watched the clock tick away but I knew what time it was. I was just unwilling to face it. I knew by dawn it was time to quit. In the bleak hours of the mid-night, in the hour of the wolf, when every dread and regret rises up to be counted and beat back, I saw the clear and constant pattern of my life. When the challenge was gone, I'd move on. When it was no longer fun, I left. When it was hard, I quit.

Seven months in a job, and I'd either have to commit to the politics, seminars, new skills, and trainings, or I could call it done and tell myself I was a jack-of-all-trades, when, in fact, I was a quitter.

I once read about the ninety-ninety rule. It said that the first ninety percent of a project's development required ninety percent of the effort, and the last ten percent, required another ninety percent effort. It meant that the effort it took to get a project ninety percent of the way done was about the same as it took to finish the last little bit. Giving up at ninety percent made ergonomic sense, if you didn't mind never finishing anything.

I got up when I had no more shadows to count, and the light streaming through my window was too tinged with the red of my tired eyes. I decided to be busy, to put off my defeat a few more hours by being useful and unloading a box or two.

Nancy had gotten me enough furniture to hold a lot of things; shelves for my trophies, DVDs, and books, and places for me to ditch the remains of a thousand interests I'd abandoned at ninety percent. She knew me well.

I hung my best oil painting, the last one I'd done, where I thought I showed real talent before never picking up a brush again. I found the novel I'd written, edited once, and abandoned. I found the books on car repair I'd purchased en masse, determined to restore a '66 Mustang my neighbor had offered me. The books were pristine. I never got started with that one. I gave up at ten percent there.

Every box had reminders of my inability to specialize. What I once saw as a strength, I now saw a fatal flaw that would betray an auburn-haired girl who had waited for me.

My relationships had always been selfish. Before Nancy, I'd gone through love affairs with the same level of commitment as my jobs and hobbies. Marrying Nancy was the exception. She caught me in a weak or strong moment, I'm not sure which. It was a change from the usual, but when it got hard, I was ready to leave. It was Nancy that kept it together. And she kept it together by making it easy for me. If it had been hard, I'd have left. I resisted hard. I left hard. I ran from hard. I gave up when it got hard.

And I was in a hard place.

I had no leads, no help, no hope. I knew what I was going to do. What I was good at. What I always did. But I couldn't make myself commit to my natural weakness, so I dug through more boxes.

Many of them were mussed up, as if they'd been opened and searched after they were packed. My first impression was that Mudge was messing with me. I still hadn't figured out why his famous aplomb had deserted him the other night, and thought that maybe he had formed a lower image of me by rifling through my possessions while I was playing "don't drop the soap" in County. Then, in my pornography box, the one box I had personally packed and sealed with double layers of tape and marked "private" and "socks," I found a ticket from the police stating that the contents of this box, all except the sweater I'd used for padding, had been confiscated as "evidentiary material."

That couldn't be good news.

I had nothing illegal, but I had more than my share of pseudo-bachelor comfort literature collected from the far reaches of the Internet. In the evidence box Mollif had left me, I'd seen a cryptic report that certain things of mine had been seized. It had promised an inventory, but it hadn't been completed by the time Mollif got it to me. My guess was that the clerks cataloging my ten years of classic skin mags and ripped DVDs were taking their time with the list in a dimly lit room in three-and-a-half-minute shifts.

The confiscation deepened my already gloomy mood. Sweet and McGraw would paint me as some kind of sex fiend. At best, they'd say things got out of control, and I accidentally killed Rose in a fit of lustful abandon. That was the theory Dara had thrown at me between eggs. More likely, they'd paint me as a killer rapist living out fantasies portrayed in close-ups of latex-clad Swedish models.

Meanwhile, I had no suspects. Carlos and Harris had not only been on the top of the list, they'd comprised the whole of it. If what they told me was true—and I tended to believe it was—I had nothing. I didn't know where to turn. I could spend the next week checking Harris's alibi or trying to make a case that Carlos, who'd bailed Rose out of jail and protected her, later decided to kill her.

Detectiving was hard.

To make matters worse, and things could always get worse, the calls I'd made to lawyers were frightening. Everyone was eager for the case and claimed intimate familiarity with it. All were willing to get right to work, once their retainer was paid. I measured them by how convincing their initial lies were. If they could make me believe they'd actually heard of me, they got five points. If they actually made me think they thought I was innocent, they got ten. If they could make me feel that they actually cared, I gave them twenty. No one had scored above zero yet, and I'd called a dozen.

Some of the lawyers were ridiculously expensive, and the rest were ungodly expensive. Even on the cheap, with a plea deal and delaying motions, I'd have to sell my house at the least. If things got messy and I insisted on innocence, we would go to trial and possibly appeals. In that case, I'd be looking at complete bankruptcy.

I mentioned that prospect to one lawyer, a Mr. Threshershark Von Bloodstain, Esq., I think was his name. Without batting a telephonic eyelash, he reminded me that being broke was better than prison and referred me to a bankruptcy lawyer whose number he knew by heart.

I looked around my cluttered but empty house, and for the first time since I got out of the clink, I felt lonely. I missed Nancy. I missed Randy. I never did much with either of them, but knowing they were there had always been a comfort.

I ordered a pizza and assembled my drum set. I beat out a few rhythms I taught myself during my drummer days—days Nancy couldn't get through fast enough—and I let my mind go blank.

The bell rang. I answered it still in my robe and underwear. Pizza guys are used to that. I know; I used to be a pizza guy. It wasn't the pizza guy.

Junior Detective McGraw stood in my doorway. His trench coat looked like he'd slept in it in the trunk of a car.

"Detective," I said cheerfully, "working undercover at the homeless shelter?"

"Zip it, Flaner. And close your robe before I arrest you for indecency," he said, trying to push his way past me into the house. I stepped in front of him, barring his entrance.

"Don't you have to be asked in? Isn't that the rule among you vampires?" Thinking about lawyers all morning had naturally put me in a Hammer Horror state of mind.

"Do I look like a vampire to you?"

"Not with that fashion sense, but I still think you have to be invited in. Unless you have a warrant. Do you have a warrant?"

"We already searched your things, Flaner. We got plenty to hang you with."

"Well, if you found enough to hang me, that explains what happened to all my nylons, but you still need a warrant to get in today."

"Do you have something to hide in there?"

"Whoa, that was a close one. I almost talked. Nice try, detective." The neighbor girl was out on her lawn again pointing to my open robe and trench-coated visitor.

"Just let me in, Flaner, so we can talk. I don't like standing on the porch."

"No."

"I can go get a warrant if I want to," he said. "I know a judge who'll sign off on anything I say over the phone."

"No. I just had the place fumigated, and you look to have fleas. Say what you have to say now, and then leave. And, for the record,"—here I shouted very loudly so the neighbor girl and concerned father could hear—"I do not give you permission to enter my home!"

A dented Volkswagen Jetta with a pizza sign bungeed to its roof pulled up. A kid with hair in his eyes, pants sliding down his legs, and a baseball cap at twenty-nine degrees off straight, trotted up with a pizza box.

"Come right in," I said, letting him in.

"Let me take care of this." I closed the door in McGraw's face.

I told the pizza guy to wait in the kitchen and gave him a Pepsi. I went to the bedroom and pulled on a pair of jeans and a T-shirt. When I came out, McGraw was pounding on the door and ringing the bell.

"That dude's still on your porch," said the pizza guy. "What's his problem?"

"Cop," I said.

"No shit?"

"No shit."

I paid for the pizza and opened the door on McGraw's fist. He nearly landed a punch on the hapless courier, but he ducked under McGraw's arm before skipping to his car.

"You still here?" I said.

"You better learn some respect," he said, his fury visible in his trembling upper lip. "I understand you've been doing a bit of witness tampering."

"It's called investigating. It's what detectives do. You should look into it."

"Cut out the smart-assness," he said.

"You do have a way with words, McGraw. But I'm not convinced I did it, and since you're too stupid and too lazy to find the real killer, someone has to step up for truth, justice, and the American way." My breast swelled, and I put my fists on my hips.

"You need a license to be a detective in Utah," he said.

"Do you have one? Must not be hard to get."

"I'm a cop; that's better than a detective."

"I'm not breaking any laws," I said.

"Everyone breaks laws," he said with a sneer.

"Are you going somewhere with this, or is that all you got?"

"I mean, you can be arrested again, Flaner. You can cool your heels in jail until court time. I could violate your bail anytime I wanted to."

"If you want to violate me, buy me a drink first. Otherwise, beat it, or I'll report you for police harassment."

"You'll never make it stick," he said a little too quickly.

"I wouldn't be the first to make an official complaint against you, would I?"

He squinted.

"If you get too many of those, even your cousin won't be able to save you. You'll be writing parking tickets in school zones before you can say 'public safety oversight board.'"

I'd hit a nerve. His lip quivered. His inexperience had obviously shown itself before my case.

"It was nice visiting," I said. "Ta-ta."

"A witness list is coming out on Monday," he said before I could shut the door on his face again. "You better stay away from them if you know what's good for you."

"Do you practice these lines in the mirror?" I asked.

"No," he said in weak denial.

"Goodbye." I closed the door on his face for the second time that morning. You have to enjoy the little things in life.

"And don't leave town," he said from the porch.

McGraw had challenged my cowardice, and I was angry. I stabbed my hands in my pockets and stormed through the house. I felt my finger slide into the top of Rose's finger trap. I withdrew it and looked at it. It mocked me obscenely. It was on my middle finger of course.

"I am not caught!" I said to the toy. "I will get out of this. For Rose, if not for me."

I thought of McGraw and felt my face get hot. This was the guy who was charged with finding Rose's killer? The injustice flew me into a rage. When I added the fact he was actively trying to stop me from finding the killer while wearing such horrible clothes, I went mad and did something stupid.

I removed the trap, went straight to the phone and called Morris Mollif.

"Mollif here," he said like a beaten serf.

"Morris? It's Tony. Tony Flaner."

"Hello, Tony. Have you found another lawyer yet?"

"No. I'm keeping you."

"Why would you do that?" I could hear tears in his voice.

"Because you raise the stakes," I said. "Because if I take a plea, I'll have to confess to something I didn't do. And I won't."

"It's easier."

"Exactly," I said. "I won't deal. I don't want to get off on a technicality, which some high-price lawyer will surely find, particularly with McGraw. I don't want a pardon. I want to find Rose's killer because Rose deserves it. Plus, I started it, and I'm not giving up. Not this time."

"You do realize you've been indicted for murder, right?"

"I am aware of that," I said. "I saw it in the paper while I was hiding from a Tongan separatist in the prison library."

"And how do I help any of this?" Morris asked.

"You've already given up."

He didn't deny it.

"If I don't succeed, I'm toast," I said.

"I wouldn't go that far," he finally said in his own defense. "I am a lawyer. I can find technicalities, too—put up a good fight and all that. I just have to tell you that it's not going to be easy. I'm not your best bet."

"Maybe you need something hard yourself," I said.

"Thanks, but I don't go that way."

"There, you see? You do have a sense of humor," I said. "I mean, you're like me. You've made a career out of taking the easy way out. This is your chance to . . . to not to."

"And that's why you want me?" he said. "To redeem me?"

"I don't know," I admitted. "You just feel right. The right lawyer at the right time. Besides, I don't have time to break in a new guy. And I can't afford what they'll cost. If I hire one of them, I lose by financial default. It's all so unfair. I don't need a super attorney. You'll do."

"With that kind of confidence, how can we lose?"

"Exactly," I said. "You're up against a petulant, lazy detective and a green district attorney. They pinned it on me because it's easy. We'll beat them by doing it the hard way."

"You ever heard of Occam's Razor?" he said. "Easy is usually true."

"But I didn't do it," I reminded him. I was sick of reminding him. "And I'll catch the guy who did."

"Highly unlikely. The best you'll do—the best anyone ever does—is collect enough evidence to form a case of reasonable doubt. This isn't the movies, Tony. Bad guys get away, and good guys get sent to prison, especially if they're too proud to take a plea. It happens all the time."

"Not this time. I am the guy who won't take a plea, because he's fucking innocent," I said. "I'm also the guy who catches the guy who did it. I'm that guy."

"In the long run, it's usually better to take a plea and just put it behind you."

"Usually, but not always."

"My mistake. I meant 'always.' Get a good attorney, Tony."

"Nope. You're my man. I'll collect the evidence, you present it. You know the ins and outs of the courthouse better than the janitor."

"Tony, you're making a mistake."

"Probably," I admitted. "But if they bankrupt me, I lose. If they kill me, I lose. If I go to jail for more than seven months, I lose."

"Why seven months?" he asked.

"Never mind," I said. "Besides, I think you need a win, and this one will be easy."

"I thought we didn't like easy?"

"My mistake. I meant 'fun.'"

"It won't be. Capital cases are always murder, if you'll forgive the pun."

"I won't. I'm offended."

"Good."

"Keep buying me time," I said. "I need to sort things out, and I think McGraw will try to lock me up again to keep me from making progress. He is more concerned about a conviction than the truth."

"So you do understand the legal system," Morris said. "That's good."

"Do you like your job?"

"No," he said without hesitation.

"Let's win this one. It'll make a name for you and you can get a private practice."

"It doesn't work that way."

"It does if you win a big one. People will be asking for you."

"Is this big?"

"It could be," I said. "We could make it big."

"That would be a huge mistake, Tony. If it gets big, the DA himself will step in, or at least a more seasoned lawyer. We have to keep Sweet."

"Ah-ha! I caught you planning the defense."

"An aberration. A momentary lapse of reason. Temporary insanity."

"You're up for it," I said.

He sighed.

"Please. It could be good for you," I said.

"It won't be."

"Are you refusing to represent me?"

"No," he said sighing again. "I'd have to show cause to the court."

"Good. We're a team. I'll get the evidence, you present it. I'll be free, you'll be feared. It'll all be great."

"Your naivety is matched only by your stupidity."

"Tell me what you really think," I said. "No need to hold back with me."

"McGraw will get a restraining order on you if you approach a witness after the list is out."

"Then you will have to interview them, right?"

"Don't do this to me, Tony."

"Okay, I'll keep you out of it," I said. "There're only a couple of people I haven't already seen who could be on the list, unless it's the entire phone book."

"It might be," he said.

"Then make them shorten it. I assume you can make them show cause for each name."

"I could, but it would inconvenience me greatly."

"But them more?"

"Probably."

"Perfect," I said.

"Tony, I hate you."

"No, you don't. I'm a breath of fresh air."

"I know how to delay. They're green. Like you, they're under some misguided idea that justice is on their side. Besides, I've told them you're seeking new counsel like a sane person. They're probably waiting to hear from them."

"So it's a staring contest?"

"Sweet will come around when her case load catches up to her. She'll try to clear a few files off her desk in a month or two when she has a hundred like this. If you can keep out of trouble that long, I'll be able to bargain then."

"No bargain," I said. "I'm innocent."

"Innocence proves nothing unless you can prove it, and then it doesn't always take."

"Just keep them off me, if you can," I said.

"Have you found anything useful, by the way?"

"Not a thing."

"You should get a good lawyer."

"I have one," I said.

He sighed into the phone. I was beginning to think it was his standard method of respiration.

"Morris," I said, "have some faith in me. I'll send you a business card. It explains everything."

"I'll try," he said. "I guess after you're convicted, you can always appeal on the grounds you had inadequate council."

"That's the attitude."

"Goodbye, Tony."

"Goodbye, Morris," I said. "Talk to you later."

"Apparently so."

I hung up, sat down slowly, and ate some pizza.

I chewed slowly and carefully. I had quit quitting. I was in unchartered waters now, the last ten percent.

CHAPTER TWENTY-FIVE

I had a day and a half to talk to everyone who might be on McGraw's witness list. With any luck, Melissa was over the shock of her lost lizard. And gerbil. I called her home but got no answer. I didn't leave a message, though the machine begged me to do so in a heart-breaking, desperate voice that smacked of chronic loneliness over a dog whimpering in the background.

I called Mountain Dell Hospital.

"Hi, this is Tony," I said to her floor supervisor. "Is Melissa working today?"

"Ah, no, Tony," she said tentatively. "Melissa is scheduled for the graveyard. She won't come in until seven."

"Oh, that's right, I forgot. Thanks." I could tell the woman on the other end wasn't used to receiving calls for Melissa. I wasn't surprised she was surprised.

Graveyard shift started at 7:00 p.m. I got there at nine so she'd be settled in. I worked in a hospital once and knew how hectic it was around shift change. Besides my tenure as orderly/CNA, my pyrotechnics hobby put me in the ICU overnight and on the medical/surgery/shut-up-and-heal floor for three. My eardrums came back before my eyebrows did.

For Halloween one year, I wore a set of green cotton scrubs with a lab coat and a "Hello, my name is Dr. Kevorkian" sticker on the breast. I spent the whole time asking partygoers how they were feeling. I still had the scrubs and wore them to the hospital sans lab coat and name tag. I was in disguise.

No one batted an eye when I entered the building, moseyed into the staff elevator, and rode it to the fourth floor. Mountain Dell wasn't the largest hospital in the valley, or the nicest. It wasn't the newest or the cleanest. It was, however, one of the cheapest and had earned plenty of free publicity the previous year when a rampant staph infection sent half the nurses home and the other half on strike until the whole building had been evacuated, covered in plastic, and cleaned with chlorine gas by men in blue hazmat suits. Occupancy had been slow ever since.

The fourth floor was a potpourri of post-surgery patients, "frequent flyers," and crazy people who didn't fit into the narrow requirements of the other floors. I walked up to the desk like I knew my way around.

"Hi," I said.

The woman didn't look up from her work, but mumbled, "Hold on a minute, will you?"

Down the hallway, someone screamed, and the woman behind the desk ducked behind her papers. The noise sounded urgent. Forgetting I wasn't really an orderly or a nurse or Dr. Kevorkian, I headed toward it.

The shouts led me to a woman strapped to a bed. She had crazy eyes, crazy hair, and crazy spit shooting out of her crazy mouth. Her hair was black with three inches of gray roots. Her teeth—what were left of them—were yellow and gray, and she smelled like she needed a new diaper yesterday.

"Who the fuck are you?" she yelled when she saw me. Though I'd taken my time locating her and the noise never ceased, no one else was in the room.

"I'm Tony," I said.

"I want my goddamn medicine, you fucking prick!"

"Now be nice," I said.

"Rape!" she yelled. "Help, I'm being raped! Help!"

I stepped back into the hall and bumped into someone. I whirled around and was face-to-face with Melissa. She glanced at me and pushed into the room. She looked like she'd been crying, so I recognized her instantly. Halfway to the crazy woman, she remembered where she'd seen me and turned around.

"Hi, Melissa," I said, handing her my card.

"Murder! Rape! Help!"

Luckily, it wasn't Melissa screaming.

She looked at the card and then at me, then down at the card, and then up to me again as if checking each word against my face for verification.

"I just want to ask you a few questions."

"Goddamn, cocksucking, motherfuckers! Rape! Rape! Rape!"

I put on my innocent face.

The woman thrashing on the bed lifted her head off the pillow, horked up something nasty from the back of her throat and took aim at Melissa. Melissa closed the door just as a mucous blob splatted against the wire-meshed window and oozed down the door.

"Just for a minute," I said. "Do you have a minute?"

She looked at me, then back at the woman through the window, who was reloading, and gestured me down the hall.

"Everyone says you killed Rose," she said. "Why should I believe you?"

"Read my card again," I said.

"That doesn't prove anything," she said. She was smarter than Tonya, but that wasn't saying much.

"The police asked me about you," she said, handing back the card. I held up my hands for her to keep it.

"Rape! Murder!"

"I guess I'm asking you to trust me," I said.

"Help, they're killing me! Call the fucking police! Help, you cocksuckers!"

We found an unoccupied room. She pulled the door shut, and we sat in visitors' chairs that smelled like a swimming pool.

"Did you call here looking for me?" she asked.

"Yes."

"Did you tell my supervisor that you were my boyfriend?"

"No, just that I was looking for you."

"She thinks you're my boyfriend."

"Even after you told her I wasn't?"

She looked at her hands folded in her lap. Satisfied with the arrangement, she changed the subject. "What do you want?"

I scooted my chair closer, needing to be more intimate. Melissa seemed sensitive, rape and murder allegations notwithstanding.

"I'm talking to everyone I know who knew Rose so I can find the real killer," I said.

"Isn't that the police's job?"

"You'd think so, but they have other ideas. It's just me."

"I knew Rose a long time. I always told her that if she kept breaking hearts, one of them would break her," she said. "But I guess guys like that. They like girls who'll dump them. Loyal, dedicated, long-term, caring girls just aren't attractive."

"They are," I said. "Just not to the kind of people Rose liked."

I could tell she didn't know if I'd complimented her or not.

"Do you know anyone who might have been particularly broken hearted? Violently so?" I asked.

"We didn't talk much. We knew each other in school, but didn't hang out together, really. I'd call her when I was depressed. Well, more depressed than usual. She was a good friend. She'd call me if there was a big party or something happening where I might meet a nice guy. I never did, of course. Nice guys don't exist."

"Tell me about high school," I said.

"Rose was one of those girls who started high school as the ugly duckling and left a swan. No one would talk to her freshman year because she was so skinny. No one but me, of course. I knew what it was to be unpopular. I had a weight problem back then. Also then," she corrected herself with a sniffle.

"When boys started liking her, and popular girls started talking to her, she stayed friends with me. I know that she got shit for it from Marci and Ginger, but she stayed my friend and took me on group dates and stuff. If it hadn't been for her, I'd probably still have my virginity." She blushed. "I shouldn't be telling you these personal things."

"I'm not judgmental," I said. "I know a lot of lesbians. Was Rose always bisexual?"

"No." She looked horrified. "I didn't lose my virginity to Rose. She wasn't a lesbian. She invited me to a Senior Party where Roger Carmical took me into his parents' room."

"Oh," I said.

She sniffed back a sob while I concentrated on the screams of rape and murder coming from the hall. Someone in another room joined in with a shrieking chorus of, "Won't someone help that poor woman?"

"Rose always had big ideas," Melissa said. "When her parents died, she kinda went nuts. She became a real loose girl there for a while. Her grades suffered, but then, all of a sudden, she snapped out and said she'd do things her way. She started to work on her big ideas. She got through college and limited herself to one boyfriend at a time."

"What ideas?"

"Independence," she said.

"What's so big about that?"

"We grew up in a tight-knit Mormon community. Two neighbors on my block were polygamists. Rose didn't live but a street over. The culture was the same. Women were defined by men. That's just how it was. Rose planned on marrying and settling down. After her parents died, she threw that out with her *Book of Mormon* and made her big speech about independence. And did it."

"You envied her," I said, finding a new suspect.

"Everyone did," she said. "I don't know any girl who didn't want to be Rose. She had no job, but always enough money. She had no man, but interesting men. She was fun and lively, and sinned openly while we did what we were told."

"By sin you mean sex?"

"That and drugs," she said. "You know she sold drugs to get through college?"

"I heard that," I said.

"Her grades tanked after her parents died. She lost her scholarship and was going to have to leave. She worked part-time at a bookstore, but didn't make enough. She applied for loans and grants and then gave up. She dropped out for a quarter and then came back with a full load, paid tuition, paid fees, and no more job, except selling pills. She was still a good person. She didn't sell anything illegal, just not prescribed."

"I heard she sold illegal drugs. Carlos told me." The name didn't draw a reaction.

"Yeah, she did that recently, but in college she sold prescriptions exclusively. Mostly amphetamines for studying, but also some pain pills, even antibiotics for kids who had to get rid of something and couldn't go to their family doctor."

And now the question I'd been waiting to ask. I took a deep breath and concentrated on Melissa's face, ready to detect the lie.

"Did you supply her with the drugs?"

Her wet eyes went wide. "No," she said earnestly, tears gathering. "Why would you even ask me that?"

"It's an easy connection. You work in a hospital. Rose sold pills. Carlos said he didn't give them to her."

"I didn't work here then. I just got this job. In college, I worked at the campus food court, and Sears during the holidays."

"Oh. Do you know where she got the pills?"

"No. I never asked, and she never told."

"Okay, uhm. What about recently? Who do you think might mean Rose harm?"

"No one," she said.

"Won't someone please help that poor woman!" The screaming was right outside the door where a head-bandaged woman in an open hospital gown stood bare-assed holding an IV above her head.

"Do you know a guy named Harris? Luke or Justin?"

"I know Harris. He was a prick. Rose talked about him. Luke is a guy at the club where you hang out. They had a fling. I don't know Justin."

"Anyone else she hung out with? Other girlfriends?"

"Tonya and Patricia were at every get-together. Back in college, she saw a lot of Dara. Rex and Simon were at all the parties then, too. I didn't like them. I haven't seen them in forever."

"Who're Rex and Simon?"

"Boys from college. Rex Merkin and Simon Petersen."

"What's their story?"

"Simon moved down to Provo to work with his father at Peterson Plumbing. I think Rex is still in town."

"What does he do?"

"He works in a grocery store. I see him once in a while. He's still in school. A slow learner, I guess. Rose dated him for a while. He has a place in the Avenues on K Street and third, an old, white apartment building. He's lived there forever."

"How do you know he still lives there?"

"Ra-ape!" The word rang down the corridor like it was the name of a lost puppy.

"I guess I don't. But I think he owned it. His parents gave him the apartment for graduation. He talked about it."

"Were Dara and Rose close?" I asked.

"Yes," she said with some bitterness. "Kindred souls if you ask me, just opposite extremes. I know Dara's your friend too, but she can be a cruel bitch."

"I'd have to agree with you," I said.

"I didn't know Rose as well as I would have liked." She began to cry. I wondered why it had taken this long.

Instinctively, I put my arm around her. At first she resisted, then she melted like microwaved ice cream in my arms and boobed onto my shoulder for five minutes. Before she was done, I found myself crying, too. An emotional reservoir of pent-up stress and mourning gushed back onto Melissa's shoulder.

Eventually, we pulled apart. Her makeup was a complete mess. She looked like Picasso's oilcloth.

She reached for a Kleenex and blew her nose. She got up to fix herself in the mirror, and I got a drink of water from the tap.

A minute later, we stole out of the private room like two clandestine lovers. If anyone noticed us, they'd surely think we'd been getting it on. No one noticed us. Everyone was standing at the crazy woman's door.

Melissa took a deep breath and marched up to it. She pushed her way past the assembled staff and curious patients.

As I passed the door on my way out, I saw two uniformed security guards and three large orderlies standing by the bed.

"There!" screamed the crazed woman from the bed trying to point with a restrained arm at Melissa. "There's the ugly man who raped me!"

I could hear Melissa's terrible sobs from the elevator.

CHAPTER TWENTY-SIX

Sunday morning, I kicked boxes Pelé-style down the hallway from the bedroom. I nearly kicked one straight into his head before I noticed him.

"What the hell are you doing here?"

"Mom said I need to spend some time with you," said Randy, not looking up from his phone.

"How long have you been here?"

"Not long. I heard you singing." He tapped his screen, and I heard a *swoosh* of a text going out into the digital aether.

"How'd you get in?"

"Mom has a key."

"That's interesting."

"Glad you didn't change your Wi-Fi password," he said to his phone.

I went into the kitchen for caffeine and toast. "Why didn't anyone call?"

"I dunno," said Randy, blindly sliding into a chair.

"I have some things to do today," I said. "I guess I can use the company."

"Just tell me where the remote is, and I'll chill here," he said, tapping buttons.

"No. I think spending time together would be good."

"Come on," he whined.

"Nope. Father-son time. Your mom commanded it."

"But it's Sunday," he said, and finally looked at me. It was getting serious. "I just want to play with my friends. I brought discs and everything."

"What game do you need to play so badly?"

"Colonies, mostly. There's a new patch I want to check out. But I brought some other stuff if the guys want to play an FPS or Sim."

"What guys?" I tried to slam an entire Redbull in one swig, but my esophagus rebelled.

"The guys. You know—the guys. The guys I play with."

"Have you ever met them?" I coughed.

"In person? No."

"What's so damn cool about Colonies?"

"It's an awesome game, Dad. Today's the regional finals for the nationals next week. I want to lurk the games and pick up some strats."

"What?"

"You can sign in and watch the actual games as a lurker. You can comment in a chat room or link to professional commentators and chill with them."

I was proud of myself. I understood nearly half of what he said.

"So it's televised?"

He made no attempt to conceal a look of disgust.

"Dad, it's online," he said, but then corrected himself. "At least in America. In Thailand where Colonies is practically the national sport, it's televised. That's where the World Challenge will be."

"They televise a video game?"

"In Thailand."

"Can you download the games and watch them later?"

"Yeah, of course. And you can zoom in on different units, check out the strategies and everything. The whole thing is recorded. Free downloads."

"Great," I said. "You can watch them later then."

"Are you kidding?" Loud whining and eye contact. He was in full panic mode.

"Nope," I said. "You're coming with me for some quality drive time."

"It was Leafcaller's idea," he said, hoping to escape that way.

"You call him that?"

"Mom makes me."

"You can tell me all about it in the car."

He didn't. He was sullen and pouty. I pointed out local landmarks, like the prison, tailings dump, and waste treatment plant, but he kept his eyes glued to his phone. When I turned the radio up and tried to start a sing along, Randy produced a pair of earbuds and plugged one end into his smartphone and the other in his head.

Randy didn't even ask where we were going or why. His time was being wasted with me; that's all that mattered. I didn't take it personally. I was a teenager myself once.

Peterson Plumbing was open on Sunday, a rare creature for Mormon Utah County. A call before leaving the house confirmed I'd find someone there. My plan was another background check on Rose. I considered a plethora of cover stories to get his address if the address listed in the phone book for S. Peterson wasn't his. I favored the one involving circus clowns. No one ever suspects circus clowns.

It was housed in an industrial building in a residential area. Chain-link fence topped with razor wire surrounded a gravel storage lot where pallets of white PVC piping stood next to rusting vintage cars from Carter's administration.

Randy got out with me. He limped from cramps in his legs and the strain in his back from sitting awkwardly askew in the passenger seat, deliberately turning his face from me. He followed me into the office. I think he needed a bathroom.

A middle-aged man with a stained, button-down dress shirt read a catalog behind the counter.

"Can I help you?" he said without conviction.

"I'm looking for Simon," I said. "Simon Peterson. I was told he works here."

The man gave me a long hard look. He looked at Randy and then back at me, still hard.

"What do you want with Simon?" he said, growing larger in his chair.

"I want to talk to him." I said.

"How do you know him?" There was malice in his voice, a tenseness in his body, and threat in his eyes. Randy took a fearful step backward.

"You must be his social secretary," I said. "Is there any chance I can talk to him directly, or must everyone he meets pass an oral exam?"

He stared.

"Should I return with a letter of introduction? I think I can just catch the Regent at home if I hurry." He didn't understand the comment, but he got the tone.

He snarled. I glared.

I was angry at this man, not for wasting my time, but for intimidating Randy. My paternal reflex was to defend him, and my weapon was always sarcasm.

"You some kind of faggot?" he asked me.

"What kind are you looking for? Maybe I can hook you up. Do you have money?"

The man stood up, red-faced. His hands clenched.

"Is Simon here or not, bucko?" I held my ground confidently because there was a counter between us.

"You don't know shit," he said.

"Give me a chance. We just met."

Through a sneer, he said, "Simon's dead."

"What? Dead? I didn't know that."

"I can see that," he said. "Been dead two years."

"Why didn't you just say so?"

"He hanged himself when his dad found out he was a faggot."

The information silenced me for a moment, then I asked, "What's his father's first name?"

"Steve. Why do you want to know that?"

That would be the S. Peterson in the phone book, I thought. I saw no reason for the bigot to lie. This was literally a dead end.

"Well, if Simon's not around, I guess we'll be going," I said.

"What did you want with Simon, anyway?" he asked.

"Nope. I'm not talking to you anymore," I said. "You've been a thoroughly unpleasant person."

I opened the door for Randy, and we left. The man was at the door watching us when we pulled out of the yard. Something twitched in the back of my mind, but I couldn't catch it.

"What a jerk," Randy said.

"Totally," I said in my best Valley Girl.

"You cut him pretty good, Dad," said my son with a hint of admiration in his voice.

"Simon was a friend of Rose Griff's," I said, giving Randy one of my business cards. "I'm trying to find out about her so I can find who really killed her."

"Sounds like a good idea," he said. "You think Simon's death is related?"

"No," I said. "Well, maybe. Who knows? It's interesting, though, isn't it?

"So now what?"

"We're going to the Avenues," I said. "Another lead."

"Cool," he said.

We drove the deserted Sunday freeway back into the city.

"So tell me about Mudge," I finally said.

"He's moved in, you know. He was evicted from his place. He said it was some kind of hate crime, but I think he hadn't paid rent. He doesn't seem to have any money. He's always borrowing it from Mom."

"Doesn't he have a job? A business? What does he do all day?"

"He goes out. I don't know where, but he goes. He teaches yoga at the Rec. Center a couple times a week at night. He lost a lease at some strip mall. He said he was 'defeated by capitalism,' whatever that means."

"Is he nice to you?"

"Overly," Randy said.

That was something, I guess. "Is Mom happy?"

"She's different. She's trying to loosen up and feel the 'genius of living,' she says. She burns a lot of incense and meditates, holding a big rock in her lap, humming 'Ohm' through her nose."

"What happened to my room?"

"Oh, that's Hank's now," he said.

"Hank, huh?" I mused. First names now. "So they don't share a room? Your Mom and Mu . . . Lea . . . Hank?"

"They have visits," he said.

The reptile stirred inside me. It wanted blood. My inner caveman reached for his club and flexed his hair-grabbing knuckles. I took a deep breath, forced a smile, subdued the beasts, and let it drop.

"Let's get some food," I said.

"Meat?"

I nodded.

"Hell yes," he said.

We went to a hamburger joint we liked because it had more Elvis memorabilia than Graceland. It was called the King Diner after its owner, Igor Meloquivitchson, if any attorney asks. It was a cultural lesson in kitsch, good food, and rock and roll.

I was still thinking about Nancy and Mudge when we walked in. "Heartbreak Hotel" played from a corner jukebox.

I fetched our lunch—generous burgers perched atop nests of French fries in red plastic baskets. Randy looked up from his phone when he smelled the charbroiled meat. Nancy had imposed strict vegetarianism. Randy made me promise to keep our carnivorous consumption to ourselves. I was happy to do it.

"Simon Peterson's obituary doesn't list cause of death," he said, showing me his phone display.

I took the device. He'd linked to the Internet and searched the newspaper archive while I was in the bathroom. It was only a couple of lines about the untimely death of a young man. No mention of time or place. There would be no viewing and family only at the internment. It backed up the bigot's story, as far as that went.

"You're pretty good with that," I said, meaning the phone.

"No biggie." He squirted ribbons of ketchup into his basket.

"So who's this other guy?" Randy asked.

"Just someone who knew Rose in college," I said.

"That's it? That's all you know about him?"

"Yeah, pretty much. I'm running out of leads."

"Is he a suspect?"

"I have no suspects anymore," I said through a mouthful of greasy heaven. "Last week I thought I had the guy, but it wasn't him. Then I thought I had the guy again, a different guy, but it wasn't him either."

"That sucks. What do the police think?"

"That I did it."

"So you're screwed?"

"I'll have my day in court."

"So you're screwed." Smart boy.

"I'm not dead yet," I muttered.

The jukebox flipped to a new record. Vinyl scratches underlined the familiar strains of "Jailhouse Rock" and I was certain then that the god of irony was visiting the King Diner that day, probably for the onion rings.

Randy and I talked about school and girls, more the former than the latter. I felt the paternal need to impart on my son all I knew about women. "Beats me," I said.

"Let's go check your next clue," said Randy as we left the King Diner full and happy, the jukebox playing "Suspicious Minds."

* * *

The place was as Melissa described it—an old white apartment building. It had four stories, built in the late forties and renovated at twenty-year intervals. It was a decade overdue.

The cement steps flaked like exposed shale under our feet. The paint was peeling and rust appeared in streaks where no metal was visible or suspected.

Inside, a bank of mailboxes listed the names of current tenants in a hodgepodge of different handwritings and label makers. Rex Merkin was on the third floor, room C. Randy and I went up together.

We found Rex's room by the crowd in the hallway. Five guys stood outside an open door puffing away on cigarettes and drinking imported beer. They hardly acknowledged us as we peered around them to match the number on the door with Rex Merkin's address. Another crowd of people stood inside, silently engrossed in a TV show. I thought I recognized some of the faces in the room, but I didn't know from where.

Since the door was open, we went in.

I was trying to place the faces when Randy pulled on my sleeve and gestured to the front room.

A flat-screen television hung on the wall and beamed video of a computer game. Set at a right angle to it, against the wall, was a computer display with the same images. A man in headphones sat in front of the computer manipulating the view with mouse clicks and dexterous keyboard chords. His computer screen was mirrored on the wall for all to see.

"That's Colonies, Dad," Randy whispered to me. I nodded. The game's popularity was becoming annoying. Even I recognized it.

"What did you say this guy's name was?" said Randy.

"Rex Merkin," I whispered.

Randy pointed to the screen. I shook my head not understanding.

"RexingBall," Randy whispered, pointing to the upper right hand corner of the display. "That's the handle of one of the better players in the state. You think it's the same guy?"

"What does he look like?"

"Don't know, Dad. I just know the name."

The screen flashed from one building to another. A swarm of birds swooped down on a rock building and suddenly the words "ZotroN is Victorious" appeared on the screen, and everyone clapped.

"Did he just win?" I said.

"No. He's lurking. Scoping out the competition."

"Is this live?"

"Yeah, I told you," he said.

The man at the computer desk took off his headphones and stood up.

"You've got that guy, easy," someone said to him.

He nodded.

"Wreckers rule!" hollered a drunk bystander.

Then I recognized where I'd seen the faces—the Midvale Cyber Café. Calvin wasn't in the room, but many players I'd seen there were. The man in the chair was the gray-haired guy I'd seen there. The man talking to him was the guy who'd shocked his balls off.

"Rex Merkin?" I said into the room.

He turned to me. His eyes widened and his lips parted. Either he was trying to place me or searching for the perfect phrase to cuss me out. For a second I thought he might scream.

"Who are you?" he said.

"Are you Rex Merkin?"

"Yeah. What are you doing in my house?"

"Can I talk to you for a second?" I said. "Just a second?"

He glanced at his cadre of fans and friends.

"Yeah, sure. I got a second." We followed him into the kitchen.

"Do I know you?" he said, after he'd shooed away two guys raiding the fridge for beverages they weren't old enough to buy.

"I saw you at the Midvale Cyber Café last week," I said. "I was talking to Calvin."

"Who? Oh, yeah, that's right." He was friendlier than he'd been that day. "I thought you looked familiar. Who's Calvin?"

"Just a guy I needed to talk to. He plays Colonies, too. Like you."

"Not like me, I'm sure, or I'd know him," he said. "What can I help you with before you leave?"

"I'm investigating a murder."

"Really? No kidding? Who?"

"A woman named Rose Griff. Do you know her?"

"Rose Griff?" he repeated, rolling the name around in his head. "Sounds familiar, but I can't be sure. I know a lot of people."

"Are you really RexingBall?" said Randy.

He looked at my son as if surprised to see him, like he hadn't noticed him standing next to me the whole time.

"Yeah," he said. "That's me."

"What do you think of the new patch?"

"Nerfs the birds," he said. "Good thing."

"You went to school with her," I said.

"I'm still in school," said Rex. "I'll finish up this year with any luck."

"It was a while ago."

He shrugged.

"She hung out with you and Simon Peterson."

"Simon died," he said. "A couple years ago."

"Yes. So you remember him?"

"Yeah, I remember Simon, but not Rose Griffin."

"Griff," I corrected.

"Sorry. Griff," he said.

"Do you remember a girl named Melissa, or maybe Dara?"

"Dara, maybe," he said. He looked over my shoulder to the TV. "Listen, I've got get back. My round's coming up."

"Good luck," Randy said.

"Thanks, but I won't need it." He took a step to go.

"Where do you work?" I said.

"I have a job at Smith's Grocery Store on ninth" he said. "Why?"

"Just curious."

"Because of the TV?" he asked.

I nodded.

"Student loans," he said. "I gotta get back."

"Here, take my card," I said, offering him one. "If you remember anything about her, give me a call. I'm trying to piece together her past, you know, looking for clues."

"Oh, yeah? Okay. No problem." He led us out of the kitchen. We were excused.

At the doorway, I stopped. Someone had lowered the lights, and the screen flashed a countdown until the beginning of the next game: "Quarter Final Qualifier—RexingBall vs. ZotroN in thirty-five seconds."

In the glow and shadows of the flickering screens, I recognized a color and a shape. My heart jumped as I placed Rex's profile and his silver hair. I saw him hugging shadows, wearing sunglasses, and talking to Rose beside the concession stand at the Hangar Rave.

"Can we stay and watch?" Randy said, craning his neck to see the screen.

"No," I said. "We've got to go."

"Why?"

"Because he's lying."

CHAPTER TWENTY-SEVEN

"If you suspect him, Dad, why didn't we stay?"

I drove Randy back to Nancy's house. I felt bad that we'd spent the whole day in the car, but at least Randy and I had talked more in those hours than we had in the previous six months.

"I know he's lying, but he doesn't know I know he's lying."

"So?"

"So, I don't know why he's lying. I don't know what it's about."

"It's gotta be about the murder," he said.

"I don't know that it's about the murder. Remember how I told you that I had two previous suspects? Well, they both had secrets too and reasons to lie. Some of them biggies, but not murder. I went so far as to accuse the most dangerous one. I felt like an ass afterwards."

"But you found out stuff today," he countered.

"Yes. I met Rex Merkin the other day at a café, and he was a total douche, but today he was nearly friendly and had free beer. He creeps me out. I have a feeling about him."

"What are you going to do?"

"I don't know."

I didn't have a plan, but I had a lead and a hunch and that made me happy. So happy, in fact, that I decided to walk Randy to the door instead of just dropping him off at the curb like Mudge had done that morning.

"You don't have to do this, Dad," he said. "I know the way to the door."

"Yeah, but I need to stretch my legs. Maybe you'll let me have a beer if no one's looking."

"Mom got rid of all the beer. For special occasions, they drink organic wine from Australia, where the water is supposed to have healing properties."

I hated to think that Nancy and Mudge had special occasions. "Okay, I'll have some of that," I said.

Randy shrugged and led me in.

The house smelled like burned cardamom. The smell clung to the walls and coated the back of my throat the instant I inhaled it. It was either cheap incense or someone had let curry get out of control.

Randy thanked me for lunch before loping up the stairs to his lonely computer. I went to the kitchen.

No one was there. A deep frying pan stood on edge in the sink; black residue clung to its inside like poached barnacles. The stove was splattered with black oil drops, and the floor was slippery. So it wasn't incense burning my lungs.

I had a lead, and I wanted to celebrate. I opened the pantry and fished behind a dozen brands of organic whole-grain pastas until I found a wine bottle with a handwritten label: Leonora Springs Winery. Red.

Just "red." Not Merlot, not cabernet. Just "red."

The corkscrew was in its usual place. I pushed the tip in but fumbled the bottle and it dropped to the floor. The bottom cracked and wine seeped out. Sturdy bottle—it hadn't shattered, but it was done. I set it in the sink to drip away and reached back into the cabinet for another bottle with the same label.

In a moment I had it open. I found a glass and poured to the rim. I had to bend over the counter to suck some off the lip before I dared pick up the glass.

Down in one gulp.

It wasn't bad. It reminded me of the cheap, sweet table wine they served at Bucelli's Italian Kitchen.

I refilled my glass.

"To Rose." One gulp.

The glass in one hand, the bottle in the other, I walked through my old house on waves of nostalgia.

Except for the sound in Randy's room, the house was quiet. Deserted. No one had told me what time to bring him back, which was fine, since no one had told me he was coming over either. Randy was old enough to be left on his own. I'd leave as soon as I'd finished my drink.

My old study was now a new study in Mudge aggrandizement. Pictures of Hank "Leafcaller" Mudge hung on every surface. He was well-travelled. There were numerous pictures of him in Mexico, some in the Caribbean, a couple in Alaska, and some clearly from Disney World in Florida. In each one, he was surrounded by different people. In most of them, the picture had been cropped unnaturally and needed special frames to accommodate the edited picture.

Half glass. One gulp.

Intermixed with photos were framed charcoal drawings of landscapes. I recognized the point of Cabo San Lucas and the skyline of Epcot Center's geodome. They weren't bad sketches, but I hated them anyway. I saw each was signed with a stylized HM in the lower-right corner, the right vertical of the H forming the first stroke of the M. A more pompous monogram I could not imagine. How could Nancy like this guy? I thought in caveman grunts.

I heard the garage door motor and left the room. For a second, I thought of hiding, but my car was parked in the driveway. Sneaking away was out. A horn blared.

I trotted to the door on unsteady legs. My head swam from wine. My tongue felt thick and numb. The wallpaper designs moved like living things and color from the carpet peeled itself free and wrapped around my ankles. I was aware of a skinny man with a cigarette holder, yellow sunglasses, and press credentials whispering in my ear me about bats in the desert. Don't stop!

Outside, a white buffalo nosed up to my Prius's bum and honked in a feral mating ritual. The white animal rumbled and snorted. I watched and waited. Any moment now, I knew, the white beast would try to mount my delicate pet. I was eager to see if my docile little car would accept the advances of such an obnoxious mate.

"Move your goddamn car!" yelled the beastial suitor. The Prius held still, coy and calculating. Then, a door opened and Mudge from a cavity inside the beast's head yelled at me, "Move your goddamn car! You don't live here anymore!"

What strange brutish rites these were. Fascinating. What did the sounds mean? Were the colors important? Where were the bats?

"Tony fucking Flaner, move your goddamned car!" the beast yelled at me.

Suddenly, I realized my interpretation of events had been incorrect. These were not wild animals. They were automobiles.

I put the bottle and empty glass on the entranceway table and jogged to my vehicle. I rubbed its roof in soothing strokes to calm it. The white randy BMW backed out into the street. I got in my car and backed out the other direction.

For a brief second, both cars stared at each other across the driveway. The mating dance had become a challenge. I patted the dashboard to steady her for the coming battle frenzy. I flashed my headlights to show I was prepared for the joust, and slid the car into drive.

In a blur, the BMW swerved up the driveway and into the garage. My little electric-hybrid four cylinder was barely off the blocks when the white beast spit out a gelatinous gob, which resembled my wife's new boyfriend.

CHAPTER TWENTY-EIGHT

"Then my hairdryer broke. The interview was in three hours, and my stupid hairdryer broke. I had to totally change my style because I couldn't blow-dry my hair. It was a mess. Then, when I got in my car, I had a dead battery. The door was open all night. So I called Bren to take me, but she couldn't right then. So I called my mom. The whole way all she could talk about was why I didn't have a husband yet and how the best years of my life were being wasted."

Stephanie's tale of horror and disappointment would shake anyone's faith. She was twenty-three years old, unemployed, and like me, this was her first Atheist Alliance meeting.

She stood at a lectern in front of the skeptical congregation relaying the long tale of woe that led her to this meeting. She was the third speaker so far. She was the most energetic, but the least interesting.

The format of the AA meeting was not unlike a prayer meeting with pews and a pulpit. The crowd was more subdued than at a revival, but there'd been several moments during the testimonials where an "Amen" or "Hallelujah" wouldn't have been misplaced.

"I went to the Nordstrom counter and said I was there for the job, only to find out that they do all the hiring in the basement." An involuntary groan escaped me.

Patricia sat behind the lectern facing the congregation. Beside her was a distinguished man chewing an unlit pipe through his salt-and-pepper beard. His tan tweed jacket had leather at the elbows, and his bushy eyebrows made him appear constantly contemplative.

Patricia saw me slip in to the meeting right after the "Positive

Affirmation of Independent Thought," when everyone held hands, lowered their heads, and chanted the mantra of the True Atheist.

"I had to walk down, like, a hundred flights of stairs in heels," Stephanie said. "It was a living hell. I was, like, all sweaty when I got there."

My hangover was mostly gone. It was the worst hangover I'd ever had, and I'd had a few beauts. I couldn't remember how I'd gotten home. Just thinking about it made me dizzy, so you can understand how Stephanie's story was making me nauseous. I reached for my phone and checked my voicemail.

"Let me be clear, you jerk. I don't like you. That's right. I called you a jerk because you are a jerk, Tony. A big, dumb jerk." Mudge either had no idea how to level an insult or he was out-of-his-mind pissed. "You can't just do whatever you want. You don't live here anymore," he screamed in the message.

The time stamp indicated that it had been left just after nine the previous night while the gnomes were torturing me.

"And what's this? Oh my god. You maggot! You just helped yourself to my private wine?" His voice spiked suddenly from petulant to infuriated, skipping peeved, annoyed, and angry altogether. "This wine costs a thousand dollars a bottle! And what's this? You broke one? I hope you die!"

There was a macabre incongruity to Mudge's repetition of the well-mannered phrase "and what's this" and the shrill insane tone he said it in.

The call ended with a crash. I imagined shattered phone bits skidding across the tiles of my old kitchen floor.

I played the next message. It was from Nancy, left ten minutes after Mudge's.

"Hi, Tony," she said calmly. I heard cabinets slamming in the background among Mudge's shrill, angry screeches.

"Randy says you came in when you dropped him off," she said in her realtor voice. "You probably should let me know when that's going to happen. It's fine with me, but Leafcaller has boundary issues."

"Motherfucker!" he screamed in the background before Nancy

muffled the handset for a minute. "I see you drank some of Leafcaller's wine," she said with calm, statesmanlike diplomacy. "I hope you made it home okay. That stuff is pretty powerful. Not at all how it looks. Call me when you get this so I know you're okay."

Nancy's voice conveyed a familiar frustration I knew from fourteen years of bad behavior. This time, however, it wasn't just about me.

While Stephanie droned on, I texted Nancy's cell phone and told her I'd made it home safely, and thanked her for the concern and for letting Randy visit.

"I ran to the bathroom after. I saw then I misbuttoned my blouse. The collar was all crooked. No one in the waiting room had even bothered to tell me and the guy just pretended not to notice. I was *horrified*." Stephanie stressed "horrified" with a generous roll of her blue-lined eyes. She'd lost the audience long before, but on she plowed.

According to "discovery" (that's the term for all the evidence the other side has against me—I looked it up) the police had talked to Rose's neighbors. They knew nothing about that night, but spewed gossip about different men visiting her. It strengthened their prostitution theory.

I considered interviewing the neighbors myself, but didn't see it panning out. They weren't there that night. Then I had a brainwave. Stephanie's imbecilic ramblings had driven my mind into transcendental-detecting nirvana, or I just thought of something obvious: the goddamn crime scene. Rose's apartment. It was an obvious witness.

"So the phone rings, and the guy tells me that I didn't get the job. I started crying. I love that store. I shop there all the time. He told me to calm down. I told him he didn't know what kind of day I was having. He said, 'Sorry.' Can you believe it? He said, *sorry*. So before he hangs up, I ask him who got the job. He told me some girl named Bren."

A gasp, a groan, and a chuckle came from the crowd.

"That's when I knew there was no god," finished Stephanie. With an air of certain triumph, she marched back to her seat. There was a smattering of applause.

The man in the tweed jacket took the podium.

"Thank you for sharing, Stephanie," he said. "Is there anyone else who'd like to share?" His voice was rich and textured. It reminded me of Ivy League professors and walnut bookcases. His beard and pipe made me imagine him in a Jules Verne novel bearing down, full throttle, into the hull of an unsuspecting munitions ship.

Patricia had eyed me suspiciously throughout the meeting. She was irritated when I'd checked my messages during Stephanie's talk. Not wanting to appear more insensitive, I raised my hand to speak, hoping to woo Patricia into trusting me.

"Yes," said the heretical pastor. "Come up."

I took the microphone off the podium and slid into stand-up.

"Hi," I said. "My name is Tony."

"Hello, Tony," came the chorus from the audience.

"I have never seen such a godless group of people in my life," I said. The crowd wasn't sure if I'd insulted them or not. Neither was I.

"So, every morning I get up from bed and fall to my knees and thank the chest-of-drawers that I'm an atheist." A few giggles. Someone recognized the format. The crowd began to sense what was happening and were grateful for the palate cleansing after Stephanie.

"It's not easy being an atheist," I said. "Coming in the library today, a blue Civic cut me off and stole my parking place. I rolled down the window and yelled, 'Go to Helsinki!' It lacked something."

Laughs.

"When someone finds out you're not of their faith, they judge, prejudge, and misjudge. They isolate, desecrate, and humiliate. They ignore you, abhor you, and finally deplore you. Can I have an amen?"

"Amen," came a response.

"Ah, caught you!" I said, pointing to a man in the third row. He blushed. The crowd laughed.

"I don't know if I'm an atheist. I haven't had to put up with what many of you have. It doesn't play in my family like others. Growing up, I thought excommunication meant hanging up the phone."

More laughs.

"Well, I just want to thank you all for allowing a curious person to visit with you tonight," I said. And then, more to Patricia, I added, "It's good to be among people who keep an open mind, think for themselves, and don't believe everything they're told."

I returned to my seat to applause, regretting I didn't have anything to plug.

Patricia was the last to speak.

"Everything you heard here today is private and confidential," she reminded everyone. Then she looked right at me. "Do you understand that, Tony?"

"I do," I said. "I won't breathe a word. I swear to God."

Giggles from the crowd. A scowl from Patricia.

"I understand," I said with more humility. Sometimes, I just can't help it.

She brought out some prepared notes and said, "We have to save humanity from its own failings. We have to stomp out the superstition that is ripping our society apart. We have to recognize our own worth and responsibility. We need to fight ignorance. We need to remove myth from our lives, our currency, and our country."

She didn't pound the podium, but I think she wanted to. She was militant. Whereas the others had spoken about personal trauma and individual challenges with faith, Patricia argued for the aggressive, and possibly violent, overthrow of the "religious state."

Most of the audience glassed over during her rant. Some lip-synced her rhetoric, having heard certain turns of phrase many times before.

"At the least," she said, "we have to fight back against the repression of the nonbeliever."

The way she said "nonbeliever" sent a creepy chill up my back.

She suggested mass walkouts of school graduation ceremonies if prayers were said. She had few takers when she noted that St. Vincent's Catholic Preparatory School for Young Girls would be handing out student achievement awards next week and the program was open to the public. "It's a perfect place to begin the public movement," she said, her chin raised like Il Duce.

I raised my hand to join the protest. I'd gladly walk out of a Catholic school program. I didn't need an agenda to do it. Boredom would get me moving.

Finally, she asked those interested to see her after the meeting and sat down.

The tweed fellow, whose name I never learned, spoke again. He announced refreshments and listed upcoming events. There was an AA picnic at the Glory of Moroni Park next Sunday, potluck-style. He added the "possible" protest at St. Vincent's on Saturday after Patricia cleared her throat loud enough to silence Gabriel's horn.

Then, everyone joined hands and repeated the "Positive Affirmation of Independent Thought" prayer, I mean, credo, and then dug into donuts.

I sipped tepid coffee while waiting for the crowd to thin and perused the literature table. I picked up *There is No Goddamn God*, but passed on *Freeing Yourself From Religious Oppression, Mormon edition, Volume 8*. I couldn't resist *An Eternity of Quiet: An Atheists Guide to Death*. The cover showed an old man in Dickensian sleeping garb, floppy hat and shirt to his ankles, spiraling down a tunnel of light to a black, empty hole.

Patricia found me as people were leaving, "What do you want? Why did you come here?"

"I swear to God I didn't kill Rose," I said. Her eyes bulged.

"Poor phrasing," I said. "I'm trying to find out who did. Could you please help me?"

I gave her my card. She read it and frowned.

"I got a call from a cop," she said. "He warned me that you'd try and talk to me. He called it 'witness tampering.' He said you were a desperate killer, digging yourself in deeper."

"It's the finger trap," I said. "Once you're caught, the only way out is deeper in."

She seemed to understand.

Patricia sat down at a table. I sat down, too.

"I've been putting together a picture of who Rose was," I said. "Do you know anyone who might have wanted to kill her?"

"Everyone liked Rose."

"I heard she had a lot of boyfriends."

"She did."

"Any of them seem suspicious?"

"There was one guy they say killed her."

"Do you have his name? Number? A card perhaps?"

She smirked.

"Do you know a guy named Rex Merkin?"

"One of Rose's old boyfriends," she said. "I haven't seen him in forever." She fished a cigarette out of her purse and then, remembering where she was, put it back.

"How long have you known Rose?"

"We met in college. I worked at a bar. She came in. We hit it off." She snipped off each short sentence like a snapping turtle lunging at a pigeon.

"What bar?"

"The Sailor."

"Did she ever bring anyone in with her?"

"Yes. Lots of guys."

She was cooperating, but it wasn't easy for her. I'd asked her to ignore the official story and believe the total opposite. In a very personal way, I challenged her faith. "Did you see a lot of her?"

"Not much. Twice last month. The club and the rave."

"Did she tell you about anything going on in her life? Something new? Something unusual?"

"She said she was going to get you," she said. "Seems like a pretty bad idea in retrospect. Her being murdered and all."

"I think it would have happened no matter what," I said.

She'd regressed back to old opinions and scowled at me.

"Why do you assume I killed her?"

"The media. That cop. My gut."

"Wrong. Wrong. And, I'm sorry to say, wrong. I didn't do it. I'm being framed. I'm also the only one who's looking for the killer; not the newspapers, not that cop, and not even your godless gut. Just me.

If you cared about Rose, you'll help me. And give Rose the benefit of the doubt that she had sense enough not to take a sociopath home with her after a drunken party. Maybe she was a better judge of character than you think. She liked you, after all."

She slouched and stared at the empty table.

"I wouldn't put it past Rose to take a sociopath home," she said. "But I'll give you the benefit of the doubt. I liked you before. I may have built you up into more of a monster than you are. Plus, the police like easy answers, and the media lies."

"Thank you," I said with more emphasis and feeling than she was ready for.

I took a deep breath to restrain my gratitude. "So, what can you tell me?"

"She said she was expecting a lot of money soon. 'Life-changing money' she called it."

"Did she say where it was coming from?"

"No."

"Did she mention any names or places?"

"No, just that she was coming into money. Oh, she said she was going to Las Vegas. Maybe that's what she meant."

"Was she a gambler? Did she go to Las Vegas a lot? Was this normal?" I could have posed the questions individually, but my mouth had seized the switch and rolled on without me.

"Normal? Yeah, she would invite us all on trips, cruises and such. We all went to Moab once. It was a rafting trip, but that was years ago. As for gambling? Like, did she have a problem with it? No. I don't think so, and I know a few people with problems like it."

I bet she did. "Who'd she invite to Vegas?"

"Don't know the whole list. It was to be an all-girls trip this weekend."

"Where were you going to stay?"

"The Rio."

"Remember the rave?" I said. "Rose had a bottle of rum. Do know where she got it? Did you give it to her?"

"No, but Rose liked rum. Spiced rum was her favorite. She always liked to end the evening with it. She said it was lucky."

"You knew this from the bar?"

She nodded. I sighed.

"Thanks for talking with me, Patricia. If you think of anything else, you have my card. Call me, okay?"

"Okay," she said. "And thanks for coming to AA. Will you come back?"

"I have other things to do right now," I said.

I stood up and shook her hand.

"I like the Sailor," I said. "Strange I never saw you there."

"Most people don't notice me there. Wrong chromosome set."

CHAPTER TWENTY-NINE

For my next witness, I wouldn't have to put on my innocent face, flash my card, or play verbal tricks for answers. I'd only have to break in, which was ever so different. Instead of facing a witness-tampering charge, I'd go for breaking and entering. Yep, my investigation was going places.

Among the papers Mollif had left me was a list of things taken from Rose's apartment as evidence. It wasn't much. There was also a description of the apartment, its several rooms, and photographs of the same.

I put the photos of Rose aside, face down, and studied the other ones. The photographer had a flare for artsy tourist snapshots: close-ups of interesting, but meaningless, things. He was impressed with the coffee pot, but not the kitchen as a whole. He liked the coffee table, but not the sofa. The bathroom shot consisted of an open door at the end of a tilted Caligari hallway. There was a subtle emphasis on the *Casablanca* movie poster hanging on the right wall. I think the photographer was trying to get into a gallery with that one.

My plan was simple: I'd go to Rose's building, get into her apartment, and find all the evidence. It was brilliant. I planned my espionage for the middle of the day. Every good citizen would be at work, greeting shoppers or shoveling coal.

I took along my digital camera, a pair of latex gloves ideal for keeping your manicure safe while scouring baked-on foods, and my lock-pick set. I'd gotten into picking locks for a while, another short-lived hobby. I still had the kit and the half-read book that came with it. I took both and added a screwdriver, butter knife, and obsolete video rental card—Q would be proud. Then I remembered how terrible I was with the lock picks and went to the garage where I added a brick and a crowbar. I put it all in a gym bag and hit the road.

I drove slowly by the apartment. It looked quiet, if not deserted. I parked my car a block away on the next street and walked back.

It was different in the daylight. I hadn't noticed it when I'd left in the backseat of a vomit-scented police car, but now I did. Signs of age and neglect countermanded my first impressions of antique charm. It bothered me. Cracks in the sidewalk irritated me. Garbage blown in the bushes pissed me off. Cracked and missing mortar made me grind my teeth. Old things aren't valued in America, even when they're very cool. Rose had valued old things, even if her landlord didn't. I wondered if the owner was deliberately letting it rot, planning to put in a Joni Mitchell's parking lot or a 7-Eleven rather than spending a dime to restore anything. Luckily, the building had been built well. It was sturdy and stubborn, fired brick and local cement. With any luck, someone would put it on the Historic Registry before it was too late.

The carpeted stairs creaked as I crept up to the third floor and straight to room six. Two things had changed since I last saw the door. First, there was a notice glued to it proclaiming it a crime scene, forbidding anyone entrance under dire warnings punctuated with legal reference numbers and statute codes. Interested parties were directed to call the police at an underlined phone number. Second, there was a hasp-and-lock set on the door in case the paper didn't do its job. Even if I'd had a key to Rose's apartment, I couldn't get in without the combination to the lock.

"Fuck," I said, flipping the padlock.

"Fuck yeah," I corrected myself, recognizing a MasterLock. Thank you useless hobbies for making me the man I am today—a third-rate burglar. I began the procedure I'd learned from the Internet before my life went to shit. A few minutes later, I had the possible numbers and tried them. The fourth set opened the lock.

"Can I help you?"

"Ahhhh!" I shrieked. I turned around too fast for my feet and fell on my ass.

A short man, a little younger than the building, stared down at me, his hands in his pockets, his wrinkled jowls flapping like a bloodhound's. He wore a checkered flannel shirt under his overalls and visible white socks in his worn, scuffed brown Redwings. His eyebrows and nostrils needed a trim, but the hair on his head was waxed down firmly.

"Jesus. You scared me," I said, regaining my feet. "Don't sneak up on people like that. You want to kill someone?"

"I didn't sneak up on anyone," he said. "I just came up to check the water line and saw you fiddling with that lock. You ain't allowed to go in there. Can't you read?"

"Yes, I can read," I said. "You must be the super. I was about to find you. Open this door for me, will you?"

"You can't go in there," he said. "Police posted that note and put that lock on it. I couldn't let you in if I wanted to."

"You mean this lock?" I twirled the opened lock on my index finger. "Yeah, I got that one. I wouldn't come all the way down here without the combination, would I?" I wasn't specifically claiming to be a policeman; I let him come to his own conclusions on that. I didn't want to get into trouble.

He eyed the lock and then looked at me, my bag, and the door.

"Can we get a move on? I have a ton of paperwork to do after this. Don't make me call the captain," I said, thinking of Captain Crunch for plausible deniability. I was like Teflon.

"Let me see a warrant and some ID," he said.

I reached into my pocket and rolled my eyes. I reached into another pocket and looked peeved. I pulled out my illegally concealed handgun from my waistband and held it nonchalantly in my palm as near the super's nose as I could and not actually hit him with it.

"Damn. Did I leave it with the bailiff at court? Or was it the squad room?" It was a question, right? Not an actual lie. Nothing fishy here. No siree.

I bounced the gun in my hand casually, feeling the weight, and twirled the lock in my other hand, feeling it spin. I waited to see if enough unintended deceit and accidental suggestion had filtered into his senescent head to convince the super I was a cop and get him to open the goddamned door before I had to make a break for it down the stairs.

"Buddy, give me a break. Just open the door. Be a good citizen. If I gotta come back here later, I might bring a building inspector or a fire marshal along to make sure everything's up to code." No lie there. I might.

He snorted in an antique language and pulled a ring of keys from his pocket. He slid one into the bolt then into the knob and pushed open the door. I collected my bag and stepped in. He made to follow me but I shut the door before he could. I threw the bolt and connected the chain.

My steps were light as I walked. My stomach limbered up for calisthenics when I saw the boxy couch again. It went into its full routine when I glanced at the door to the bedroom. I looked away, then closed my eyes, took a deep breath, and let it out slowly. That didn't work, so I tried it again. Third time's the charm. My gut waited for the judge's scoring while my heart wildly applauded.

I had to fight to get the yellow gloves onto my hands. You'd think sweaty palms would be an effective lubricant, but it's the opposite. I concentrated on shrinking the bubbles at the fingertips while the applause subsided and I felt calm enough to look around.

The kitchen was my first stop. The garbage had been taken out, but no one had thought to check the fridge for perishables. The smell nearly knocked me out. A black head of lettuce, liquefied broccoli, and a bulging carton of milk encouraged me to look elsewhere.

I checked the cabinets. Her dishes were all mismatched, but each one was a work of art. She had china whose patterns had graced the pages of a turn-of-the-century Sears and Roebuck catalog, stacked alongside indestructible Disney princess plates. The silverware also had been collected from a hundred different antique shops. The silver was tarnished, but the patterns were nice.

Her liquor cabinet was adequate for a single non-Mormon in Utah. She had all the standards: gin, vodka, and rum, but not spiced rum. She had several bottles of wine—whites and reds and pinks—and several champagnes. None chilled. She had a single bottle of Leonora Springs Winery, Red, like I'd seen at Nancy's. Just looking at the handwritten label made my head swim.

I saw the familiar Flintstone glasses mixed among crystal goblets and etched coffee mugs from Yellowstone Lodge's 25th anniversary. There were only six Flintstones. Dino and Wilma were not in attendance. Fred looked worried. He stood in the sink where I'd left him, waiting for word of his missing family.

The bathroom yielded no clues I didn't already have. The medicine cabinet was still a ghost town. The furnishings still old, white, and enameled.

The study was next. I compared the photo the police had shot with what I was looking at. They looked the same. I looked for obvious gaps in the bookshelves. The police photographer hadn't bothered coming into the room. The doorframe was enough for his aesthetic sensibilities.

The Twains had been valuable, but they were still there. Her first edition copy of *Catcher in the Rye* was surely valuable, but there it was beside Baudelaire. The computer was still there, still out of place amid the antiques.

It had to be Colonies. I thought I remembered seeing Colonies among Rose's stuff. There was something about that video game that could draw even the retro Rose into twenty-first century technology.

I wanted to see the game, to scope out its cover and see if I could discern the secret addictive ingredient that sucked everyone from Rex to Randy to Rose into its control. But the game was gone. The disc was moved.

I looked through the desk, in the cubbies, on the floor. No Colonies disc. I checked the police photo. The telltale orange and blue case was not among stack of discs shown in the picture. It was gone.

What the hell?

I went through the roll-top desk more carefully. I didn't find the disc, but I did find an interesting receipt from an attorney, Rebecca Taylor of Smith, Bannon, and Taylor. The receipt was for notarized papers which had been delivered to Rose's house by carrier the day before her death. It said "legal documents." No more. Rose had signed for them. The receipt was there, but not the papers, at least not in the desk. I took a picture of the receipt—faster than writing down the information.

I found phone bills and power bills, rent receipts, and a sticky note to buy eggs. Nothing unusual. I took pictures of them all. No bank statements. The rent receipts all listed "paid in cash." Because of Rose's purported career, I wasn't surprised she was off the grid and didn't use banks.

I found the switch for the computer. I heard the familiar chime as it came to life. The police report said that the computer was new and had no personal files on it. I recognized the background as the system default. The application folder had standard programs. Nothing unusual. No Colonies.

I checked the recent files list, and there it was. Colonies was the second to last program run on Rose's computer, yet it was gone now. To be sure, I selected the program from the list and received a message that the program could not be found. I checked the garbage. It was empty.

The last program to be used was the default web browser. I selected it from the recent application list, and it fired up with the zesty perkiness of a new computer. The home screen that greeted me was the default for a new computer. I checked her bookmarks. Nothing had been added. Then I opened the history file and surfed to the last page she'd been on: The Wreckers Guild Home Page.

The Wreckers were a Colonies gaming guild—Rex's guild. Their website was amateur and simple, hosted on a free site. It looked to have been thrown together by a kid in his basement, possibly as a homework assignment. The most recent message on the page was a poorly spelled article speculating on what the next patch would have. It was dated five weeks earlier. I took a picture of the screen to record the address and then checked out other pages Rose had visited.

She'd visited a dozen pages related to Las Vegas, the Rio in particular. She'd Googled money conversion and found a page to convert dollars into any of one hundred world currencies. That's as far back as the history went.

I shut the machine down.

The liar was now a true suspect.

The last room to visit was the one I dreaded most: Rose's bedroom. My hands were water balloons at the end of my arms as nervous sweat filled my Playtex SureGrips. The door was ajar and I walked in with my burglar bag slung over my shoulder, my hands gripping the strap like a lifeline.

The bed was made but I could trace Rose's lifeless body in the wrinkles of the bedspread. My breath caught for a moment, my heart beat a sad rhythm of loss and love, and I recalled why I was there. I got to work.

Police had found nothing of interest in any of her dressers or closets, but I looked anyway. Her underthings didn't bother me. Her shoes were plentiful and varied, but told me nothing except that I didn't understand women's fondness for shoes. The dress stopped my breathing again. There were the blue sequins I remembered shimmering at the bar, flickering in the strobe lights and swaying up the stairs, the dried corsage still pinned on the front.

I pulled down a suitcase from the top shelf of the closet. It felt empty. It was. I pulled another. Same thing. I pulled the last—a black carry-on, pull-behind Samsonite. The most ubiquitous bag in the world. There was nothing in the main compartment, but I felt a paper in the front magazine pocket. I pulled it out and nearly shit myself.

It was a large, poorly folded sheet of heavy, white, textured paper. One edge was ragged where it had been torn from a spiral notebook. Opened up, the page was eleven inches by fourteen, standard size for an artist's sketch pad.

On the paper, drawn and shaded in charcoal pencils, was a reasonable portrait of Rose sitting on a beach. A distant volcanic hilltop and palm trees put it in the Caribbean. The stylized HM in the corner put it in my craw.

The front door rattled. Someone was coming in. I heard the chain catch, and then the muffled curses of a familiar noir voice; it was either Bogey or Detective McGraw.

I stuffed the picture in my pocket, grabbed my stuff, and opened the window. I was on the third floor, but I was ready to jump if need be. My veins pumped a potent cocktail of adrenalin, confusion, and suspicion, creating a shield of madness no forty-foot fall could dent.

Luckily there was a fire escape. I might have seen it from the outside, but it hadn't registered. I stepped out onto the rusting grates as a loud rip signaled a police kick tearing the chain from the doorframe.

I scurried down the stairs to the second floor landing and didn't even try to extend the ladder. I swung my feet into the opening, turned over, and dropped to the ground. I set off running between the buildings. No windows faced into the alley, so I felt sure McGraw hadn't seen me on the fire escape.

A block away, I caught my breath, and then, as casually as I could, I walked to my car.

"Casually," I discovered, meant constantly looking over my shoulder and diving behind parked cars and thorny shrubs whenever I heard a leaf rustle.

There were no cops by my car, no boot on its tire, no ticket on its windshield. I opened the door, tossed my bag on the passenger seat, started it up, and drove away.

Ten minutes later, I pulled into a gas station and peeled off my gloves.

My hands were hot and wet, wrinkled like raisins. My head spun with coincidence, suspicion, and connections. I stared at my poor cooked fingers. I pointed each index finger to the other and touched them.

"What a complicated trap this is," I mused.

CHAPTER THIRTY

All day I pondered possibilities. I considered random happen-stance, to hired hit man, to Karmic debt following me through lifetimes. What had I done to Hank Mudge to deserve this? I must have been a really bad person.

I had to warn Nancy.

I called her at eight-thirty the next morning.

"Hello, Tony," she said.

"Hey, Nance," I said. "I think Hank killed Rose Griff and framed me for it." Small talk is for losers.

"What?"

"I thought you should know."

She took a long deep loud breath.

"Tony," she started, "I have the name of a good counselor. I know this divorce has been hard on you. You didn't take advantage of the time to prepare for it. You're acting out. I'm sorry I moved on so quickly, but I was prepared. You can't hate Leafcaller for that."

"I can if I want to," I said. "He hates me."

"Hank has some issues of his own," she admitted. "It's the negative energy you bring that upsets his harmony."

"So it's my fault he's a prick?"

"Unseen energies flow from your unbalanced chakras like rays of unhappiness and disease. Leafcaller knows that your imbalance is so bad as to overcome even his equilibrium. He's promised me to work on creating a protective aura to thwart your negative vortexes. He knows he'll have to see you again."

"You've really gone off the deep end," I said. "You scare me, Nancy. This is total bullshit. He hates me because I'm not in jail and, until I am, there's a chance he can still be nailed for murder. He's not what he appears to be. At least not to you."

"That's an unkind thing to say," she said. "If you don't want to see a counselor, I can recommend some spiritual healers who can help with your aura distribution. That might help."

"What might help is if you stop smelling the poppies and wake up to this creep. He's using you, at the very least. Why doesn't he have a place of his own? Where does he get off just dumping our son on the street and driving off without checking I'm home?"

"He doesn't believe in material possessions or ownership," she said. "When Randy got inside, he assumed you'd let him in."

"Doesn't believe in material possessions? Is this the same guy with the BMW and thousand-dollar wine?"

"The car was given to him," she said.

"By his last mark, I bet."

"Tony, you've got to release your anger."

"Good idea. Where's Mudge now?"

"Leafcaller," she corrected.

"Where?"

"He's gone on a trip," she said. "I'm not telling where."

"Because you don't know, aren't sure, or think he lied to you?"

"Because it's none of your business."

"I'm guessing Vegas," I said.

Her snort told me I was right.

"Tony, get some help. Move on," she said.

"I know it would be easier for you not to hear this. I'm sure you're wishing you'd never let me get out of jail right now, but it's not me who needs counseling. It's you. I don't recognize you. This creep you let into the house has brainwashed you into a card-carrying member of the Symbionese Liberation Army. What happened to your plans? Your discipline? Your steadiness and sensibility? I was always the flake.

You buying into all this chakra-balancing crap is making me look positively dependable."

"Are you finished?"

"No. But thanks for asking. I'm not saying that there couldn't be auras or vibrations or chakras. What I'm saying is Mudge is full of shit and full of himself, which is a tautology, now that I think about it. How much has Mudge gotten out of you so far? A lot? Who are the people cut out of his pictures in my study?"

"Leafcaller, before his enlightenment, led a less than balanced life. He's admitted that. He used to teach on cruise ships and often fell into temptation with vacationing single women. It was a bad time in his life. One he regrets. He's been very honest about it."

"Did he tell you he knew Rose Griff?"

"The girl you killed?"

"Dammit, Nancy. Don't say that. You don't actually believe I killed someone do you?"

There was silence on the line. The quietness was thorns in my gut.

"Leafcaller says your aura is muddy. Your other self might be capable of committing terrible crimes and you might not even remember them."

"Nancy, you've known me two decades. You've known Mr. Smooth-Food-Face for a couple of months. Get sober and think for yourself."

"I am thinking for myself."

"Are not."

"Am, too."

"Did he mention he knew Rose?"

"He didn't mention it."

"Don't you think it's interesting that he didn't bring it up? Don't you think such a strange coincidence would merit a mention? Something like, 'Funny thing, Nancy. I knew that woman your husband supposedly killed. I stalked her for some time after meeting her on a cruise ship.'"

"No, it doesn't seem strange, because that never happened. He would have told me if it were true. You're making things up. You're scared and desperate; you're focusing everything on me and my new life."

"Am not."

"Are, too."

"Nancy, I have proof. I'll show you."

"Get some help, Tony. I'm sick of talking to you." She hung up the phone.

I'd broken her magical, mystery calm. Great success.

The phone rang.

"Nancy, if this is some kind of tenth-step bullshit, save it for the meeting."

"Mr. Flaner?" asked a heavily accented voice, Indian or Pakistani.

"Yes?"

"Hello. This is Ganesh Lahkpa of Nephi Bail Bonds and Pawn." It was Nepalese.

"Yes, how do you do?" I said.

"I do very well, thank you very so much for asking. I hope you are doing well, as well. It does my heart great joy to know you are well."

"Joy away," I said. "How can I help you?"

"I was going over my paperwork for the bond we issued for your deserved freedom, and I noticed there is a small mistake. I have accidentally misspelled your name on one page. I accidentally added an 'e' to your name 'Tony' on page six of our agreement. I am so embarrassed. It is nothing, but my wife, she is a stickler for detail. Very useful trait sometimes, sometimes not so much. You would be doing me a very great favor if I could meet with you and have you initial the correction on the paper so the wife would be happy and domestic bliss would again reign in my house."

"Yeah, okay sure," I said.

"Very excellent," he said. "I see by your ankle bracelet tracker that I have found you at home. I will drive over right away with a pen and we will have this issue tidied up before midday. Will you be there for a short while longer?"

"Yeah, I can wait for you. When do you think you'll be by?"

"It should not take me more than half an hour to drive my car to your home. I am leaving now. See you soon."

"Okay," I said. "Goodbye."

"Goodbye."

Why couldn't everyone be that friendly and cheerful as Mr. Lahkpa? I needed to surround myself with more people like him, absorb the positive vibe of helpfulness, not the sinister aura of cheaters and liars who populate the world in voracious packs. I'd invite him to dinner as soon as all this was settled to thank him for his trust in me.

The phone rang again.

"Hello?"

"I told you it could always get worse, and you proved me right. I knew you would."

"Hi, Morris," I said. "What can I do for you?"

"Sweet and McGraw went to the judge this morning. Your bail is revoked because you talked to witnesses and committed more crimes."

"I talked to the people before the witness list came out. They were fair game."

"No. There was a girl named Patricia something on the list. They say you accosted her at the library and threatened her."

"Bullshit, I just talked to her."

"The list had been released."

"But I hadn't seen it."

"Do you really think that matters?" he asked.

"And that's enough to throw me back in jail?"

"They also claim you burgled Griff's apartment and may have taken evidence."

"No one saw me," I said.

"A janitor identified you from a mug shot."

"Fuck. What should I do?"

"You should get a good lawyer," he said. "Turn yourself in."

"Are the cops coming for me?"

"Not yet. They'll contact your bondsman first. Get him to do it. Saves manpower that way."

"I just got a call from him. Ganesh is on his way over now to settle some paperwork."

"Don't resist," Morris said. "They can get pretty rough."

"What?"

"They're coming to get you, Tony. When they get there, don't resist or they'll beat the piss out of you for practice."

"But he was so nice on the phone."

"Ganesh issues bail bonds and runs a pawn shop. What part of this career choice would make you think he was a nice guy?"

"He sounded nice on the phone."

"You're naive."

"I gotta go," I said. "Don't tell anyone I know there's a warrant out for me. Don't tell anyone we talked."

"Tony, they have your passport. You're wearing a GPS locator. Where can you go? This is stupid. Turn yourself in and get a good lawyer."

"Yeah, uhm, about that ankle thing," I said.

"I don't want to know."

"Don't give up on me, Morris. We're going to beat this."

"I don't see how."

"I need help," I said. "Help."

"Okay, I'll do what I can. Good luck."

I tossed an armful of clothes in a suitcase, a few things from the bathroom, my burglar kit and gun, and ran to my car.

I peeled out of the garage in reverse, angled up the street, and hit the garage door clicker. I sped away. The neighbor girl smiled and waved. I waved back.

I looked up just in time to see a tan Chevy Continent coming right at me. I swerved out of its way. The driver yelled something appropriate, but not very nice, then recognized me. The SUV skidded to a stop in a cloud of rubber smoke and wheeled around to follow me.

I decided the next stop sign was optional and drove for my life.

I'd seen two men in the behemoth vehicle. I knew they were massive, muscle-bound monsters without actually seeing them flex or tie lampposts into circus animals. I knew this because they appeared to be normal-sized people in that cavernous cab. That meant that they were both thyroidal, steroid, mutant freaks escaped from a government laboratory, intent on wreaking havoc to quench their insatiable thirst for blood.

And they were after me.

I was so screwed.

The stoplight was more of a suggestion than a direct command. I tried to express this opinion to the lady in the white sedan I nearly T-boned, but she was too busy rearranging hedges with her bumper to listen.

The SUV behind me may have heard her ultimate opinion of my driving, but that would be their little secret if I could help it.

I slowed enough to make a right. Rights were safer than straights—fewer flying objects.

I made another right immediately after and saw the tan Chevy tipping on two wheels to make the first turn in pursuit.

It was the middle of the day in a residential neighborhood, so traffic was light. Lots of pedestrians though. Old people taking in the air, thin women in synthetic fibers jogging one direction, fat ones in cotton sweats walking in the other. Two mothers side by side pushed side-by-side strollers behind a man being pulled by a dozen eager dogs toward a fire hydrant. The menu of potential casualties was rich. I tried to keep my speed below fifty so there'd be something to identify.

I cut a corner at the next stop sign, another right. The Prius took the curb with the kind of indifference you'd expect from a little half-electric car; the bottom scraped, the axels whined, the tires threatened to explode from the sudden edge, and the whole vehicle lurched and bucked in anger.

I didn't see the plastic garbage dumpster and couldn't have missed it if I had. I didn't break it—those things can't be broken—but I did hit it hard enough to send it flying across the street into a parked Volvo. It bounced off the Swedish steel and caromed back into the road where I hit it again, sending it over my car and into the air. I sped on.

I checked my mileage. This was doing nothing for my fuel efficiency.

In my rearview mirror, I saw the Chevy cut the same corner without as much as a bounce in the springs. It roared after me. For all my evasion, they'd cut the distance to a third of what it was when they first turned to follow.

I could hear their massive engine as the tires regained the pavement. The Chevy raced down the center line and approached the trash barrel, ready to send it after me like a waste management missile. I looked for my next right. A one-way street cut my options, and I slowed to avoid the traffic at the light, readying myself to shoot a gap or feel the trashcan in my hatchback.

I heard a boom of brown steel on blue plastic and looked in my mirror. The truck hadn't launched the can as I had. It had climbed it.

The Chevy rolled over it like it was a dune or a bull trying to mount a cow. The truck swerved and skidded. The trash barrel wedged underneath between the two axels. Their steering was messed up. Something in the undercarriage wanted to turn, but couldn't. White friction-melted plastic smoke billowed from all sides of the truck. It stopped.

The light changed. I floored it.

In my rearview, I watched two giants get out the truck, point at me, and then look under their vehicle.

Another right, and I was clear.

What a deceitful, lying creep Ganesh Lahkpa was, sending goons to drag me back to jail. And to think I was going to invite him to dinner.

Seemed like getting out of town was a good idea. Push and pull.

It was a straight line to the freeway, and I hit it at exactly the speed limit. I turned south and headed for Vegas.

CHAPTER THIRTY-ONE

I hadn't stayed at the Rio before. It wasn't on the Strip, and I'd always stayed on the Strip, thinking I'd find some of the old Frank Sinatra-Bugsy Siegel vibe there. Never happened. What I found were bands of insistent men handing out flyers for escort services to be dropped two paces away and to be blown down the hot desert streets like obscene autumn leaves. Vegas had its own nature.

The Rio was nicer than the places I'd stayed before. No flyers and enough parking for a World's Fair. I backed my car against a wall and used a screwdriver to remove my front license plate. I could have asked a valet to do it. This is Vegas; they wouldn't have batted an eye. But I was cheap and saved the tip.

I followed the carpet-induced hallucinations to the registration check-in line. Two men waited in front of me. They were arguing gambling tactics.

"You can't stop gambling," said the first one. "If you don't gamble every day, how will you ever know if you're on a winning or losing streak?"

The other man weighed the impaired logic and sighed. "I have got to break even today," he said. "I need the money."

"I know what you mean," said the first. "You know, I don't mind losing bets; it's the money that bothers me."

"Yeah, me, too," agreed his friend.

And thus the city of Las Vegas thrives in the desert.

"I'd like a room near my friend, Hank Mudge," I told the woman at the counter. She was coffee-colored and slim. She had big eyes and a big smile. Hormones I thought I'd outgrown made me suck in my gut and lower my voice an octave.

"What did you say the name was?" She spoke with a Caribbean accent that fluttered my heart.

"Mudge. Hank Mudge. He sometimes goes by the handle 'Leaf-caller.'" I spelled the names.

"Your friend is not staying here and has no reservations," she said.

"Oh, I guess I beat him here," I said. "I don't have a reservation either. What do you have?"

"It's good you checked in today. Tomorrow we'll be booked up for sure. I have a suite on the fifteenth floor. Smoking or non-smoking?"

"Non," I said. "Will I be able to stay past tonight?"

"Yes, but we are filling up. How many days?"

"I think through Sunday, unless I get cleaned out right away."

Connecting the length of my stay to my gambling success gave her pause. She wanted to record me as a one-nighter, but relented and set me up through Sunday.

"So what? You got a big convention coming in?"

"Yes, a tournament," she said, taking my credit card. I should have paid cash to cover my tracks, but alas I hadn't any. I'd backed my car against a concrete wall and ripped off the license plate so no one could find me, and here I was using my credit card at the Rio. "Is it too late to sign up?" I asked. If it was blackjack, my card counting skills might earn me my mental money, but it was surely Texas Hold'Em. Everyone plays Texas Hold'Em now. They practically have an entire cable station dedicated to the game.

"Afraid so. Invitation only." She handed me my Visa and a room keycard in a paper envelope. "Enjoy your stay. Good luck."

Up in my room, I threw the bolt on the door, my bags on the floor, and my tired body onto the bed. The escape and the drive had taken something out of me I'd only find again after a short rest. I was asleep before I realized how much I needed it.

* * *

The room was dark and unfamiliar when I awoke. I was disoriented for a moment and thought I was in jail again, but I recalled it had never been dark in jail. It was dark here. I recalled where I was, slid off the bed, and threw open the drapes. This was Vegas at night. Opening the drapes in the dead of night was the surest way to get light into the room.

Blinking billboards advertised the "loosest sluts in town" before I corrected my spelling. Streams of white headlights flooded the room from one direction while red ones shined from the other. I found a real light switch.

It was one in the morning. Time to get up.

This is the city that never sleeps, with all due respect to New York. Vegas doesn't get warmed up until midnight. Real players don't come out before one. This was magic hour when the grown-ups come out to play.

Mudge wasn't at the Rio, but I thought he was coming. It was only Thursday, well, Friday morning. He could still check in. I couldn't connect Mudge coming to Vegas with Rose's plans for a girls' night out, but I was here to try. I kept Rose's appointment, sans the girls. Mudge was somewhere in town. The coincidence made my mind ache, but I was getting used to that feeling.

I caught a shuttle to the Bellagio. A pack of frat boys loaded up behind me. A man in a golf cap and penny loafers snored in the back-bench seat, his legs crossed in the aisle.

"It's going to be awesome tomorrow," said one of the twenty-somethings.

"Hell yeah," his friends agreed.

"We gotta be sure we're up by noon or we'll miss the draw."

"Fuck yeah," his friends agreed.

I thought of haggard, alcoholic, cowboy-hat-wearing poker pros who'd have to face off against this mob of computer-trained mathematics majors in a Hold 'Em tournament tomorrow. Steely eyes against crooked baseball caps. It would make for good television. I wanted the old-timers to win.

I hadn't any plans at the Bellagio. It was just the first destination of the first shuttle I could catch. I didn't feel like driving or paying for a cab.

Once inside, I walked to the deserted registration desk and asked for Hank Mudge. He wasn't there. Leafcaller also hadn't checked in. I admired the glass chandelier for forty-eight and a half seconds and left.

I walked the Strip. It was hot. Black asphalt radiated stored heat from the day's desert sun like a hotplate cooking bacon. I ducked wide-eyed tourists, porno pamphlet pushers, and staggering drunks. A gaggle of cameras attached to Asian schoolgirls giggled and ignored eight septuagenarians carrying plastic tubs of quarters and arguing over cab fare. What a place. I stopped in every hotel I passed and asked after Mudge. Nothing.

Hours later, I was at Caesar's Palace for a drink. I took a bourbon shot and then another. It was easier to one-gulp a shot of whisky than a peach daiquiri, so I went with that. I slammed the drink down in a single go as Rose had showed me. It kept my mind focused and my vision blurred.

Behind the casino and bars, Caesar's has one of the most upscale shopping malls on the planet, the Forum. Dubai might have better now, but I bet they came to Caesar's to see how it was done.

I liked walking the Forum, window-shopping at the things people who have more money than sense liked to buy. I followed swarms of sobering tourists doing the same, not daring to enter any shop, not wanting to even suggest they'd buy anything.

I passed a bar and went in for another shot. But I was wrong. It wasn't a bar at all; it was an upscale liquor store. A slender, big-eyed blonde, who looked an awful lot like a model from my seized pornography collection, asked if she could help me.

"I'm sorry," I said to her boobs, which obviously wanted attention, trying so hard to escape the woman's tuxedo vest. "I thought this was a bar."

"You'll have to go back to the Casino," she said.

"Okay, thanks," I said to her eyes with Herculean control. Then

I had a thought, which surprised me considering where most of my blood had gone.

"Have you ever heard of a place called 'Leonora Springs Winery?' Expensive wine, cheap bottles, hand written labels?"

"We refer to it as 'Laudanum Springs Winery' around here," she said. "I've seen it, but it's illegal."

"Tell me about it."

"It'll cost you some money if you can find it," she said. "I could give you a name of a smuggler, but don't tell anyone I told you. He might be able to help, but no promises." She reached for pen and paper.

"Why is it illegal?"

"It's spiked with narcotics," she said. "I wasn't kidding about the laudanum. It's worse than Absinthe ever was. It's high-proof wine, opium, and who knows what else. It'll get you there with a single glass, if you know what I mean."

"I'm afraid I do," I said. "It's from Australia, right?"

"Right. But it's illegal there, too. For export only."

"How much is a bottle worth?"

"It's shit wine. It's all gimmick, but a bottle still goes for a thousand dollars. Maybe more. Never heard of it less than nine hundred. Expect a grand, maybe eleven hundred if you're buying singles."

She slid the note to me.

"Thanks," I said.

"You're welcome."

I couldn't resist. "Do I know you?"

She studied my face as I studied hers.

"Probably," she said. "But we've never met."

"Thanks for all you've done for me," I said. "Not just today."

"You're welcome."

I walked out the store stiff-legged and glad.

An abstract fountain in the corridor activated, sending plumes of water over colored lights choreographed to music. I found a bench and sat down to watch. The air was made cool and moist, a calculated contrast to the outside world.

I looked at the paper the girl had given me. It had a Nevada area code. I didn't recognize the phone number, but the name "Leafcaller" rang a bell.

The fountain show wasn't bad, kind of a mini Bellagio thing to "Pachelbel's Canon."

When it was over, my penis had relaxed, but my legs were sore from all the walking I'd done. My thoughts weren't on boobs any more as much as one boob in particular, who had some answering to do.

It took me forty minutes, but I finally found an exit out of the casino. They make it very hard to leave. That, no clocks, and carpet that can cause seizures are the three pillars of American Casino psychological torture. Someone should call another Geneva Convention to deal with such things.

I found the free-shuttle station far away from the door. They dropped you off in front, but loaded you up in an alley by a dumpster so the cabbies wouldn't riot and the muggers could pick the bones of the busted stragglers far from the glittery lights.

It was the same van as before. The same man snored in the same seat in the same position as before. We made several stops. It was past four and the people who boarded the bus were beaten and tired. One tired guy actually had a black eye where he'd actually been beaten.

The group of frat boys from before were collected at the Flamingo. They staggered in and fell into the seats, reeking of cheap booze and sugary mixers. They were the city's new favorite clientele—young, dumb, and full of cum, as Dara said in one of her bits. Muppets without the cognitive power of their foam counterparts. Here they were, the perfect dupes. Any cash they hadn't drank had been left on a piece of green felt in the last few hours. They'd be shot for tomorrow's poker tournament. Go old-timers!

"I'm so trashed," one of them said.

"Noon, is it?" said another. "How long is that?"

"Eight hours," said a third, more alert than the others. "Plenty of time to recover."

"What's the most we'll miss if we sleep 'til one?"

"We miss the pairings and might not get good seats."

"We can still watch it online. Can't we?"

"Who knows when they'll post the games," said the soberest one. "That's why all the players will be in the audience. It's our chance to meet them."

"We paid for the damn passes," slurred a belligerent one. "We better fucking use them."

"I wanna sleep."

"The first ever American National Colonies Tournament, and you're actually thinking of missing some of it?" said the sober one.

"What?" I said. "Did you say Colonies? The National Colonies Tournament is in town?"

"Duh," said the belligerent one.

The sober one said, "You know Colonies?"

"A little," I said.

"Well, yeah, the national tournament is at the Rio this weekend—Friday, Saturday, and Sunday. Winners go on to World. Big money on the line. A million dollar purse."

"That's a lot of money," I said.

"Hell yeah," hooted the other drunk, making sure I knew he was still there ready to fight me.

It wasn't poker. It was Colonies. And a million dollars. That's a lot of money. Life-changing money.

CHAPTER THIRTY-TWO

I stumbled into the lobby the next morning at half-past eleven. The hotel was packed. I put the patrons' average age at nineteen, two years shy of legally entering the casino. But they weren't here to gamble. They were there to celebrate a computer game Vegas hadn't figured out how to exploit yet beyond hosting.

The tournament was part competition, part convention, part trade show, total geek fest. Unlike Sci-Fi conventions I'd been to growing up, there were females here. Amid the scores of husky, black T-shirted males strolled a slender eighteen-year-old beauty in a blue monocle, brass brazier, and burgundy velvet skirt. Her midriff was exposed and shapely, a silver ring looped through her belly button. I recognized the style: Steampunk. I didn't know how it fit with the tournament, but I didn't care. Along with the rest of the panting males in the hotel, I was just happy to look at her.

I bought a weekend pass at the door. My credit card still worked. That was either encouraging or threatening, depending on how far I let my paranoia run.

I followed the crowds along a hallway lined with new game vendors, used-game vendors, special-edition game vendors, T-shirt vendors, button vendors, accessory vendors, gold-coated cable vendors, book vendors, Futurama figurine vendors, and a table offering free deodorant to all attendees. If you've ever been to a fantasy convention, you'll recognize the need for the last thing.

Walking behind the flow of stinky people too proud to accept gifts, I shuffled into the auditorium. It was massive. I may have seen a boxing match broadcast from here on TV once. It hadn't done it justice.

Rows of seats descended into a basement amphitheater where, upon a raised dais, two computer stations stood. Announcers sat on the floor, their backs to the platform. They wore microphoned headsets and looked into cameras that televised them onto a giant four-faced JumboTron hanging over the platform like a suspended Borg ship mid-crash. Other displays hung from the ceiling at strategic viewing locations to offer a clear picture of what was happening below. The resolution was impressive. There wasn't a bad seat in the house, but I didn't know what there was to look at. Two guys sitting at computers wouldn't be interesting, no matter how clearly you could see their swollen pores.

It was open seating in the bowl. Floor seating was reserved and came with special tickets. My drunken van friends were probably down there. I found a place close to a door where I could see and still be able to exit quickly. Interpol was nearby, dragging their nets.

The cube displayed towering fifteen-foot faces of an Asian man with narrow black glasses talking to a Californian punk, who sported bleached hair teased into three-inch spikes.

"With the newest patch only a week old," said the blond, "it's anyone's guess who'll come out on top."

"Nachozman was heavily favored before the patch," said the Asian in English too precise to be his native tongue. "But he nearly didn't make the qualifier and plays today as a wild card."

"Goin' to be some amazing matches," encouraged the punk.

"Yes, they will be very exciting," agreed the Asian.

Typical sportscaster time-filling, dribble banter. E-sports had promise.

The first game featured Nachozman against a kid so young he needed a hall pass to reach the dais. His name was PekatchooDrone.

The players took the stage at opposite computers. A ring man in a black and white striped referee shirt went over the rules like before a prizefight.

"These matches are best of three," he said. "Players will be wearing noise-canceling headphones throughout the games to aid their concentration and to keep out any information from the crowd or commentators. Nachozman will play Lizard and PekatchooDrone will play Spiders. Let's get ready to Colonize!" he yelled.

The screen changed from close-ups of the contenders to game display. The players were boxed in a corner of the screen. Numbers appeared and counted down from ten to one, and suddenly the game was on. The crowd cheered.

What the audience saw was not what the players saw. The commentators controlled the view and had full access to the battlefield. They popped around it, examining each player's moves, tactics, and outcomes.

Nachozman's eggs hatched before the spider cocoons, and his economy was better, having absorbed more "fungus" than PekatchooDrone. Several lizards went "jungling" for a while until they morphed into "Greater Biters" and set a picket around the spider nest.

Hoards of little spiders—a cloud of them—fell upon the lizards, but were quickly dispatched. The lizards moved to invade the nest and were caught in a web, while several mother spiders ripped them to shreds in animated gore.

Meanwhile, some of the lizards had evolved wings and began a circuitous trek around the map to attack the spider nest from an unguarded quadrant. An invisible spider crept into the Lizard base and saw the wing evolution, and all hell broke loose at the spider's base. Web barrier defenses were frantically thrown up around the unfortified perimeter, using up much of his fungus in the process.

Several flying lizards, appropriately called "dragons," got caught in the webs and were killed, making the rest retreat to harass worker spiders foraging for fungus.

Eventually, a giant tarantula spawned from an orange cocoon and dominated the screen. Clouds of little spiders, like the ones eaten earlier, floated around it as a cloud creeping across the map. Lizard scouts saw it coming. When it was halfway there, a reinforced squadron of dragons gnawed through the webbing and attacked the main base.

The behemoth spider hesitated for a moment as the young player weighed defense verses offense and finally pressed forward.

"It's a base race!" exclaimed the announcers. The crowd went wild. Images of spider buildings under assault from dragons on one side were shown split-screen next to spiders swarming over lizard architecture. The battle raged. The crowd cheered.

Suddenly, a hole opened beneath the orange spider, and a swarm of writhing snakes appeared and fastened onto it. The spider was taken down in short order, and the attack was over. At the spider nest, two remaining dragons destroyed the last building, but the game didn't end.

"Nachozman has to find the spider expansion quickly if he's going to win this. It's not over yet," exclaimed an announcer.

Indeed, the spider had set up a second base in the forest. Frantically, the lizards spread out in a picket, searching for the secret base.

"It's all in now," said the Asian. "If PekatchooDrone can spawn his cocoons, Nachozman is done."

A phalanx of six-legged alligators found the nest and immediately chewed on the unhatched spiders seconds before they hatched.

"GG" appeared on the screen in webbed letters as PekatchooDrone surrendered the first game.

The reply, "GG," was in scaly letters.

The game was exciting. It took only eleven and a half minutes, a middle-length game, I learned. The announcers admired how Nachozman had resorted to his "old school" methods of early harassment and wings to carry the day.

There was something to this game, I realized. I always understood how people liked to play games like Colonies, but now I understood why people would pay money to watch other people play them. It was cool.

I stayed for the rest of the match. Nachozman lost the next one in an epic forty-five-minute affair, during which every unit had been evolved, every possible base had been colonized, and all the fungus harvested. After all that, it came down to three lizards versus six spiders, the lizards winning until a final web slowed them enough for the ranged venom strikes to take them down. Nachozman surrendered.

The last game was only four minutes. PekatchooDrone had gone for fungus while his opponent had made soldiers and emptied his base in the attack. It was over before everyone got back from the bathroom. Nachozman—the underdog, wild card, old-school player, advanced. Somehow that made me feel good. Yep, it was a sport.

I left after that to explore. I found a full-color, forty-eight-page program of ads at the information booth for a mere twelve dollars. Seemed reasonable; there was a pizza coupon on page sixteen.

I found breakfast in the hotel café and perused the program. The tournament brackets were listed along with projected start times for each match up. A map of the tournament venue showed several other rooms where games were being played besides the big arena. Only the special matches were in the auditorium. I recognized the brackets format from office basketball betting. Attendees could fill in the diminishing tree to the finals if they had a pen, which I doubt many attendees had, having forgone them for keyboards long ago.

In the Blue bracket, RexingBall was facing NoodleBite in the Macau Room in an hour. What a splendid coincidence, I thought. But how could Rose have known that Rex would make it this far? He had barely made the cut earlier in the week. The coincidence was too great. And then there was Mudge. Another splendid coincidence to grind my little gray cells.

As if I needed another coincidence, a full-color ad on page twenty-seven gobsmacked me upside the head with a picture of an ice castle I'd visited the week before: "Chronoboost, Inc., Headquarters in Utah," read the caption. While the waitress ruined my perfectly tailored sweet and creamy coffee with a free black tar refill, I read how Chronoboost was one of the many software subcontractors employed by Stormfront, the makers of Colonies. The company had a table in one of the halls. I left my ruined coffee in search of the Chronoboost table.

I found it in a room of vendors by a framed picture of their blue building as if their leased office proved some technological achievement. I didn't see Justin, but the man sitting there was familiar. It was the black guy who'd told me to fuck off in a stress-induced rage when I asked after Justin. He seemed calmer now.

The man's name tag said "SlyStack." I remembered his cubicle had said "Mallory."

"Are you playing in the tourney? I assume that's your username on your tag."

"I'll get in a few games, but I'm not in the tournament."

"Tough competition," I said.

"You can say that again. Even if I was good enough, I couldn't compete professionally. Conflict of interest and all that."

"You had to sign something?"

"Everyone does. It's industry standard."

"You don't remember me do you?"

"No," he said. "Haven't a clue."

"We met last week. I visited Chronoboost, the most secure software company in the world, and asked you about Justin. You told me to fuck off."

"Did you?"

"I left you alone, if that's what you mean. But I haven't been laid in fourteen months." I knew this because I'd calculated it that morning after dreaming of the woman at Caesar's. Nancy told me the date before jail, and I'd added the weeks after that to arrive at fourteen months, give or take a few hours. It had been the longest dry spell in my adult life and made me easily distracted by Steampunk beauties, Caribbean queens, and liquor store retailers.

"Bummer," he said. "Sorry I was rude."

"No worries," I said. "So where's Justin? Watching the games?"

"No, he's back in Provo."

"He's not here?"

"That's what 'back in Provo' means. Not here. Not in Las Vegas. Provo is in Utah, you see, so he's probably in Utah." I was happy he'd overcome his grief at being rude to me before.

"Why didn't he come?"

"Justin is a junior programmer," SlyStack explained as if I were simple. "He doesn't get to go to things like this."

"I thought his work was integral to the Stormfront account."

"No," he said.

"But he was helpful in the project, right? For the new patch?"

"So was the pizza guy," he said, "if you broaden your scope of helpfulness wide enough."

"He didn't design anything meaningful?"

"He copied and pasted old code into the new patch," he said. "Why are you interested? What are you getting at?"

"Nothing," I said. "I guess I got the wrong impression of what Justin did. It would seem he was bragging."

"I wouldn't put it past that pasty-faced kid for a second."

"Is he paid well?"

"He told you he was, huh? None of us are paid well," he said. "But I'm paid a hell of a lot more than he is, and I'm not rich. Seniority counts and responsibility counts. Justin has neither."

I shook my head and rolled my eyes in disgust. SlyStack shook his head in sympathy. His low opinion of Justin reflecting on me.

I left the Chronoboost table for the Guild Rooms, relieved I hadn't run into Justin. I felt like I was standing in the middle of cyclone, witches and houses and faces I knew whirling around me in unmatched, furious clutter, morphing into new characters. I didn't think I could handle another coincidence right then. I was wrong.

There was Calvin strolling up the crowded hallway, his pierced lip glittering in the light of the stained glass sconces. His tattoo was on full display with his hair tucked behind his ear. His arm was around a tanned, blue-eyed brunette in a yellow sundress and sandals. It wasn't Tonya. I stopped and stared. He didn't see me until he walked into me.

"Watch where you're going," he said, and then recognized me. His face went white, and he withdrew his arm from the girl with a whip-like snap.

"What are you doing here?" he demanded.

I glanced at the gum-chewing brunette who popped a bubble the size of a softball before smacking it back into her mouth. She looked at me and then Calvin and popped another bubble.

"Checking things out," I said coolly, but my mind was racing to fit this new data into a plausible theory.

"Me too," said Calvin.

I admired his torn jeans and sleeveless Tony Hawk T-shirt.

"So have you found the killer yet?" he said. I don't think he intended to be so blunt, but I'd flustered him.

"What killerrr?" asked the brunette, holding the last syllable just long enough so no one mistook her for an intellectual.

"I'll tell you later," Calvin said to her.

She popped another bubble.

"No, actually, I haven't," I said. "I'm still looking. Do you have any leads for me?"

"No."

"How about Tonya? Is she here? I'd like to talk to her again."

"Who's Tonyaaaa?"

"A mutual friend," Calvin said directly to me, accented with a wink. "No. She's back home. Couldn't get off work. She's not into this shit anyway."

The crowd surged. A match had finished, and the hall flooded with people. We were pressed together.

"Are you in the tournament?" I asked Calvin.

"No. Just chillin'."

"And you?" I asked the brunette.

"Am I what?"

"In the tournament?"

"No wayyy," she said. "This is just too nerdyyy."

People pushed around us. We weren't moving with the flow. The crowd pressed in. I had to fight to keep from moving with them. Calvin stood there uncomfortably. The brunette was confused. She looked used to it.

The space between us shrank as each passerby nudged us toward the lobby.

I was pushed forward and nearly off my feet. A sudden sharp pain stuck my left butt cheek, and I spun around to see who did it. The moment I shifted my spot, the throng surged with purpose past me.

"What the hell is that?" said Calvin, pointing to my ass.

"My ass," I said. "Some prick stuck me with a hot pin to get me to move."

"That's not a pin," said the brunette. "It's some kind of a shot thingeyyy."

I reached around and felt something hanging from my pants.

"She's right," Calvin said. "It's a hypo. It's broken."

I felt dizzy and grabbed Calvin's shoulder for support.

"Be a dear and pull it out for me won't you?" I said.

He reached around, and I felt a needle slip out of my muscle. He held it in front of me. I tried to focus on it, but my vision blurred. Sweat erupted all over my body like I was a squeezed wet sponge.

"Do you have diabetes?" Calvin said.

"What?" I heard myself say, and then saw myself at senior prom in my father's car, willing the courage to approach Natalie Connor's front door with a bouquet of flowers big as an umbrella.

I felt myself fall in a dream and then the liberation of a single shoe sliding off. The toe-wiggling freedom was quickly replaced by a burning at my heel. I had a bullet scab there, I remembered, and I felt it scrape off on the barbwire fencepost at my uncle's farm. I think it hurt. But I had worse problems.

Natalie Connor was allergic to flowers. Every spring and summer she had to go to a special clinic for shots or live in a plastic tent. I didn't know that. I only knew her father took one look at me, one at the flowers, and ripped them from my hand. He hucked them halfway to my dad's car. I'd gripped them too tightly in my sweaty teenage eagerness, and a thorn ripped my palm open when he yanked them away.

Someone called for a soft drink. That wouldn't stop the bleeding. I needed a bandage. I sucked the wound and tasted blood, which turned to cola. My blood fizzed in my mouth and ran down my chin.

Natalie came to the doorway in her pink prom dress. It matched my baby-blue tuxedo. We'd be a cute couple. But my blood still ran down my hand and my face, and grew grainy and scabby in my mouth.

Her hands flew to her face when she saw the blood. "It might need stitches," she cried, drawing me into the house. Her father looked a lot like Calvin. He made me drink a glass of sugar water. I guess he was sorry for cutting my hand. He was only trying to protect Natalie. I'm sure he was also worried about my intentions with his daughter. Any father would be. He didn't know she'd already lost her virginity to Scotty Patrickson the summer before. Scotty told me about it. I think he also mentioned the flowers thing. I must have forgotten about that.

CHAPTER THIRTY-THREE

I can't say I woke up in the hospital because I don't think I ever went to sleep. I paraded through a history of high-school humiliations scattered among visions of paramedics and casino ceilings. I failed my first driving test in an ambulance, and farted in French class while some guy told me to hang in there. I threw up in the cafeteria, and watched the walls change from Ms. Steinman's algebra class to hospital room, then back again. When the hospital lingered long enough for me to find purchase, I forced myself out of teenage angst and into adult recovery.

I was flat on my back, naked except for a narrow cloth over my privates, which meant I was still naked, just not exposed. The room was brightly lit. Tubes led from my arm to plastic bags hanging on a steel arm attached to the bed. A white wired clothespin pinched one finger. A plastic tube ran under my nose and tickled it. My heel hurt and my ass hurt, and I had a headache that made other headaches scared.

A tanned woman with straight black hair, ebony eyes, and a lab coat strolled in like she was running an hour behind.

"Mr. Flaner," she said in a British accent, "good to see you awake."

"Namaste," I said.

"Namaste," she replied. "How do you feel?"

"Pain in my ass, head, and heel."

"That's to be expected. I'll get you something for it." She leaned forward and pulled at my eyelids.

"So," I said slowly. "Who are you?"

"I'm Dr. Singh," she said.

"And why am I here?"

"Hypoglycemia," she said.

"I think I was stabbed," I said. "I'm not hypoglycemic."

"You were after a shot of insulin," she said. "Which makes this a crime."

"Crime?"

"Unless there's some plausible explanation for you backing into an insulin syringe, I'd say someone tried to kill you."

"With insulin? That's a good thing isn't it?"

"If you need it, it is. If you don't, it's deadly in large doses. It drove all your sugar into your cells. Starved your brain. Did you hallucinate?"

"Oh yeah."

"You're lucky to be alive. Two things saved you. First, the needle broke before the entire syringe was emptied. Second, your friend has some experience with diabetics and knew to get you sugar. He saved your life."

"Shit."

"Pepsi, but close enough," she said. "Insulin overdose is a bad way to die. It's hard to detect even post-mortem."

"So, what now?"

"You're through it. We'll keep you one more night and you can go home tomorrow."

"I think I want to leave now," I said.

"That would not be advisable," she said. "And there's a policeman who wants to talk to you. Also a hotel detective."

"I don't think I want to talk to the police," I said.

"I can't keep you," she said. "Do you want to see your friend?"

"I have a friend? Yeah, send him up."

"Good luck, Mr. Flaner," she said, turning to go.

"Doctor," I said. "Where does one get a syringe full of insulin?"

"They're very common: hospitals, pharmacies, clinics. Some hotels keep some on hand for emergencies."

"Okay," I said.

"Good luck," she said. "I'll send a nurse to unhook you."

I tried to think of this as a new clue, the way Marlowe or Mike

Hammer would know they were getting close when someone took a shot at them. Someone had taken a shot at me, but instead of busting a cap in my ass, they'd broken a needle in it. Intellectually, I was excited. Emotionally, I was scared. Things were getting worse, as Mollif would have pointed out. I was deeper into the trap than ever and about to go further still under the metaphorical direction of a Chinese paper puzzle.

Calvin poked his head in the door, his hands in his pockets. "Dude, you okay?"

"Calvin, I think you're my new best friend. How'd you know what to do?"

"My mom takes insulin. I've seen it before."

"That was lucky."

He shrugged. "Someone tried to kill you, didn't they?"

"Looks like," I said. "See if my clothes are anywhere. I need to get out of here."

He went to a cabinet and threw open the doors. "Do you think they'll try and kill you again? Is that why you're leaving so fast?" He didn't seem fazed by my instructions or plan. My respect for Calvin rose as he showed levels of complexity belied by his choice of girlfriends.

"To be honest, Calvin," I said, "I'm on the run. They revoked my bail for talking to Patricia."

"Just for that? Why?"

"That and burglary. But mostly for trying to mess up their case against me. I don't want to talk to cops right now."

"I made a report," he said.

"That's good. And you saved my life, which means I'm honor-bound not to suspect you."

"Me? For what? For trying to kill you?"

"Me, Rose, JFK, whoever," I said. "Where's my shoe?"

"We lost it at the hotel when we dragged you away. Why would you suspect me?"

"You're here, and this is where the clues have led me," I said. Calvin's eyes widened. "Don't worry. You're not alone. It's a regular suspects convention here. I got to get back."

A nurse came in and quietly removed the tubes from my arms. She made me sign a form stating unequivocally that I was a complete moron for going against the doctor's orders and leaving the hospital. I asked for a discreet elevator. The nurse raised an eyebrow, but showed us to the staff elevator, swiped her card, and pushed "lobby" for us.

Calvin drove us back to the Rio in the mid-morning glare. I'd been forty-two hours in the hospital—over a day and a half. Quick work for near death, I figured, but there went my Vegas getaway.

"I'm here for the tournament. I didn't know anything about Rose's girl plans," Calvin said. "Tonya never mentioned it."

"Speaking of Tonya," I said. "I assume that what happens in Vegas should stay in Vegas?"

"Straight up."

"Straight up," I said.

We stopped for a new pair of shoes for me and a bottle of bourbon for Calvin. I didn't know how else to thank him.

"I was headed to the Guild Room when I ran into you," I said. "Where were you going?"

"I was showing Debby around. Nowhere in particular."

"What happened to Debby?"

"It got too intense for her. She bailed."

Calvin walked with me. It was like he felt responsible for me now and was afraid to let me go anywhere alone. He even followed me into the lavatory where he only washed his hands after checking the stalls.

We went down the hall where I'd been attacked. Several people recognized me and pointed, muttering to their friends.

"Guess it was quite a scene, huh?"

"Yep. Who's Natalie?"

"No comment."

The Guild Rooms were an array of booths decorated with hand-painted, plywood, heraldic devices and threatening images, each proclaiming their supreme dominance in the virtual world of Colonies. I recognized only one, the Wreckers, Rex Merkin's guild.

"Are these all the guilds in the country?" I asked.

"Hell no," Calvin said. "These are only the ones with players in the tournament. Most players don't have guilds."

At the Wrecker's booth, there was a skinny guy with an asthma inhaler and the boy who'd always be known to me as the guy who had attached wires to his testicles.

"Beat it, Calvin," he said as we approached. "Arsonists didn't make the cut. Never will."

"Fuck you, Trent," said Calvin.

"Where's Rex?" I asked. "He's the only one from Utah to make it this far, isn't he?"

"Only one from the whole state."

"And by state, you mean Utah. Which is what I said."

"What are you, a smart-ass?"

"What are you, an idiot?"

"Good one," said the asthmatic. What a zinger.

"So where is he?"

"His match starts in fifteen. He's already made it to the quarters," the ball-charger boasted. "He's going all the way to Bangkok."

"Good to hear he's still in it," I said. "Shouldn't we all go cheer him on?"

The Wreckers didn't know what to do with my proffered camaraderie. I guess the schism between the two guilds ran deep. Jets and Sharks all over again, but without the dancing.

We left them scowling at us and went to the auditorium.

"Rex is a fluke," said Calvin. "It's a miracle he made it to this tournament. He's not that good. It's a fucking double miracle he's made it to the quarterfinals. I'll be happy to see him burn."

"But he's from Utah. Where's your loyalty?"

"You don't know Rex Merkin," he said. "He's a double fucktard with syrup."

"I met him."

The familiar e-sports casters were on the screen announcing the second quarterfinal match between RexingBall and Tichi. The screen showed a plump, curly-haired, nineteen-year-old with freckles take on a computer station. Behind him came the familiar silver dome of Rex Merkin. He wore a cheap, silkscreened, green jacket that hung on him like a towel on a shower rod. The announcers commented on it.

"RexingBall is serious," said the Asian. "He already has sponsorship."

The camera followed him up the stairs to the platform. The back of Rex's windbreaker read "GBM LLC WTF LOL."

"What's with the sponsor?" I said to Calvin.

"Hell if I know," he said. "Maybe he needed money to make the trip."

"LLC is Limited Liability Company, a corporation," I said. "Do you know what the other stuff means?"

"WTF is 'what the fuck;' LOL is 'laugh out loud.' Internet slang. Don't know the other. I'll check the net."

He produced a smartphone like Randy's and Googled as the match started.

"RexingBall is a surprise newcomer," said the Asian announcer.

"He has skills," droned the spiky-haired blond. "But will they be enough?"

"He's the oldest player in the tournament by four years," said his companion, reading something off a laptop. "If he wins here in Las Vegas, he'll be the oldest player in Thailand as well."

"He has skills."

"It's not internet slang," said Calvin. "The Urban Dictionary didn't know it, so it's something else."

The game was relatively short. Rex fought off an early rush by the skin of his teeth and then built up his forces with singular intensity. In a matter of minutes, he was out-harvesting his opponent, spending fungus resources to build a single, unstoppable attack force that jumped through the jungle in ever-reinforced steps until he overwhelmed Tichi's main base. GGs were exchanged, and they set up for the next match.

"That was impressive," I said. "He's got skills."

"Lucky," said Calvin. "I don't know how he survived that initial push. He should have been barbecued by the flamethrowers. Watch. He'll lose the next one."

He didn't. Rex built up a defense early this time and was ready for the early rush that never came. Meanwhile, both players moved to expand without confrontation. Fifteen minutes into the game, Rex moved out, but was flanked by Tichi. The battle was fast and furious. The commentators went nuts at the number of units being lost on both sides. They wrote Rex out of the game the instant it began, but admired his spirit in fighting on. At the end of the fight, only Rex had surviving units. Tichi GG'd and they shook hands.

"Fuck," said Calvin. "How'd he do that?"

"He outplayed him," I echoed. "He's got skills."

"I guess," said Calvin, shaking his head in disgust.

They proclaimed RexingBall the winner and set up for the next match. We were told that all tournament games would be posted online before midnight, thanks to their technical sponsors.

I had nowhere to go, and walking made my heel hurt, my ass hurt, and my head hurt. I found a twelve-dollar program on the floor.

"Wait. The winner gets only a quarter-million dollars?" I said. "Two hundred and fifty thousand? Second place gets one hundred thousand and third only seventy-five thousand dollars? How're they calling this a million dollar prize pool?"

"Don't know. Seems kinda low."

I found it in the small print. All participants won a shopping gift certificate to Stormfront's online store, where they sold games and accessories. The winners also received first class round-trip airfare to Bangkok, luxury accommodations, and guaranteed prizes there. Put all that together, along with a free order of Crazy Bread and a Big Gulp, and some accountant had come up with one million dollars.

Spiders fought birds on the big screen. Birds dove and circled around an advancing goose bump-raising army. Occasionally a spider pulled a bird out of the air and fed on it. The crowd cheered. It chewed.

I was working on the assumption that the life-changing money Rose had mentioned might have been a share of the winnings, but two hundred thousand wasn't life changing. It was a lot, but not that much.

"How much is the world prize?" I asked Calvin.

"Don't know."

"Look it up," I said. "On your phone."

The game raged on. Calvin didn't appreciate the distraction, but pushed the requisite buttons anyway.

After a moment, he said, "One hundred million for the winner."

"What?"

"Sorry, one hundred million Baht. That's Thai currency." He punched more buttons.

"It's about three million dollars," he said.

"That's life changing," I said.

"I'd take it."

The first game ended with the traditional GGs, one feathered, the other webbed. They went immediately into the second game on a new map.

"Calvin," I said tentatively, knowing every syllable I uttered interrupted his viewing enjoyment. "Is it possible to cheat at Colonies?"

"I don't see how," he said. "It's a computer game."

"Is it possible?"

"No. Everyone has the same program, the same patch, the same version and all that. There may be people who have a special keyboard at home, but at tournaments, the computers are exactly the same."

"Has it ever been tried?"

"I once heard about a guy in Maine who set up a bot, a kind of mini-program that fixed pairings, but Stormfront came down hard. Altered games can't access their servers. So if you hack it locally on your home computer, you can never go online. And that could never happen in a tournament. There's no getting to the program, and the servers would cut the connection if there was any deviation in copies. It's pretty tight."

Calvin looked at his watch and said, "I've got to head out. I've got work tomorrow and a drive."

"Go ahead, dude," I said. "I'm good."

"Nothing to Tonya, remember?"

"It's all good."

It had been silly to have him hovering over me like a mama hen, but once he left, I felt a tremor of fear and vulnerability.

I felt exposed, so I went to my room.

A bulging, black ex-boxer with cropped hair and a business suit sat on my hotel bed. He responded calmly to my screaming retreat into the hall.

"Mr. Flaner. Calm down. I'm Mr. Tennin, hotel detective." He held up an identification card. "I want to talk to you about the incident Friday."

"Are you allowed to just come into my room like this?" I said.

"Yes."

"Well? Okay then."

The interview was short. He apologized for the scare and said he'd missed me at the hospital and wanted to know the facts about my assault. After a while, I calmed down and entered the room. I told him what I remembered, which was a hell of a lot less than what Calvin had already told him.

He took notes, acted concerned, and went out of his way to assure me that such things are unheard of in modern Vegas. He lied well. He probed the likelihood of a lawsuit against the hotel. When I forgave him and his hotel, he relaxed, apologized, and comped my room. He even gave me a voucher for another weekend.

"There's a policeman that wants a statement from me, too," I said. "Could you get with him and tell him what I told you. I'd rather not be bothered."

"Not a problem, Mr. Flaner," he said. "I'll take care of it."

Vegas—where hotel cops trumped real ones.

As much as I was tempted to feed off the free buffet and trash my comped room for a week, I had to get back to Utah. I needed to find Mudge, and I knew where he lived.

But first I watched RexingBall go up against Malixxx for the big prize in the best of five.

The match went four games. Malixxx accepted Rex's GG and was crowned the North American champion. I was confused.

The announcers congratulated the winners. Both Malixxx and Rex, along with an alternate would be competing in Bangkok next week for the World title. A bikini-clad, artificially-endowed, ex-stripper presented the winners with oversized checks and gave them each a big wet kiss on the mouth which raised a roar in the pubescent hall.

The lights came up, and the crowd milled away. Meanwhile, in a post-game show that would appear on the net along with all the weekend's games, the commentators recapped the tournament and speculated on the Americans' chances in Thailand.

"The American team has skills, but they have no chance to win," said the American.

"Afraid not, but that's not the point," said the Asian. "If they make a good showing, maybe eighth place or so, America will be well represented."

"They have skills."

CHAPTER THIRTY-FOUR

"You think a lot of yourself, don't you?"

"It was just a question," I said.

Morris Mollif sighed. "You're making things worse, that's all. Yes, the police will arrest you if they find you. But no, there isn't a special task force in hot pursuit of you. You're not that important."

"But they know I'm on the run?"

"Ganesh Lahkpa reported your flight and tampering with your ankle bracelet. He also started a claim against you for damages."

"For what?"

"Something about a trash can."

"Typical."

"So are you coming in?"

"No. But I am coming back."

"Where have you been?" asked Mollif. "You didn't leave the state, did you?"

"Uh, no?"

"Good, because if they can prove that you left the state, you'll be facing interstate flight charges on top of everything else."

"So it's a good thing I didn't leave the state, go to Vegas, get assaulted—nearly murdered, make an official statement about it to a hotel detective, and then, through him, to the Clark County Sheriff's Department?"

"Yeah, it's good that didn't happen. That would be bad."

"Medical records proving I was there?"

"Good thing those don't exist," he said.

"Cool," I said, feeling myself slide deeper into the trap. "Do you have any good news?"

"Actually, Tony, I do," my reluctant attorney said. "The toxicology reports came back."

"Toxicology report?"

"There was one for the victim in the prosecutor's file. You said a medic treated you."

"And?"

"The medic took blood samples from you then. I don't know if he was told to or did it on his own, but it's a lucky break for us. I chased the medic down and found the report. Your system was swimming with tranquilizers. With an expert witness, I can prove, as far as anything can be—which isn't always enough—that you were unconscious at the time of the killing. The metabolic breakdown is conclusive, according to my sources."

"That's good," I said.

"Problem is, the prosecution will try to deny the report, attack the witness, and then claim you took the drugs yourself after killing Rose. They might claim you have a tolerance or otherwise faked the metabolites."

"That's pretty far-fetched."

"Count on it. Evidence doesn't always get admitted, or understood. Where's your cell phone?"

I was calling from a pay phone. "I left it at the house. Is my house being watched, do you know?"

"Might be. Ganesh is motivated."

"I'll be careful," I said.

"Tony, you don't have long. Do whatever you have to do fast. Do you have any leads?"

"It's a nest of snakes," I said. "Nothing straight yet."

"Were you really attacked in Vegas? Someone tried to kill you?"

"Looks that way."

"Why don't you come in, Tony? I've got enough for reasonable doubt."

"Nope. Thanks. Talk to you later."

I hung up the phone and stepped into the heat of a Saint George gas station parking lot. I'd stayed at a motel on the Utah side of the border and had a cheap, heart-clogging breakfast in a café that smelled of burned coffee, diesel fuel, and unbathed men before calling Mollif.

I stopped only once driving home for gas and a life-scarring adventure into an unattended bathroom on I-15. I drove by my house three times before deciding it was safe. I clicked the garage door opener and slipped in before it had finished opening. I was in the house behind a locked door before it shut.

I held my gun in both hands, barrel pointing upward. Keeping my back to the wall, I slid around the doorway, like Starsky—or was it Hutch? I snapped around the corner, pointing the gun out in front of me in a braced wide-stance shooting posture. I surveyed my living room. Nothing worth shooting, I decided. If I thought my back could have stood it, I'd have done a Shatner roll to the kitchen; instead, I just tiptoed. Another TJ Hooker pistol-wave cop-pantomime and it was clear. I kept up the belligerent gun brandishing act into the bedroom, bathroom, and study. By the time I checked the basement, the gun dangled one-handed at my side. It was holstered when I came back upstairs.

No one had been there as far as I could tell. My legal papers were as I'd left them, my bed as unmade as before, my boxes still strategically pushed out of the flow of traffic. I found my cell phone in the bathroom beside the toilet where I'd forgotten it. I had several messages. The battery light flashed on the screen for one instructive instant, and then the entire gadget went dark.

My dead cell phone number was on my "I did not kill Rose Griff" business cards. Any leads would land there.

I plugged the phone into a charger, showered, and changed. I had a bruise on my ass where the needle had gone in. My heel was also complaining. The scab over the gunshot wound had been torn off, and it'd bled into my sock though the unchanged hospital bandage. I only had finger Band-Aids. I wove them into a net and stuck it on my heel before carefully pulling a new white sock over it.

I checked all the bolts and windows before sitting down at my computer and calling up corporate listings in a dark-curtained room.

GBM LLC was a current, privately-owned, limited-liability company located in Utah. It was created three months ago, and it had no public offices. The bylaws were the standard minimum requirement produced automatically online. The stated purpose for existence was "sponsorship." It was a for-profit corporation, so they expected money to come in. The LLC's contact address, phone number, and board of directors were all part of Smith, Bannon and Taylor, attorneys at law. Rebecca Taylor was both president and reporting officer. Their office was suite 307D in a small business park in a medium income corner of a dying suburb.

I called the law firm and asked to speak with Rebecca Taylor. The receptionist challenged my reason for calling. I said I needed her A.S.A.P. about BGM LLC O.K., FFS?

I was put on hold where a saccharin remake of "Last Train to Clarksville" upset my digestion.

A curt voice met me at the station. "This is Ms. Taylor," it said.

"Hello, Ms. Taylor. I'm calling about the BGM LLC. I was hoping you could tell me about it." Again, too late, I realized I had no idea how I was going to manage this call.

"Who is this?"

"I saw the name at the National Colonies tournament in Las Vegas and wanted to know what it means."

"I have no comment," she said.

"What? Why? The man who your corporation sponsored came in second. He's going on to the world championship. Doesn't that merit a press release, at least?"

"Really? Second place? I hadn't heard. But I can't comment. BGM is a privately held company and doesn't seek publicity."

"Can I quote you?" I was a reporter. Smooth move, Tony. Score one for winging it.

"No. No comment."

"Does BGM sponsor other Colonies players or other games?"

"No," she said, then corrected herself. "No comment."

"I don't understand all the secrecy. You make it sound like you're hiding something."

"We have nothing to hide. I just can't tell you anything without approval from the board."

"Who's on the board?"

"Give me your name and number. I'll contact the principals and see how they want to proceed," she said.

"My name's Easy Marlowe," I said and immediately regretted it. If she read any crime fiction at all, I was busted. Winging it fail. I gave her my cell number, and she hung up without a goodbye.

My next call required me to hide my phone number. I called my cell phone carrier first to find out how to do that. They gave me the series of commands, and I dutifully made the call.

With another jolt, I realized I had again made a call without planning first.

"Fuck," I said.

"Hello?" came the hated, familiar voice. "Did you just say 'fuck?'"

"Sorry," I said in a deep voice.

"Who is this?"

"I'm calling about some special wine. I'm told you can get me some?"

"Who gave you this number?" said Leafcaller.

"I was sworn to secrecy." I sounded like I was choking on a potato.

"What's your name?"

"Mr. Smith." The potato slid lower into my esophagus.

"It's pricey. If I can lay my hands on any, they'd be a thousand dollars a bottle."

"I want four." I was full-on Jabba the Hutt.

"Where are you?"

"I'm in Salt Lake City, but I can be in Las Vegas by tomorrow."

"No, Salt Lake City is good. I'm in Salt Lake now. Give me your number, and I'll call you back when I have some."

"I better call you. When can we meet?"

"Call me around nine, and I'll see what I can find."

"Okay," I gargled and hung up.

I was working a plan to meet Mudge outside of my old house and confront him. Maybe he'd put up a fight, and I'd get to beat him senseless until he talked, maybe even if he talked, while he was talking, and then some more after he had finished. This was my best plan yet. The reptile and Neanderthal inside me applauded wildly.

I was ready to leave when there was a knock on the door.

I crawled to the curtains and peeked out. I saw a tan SUV parked in my driveway, blue plastic streaks on the bumper.

On hands and knees, I went to the bedroom and collected my burglar bag. I headed to the back porch, positive they were going to kick in the front door any second.

I turned the corner in the living room and froze. A man was on the back porch. He cast a clear shadow on the drapes. His hands were cupped around his eyes and his face was pressed to the glass. The curtains were drawn, but there may have been gaps.

I dashed back the way I came and fell to the ground. I made a noise. It was muffled—soft belly on soft carpet—but I'd heard it and was pants-pissing scared they had, too.

I held my breath and listened to the knocking and bell ringing. Then the phone rang. I let it ring. Then my cell phone rang, and I let it ring.

Though freethinking infidel scientists would say it was only ten minutes, it was a lifetime later when I heard the SUV finally pull away.

I wasted no time. I threw my refilled suitcase and burglar bag in the backseat of my car and was on the street before you could say, "Run for your life."

A lead had been niggling me, if that's a word, and I figured then was as good a time as any to follow up on it.

I parked near the Sailor, up against a wall, beside a rotting wooden fence and a heaping garbage pile. The place offered a greater-than-average chance for a car break-in, driver mugging, or terminator arrival. I took my chances.

I walked swiftly into the Sailor. I planted myself in a back booth on the wall with the kitchen door to my right and a good view of the entire place. The detective table, I decided. I ordered a club soda and tipped generously. I watched and waited.

Patricia came on duty thirty minutes later. She didn't notice me for another ten; when she did, she stomped straight to my table and hovered over me with her arms on her waist, looking like an angry nanny.

"What do you want?" she demanded.

"I need to talk to you again," I whispered.

"The cops were by. You know they're looking for you? They told me to call if I saw you."

"But you don't see me, right? I mean, it might be me, but it might not be, right? Right? Right?"

"Wrong." She turned to go.

"It's about Simon," I said to her back. "I need to ask you about Simon."

She turned back. My innocent face was ready, but my hips were angled toward the kitchen door.

"Give me five minutes," she said and left.

Since I'd arrived, a third of the tables had been occupied and more people were streaming in. They were mostly men, but some female couples drank fruity drinks, while men dressed as women enjoyed even fruitier ones. I sipped my club soda and waited.

I thought Patricia and I had ended on good terms, but the police had shaken her faith. I watched her like the jittery fugitive detective I was. I didn't see her pick up a phone, but when she went in the back room I lost sight of her for five excruciating minutes. I imagined SWAT team commandos taking up sniper positions in nearby buildings while a hostage negotiator cleared his throat outside and put fresh batteries in his bullhorn.

She came back with an armful of bottles and set them on the counter before putting them behind the bar where they belonged. I pretended not to be nervous. I pretended I wasn't about to run through the kitchen door and out the back alley.

The waiter brought me another club soda and when he turned to go, a man was standing behind him.

"Hello," he said. "Remember me?"

I shook my head.

"My name is Pratt, Joshua Pratt. I saw you at the AA meeting last week."

"I don't remember you, but your name sounds familiar."

"I'm Joshua Pratt, junior."

"Wait. Are you related to the Mormon Joshua Pratt?"

He nodded unenthusiastically. "He's my father."

Joshua Pratt was a minor LDS luminary. He was in the high Mormon hierarchy somewhere, but I couldn't tell you where. Wherever it was, he wasn't satisfied with it. He wrote two books a year about faith, Mormonism, conservatism, and white male superiority, which I bet he thought made him a darling in the church. In my circles, he was a grinning symbol of intolerance, a desperate fame-hungry zealot with aspirations. I think he did a radio talk show, too.

"Hi," I said.

"May I sit down?"

"By all means. How's your dad?"

"Hell if I know."

"You're an atheist," I said. "He's gotta love that."

"He's better with that than with my homosexuality."

Spit-take. I blew club soda over the front of him.

"You didn't know?"

"Of course, I did. I'm a detective. I was putting out a fire. Your buttons were burning."

He wiped himself off with a napkin.

"Pat says you want to know about Simon. I know about Simon."

"Yeah."

He had a wistful air about him, a grim acceptance even a mouthful of warm, bubbly water couldn't move.

"Simon and I were a couple. We helped each other through some tough times."

"Did you know Rose Griff?"

"I knew her through Simon. He liked her, and so I liked her. She was killed, too, right?"

"Yeah, they think I did it." I waited for his surprise to fade. "Why do you say 'too?' I thought Simon committed suicide."

"He did. He hanged himself. When his family found out, it was bad—really bad. They made him confess before church leadership and promise to give up his life of sin. He couldn't. It shamed him so much, it killed him."

"Why'd he come out?"

"He didn't. Someone outed him. Someone sent an anonymous letter with a photo to his father at work."

"Who would do that?"

"I've thought a lot about it," Joshua said. Emotion cracked his voice. "Simon needed money before it happened. First, he needed five thousand dollars. He never told me why. He borrowed it, and then things were normal for a month. Then, he quietly said he needed ten thousand dollars more. He made it sound like he was behind on a payment, but didn't say for what. We were all strapped then though, and he couldn't get the money."

"Blackmail?"

"That's what I think now," he said. "About a week after he asked for the ten, he stopped coming to Salt Lake and stayed in Provo. He dropped out of school. I called him and knew something had happened. He wouldn't see me. Said it wasn't safe. I stayed away for two weeks—two weeks that must have been total hell for him. I finally snuck down and caught him after church. He told me that someone had outed him. He said it was someone we knew because no one else could have gotten close enough to take those pictures."

"Rose?"

"No," he said. "She's the one who gave him the five thousand."

"Dara?"

"You know a lot about our group," he said. "But no, I don't think it was Dara; she's half dyke herself."

"Was Rex around then?" Joshua's reaction told me all I needed to know. "You don't like him?"

"What's to like? His cheap gay bashing? The way he never picked up a check? The way he lorded his family money over us?" Joshua literally spat in disgust. The gesture surprised me, and I couldn't take my eyes off the spot on the floor. Talk about old school.

"I tolerated Rex because Simon did. Simon did it for Rose. I don't know what Rose saw in him."

"Rex had money," I said. "So it couldn't have been him."

"I heard he was cut off," Joshua said. "Survived on a minimum allowance. He had to work at a grocery to meet his expensive tastes."

I remembered the television and computer bay in Rex's apartment, the free beer and piles of pizza being consumed by his adoring fans, who didn't look like they had bus fare, let alone pizza money.

"Do you see much of Rex anymore?"

"I haven't seen him since Simon needed the first five thousand dollars," he said. "But if I do, I'd like it to be dark." Tears rolled down his cheeks. He sipped his drink, a rum and coke. I didn't know what to say.

After a minute, Joshua said, "I didn't hear about Simon's death for two days after it happened. That was the day I told my father, the great Joshua Pratt, Senior, that I was an atheist and a homosexual. I dared him to say a fucking word. I would not go quietly into my grave to save the family honor."

"And he's okay with that? Good on him."

"Hell no, he's not good with that. But we have an arrangement; I stay low, and he stays out of my life."

I sipped bubbly water.

"Didn't mean to dump all that on you," Joshua said. "I'm still raw over the whole thing."

"Understood," I said. "Thanks for telling me."

"You think this is related to Rose's death?"

"Honestly, I don't know, but Rex Merkin keeps blipping on my radar. I wasn't impressed by him, and no one else has a kind word to say about him."

"That's all?" he said.

"And he lied to me," I said. "And a couple other things I can't fit yet."

"Getting whoever outed Simon won't bring him back, but I'd like to think there's justice in the world."

"I haven't found much of it in the legal system," I said, "so the world is where we have to look for it."

It was eight o'clock. Time to think about Mudge.

"Do you know a guy called 'Leafcaller' or Hank Mudge?" I asked on a whim.

"Cruise ship gigolo?" he said. "I've heard of him. Used to work out of Uintah Travel before they were put out of business by the Internet. Don't know what he's doing now."

"He's fucking my ex-wife."

"Oh."

CHAPTER THIRTY-FIVE

I approached my car cautiously in case someone was lying in wait—or waiting to lie, as the case would be. Luckily, no one clubbed me with a tire iron or appeared in a lightning storm to find Sarah Connor. I stepped in and started it up. My phone rang. It was an unfamiliar number. I let it go to message. They left no message, but I had a few from the weekend I'd forgotten to check.

"You goddamn son of bitch." It was from my bail bondsman. He wasn't as friendly as before. "You think you so smart, you cocksucker. When I catch you, I'll beat you and feed you to tigers if you don't get your ugly asshole to my office this minute! I'm out big money if you fuck with me. I'll murder you and play football with your head!"

Next message. "Hello, Tony, this is Ganesh Lahkpa, your bail bondsman. I'm sorry about my call to you yesterday. I was having a very bad day. My wife and I are quarrelling, and it was ever so shameful of me to take out my own personal, emotional problems on an innocent man such as yourself. Please forgive me. I am so ashamed. It is important that we discuss changes in your case. The judge wants certain conditions, but just because the judge says something doesn't mean it can't be negotiated. Come to my office, and we'll discuss our options. I'm very confident we can keep you out of jail. No problem at all. Give me a call as soon as you get this message, and we'll arrange an appointment to get this all squared away."

Fat chance.

"Hey, Dad, it's me. I'm chillin.' I'm sick of Leafcaller. I'm jonesing for a cheeseburger. If you get this message before it's too late, come get me. I need meat."

"Hello, Mr. Flaner, just calling to make sure you made it home, and you're feeling okay and all that." It was Calvin. "And, uhm, I'd really appreciate it if you kept the whole Debby thing between us. You said you were good with that. And you should know, I guess, that Tonya found some ticket stubs in my wallet for that car museum in Vegas. Two tickets. I told her I went with you. If she calls, back me up, 'kay? Thanks, dude."

There was a hang up from a number I didn't recognize. It called again an hour later and hung up again without leaving a message.

"Hello, this is the gas company," said a hesitant male voice. "We're scheduled to check your house for code violations. Please be home on Monday at 10:00 a.m. to let us in. Thank you."

Fat chance.

"Tony, some men are looking for you," said Nancy. "An Indian fellow called. He seemed friendly, but I don't know. Then two large men came to the door and asked for you, too. What's going on?"

"Mr. Flaner, you'll be pleased to know that your name has been drawn in our Best Buy home entertainment center giveaway. You won a fifty-two inch LED flat screen TV, BluRay DVD player, and Bose speakers. To claim your prize be at the Best Buy on twenty-eighth South at exactly three o'clock today. If you're not there on time, we'll have to give your prizes to the second place winner. See you there."

Fat chance.

Another hang up. Same number as before. Then another an hour later. I checked the number. The hang up number was the same as the one I'd just ducked. It didn't match the Best Buy number or gas company number, which happened to be the same numbers. Go figure.

* * *

My old neighborhood was unchanged, but I found it alien and unwelcoming. My relationship to it had changed. I was an intruder now. I parked two blocks away in a church parking lot, under a tree, backed against a fence.

I needed to talk to Randy, but according to Facebook, Randy had lost his phone and was waiting for the new model coming out next week to get a new one. I didn't dare call the house or approach the door. Nancy thought I was crazy and acting out. Mudge might be the guy I was looking for. If I met either, I didn't think I'd see Randy.

I snuck through a neighbor's backyard. Nancy's house, my old one, was lit up like a jack-o-lantern.

I skulked along the fence by newly planted bushes and seasonal flowers. In the dark it was hard to see obstacles, so a garden gnome caught me square in the shin and dropped me on my face. I mumbled a curse into the back of my hand and wondered if the iron garden gnome was an ornament or a new security feature. I felt a lump on my leg start to swell.

There was movement inside. A shadow crossed the sliding door, and another moved in the kitchen. The upstairs was dark, but that was only the master bedroom from this side.

I glanced at my watch. It was exactly 8:30 p.m. A spike poked me in my crotch, and I rolled over just in time to see the one-eyed sprinkler take aim and spit at me. It hissed and then shot water in spurts, then streams, across the lawn. Nancy had changed the watering schedule. Only half drenched, I dashed to the side of the house.

Back in my day, before the organic reconstruction, I'd kept a door key hidden in the wall by the back door. It'd come in handy when I locked myself out of the house, a phenomena that happened with some regularity and which Nancy said was a defining characteristic of my existence. I didn't understand what she meant, and she said that was also a defining characteristic of my existence. If I was lucky, she'd neglected to change the backdoor lock, and if I was really lucky, she'd forgotten about that key. I wasn't lucky.

There had to be a key, though. Nancy had always been adamant that we have one for Randy, if not me.

Nancy appeared in the kitchen window, and I ducked behind a potted tree. I heard voices inside the house. Nancy was yelling for Randy to come down and eat. I couldn't see Mudge, but I sensed evil, so knew he was nearby.

The tree I hid behind was new, a maple with tiny leaves in a big pot. The planting tag was still on it. The tree cost three hundred dollars and had four pages of care instructions. It was three feet tall.

In the pot, at the base of the tree, sat a single plastic rock.

"You've got to be kidding," I said, picking it up, sliding open the compartment, and retrieving the backdoor key.

I saw my son go into the dining room followed by Nancy carrying a steaming casserole pan. I ran to the door.

In a moment, I was in the back hallway. I quietly took my shoes off. My wet socks were better than my muddy sneakers. Step by squishy step, drop by sprinkler-soaked drop, I tiptoed to the base of the stairs and then took them three at a time, lithe as a jaguar, silent as a shadow.

Still the ninja, I slipped into Randy's room and closed the door behind me. His room was messier than last time, but still cleaner than it ever was when I lived there. The stack of hard drives I'd noticed before was nearly gone. Only five remained. His computer was on. I sat down to wait.

The screensaver of ever-changing fractals dissolved to a desktop when I shifted the mouse. The revealed screen showed Randy's online banking page. He had eight thousand three-hundred twenty-two dollars and sixteen cents in an account I didn't know about, in a bank that wasn't in the country.

One of the new external hard drives was attached to the computer via a short, thick cable. A green light flickered on its case, and I could hear the quiet whirl of the internal mechanism.

I looked under the bank page and found a copying utility program. Randy's third hard drive was being mirrored to the external one. The third drive, called "Drive X-1" was full to its five-hundred-gigabyte capacity. "Time remaining for copy: Four minutes."

While I waited four minutes, I looked around my son's room with heightened curiosity. He had a closet full of cardboard mailing boxes and a bag of Styrofoam peanuts.

I smelled rank pasta, garlic, parsley, and what I imagined was over-ripe cauliflower, and wished I'd brought a cheeseburger with me. Poor Randy, I thought.

When the copy was finished, I opened the external hard drive. It had a long list of numbered folders, one through two hundred thirty-eight. I opened the first one. A list of image files popped up. I clicked one. I saw feet. I clicked on the next one. More feet. Fifty-six pictures of feet. The same feet. A woman's feet. I opened folder ninety-five. Feet again. Different feet. A woman again. Feet with heels. Feet in slippers. Feet in the sand. Close ups of the toenail. Wide shot up to knee. Folder one hundred sixteen: black woman's feet. In flip-flops. Up to the shin. Against white sand. Standing on tile. Bottoms of feet. Blue toenails. Red toenails.

It was feet fetish porn. Not pornography in the strict sense, but what else could it be? The collection was staggering. Randy hadn't taken the pictures. He'd never been to Rome or the Bahamas. He didn't know two hundred thirty-eight different women.

Feet. My son had five-hundred gigabytes of feet pictures. And he was making a copy of them.

"What are you doing here, Dad?" said Randy at the door. His eyes were wide and telegraphed guilt.

"Keep your voice down." I gestured for him to shut the door. "I need to talk to you."

He shut the door and reluctantly sat on the bed, his eyes shifting between me and the computer screen.

"First, two questions. Where'd you get all the money, and what's with all the feet?"

"Am I in trouble?" His lip quivered.

"Tell me," I said.

He took a deep breath and exhaled a defeated sigh. "I'm selling copies of my collection online and hiding the money in a Caymanian bank to avoid taxes."

"Oh," I said. "That's nice."

Randy waited for it to sink in. After a moment, enough of it had to prompt a follow-up question. "Where did you get it?" I asked.

"I've been collecting for years. I traded parts of my collection for other parts. After a while, it got really big and I stopped trading and started selling."

"How much?"

"The drives cost me sixty dollars and postage is usually around fifteen. They sell for four-fifty."

"Four hundred fifty dollars?"

"You think it's too much? I thought so, but I haven't had any problem selling them. I think the price attracts buyers, actually. I use a post office box in a Wrap-and-Ship store under an assumed name and handle all the money through dummy PayPal accounts that filter straight to Grand Cayman. When I need supplies, I charge them on my Caymanian Visa."

"Oh. I see," I said, nodding. "How many have you sold?"

"Over nine thousand dollars' worth. Are you mad?"

"I don't know. I don't think so. I'm stunned. I'm shocked. I'm impressed. But I don't know what to think about all the feet."

"I don't get it either. It was a game, you know? How many pictures of one woman's feet could I find. Then people wanted to see it. It kinda snowballed. It's weird. Some people like it. I like boobs myself."

"Are there boobs in there somewhere?"

"Nope. Just feet. Not even faces. Nothing above the knee. It's a rule."

Words failed me. I was awash in pride and horror at my son's computer antics, splashing around flummoxed, clueless, and speechless. My mouth opened and shut several times, and my face knotted up into a dozen different expressions before Randy bailed me out.

"Why did you come here, Dad?" he said. "Is something wrong? Why are you wet?"

"I need your help," I said. "I snuck in through the back door. The sprinklers came on."

"What do you need?"

"Do you still play Colonies?"

"Of course," he said. "It's more than a game, more than a sport. It's a way of life."

"Sad as that sounds," I said, "I'm glad to hear it."

"Why?"

"Did you see any of the games played in Vegas at the national tournament?"

"Some."

"Well, I was there. One of the players interests me."

"RexingBall?"

"Yeah," I said. "Remember I said he lied to me? Well, he keeps showing up. He came in second at nationals."

"Ah, you spoiled it," he said.

"Sorry. I want you to examine his games. Could he be cheating?"

"What? I don't see how."

"Neither do I. That's why I need a smart player to look at it."

"Okay. Maybe I'll ask a few of my friends to help. How do you think he's cheating?"

"No idea. But no one at the tournament gave him a chance in hell, and he comes in second place. He got a hundred thousand dollars and an all-expense paid trip to Bangkok."

"Okay, Dad, I'll get right on it," Randy said. "Are you going to tell mom about the feet?"

"Is there anything illegal in the pictures? You know, anything that can get you arrested?"

"No, I don't think so. I sell discs, not content, see? I just forget to erase them first." I knew where he got that kind of thinking.

"Good. No problems there. Is the banking legal?"

"Does laundering money in off-shore accounts count as illegal?"

"No. I can't see how. Are you ripping people off?"

"No way, Dad. This business is word of mouth. Everyone's satisfied.

Money-back guarantee. The only thing I do is add a little bug on the hard drive to mess up mass transfers so they can't copy the whole disc at once. One picture at a time is okay, but nobody is going to copy five hundred gigs of pictures one at a time. It keeps me in business."

"I'd like you to set a goal and then get out of the business," I said. "Say ten thousand and then find something else. It's a little seedy and dangerous, and you can't even drive yet."

"Okay, ten thousand dollars and I'll stop. When I can drive, I'll be able to buy my own car."

"Better save it for a rainy day," I said. "Let your mom buy you a car."

"Yeah, don't want her to get suspicious."

"How's Mudge treating you?"

"He's sickly nice, then stern. I say good morning to him, and he gives me a long-winded heart-to-heart about the real meaning of morning and the glories of sunshine while I'm trying to choke down a bowl of roots he calls breakfast. Can I live with you?"

That was the nicest thing my son had ever said to me.

"Not right now," I said. "When I'm clear of this mess, we'll look at it again."

I sat down next to my fetish-trafficking son and gave him a big, long hug. He hugged me back. I held him until he squirmed to get away. I caught a glance of my watch. It was five past nine.

"Oh shit," I said. "I gotta call Mudge."

Randy watched suspiciously as I flipped open my phone, blocked my number, and called Leafcaller's Nevada number.

I heard Mudge's phone ring downstairs.

"Hello," he said.

I swallowed another potato, donned my Jabba suit, and said, or rather gargled, "Hello, Leafcaller. Did you get the wine?"

"Yes, I have four bottles I can let you have," he said.

Below me, I heard the front door open and close. Then, over the phone, came the sound of a passing car I watched through Randy's window. "But I've got to ask twelve hundred apiece for them," he said.

"You said one thousand before."

"Sorry." He didn't mean it.

"Ten-fifty."

"We'll talk when we meet," he said. "Where are you?"

"I'm staying at the airport Marriott."

"I didn't know there was an airport Marriott here."

There wasn't. It was the first thing to pop into my head.

"It's a Marriott," I said. "I came here from the airport. I just assumed."

"That's got to be the downtown Marriott. What room are you in? I'll come by."

"No. How about we meet at a bar."

"I know a place," Mudge said. A dog barked. I heard it in stereo from the phone and Randy's window.

"I saw a place," I said. "The Sailor."

"The Sailor? Really?"

"Yes, I was there earlier. I liked it. Is that a problem?"

"No, I guess not," he said. "If that's your kind of place, fine."

"What does that mean?" I might have been playing my part too well. My opium wine-buying Jabba was becoming enraged at Leaf-caller's bigotry.

"Not a problem," he said. "I'll meet you there in an hour."

"Very well. I'll see you there."

"How will I know you?"

"I'll be wearing a red chrysanthemum," I said.

I closed the phone. Randy stared at me.

"Don't tell Mom," I said.

"Okay."

Mudge left five minutes later.

"I gotta go, son. I'll call you later."

"Sure."

"I'm going to hide in the bathroom. Call your mom up here and distract her. I'll escape then. Oh, and here's the backdoor key."

I tossed it to him. He caught it and laughed.

"I told Mom that was the lamest hiding place," he said.

CHAPTER THIRTY-SIX

The familiar white BMW rolled into the Sailor lot and parked under a burned-out streetlamp ten minutes after I got there. I put my holstered gun under my windbreaker and left the car as Mudge got out of his. I waved while I trotted up to him all warm and friendly.

"Hello, Mudge," I said when he recognized me. His look of surprise and hatred made me warm inside.

"Tony?"

"Hey there, sport. Fancy meeting you here. You got a minute? I'd like to talk to you."

"Actually, no. I'm waiting for someone." He got back in his car. I stepped around and let myself in the passenger side.

"Good idea. This is more private," I said.

He took what I can only call a deep, cleansing breath and spoke to me in soothing tones like I was a confused badger he was guiding out the door with a broom. I like badgers.

"Tony, my friend, we should talk. I have forgiven you all your little tantrums. I've moved above it all. You're right. We should have a long dialogue to discuss our future and get in touch with our feelings. I can help you through this difficult time. I'm a master of energies. I promise I can help you. But not now. I have an urgent appointment and mustn't be late."

"You're a master of bullshit," I said. "Turn on the car. Let's drive."

"Sorry, Tony. I just can't right now." His calm changed to concern, then worry, then fear as I produced my gun.

"You're here to meet me," I said as Mr. Smith, a.k.a. Jabba, the potato eater. "Keep your left hand on the wheel at all times. Turn on the car. I'm asking nicely."

He did as I told him.

"Now back up and get on the freeway. Head up Little Cottonwood Canyon, you know, the steep one. We'll talk as you drive."

He drove, but we didn't talk. I didn't point the gun at him. I figured if I never actually threatened him, never aimed it at his, big, fat, shootable head, I'd have plausible deniability when he reported me to the police. Yeah, I know. But I went with it anyway.

There was a sack in the backseat, a natural hemp thing that would have made a fine Depression-era feed bag if it didn't have "Go Green!" stenciled on the side in tall, smug letters. Inside were four bottles of laudanum wine. I lifted one out and looked at it.

I said, "You know, I have no recollection of getting home the night I drank some of this shit." The car began its ascent up the canyon, the incline slow and steady but growing steeper by the mile.

"It's powerful stuff," he said. "I would have warned you, but of course I didn't know you'd just help yourself."

"That was bad manners."

"No hard feelings, buddy." I could see his forced smile in the headlights of an oncoming truck. The smell of burning brakes wafted into the cab as it passed.

"Turn right here, at the Becker Campground," I said. He did.

I directed him to a campsite far in the back. I didn't pay the camping fee. It was late and dark and a weeknight, and I'm a rebel who likes to stick it to the man.

Mudge stopped the car, and I asked him to kindly keep one hand on the wheel at all times. Just a request. If he chose to interpret it as a threat, to believe there was some kind of "or else" implied, what could I do?

I rolled down my window and breathed in the moist mountain air. I could hear the rushing creek behind the trees.

"I see a new chance for us, Hank," I said. "Do you mind if I call you Hank?"

"No, but I prefer Leafcaller," he said.

"Great. Then I'll call you Mudge," I said. "Let's toast our new beginnings." I took a corkscrew out of the bag and went to work on the wine.

Mudge flinched when I opened it.

"I don't have any glasses, just swig from the bottle." I handed it to him. He took a small sip.

"No, drink up. This is a celebration. I even brought a noisemaker." I showed him the gun to put his mind at ease that it was there solely for a celebratory firework. I think he may have misinterpreted my message, but he drank a deep draught anyway.

"The thing is," I said, "I almost never black out from drinking. But lately I've been losing my mind quite often." I left it at that for a beat, to collect my thoughts. I hoped he didn't read more into my personal confession than I'd meant. I think he might have. I saw a bead of sweat trickle down his temple.

"For instance, the other night when I drank this and blacked out, I had a kind of déjà vu. It reminded me of another time when I drank something and blacked out. Can you guess when that time was?"

"Your honeymoon?"

"Eh, no. But close." Nancy, the blabbermouth. In my defense, we'd partied hard that night. It wasn't my fault. "Drink up. Go ahead."

He did.

"What I was thinking about was the night I spent with Rose Griff. We were drinking and then blacked out, just like with your Australian wine. I found out later that there was more in our drinks than just alcohol, just like with your Australian wine. Which makes me wonder if there might be a connection."

"Tony, no, I don't . . ." He didn't finish his sentence, but the pleading tone conveyed his thoughts. I didn't care.

"You don't what? Remember Rose? How could you forget her? She was unforgettable."

Indignantly, he said, "What are you talking about?"

I cared less for his indignation than his pleading. The man could change moods faster than an FM dial.

I reached into my pocket and brought out a piece of drawing paper. I snapped it open with one hand, my other on my noisemaker. You never knew when you'd want to yip it up.

"This, Mudge, is your smudge." I'd waited days to say that. It wasn't as fulfilling as I'd hoped. "I found this among Rose's things," I said. "I'm guessing you drew it on a cruise where you met her, probably while you were robbing another woman. I think it's Jamaica, but I could be wrong."

He looked at the picture and then at me.

"Drink another," I said. He did.

"I can explain." Fear slurred in his voice.

"That's why we're here," I said. "Before you begin, let me tell you how I see it. There will be a short time afterward for a rebuttal."

I cleared my throat and presented my hypotheses.

"My first theory was that you are one of Satan's minions, sent to fuck up my life."

His mouth slid open like a lowering drawbridge, but nothing came out.

"So you don't deny it? I knew it," I said.

"No, Tony. It's nothing personal. Nancy and I met at yoga class. We hit it off. She told me you were on board with the whole divorce-separation thing."

"Nancy can take care of herself. And, I'll wager, she'll take care of you, too, but not as you think. No, it's Rose we're talking about."

"You think I killed Rosey just because of that picture? You're crazy." Now his mood was insulting.

"You better pray to your granola-munching godlet you're wrong there, Old Spice, because crazy people sometimes do crazy things in the mountains, by rivers, in the dark, to less fortunate people."

That shut him up.

"You live off women," I said. "The term, is it 'gigolo' or 'lamprey?' Pretty much the same, I guess. I got that from the walls of my old study and your cropped photos. You're not ugly, at least on the outside, and you're smooth. No, you're more than smooth. You're slick, slippery, slimy. If you can weasel your way into practical Nancy, I pity the adventurous tourists you met on cruise ships. A shark among carp."

"Not true," Mudge mumbled.

"You didn't work on a cruise ship?"

"Well, yes. As an aerobics instructor."

"Officially, but you moonlighted as an escort. Am I wrong?"

He didn't say anything. I went on. "You sidled up to rich older women who then showered you with gifts for ignoring their stretch marks, and drawing their pictures with burnt matchsticks. You found a further sideline smuggling exotic and narcotic wine. You might have even used your beguiled women to carry the stuff in for you."

Mudge moaned.

"On one particular trip," I went on, "you met a ravishing young woman named Rose Griff. She was out of your league in more ways than one. Like you, she was a scammer, but unlike you, she was a nice person. For an experiment, she may have even slept with you, kind of a dissecting-a-rat kind of thing, vile and disgusting, but probably educational."

Mudge was either balancing his chakra, shitting his pants, or thinking of an escape. Unbidden, he lifted the bottle for another pull.

"Hold up there, partner. That's enough for now. Don't want you passing out on me. Yet."

He lowered the bottle.

"You gave Rose one of your bottles of grape-flavored heroine, or maybe she just took it. Either way, I found it in her apartment. That, along with this little Rembrandt here, tells me that you two knew each other. Her friends described a creepy fitness teacher she met on a cruise who stalked her for a while. Can't think of anyone else who fits that description, can you?"

"Tony . . ."

"All polite new-age bullshit aside, you're still a man. I think. No man likes to see their lover with another man. Comparisons and all that."

I was on thin ice now. If Mudge had had his whole mind, he'd have been able to beat me with the irony of my own accusations. But luckily, thanks to an Australian pharmaceutical winery, he didn't have his whole mind just then, so I continued my speech.

"Maybe you were feeling inadequate—a feeling I'm sure you have often—and went out for a late night stalk to Rose's apartment. There you found me, the man who'd hurled stewed weeds at you only hours before, making time with your real love. You broke in using a key you had made and drugged our drinks while we were touring the apartment."

Mudge made a sound of denial, but I cut him off. "Now wait your turn. There will be a question-and-answer period immediately following the lecture. Hold your denials until then." I patted my Smith and Wesson noisemaker just for emphasis, obviously signaling to him that I'd let him hold it later after we were done. What fun.

"Once we were knocked out, your crooked little mind found her on the bed, and you strangled her with your crooked little fingers out of jealousy, revenge, and general meanness. You left me there to take the heat, thus killing two birds with one crime."

Mudge's eyes drooped under the narcotic. I could smell the sweet wine on his breath and hoped I hadn't given him too much.

"So, that's the broad strokes. Now, I have a few questions. I told you there'd be a question-and-answer period. Here it is."

"But, it's all wrong, Tony," he moaned. "You've got it all wrong."

"First, I understand why you took the bottle and Flintstone glasses. What I don't get is why you took all her pills and her computer game. Was it to throw suspicion off yourself, or was it because you needed the drugs and wanted another copy for multiplayer Colonies? Nice touch leaving the pills in my car, by the way. An obvious set up, but nice."

"Tony, I didn't kill Rosey," he moaned. "You're right. I loved her. I didn't know you were seeing her. I didn't know until after you'd been arrested. I swear to God, Tony, I spent that whole night fighting with Nancy. We didn't get to bed until after three, and we were both wiped out."

"It would have been easy for you to sneak out when you're sleeping on the couch," I said. "Nice try at an alibi, but no go."

"But we slept together," he said. "I have a rule never to go to bed mad, so we worked it out until we were friends again. We had make-up sex and fell asleep in each other's arms."

I nearly puked. "You might want to keep the amorous descriptions of my ex to yourself," I said.

"Okay, right. Sorry. I know you still have feelings for her. I understand that. That was insensitive, I'm sorry." His apology was slurred, sloppy, and heartfelt, which pissed me off all the more.

"I was smitten with Rose," he said. "I called her and tried to see her, followed her home once or twice, but it was all over. She told me to go. I always thought that after she grew up a little, she'd understand me better and I'd have another chance. But then you, er . . . I mean, she died."

"Was I right about the cruise ship and the wine?"

"Yes. I don't have many left. That's why I was so mad when you wasted two bottles. I'm trying to get Nancy to go on a cruise so I can pick up some more in Nassau. I only have the four—three—bottles left. I'm trying to get twelve cases."

"And the gigolo part?"

"Tony," he said, "I taught aerobics for a few years on a cruise ship. They encouraged me to entertain the single ladies. It was part of the job. If I picked right, I got taken care of. It was a job. I made women happy; they gave me things. They wanted to."

"So what happened?"

"I went to the beach with Rose when I should have been banging a senior executive's wife on a girlfriend getaway. I got fired."

He put the bottle between his legs and supported his tired left arm with his right.

"Tony, I don't know anything about glasses or games or pills or anything. All I know is that you were arrested for killing a girl I cared about, and that made me a little testy toward you. I lost my cool because I'd convinced myself that you'd done it."

"What changed your mind?"

"I can tell you're not the killing type," he lied.

"Why didn't you tell Nancy about Rose?"

"The same reason I don't talk about other women to other women. It's not polite."

"But the coincidence of me killing the love of your life didn't even merit an aside?"

He whirled at me with rage in his eyes.

"That wasn't a confession, Mudge," I said. "It was hypothetical. I haven't killed anyone. I was just pointing out it was something you might have mentioned."

There was real hatred in his glossy eyes for Rose's killer. His mood shift was exonerating. If I'd confessed straight up to him just then, I had little doubt he'd have lunged at me, gun and all, and ripped the chi out of my third eye with his bare, manicured hands.

"What good would it have done to tell her?" he said. "It might even have made things worse for you."

"Or the cops might put together a story like I did and implicate you."

"Yes," he slurred.

"Why were you in Vegas this weekend?" I said. "And I might add that I was in Vegas myself, too. Your story better match with what I saw." I didn't say "or else," but it would have fit there.

Mudge looked at me with unfocused eyes. If he suspected my bluff, there was no way those peepers were going to confirm it.

"I was seeing Janet Onapopolis. Her husband owns all the Kabob Castles in town."

Everyone knew the Kabob Castles. Any parking lot with six free spaces sprouted one like a weed. They were drive-through-only grease shacks with decent gyros. Hippies stood in line at the backdoor for used grease to use in their biodiesel VW's.

"You were stepping out on Nancy?"

"Yes. Janet's married. We have the occasional rendezvous."

"What did you tell Nancy?"

"I said it was work."

"At least you weren't lying," I said. "Where did you stay? Under what name?"

"Mandalay Bay, penthouse suite. Her name."

"How much did you make?"

"I came home with three grand and a new gold chain. I told Nancy I won at poker."

"And she believed you?"

"I think so." There may have been contrition in his voice, but it was masked by thickening consonants.

Tears squirted from his drooping eyes. "Are you going to kill me?" he said. "You can't think I'd do anything to Rosey, can you? You knew what a breath of life she was. I loved her."

I watched him weep. The wine had pierced a dam of grief, naked and bare. I didn't try to stop it. I let him cry. I didn't say anything when his hand came off the wheel to fish for tissue in the door pocket. I let him cry.

I rearranged ideas and moods, and remembered Rose in her blue dress. Mudge filled a tissue with a snort that would attract rhinoceroses.

I said, "Does the name Rex Merkin mean anything to you?"

He shook his head. "No. Who is it?" He sniffed and swayed in the seat.

"Get out of the car," I said. "It's time to take a walk."

Fear twisted his face like a tightening knot.

"No, Tony. You don't want to do this."

"Calm down, Mudge. We're just going to walk around. You need to sober up."

CHAPTER THIRTY-SEVEN

"Why would a gamer need a sponsor?"

"You talking about the Vegas thing again?" said Standard. He was obviously uncomfortable in the back seat of Garret's car. Perry sat next to him, crowding Garret's space, nearly lying on top of him, bracing a pair of binoculars against his shoulder.

"Yeah. What does a sponsor get out of sponsoring someone?"

Garret spoke from the driver's seat. "I watched a poker tournament on ESPN, and most of the players had hats advertising poker websites and casinos. It's advertising. Since the camera is going to be on the player, they're a walking billboard."

"Like NASCAR," said Standard. "The stickers mean money. The bigger the sticker, the more the sponsor gave. It's buying publicity."

I'd called everyone together under "Operation Jell-O" for a Dara intervention. I'd called Perry from my room at the Rest Easy Motel next to an understaffed Denny's undiscovered by the city's health inspectors. I'd stayed there because I'd been afraid to go home. Lahkpa's goons were watching it.

Mudge had drunk too much to drive. We walked the dirt paths and over the bridge spanning the rushing snow runoff. He told me he loved me in the way drunks have since Bacchus introduced fermentation to mankind. He promised me that he harbored no hard feelings and hoped I'd find "Rosey's" killer. He was the only one who called her that, which said something.

I poured him into the back seat and drove him home. He sobbed and blubbered, denounced his infidelity to Nancy and told me how much he loved me again. Then the devils came, and he shrieked while they nibbled on his legs, which had fallen asleep under his twisted body.

Nancy helped me get him to bed and drove me to my car. I told her I'd taken the initiative to make friends with Leafcaller. It hurt to call him that, but it sold my story.

I'd asked her about the events after the first dinner party, and she confirmed everything Mudge had told me, including the make-up sex. God help me.

I didn't tell Nancy about Mudge's involvement with Rose. I didn't tell her about Mudge's lampreyism, or his recent affair in Vegas. She'd suspect my motives. She'd work it all out eventually.

"She should be coming out any time," said Perry. "She's a creature of habit."

"No she isn't," said Standard. "She's nearly as unpredictable as you."

Garret's little car was parked across the street from Dara's duplex. We'd been there for over an hour. We'd seen movement inside through the curtains but couldn't be sure it was Dara. There was some suspicion that this wasn't even Dara's house. Perry said it was but admitted it had been a while since he'd actually been here. He remembered it as blue, not white, and hadn't there been a fence?

"Screw this," said Standard. "Let's just go knock on the damned door."

"The house could be watched," Perry said, not for the first time. "Do you want to get Tony sent to prison?"

"The house is being watched," said Standard. "By us."

"I agree with Stan," said Garret. "Let's just go. I'm missing work."

"Okay." I got out of the car and jogged across the street, followed by a tight cluster of my three friends.

I rang the bell. The three held back. Perry still had the binoculars and pointed them at me. He was three feet away. I heard steps inside the house. I grabbed Garret and pulled him to the door, and ducked behind Perry.

"She'll shit if she sees me first," I said. "You get us in."

Garret was petrified. Critter could have talked his way into the

Oval Office, but Garret was intimidated by shellfish. Critter had stayed behind in the car.

The door opened. Dara stood in a knee-length T-shirt half tucked into pink shorts. She was barefoot, which made her even smaller than we were used to. Her makeup was a day old, smeared and blotched, and her hair had a ridiculous one-sided flop that only sleep could manufacture.

"What the fuck are you doing here?" she demanded. Even just out of bed, looking her worst, she was a firecracker. We all took a step back.

"Uhm, Dara. How are you?" stammered Garret. "You're looking fresh today. We hope you slept well."

Perry watched her through the binoculars. She was four feet away. I don't know how he focused them.

Without a word, she went to close the door.

"Wait," I shouted.

Dara whirled around.

I stepped out from behind Perry, who turned the black lenses on the back of my head though he had to search to find me.

"Dara this is an intervention." I pulled Standard and Perry alongside me. "Can we come in? It's important. We care about you."

Perry watched her reaction closely. I took a step forward. "Dara we need to talk."

"Tony Flaner," she said icily. "You've got balls of steel to show up on my doorstep." I wondered if balls of steel were better than the coconuts Carlos said I possessed.

"Dara, I need some answers. I'm getting close, I can feel it. I just need to ask some questions."

"You gotta let us in, Dara," said Perry under his lenses. "It's about solidarity. Tony's a wanted man. We have to help him."

Surprisingly, she stepped aside and let us come in. I followed Garret onto the split-level landing. Perry walked into the doorframe and finally lowered the binoculars long enough to enter the house.

Upstairs we found a secondhand couch, a worn fabric chair, and a coffee table dimpled with cigarette burns in front of a modest TV. The kitchen and dining room were to one side, a short hallway, I supposed, led to a bedroom. We never saw the lower level.

"You have to forgive Tony," Garret said sympathetically. "It's time."

"Shut up, numb-nuts," said Standard. "Tony's done nothing wrong. What does he have to be forgiven for? Getting pelted by eggs?"

"Oh, right," he said.

"What Garret meant," said Perry, watching our parked car through the curtained windows, binoculars once again pressed to his face, "is that you need to stop being such a bitch and believing every lame cock-and-bull lie propagated by the corporate media. I've told you how they manipulate us. I've told you about the x-ray satellites and subliminal conditioning frequencies. You've got to fight the control and think for yourself. The world's on fire, and you won't see the flames."

The room fell silent, all eyes on Perry. I remembered the van parked in front of his house.

"Thank you, Dr. Strangelove," said Stan.

"But he's right," I said. "About the beginning at least, for sure. You've got to put it into your mind that I didn't do it."

"Are your feelings so fucking fragile that you have to come to my house at all hours of the goddamned morning to make nice?" she asked. "What a dickless wimp."

"Actually, Dara, it's past ten, nearly eleven," said Garret.

"When I want your opinion, I'll ask a lamp," she said, flopping onto the couch. Then, looking at me, said, "What do you want Flaner? An apology for the eggs?"

"That would be nice, but I need answers more."

"You bruised him all over you know," said Garret. "You hurt him. Look at his shin."

"Actually, she didn't do that one," I admitted.

Everyone then looked at my legs, and I wished I'd gone with jeans instead of shorts. I hadn't shaved in weeks.

I said, "Dara, tell me about Simon, Rex, and Rose."

I could tell she was about to level a burning barrage at someone, but my question deflected it.

"What the fuck does that have to do with anything?" she said. It still surprised me when so much casual swearing came from that little girl body. Her pillow bob drooped a little, and for the first time, it seemed, she noticed she hadn't put herself together. She ran her fingers through her hair to tame it and failed.

"I hear you four used to hang out at the Sailor," I said.

"Rose knew one of the Sailor's bartenders. Got us discount drinks."

"Patricia. Yes, I talked to her. But I'm interested in you four."

"And this is related to Rose's death?"

"Maybe. Tell me about Rose in college."

She leaned back and produced a pack of cigarettes from under a couch cushion. She struck a match on her fingernail and lit it. Perry had reversed the binoculars and was now surveying the room from very far away. Stan leaned against a wall looking as bored as he dared without being rude enough to invite comment. Garret sat on the sofa next to me.

"Rose and Rex were in business together," she said. "Rose needed some money after her parents died, and Rex needed some money after his parents cut him off. It was an easy pairing."

"Rex is a conman too?"

"No. Did I say anything about a fucking con-man?"

Everyone shook their heads.

"Rex stole drugs, and Rose sold them for him. Pharmaceuticals, pain pills, and speed mostly. Sold them to the kids on campus. It worked for them. Rose made it through college, and Rex could live his stuck-up lifestyle without his rich parents' support."

"How rich were they?" asked Standard. I didn't think he was paying attention.

"I don't know. Seven. How 'bout seven? They were 'seven' rich. How's that?"

I said, "What was the deal with cutting him off?"

"Rex's parents expected their little prick kid to actually go to college. Of all the nerve. When he had to drop out after a quarter because he never went to classes, they cut him off from anything but essentials.

He didn't like that. Threw a shit fit. It was hard to feel sorry for the jerkoff because bare minimum for him was still more than I made at all my jobs, and Rose was dealing with her parents' death. Spoiled little rich fuck."

"If you hated him so much, why didn't you say anything?" asked Stan. "I can't see you putting up with it."

"Oh, I said plenty. I tolerated him for Rose. I don't know why she did. Maybe he was a project. Rex was a jerk. All guys are jerks. He at least was obvious about it. That might have helped."

"So Rex turned the corner with Rose's help and got back in his family's good graces," I offered. "What then?"

"You like to make up your own fucking stories, don't you, Flaner?" She took a long drag on her cigarette. "Rex isn't the turn-a-corner kind of guy. He doesn't change. Not his style. The money kept him afloat, but it wasn't steady and took too much work. He hooked up with a couple of teacher assistants and pulled his grades up."

"Tutors?" I suggested, but knew I was wrong.

"Cheaters," said Dara. "They gave him the answers and scored him up."

"What kind of money do you need for that I wonder?" asked Standard. "Man, I couldn't get half a percentage in PE with a gun."

"I always did well in school," said Garret to no one in particular.

"Probably wasn't as much as you'd think. Teacher assistants get paid fuck-all," she said. "Even with his parents paying him to breathe, he still needed money. It got bad when Rose stopped selling for him."

"Why did Rose stop?"

"Too risky, I think, or she finally just got sick of all his bullshit. There were always money problems around him. He's greedy—didn't play well with others."

"What did he do?"

"He didn't say, and I didn't give a shit. It might have been just another fucked-up excuse not to buy the drinks. Damn, cheapskate, rich prick."

"And Simon? Tell me about him."

"Simon was a shy kid," she said.

"Rex knew about Simon's conservative family, didn't he?" I said. "He knew that they didn't know about his orientation, right? Could he have taken advantage of that?"

She leaned back in her chair and eyed me suspiciously.

"Perry," she said. "Go in the fridge and bring me a Diet Coke."

"And if I don't?" Perry asked, examining a still life with fruit hanging on the wall from half mile away.

"I'll get it myself and accidentally kick you in the balls so hard your grandkids will limp."

Perry went to the kitchen.

"Anyone else want one?" she asked.

Everyone did.

"Joshua Pratt," I said to Dara watching for a reaction.

"What about Joshua Pratt, Sherlock?"

"He was Simon's lover. He suspects Simon was outed by a blackmailer."

She dragged on her cigarette and held the smoke like a hit of pot. She looked at me, the wheels turning in her head. Perry arrived with cans for all of us.

"Fuck," she said, and I knew she thought it was possible.

"Did Rex and Rose have an affair?" I opened my soda.

"An affair?" she laughed. "Single people don't have affairs, stupid. They have flings. But, yeah, I think they did it once or twice. It didn't take. It never did."

"But they were still friends?"

"Yeah. Rose even slept with Simon once, but we all knew it wouldn't work. He was the last to know he was gay. Rose proved it. By the end of his first quarter, away from his parents and out of Provo, he figured it out and became a card-carrying, closeted homosexual."

"When did the group fall apart?"

"I'm not sure it ever did. During the heyday, we all crashed at each other's places, you know. Practically communal living. It just faded. Our lives just took different paths. We didn't meet as much as we use to. I can't tell you the last time I saw Rex. Rose and I saw each other more often, but even she was scarce."

She smoked and sipped her soda. Perry found a stain by the wall and examined it for clues. I waited for a brainwave.

"Wait," she said. "That last time she came to the club, Rose mentioned she'd seen Rex recently. I was trying to talk her out of hitting on you when she said he'd been in touch, obviously to change the subject. She said he was the same as he ever was, spending more time on his computer than in his books."

"Dara, think hard. That night is important. What else did she say?"

"She said you were cute and available and now was her chance."

The guys looked at me, wondering what it was I had that would make a woman say that. I blushed.

"She said she was onto something big, about to get a lot of money."

"What was it?"

"She didn't say. She said she'd tell me about it on a beach somewhere."

"Nothing more about Rex?"

"No. But it was weird she'd seen him again. Don't know how their paths could have crossed by accident. I thought Rose was done with him."

I sipped my Coke. Dara leaned back and thought.

"There was a rumor in college that Rex had raped a girl," she said. "I didn't know the girl. None of us did."

"Except Rex," put in Garret.

"Thank you, Captain Obvious," she said, shooting him a glare that would make Nancy proud.

"It was over as fast as it started," she said. "I heard the girl was bought off and moved out of state. His parents took care of it sophomore year. That was a while ago."

"He's still in school, though. So it couldn't be that long ago," said Garret, counting on his fingers.

"He should have graduated ages ago," Dara said. "He just can't pass his exams. Too much cheating and not enough learning. I knew it would catch up to him. I think he likes the college life. He isn't the kind of guy who craves responsibility. He's a never-grow-up type. Rose was kind of like that, too. Rose lived in the same apartment she had during college, and I'd bet Rex still has that same pasty apartment he had."

"He does," I said.

"Also, Rex is motivated to stay in school. I know for a fact that once he graduates, he's going to be absolutely fucking buried in student loans. He took his family allowance and spent it. He paid for college, all ten years of it, with student loans."

"God, good idea," said Stan. "I wish I'd have thought of that. I don't blame him for staying in school. I'm still paying on my loans."

"What did you study?" I asked.

"One year of theatre, one of pre-law, one of business, and one of binge drinking."

"Well rounded," said Perry.

"Quite," he said.

I knew my friends were getting antsy. They didn't like conversation that didn't involve them directly. Except for Garret without Critter, all yearned to be the center of attention in an unhealthy, stand-up-comic kind of way. Their patience was running out.

"Dara," I said. "Was Rex violent?"

"There were those rape rumors, but I never saw him do anything violent. He was calculating, and a lazy fuck, but not necessarily violent."

Perry finally lowered the binoculars. "Rex is Tony's number one suspect right now," he said.

"His only suspect," corrected Standard. I regretted telling them so much about my investigation.

"Yeah, I figured that," she said. She hadn't sworn in minutes. I took that as a good sign. "What've you found?"

"I've pulled every string I can, getting deeper and deeper into this mess, and the only string that still throbs is Rex's."

"I can tell you one thing," Dara said, exhaling a stream of blue smoke from her third cigarette. "We all had keys to each other's places. I've lost mine. Rex might not have."

"Opportunity," I said to myself. "So Rex worked in hospital during college? That's where he got the drugs? How'd he lose that job?"

"He never lost his job. He never worked at a hospital. He works at a grocery store. Part of his training, I think."

"He's studying to be a grocer?"

"No, dipshit," she said, returning to her old self. "He works at the pharmacy. He's studying to be a pharmacist."

CHAPTER THIRTY-EIGHT

The boys dropped me back at my roach motel; they all had places to be. It was after noon, and I had burglary on my mind. With any luck, Rex would be at school, or work, or dead maybe, dangling over a guilt-filled, notarized confession to Rose's murder.

I was throwing my dirties into a bag when my phone rang. I felt lucky, so I answered.

"Hello," I said.

"Who the fuck do you think you are, getting all up in my shit like this!"

"Mom?"

"No, asshole. You know who this is." Actually, I did. My mind had been focusing on no one else since I'd left Dara's, I put a face to the voice on the first syllable.

"Is this Rex Merkin?"

"Damn right, shit-licker."

"I think you've misdialed. This is Tony Flaner. The Tourette's outbreak hotline is one-eight-hundred-EAT-SHIT."

"Flaner, or should I call you Easy Marlowe? What the fuck are you doing following me?"

"Interesting," I said. "I didn't know I was. I'm looking for Rose Griff's killer."

"The fuck you are," he said. "You're getting all up in my shit. Why? Are you working for some other guild? The Arsonists maybe? Are you trying to undermine my game? Or are you just some kind of sick stalker?"

"Are those my only options? What happens if I guess wrong? Can I phone a friend?"

"I'll have you thrown in jail for slander, you motherfucker. My family is powerful. I am not to be trifled with."

"I wouldn't trifle you with a borrowed dick," I said.

"You asshole! I'm calling the cops. You're going to fry for killing Rose."

"Actually, Utah doesn't have —oh, never mind," I said. "So, now you do know Rose?"

"Yes, I know Rose. I never said I didn't."

"Uh-huh. So, that was you talking to her at the hangar rave?"

"How'd you get out of jail, anyway?" he said, ducking the question. "I didn't think they let date-rape killers out of jail."

"Innocent until proven guilty. It's a quaint notion, but still has a devoted fan base."

"Go ahead and play cute all you want, Flaner. I'm not afraid of you. You're messing with the wrong guy."

"Why all the hostility? We were practically chums the last time we talked."

"I'm hostile because every time I turn around, there you are. You show up at my café, you come to my apartment, I see you in Vegas."

"So you saw me in Vegas? Why didn't you say hello? Or did you?"

"Don't be smart, Flaner."

"One of us needs to be."

"I'm calling my lawyer after I hang up."

"Would that be your family's high power rape-defense attorney, or the lovely Rebecca Taylor of Smith, Bannon and Taylor?"

"I don't know any Rebecca Taylor. My family has real attorneys who will lock you up for a long time."

"Take a number."

"I'm warning you, Flaner. If you don't leave me alone, I won't be held responsible for what happens."

"From what I've heard, it doesn't sound like you've ever been held responsible for anything."

"What are you trying to do, scare me?"

"I'm busy now, Rex. Can I ignore you some other time?"

"Are you trying to squeeze me? Trying to get some money out of me because you know I have some? Well it won't work."

"How much will you give me?"

"What?"

"How much are you offering me? You know, to look for Rose's killer somewhere else?"

"Go fuck yourself," he said, and hung up, but there had been a moment of hesitation before he did.

No sooner had I narrowed it down to Rex Merkin than the charmer calls me up and all but confesses. Sometimes things just work out. I felt the finger trap loosen for the first time since I got in it.

My phone rang again. I picked up.

"Hello, no swearing please."

"Thank God," said the caller.

"Was that a heartfelt prayer, or are you taking the Lord's name in vain? I'd hate to think you already broke the only condition I had."

"What?"

"Who is this?"

"Mr. Flaner. This is Justin, Justin Bertone. You talked to me about Rose Griff, remember? I work at Chronoboost?"

"Yes, I remember, Justin. How are you?"

"My friend Mallory said he saw you at nationals in Vegas."

"Yeah, I saw Mallory."

"He said someone stabbed you. Is that true?" There was urgency in his voice. He was calling from the number that'd rung my phone for days, never leaving a message.

"Yeah. Someone jabbed a hypo full of insulin in my ass. I was lucky it didn't kill me, but it could have."

"Oh, God," he said.

"That's kind of what I thought. Why are you so interested?"

"I can't talk to you now. Can you meet me? There's a little café I know called Melanie's. Do you know it?"

"I can find it. When do you want to meet?"

"Soon. Lunchtime. Say, one thirty?"

"I'll be there at one thirty."

"Okay." He sounded relieved.

Things were getting interesting. I looked up Melanie's in the motel phone book before I checked out. Actually, I ripped the page out and put it in my pocket, detective style. I dropped my key off and got in my car when my phone rang again. I was very popular that morning.

"Yes?" I said.

"Mr. Flaner?"

"Who's calling?"

"This is the law firm of Dewey, Cox & Leik," a stern voice informed me.

"You've got to be kidding. That can't be a real name."

"It most certainly is a real name and a real law firm. A very powerful law firm, I might add. I assume this is Mr. Flaner."

"What do you want Leaky Dewey Dick?"

"That's Dewey, Cox & Leik," he corrected. "My name is William S. Cox. I have been informed by my clients, the Merkin family, that you have been harassing them, threatening slander, and attempting to extort money from their son, Rex."

"Really? That was fast. Did you talk to the actual family or just to the test-cheating, rapist boy, Rex?"

He hesitated. I was getting a lot of play from that old rumor.

"If you continue to bother Mr. Merkin, his family, or his interests, we will be forced to take steps." He paused for his words to sink in.

"Wow. Steps, huh? Is that what constitutes a threat in your social circle?"

"I am very serious, Mr. Flaner."

"I know you are, Mr. Cock. I'm just collecting my thoughts." I cleared my throat. "Eh-hem. Here goes. You suck, Cox. I laugh at your threat. I will not be intimidated by 'steps,' no matter how steep the incline or wet the pavement. You cannot menace me because I have

345

bigger problems than a stuffed-shirt, east-coast, over-educated, lap-dog, pin-headed penis taking orders from a spoiled drug pusher in Utah."

I took another deep breath.

"I suggest you see a doctor about your dripping privates," I said. "Sounds like syphilis to me, probably contracted from your sister, and she from a donkey in Tijuana. She's very talented, by the way. I caught a matinee last month; she and your mother really know how to work a tequila bottle."

"I beg your pardon," he stammered.

"Good. Okay, I forgive you. But don't call me again." I hung up.

The phone rang a minute later. I refused the call and blocked the number. If they wanted to bring heat on me, they'd have to get in line.

I drove to Melanie's. My phone didn't ring again, but I avoided every tan SUV I saw like it was radioactive.

I arrived at the café at 1:10. I got a booth in the back where I could watch the parking lot and the café while having easy access to the kitchen for an escape. My usual seat.

I was nervous and fed my nerves with strong coffee and heavy cream. I waited. Justin's call was unexpected, but it saved me the trouble of looking him up again.

I sipped my coffee and compared each patron against my idea of cop, killer, and bounty hunter. The café smelled of grilled cheese sandwiches and low-sodium chicken noodle soup.

At 1:30 my gut twisted. At 1:35, I sat on the edge of my bench, my knees bent, ready to run. At 1:40, my legs relaxed, but my stomach churned in a gnawing hunch. At 1:50, I dropped a ten on the table and went to my car.

* * *

There were two fire trucks and an ambulance at the front door of Chronoboost.

I parked in a handicapped spot and darted into the building. The receptionist was gone and the doors were open wide. I could see a crowd of people rubbernecking a nightmare in the back. I knew the spot. It was Justin's cubicle.

Two paramedics lifted a flaccid young body onto a gurney.

"Ah shit," I said, recognizing Justin.

"Make room, people," commanded a medic.

"Is he dead?" I asked.

"We don't generally put oxygen masks on dead people," he said. "Get out of the way."

He was still and lifeless, but he did have a mask over his face, and I saw a film of moisture within it. He was breathing, if only a little.

They wheeled him out quickly, urgently, I'd say.

I saw a familiar face in the crowd.

"SlyStack," I said. "I mean Mallory. What happened?"

He said, "What are you doing here?"

"I had a lunch date with Justin. When he didn't show up, I came here. What happened?"

"Man, I don't know. He's been feeling poorly for a while. He was on some meds, but they weren't working. He'd been in the bathroom all morning. When he finally came out, I heard him puke into his trashcan. Hell, the whole office did. It was loud. And if they didn't hear it, they sure as hell smelled it. Brad told him to go home. He was packing up when he fell over. He had some kind of epileptic spasm and then passed out. We called nine-one-one."

I heard sirens flare outside and then listened to them fade as the ambulance sped away.

"Bad stuff happens around you," Mallory said.

The crowd at Justin's cubicle dispersed into smaller gossiping groups. A fireman in beige rubber gloves and a notepad took statements from witnesses who told much the same story Mallory had.

I dropped into Justin's chair. The smell from the trashcan made me turn away. I saw the Tesla brochure and picked it up to fan the air currents away from me. I opened up to the page where he'd listed prices. It was as I remembered it, but a new column had been added. "Progress: 50,000."

"Oh," I said to the foul air. "Interesting."

I opened drawers and saw pencils and discs. I searched the desk, lifted up reams of paper with indecipherable computer code, and found nothing. I looked under the desk, but couldn't handle the smell. I pulled the trashcan out and moved it into the hall. A paper in the bin caught my eye.

It was a doodle. A piece of yellow legal pad with black felt-tip scribbles on it. My number was on it, along with the name "E. Z. Marlowe." He'd gone over the characters several times with the pen. The lines had bled from the vomit, but it was surely my cell phone number and the alias I'd given to the lawyer.

Below that was a picture of a bird attacking a lizard. Two cartoon fighter planes strafed them both. It reminded me of the cover of my fifth-grade school notebook. There was more on the paper, but it was fouled.

This was no time to be squeamish; the fireman had seen me. Mallory had pointed out the cubicle to the medical investigator, and I was surely on the list for a visit.

I fished the paper out of the basket and scraped half-digested scrambled eggs from it with the side of a manila folder marked "Timestamp Binaries" I hoped wasn't important.

Beneath Justin's lost breakfast was a smoking gun. It was a crude doodle, and the ink was smeared and blotted, but it was definitely a smoking gun. The hand-drawn revolver pointed to three letters "BGM" written vertically on the page. The letters were a kind of sigil and resembled a man with a big chin and wide stance. The letter man had been shot by the gun right in the heart. The picture showed the bullet ripping through the G, caught mid-flight in splashing blood-splatter.

Below the macabre drawing was a string of characters I didn't understand: "S-O-M1 CP @ 2." He'd written the string at least thirty times, repeating them in one long, unfathomable line of text like he was memorizing a catechism or writing a dirge.

I sounded out the letters. "Someone see pee at two?" It didn't make sense, but the rest of the page did.

I lifted my face from the paper, forced away from the sour smell and new leads in my thinking. My muscles tightened, my neck straightened, my chin rose. I looked at my reflection staring back at me in Justin's dark computer monitor and absorbed the information.

I glimpsed orange plastic behind a speaker on the desk. I remembered Justin kept a bottle of pills there. I reached for it, wrapping my fingers around it in a fist, and drew it out.

Slowly I opened my hand to read the label.

"Amoxicillin: take one pill three times per day. Finish entire bottle." I read the rest of the label, the names, dates, and places, and felt my heart miss a beat.

"Oh my god," I exclaimed.

"What is it?"

I spun the chair around to face the fire investigator with the beige gloves. He was bigger than he looked from across the room. He was six-and-a-half-feet tall, but he looked ten from my low chair. His brown mustache was full and trimmed, his muscles filled out his shirt, and his eyes looked into me like I'd been caught with a can of gasoline and a Zippo.

I placed the paper from the bin on Justin's keyboard and stood up.

"Leave this here," I said. "I'm calling Detective McGraw. He'll need to see this."

"What? Who? A detective? What are you talking about?"

"No, maybe not McGraw," I said more to myself. "I think I'll call District Attorney Sweet."

"The district attorney is sweet?"

"Yes and no."

"Wait, are you saying there's been a crime here?"

"Oh, yeah," I said. "How's Justin?"

"Who?" I'd rattled his cool professional control.

"Justin Bertone— with a 'B,'" I said. "The man you wheeled out."

"I don't know. He'll be taken to the medical center. The medics don't know what's wrong with him. He was having problems breathing, but he's in good hands now, and the doctors will figure it out. He'll be fine."

"I doubt it. But this will help." I tossed him the bottle. He read it.

"This is good to have," he said tentatively. "I'll tell the hospital he's already on a course of antibiotics."

"No," I said. "You have to get that bottle tested right now. I'd bet my bottom dollar those aren't antibiotics. It's poison. Justin's been poisoned with whatever is in that bottle. It's attempted murder."

"What makes you say that?" he asked.

I pointed to the label.

"I know a guy who works at that pharmacy."

CHAPTER THIRTY-NINE

Morris should have been the one to make the call, but he was in court, and I couldn't wait. I called the District Attorney's office from my car and followed an endless audio menu of transfers until the stony persecutor picked up.

"Hello, this is Sweet." Her voice was gravely and rough, and immediately reminded me of her block-like visage. If a piece of sedimentary rock ever became an assistant DA, it would sound like Ms. Penelope Sweet. I couldn't entirely discount the possibility that this had already happened.

"Hello, Penelope, this is Tony Flaner."

"Mr. Flaner, you shouldn't be talking to me. You can be put in jail for this kind of behavior. You're already in more trouble than when I last saw you. You're only making things worse."

"A simple 'hello' would have worked," I said. "Morris is in court, and I need to tell you something. Now let me talk. I know you'll hold everything against me, but this is important."

"Hello, Mr. Flaner. What do you want?"

"Remember when I said that I didn't do it, that I didn't kill Rose Griff?"

"Yes, I remember."

"Well it's true. I've been digging, and I've found some very interesting information."

"I'm sure you have."

"Don't dismiss me." It was like talking to a rock. "A kid named Justin Bertone was taken to the hospital today. He went to the City

Med Center. I think he was poisoned. I gave a suspicious pill bottle to a Captain Olsen. He's with the fire department in Alpine. He's expecting your call."

"And this is related to your charges?"

"Yessir, you betcha. Also, if you call the Clark County Hospital, you'll see that I was admitted for poisoning last weekend. There was an assault on my ass, and it nearly killed me."

"I see."

"Don't worry. I'm all right now. Thanks for asking."

"I'm glad you're all right," she said. Could I hear a crack in the stone? "Isn't Clark County in Nevada?"

"Might be," I said. "There's a piece of paper I dug out of Justin's garbage at Chronoboost. That's where he works. It's in Utah County, but I bet you can get permission to go down there."

"This isn't the twenties, Mr. Flaner. County lines don't stop the law."

"Well, that's good. Captain Olsen called the cops when I said there was an attempted murder. He said it was normal procedure. I said I had to make a call and I bolted, so they're probably looking for me."

"A lot of people are," she said.

"One found me in Vegas. I think it was the same guy who poisoned Justin and killed Rose."

"Do you have proof of this?"

"Some, but not enough. Yet. Like I said, there's this paper at Justin's work. I dug it out of his trashcan. Just some doodles, but it's very telling and very smelly. He puked on it before he collapsed."

"Did you plant it there?"

"No," I said indignantly. "Try, for just half a second, to imagine me innocent. Take a deep sedimentary breath, and open your mind. Are you doing it? Good. Anyway, the puke happened before I got there. I can't think of a better or more disgusting time stamp, can you?"

"What does this note say?"

"It has my phone number, and some code, and I'll explain everything after I get the final pieces in place. In the meantime, it's important that you get this paper. It's important to me and to you. And Olsen saw it," I said, "so it better not disappear."

"Don't be offensive."

"Can't always help it."

"How is this paper important to me?" she said.

"Even with my weak attorney, whom I think everyone underestimates, there's enough bad police work and extraneous circumstances to let me walk," I said. I wasn't entirely sure of it, but when Sweet didn't immediately contradict me, I felt better about things.

I went on. "I understand you're new, like McGraw. You both need a win, and you think you can do it on my back with very little work. McGraw does, anyway. I think you're a better attorney than he is a cop, which isn't saying much, I admit. But you didn't get where you are by having cousins in high places. You don't need to lose a murder case. You need to win one, and I can give it to you."

"You're talking pretty big for a fugitive, Mr. Flaner." Her voice was cold and professional. She was hard to love.

"What? No, I'm out on bail."

"Don't play dumb, Mr. Flaner. It doesn't suit you."

"That was the nicest thing you've ever said to me."

"You're welcome."

"Go get the paper and keep it. I'll turn myself in soon," I said. "There's only one piece left to find. It's a big piece, the long connecting piece the rest hangs on. Kinda like an axel."

"I'll call Captain Olsen and visit Chronoboost."

"Good. Also, talk to Justin Bertone if you can. If he wakes up. I think he was going to tell me something important today, but he didn't get the chance."

"I'll see if I have time."

"Make time for it. If one murder and two attempted murders won't get you moving, what will? An earthquake? If you don't look into this, I'll call the papers, and my congressman, and my aunt Selma, who can't keep a secret to save her life. She's the worst gossip this side of the

Rockies. Of course, I'll do all this after I cry myself into a migraine at the state of our legal system."

"Don't be so dramatic, Mr. Flaner."

"Don't be so hard-headed, Ms. Sweet. Did you write everything down?"

"I did," she said.

"Good." I hung up.

A part of me said to give up then. It hadn't fazed me during the conversation, but Sweet's announcement that I'd made things worse for myself rang in my head like a dizzying concussion. I was playing a dangerous game. I was playing detective, pretending that good guys win and amateur private detectives solve crimes. I had no hard evidence to prove my innocence, let alone indict someone else. And I was no longer innocent.

I may not have killed anyone, but I had committed unlawful entry and burglary. I had knowingly eluded lawful arrest and crossed state lines. That couldn't be good. I'd made contact with the prosecuting DA and talked to her even after she warned me that it was possibly a crime to do so. I'd fled a crime scene at Chronoboost and illegally searched Justin's desk. I'd fled a hospital after an attempted murder without making an official statement, and took a terrycloth bathrobe and two towels from the Rio Hotel and Casino. I'd impersonated a policeman several times and kidnapped and drugged my ex-wife's lover. A reasonable person might even misconstrue my actions towards Mudge as assault. And I wasn't finished yet.

No, I couldn't call myself innocent. I was in deep now, my fingers almost touched. It was hard and dangerous, and I'd never gone this far or this deep into anything before. It wasn't that I was forced to go on, or even that my life's compass of pushing and pulling was at work. I'd followed a new, blind stubbornness I didn't know I possessed. It was a side of me that would have made Nancy proud, might have even saved our marriage. It was decisive, and "all-in," and not like me at all.

For the first time since the dead-end with Harris, I almost gave up. I considered just going to Sweet, telling her what I knew, and letting other people settle the matter for me, one way or the other. They might even figure it out the way I thought it should go. They might. But they might not.

I needed to see this thing through. For Rose. And for me.

I still kept the finger trap in my pocket. I looked at it and saw it in a new way. It could connect and trap two people as well as one. I saw Rose's finger in one side and mine in the other like when she'd given it to me that crazy night a lifetime ago. Neither of us would be free without the other.

Deeper I went.

I drove by Rex's place that evening and saw lights blazing in his windows. The red setting sun reflected off the chipping building, making it look like an inflamed zit. I sat across the street in my car watching the shadows move in his window. At one point, a figure looked out. It may have been Rex. He may have seen me.

A short while later, I heard a knock on my passenger door. I saw only a silver belt buckle through the window.

"Hello?" I said. "What do you want?"

"Whatchu doin' here?" a man asked in a twangy southern accent. "Come out of there so I can see you."

It wasn't a cop, and Lahkpa's goons would have already dragged me out by my vocal cords. I got out. I didn't see the other guy behind the car until he grabbed me.

I was pulled off my feet from behind. I crashed onto the pavement after sliding down the car door. I didn't enjoy the experience.

"What the hell?" The stranger who'd pulled me down planted a heavy toe into my gut. My diaphragm exhausted my lungs to make room for the shoe.

I rolled away, and the next kick caught me in the ass. Plenty of padding there, but the bruise from the hypo didn't approve.

I rolled over and got to my feet

The one from behind was a young kid, twenty maybe. His Texas-talking friend with a cowboy belt buckle the size of a dinner plate was a year or two older. They weren't taller than me, but they were wider, particularly at the shoulders and thighs. These kids had either grown up in Gold's Gym or lived entirely on steroids. Either way, they were Olympic-class bullies whose muscles bulged out of their shirts like potatoes in a condom.

"Wait a minute," I gasped.

"You're not welcome here," the cowboy said.

"I'm leaving," I wheezed. Then the kicker pinned my arms in a full Nelson. I twisted and fought, but I was locked as tight as if I was chained into colonial stocks. All that was lacking were rotten vegetables and verbal abuse. The abuse I got was physical.

Cowboy gave me all he had in the gut, and my air was gone again. I bent over and looked for it under the car. An upper cut caught me on the chin, and the night filled with fireworks and iron-flavored chewing gum before fading to black.

* * *

I came to beside my car. Blood seeped from a gash in my tongue where I must have bitten it. I spit out pieces of a shattered molar and drew air into my chest in small calculated gasps—just enough to breathe, not enough to expand my chest beyond necessity. I don't remember anything happening to my ribs, but the pain and torn shirt confirmed that something bad had. Must have been kicked while I was down. Seemed appropriate.

The light wasn't much different from what I remembered before the mugging, so I figured I hadn't been out long. Maybe a minute, maybe ten.

I got to my knees and crawled to the car. The open-door alarm was still cheerfully chirping away. It didn't want me to forget to lock the car.

I swung myself onto the seat and spit out strings of blood. My mouth was thick and sticky. An approaching headache began its malevolent rumblings in the back of my skull like an army marching ever closer for slaughter. This was going to be bad.

There was no sign of my attackers. I reached for my wallet. It was there, untouched. My car was still there, the key still in the ignition. I looked at the building again and then up to the third floor, to the windows of apartment C. A single silhouette was framed in it. I couldn't see a face, but I knew it was the same person who'd called the bench-pressing buddies to pummel my middle-aged body to pulp.

I waved, then turned my hand around and offered a middle finger salute to the window. I'd have blown a raspberry if my tongue hadn't been hamburger. The figure didn't move.

I closed the door and drove to the emergency room.

I had to wait an hour, but I slept through most of it. I paid my co-pay with a credit card and told them I was mugged. They took me back and x-rayed me, prodded me, and poked me, and then I threw up on the floor. I remember apologizing to a nurse. I'd ruined her nice, white shoes. I hoped she had more nylons in her locker. I'd pay for everything, I'd said before falling asleep again.

When I woke up the next time, there was a black policeman standing over me, calling my name.

"Who's Rex?" he said.

"What?"

"You said Rex. Is he the guy who did this to you?"

I blinked and recognized the face.

"You're the cop from Rose's apartment, aren't you?" I said with a swollen tongue.

"I think her name was Rose," he said. "Yeah, I met you at a crime scene. I'm Sergeant Barkley."

"Ah shit, I knew it was a bad idea to go to the hospital."

"Why's that? You have a concussion, two cracked ribs, some dental damage, and a chunk out of your tongue. Why was it a bad idea?"

"Aren't you here to arrest me?" I felt so terrible that at that moment, I didn't care if he did.

"No. Not at all. Should I?"

Once again, I'd overestimated my importance in the crime-fighting spectrum. Sure, there was a warrant out for me, but they didn't announce it at morning roll call. If he didn't check, he'd never know. Rose and I just weren't that important. "No. We've already done that. I'm groggy," I said. "I gotta get going. I'm not done yet."

"I think you are. The doctors say you need to spend a few days here for observation."

That again?

I was in a hospital room. The second one that week. I don't remember Thomas Magnum, P.I., being in the hospital every week.

"How long have I been here?" My tongue felt foreign and over-large in my mouth. It was like I was sucking on a sensitive rib-eye steak.

"You came in about ten last night. It's nine in the morning now."

I recalled moments of consciousness when nurses took my clothes off, and I asked them if they had protection because I'd forgotten mine. I remember a male nurse waking me up every time I fell asleep and asking me what month it was. Didn't they have a fucking calendar here? I remember being stabbed in my left arm while my right was strangled. I saw an IV in one and a blood pressure cuff on the other. That explained the torture.

"Barkley, I gotta go. I'm in the middle of something. I have an appointment. Could you send in the doctor?"

"I could, but I need a statement from you."

"About what?"

"About who beat the shit out of you and why?"

"I don't know who they were. But I think I know why. And if you got me a current college yearbook, I bet I could find them under 'anabolic abusers.'"

"Why did they do this to you?"

"Because they didn't like me."

"What did you do to them?"

"Nothing," I said, "but I should have tried harder."

"They steal anything?"

"Nope. It was a hit."

"Flaner, don't be theatrical. I have to make a report."

"Okay, for the record." I told him the pieces of the story that weren't lies and wouldn't get me in more trouble. It was tricky. I told him where the attack took place, and I gave him the best description of the steroidal twins I could. When he asked what I was doing on that street, I said I was making a phone call. When he asked me how long I'd been there, I told him over an hour.

"Pretty long phone call," he said.

"I watched the sunset, too. Send in the doctor now, okay?"

He looked at his notes, glared at me suspiciously, but, in the end, fetched a green-eyed doctor in green scrubs and plastic shoes.

"Can I go home now?"

"I wouldn't advise it," he said. "You have a concussion. You seem all right now, but we'd like to keep an eye on you. Plus you have some cracked ribs, and they'll hurt like hell."

"Give me a prescription," I said. "I have places to go."

"I still think you should stay, but I can't keep you. Did you talk to the cop?"

"I did."

"Strange he came all the way out here."

"Why? He wasn't here already?"

"No. We usually just report suspected crimes, and they sometimes send out a clerk to take a statement. Real cops never come unless it's big, like a shooting, or they're going to arrest someone. And we never see sergeants."

"Did you mention my name in the call out?"

"Don't know. Probably. We usually do. In case you're a wanted man or something."

I removed my arm from the cuff and reached for the needle.

"Whoa, let me do that." The doctor unstrung me and handed me my clothes.

When I was dressed, a nurse armed with forms and waivers, pre-scriptions, and instruction sheets, waited for my attention.

I signed everything, agreed to everything, and took everything she handed me.

I walked out to the door and looked down the hallway. Sergeant

Barkley was not there. I walked calmly to the elevator and then turned and took the stairs.

Five painful floors later, I was in the lobby. I walked through the building and left through a back door, circling around. Each step reminded me that I was injured in breath-halting jolts of rib-crackling goodness. I watched my car from behind a service truck for three minutes to make sure no one else was watching it before I got in.

A pool of dried blood the size of my hand stained the seat between my legs. Similar stains adorned the inner thighs of my pants. The steering wheel was crusty with gory fingerprints.

I started the car and backed out.

My heart rate made my breathing fast. Each breath was a burden. Just about the time that catching my breath no longer made me catch my breath, I found myself again in front of Rex Merkin's apartment, ready to break the law.

CHAPTER FORTY

I hurt in places I didn't know had nerve endings. My tongue was a used milk bone. My chest ached, and my head felt like someone was pounding nails into my skull with a bowling trophy. But I could see and I could walk, and I still had my burglar bag.

I got out of my car. My phone rang.

"Hello."

"Tony. It's Morris. You called?"

"Yeah, but I got it handled."

"What did you get handled?"

"A problem."

"Did 'handling it' put you in the hospital?"

"How do you know about that?"

"Assistant District Attorney Sweet told me."

"Really?"

"Really. So what does this mean?"

"It means she didn't have me arrested when she could have."

"I'm not sure that's a good thing, Tony. Prosecutors don't give suspects rope unless they intend to hang them with it."

"So I shouldn't meet her at the oxbow?"

"Tony, it's getting worse, isn't it?"

"Yes."

"I knew it."

"You ever hear about a law firm called Smith, Bannon and Taylor?"

"Yes, they're a small outfit. They mostly do contract work. Actually, I think they exclusively do contract work."

"How about a firm called Dewey, Cox & Leik? I think they're back east."

"Seriously? That's a name?"

"Yeah."

"Never heard of them," said Mollif. "Why?"

"They might call you. I'm getting entangled with one of their clients, and they said they'd take steps."

"Wouldn't want that. Will I be hearing from Smith, Bannon and Taylor?"

"No, but they may be hearing from you, I think."

"Why?"

"It's complicated. When I have all the pieces, I'll lay them out for you, but right now I have to do something."

"What do you have to do?"

"Something stupid," I said. "Something that will probably make things worse."

"Tony, don't."

"Talk to you later, Morris." I hung up and turned off my phone.

I marched up the stairs to Rex's apartment. I had my gun. I didn't want to illegally conceal it, so I had it in my right hand, hammer cocked. Just in case.

I met no one and quickly found myself in front of apartment C with a loaded revolver in one hand and bag with a brick in it in the other.

I tried the door. It was locked. No MasterLock here. I'd have to do this the old-fashioned way.

My lock pick set came out, and I fiddled with the bolt for fifteen minutes. The spring bar dug into my hand as I probed and tripped pin after pin until I heard the luscious snap of the lock turning over. The bottom lock opened with a credit card. I was in.

I snapped my latex gloves on like Dr. Frank-N-Furter after the Time Warp and walked in.

The apartment was as I'd remembered it. The computer nook and widescreen TV were as before. The couches weren't filled with sycophantic friends swilling free beer, but they were where I remembered them being.

The TV had been big, but it was bigger now. It was huge. A label on the side told me it was new. It still had the overpriced-electronics-built-by-underpaid-Chinese-slave-labor smell. Ah, capitalism. It was top of the line. If it cost less than eight grand, I'd be shocked. Not the kind of high-definition wall display an average college student could afford. Hell, most colleges couldn't. It was the size of a billboard. I couldn't figure out how he got it in the room.

The sofa was expensive. I couldn't guess what it cost, but I figured leather wasn't cheap, and there was a lot of leather. The computer had more accessories than Paris Hilton's toy closet. The chair at the desk had a control panel on the arm. It was either from Sharper Image or the Starship Enterprise. Either way, it hadn't been free.

Empty glasses and wine bottles were scattered on every surface and overflowed onto the floor. The smell of fast-food curry and burnt toast hung in the air.

The bedroom had a king-size bed and sheets slicker than grease wadded up at the foot. Drawers in a modern chrome dresser were left open, clothes tossed out in heaps like someone ahead of me had searched it with less care than a grenade might have shown.

I found nothing interesting. He needed a maid; that's the most I got from the bedroom. His bathroom bothered me. It wasn't what I found, it's what I didn't find. There were no personal toiletries. I could find no toothbrush or toothpaste. I couldn't find a razor, comb, or brush. A half-finished bottle of shampoo was in the shower, but that was it. The medicine cabinet was bare as well. Cleaned out. I found a bottle of aspirin and popped four into my mouth, chewing them to paste before drinking from the faucet.

A side bedroom had three mountain bikes, six pairs of skis, a wall of DVDs, several piles of books, a dozen closed boxes and two racks of clothes that rolled-on castors.

I rummaged through some boxes and poked through some pockets.

He had clothes to go with each pair of skis and special biking shoes that I'd wager cost more than the bikes themselves.

A pile of recent mail lay unopened on top of one of the boxes. I helped myself.

There was an unkind note from his bank reminding him that he was overdrawn by six thousand dollars. Another bank was less friendly and told him to pay the ten-thousand-dollar overdraft immediately, or they'd "take action." I wondered if that was like "steps." I counted six credit cards with a combined balance due of thirty-four thousand dollars. A bill for last semester's tuition was marked overdue and requested a mere three thousand five hundred dollars before he was suspended.

All the poking around took a toll on my beaten body. My head pounded. My ribs felt like ground glass. The aspirin had done nothing but remind me of the chunk missing from my tongue and how much I needed a drink. I wondered if Mudge would still sell me one of his bottles.

Back in the main studio room, I found the window that looked out into the street where my car was parked. It had a commanding view.

The computer monitor was off, but I heard the spinning of the hard drive within the tower. I found the switch to the monitor on its backside and pressed it. The screen warmed up. There was an error box display. Shut down had been cancelled; something about a disc being improperly ejected.

I cleared the message box and received another one. The trash had been successfully emptied. Well, bully for it.

I cleared the trash notice and finally saw the desktop. I examined the hard drive. It was huge but empty. Nearly eight hundred fifty gigabytes were available.

I poked around the folders. The system was intact. The applications folder contained the usual programs and a few games, notably Colonies. There was a folder for saved games, but it was empty.

The documents folder had no music or movies. The photo folder had a few pictures. They were all new, based on the time stamp. Must have been importing when the trash was emptied.

I opened the photos and felt sick—well, sicker, anyway. There were ten pictures, all taken from the window to my right. Each showed my Toyota Prius lit in pimply evening light. The first showed me on the ground after the first kick. The second showed me crawling and getting up. The rest showed the beating I couldn't remember. I wanted to throw up. The last photos showed the two men waving up at the camera, and then me left for dead on the street.

What kind of a sick, sadistic bastard would take snapshots of a beating? The same kind of sick, sadistic bastard who'd arranged it. The same kind of cold motherfucker Carlos had described, who'd strangle a helpless girl.

The rest of the computer had been wiped. I'm sure a computer jockey could find something else on it, porno and plagiarized term papers, but I didn't need to see any more. My temples pulsed in barely controlled rage as I turned the monitor off and left the computer running.

The kitchen was a mess. The remains of a hasty meal were in the sink, eggs and toast by the look of it. Coffee stood cold in the coffee maker under a cabinet.

Aspirin was mortared into the cracks of my broken tooth, and I needed more water. The fridge had a built-in dispenser. I opened the cabinets looking for a water glass.

I clasped the glass and pulled it down before recognition clicked in. I turned the glass over and stared at Wilma Flintstone.

"Hello," I said.

Dino was in the cabinet too, behind a thick, deeply-cut highball glass.

I put Wilma back and searched the rest of the cabinets. Nothing. I pulled the half-full garbage out from under the sink and dumped it on the floor. Coffee grounds splatted like mud, and a cloud of burnt toast scrapings and eggshells puffed and crashed after it.

I bent down and carefully went through the garbage. I was playing a hunch, grabbing at straws, but after what I'd found in Justin's can, I was feeling lucky.

A neon green ball of paper caught my eye. I knew that color. I fished it out of the trash and fell into a chair at Rex's kitchen table. Carefully, I unfolded the paper.

It was a cocktail napkin from the Comedy Cellar. If the neon green didn't give it away, the gold lettering proclaiming "The Comedy Cellar" might have suggested a clue to its origin.

Written on the napkin in familiar heart-breaking letters, was the string of characters I had seen in Justin's office: S O M1 CP at 2. The "at" was spelled out. The "O" was in the shape of a heart. Rose had written this.

I stared at the note and took slow, shallow breaths as the aspirin found my bloodstream and cleared a little pain debris off the thinking superhighway.

The night I met Rose at the Comedy Cellar, she'd met Justin. He'd worn that stupid "127.0.0.1" T-shirt. He'd told her something at the bar. They couldn't hear each other. I remembered she'd written something on a napkin.

This was the connection. I just didn't know what the hell it meant.

I put the napkin in my pocket and left the garbage on the floor. My skull was a bone anvil, and my heart was a steel hammer. I'd stayed too long anyway. I'd been inside Rex's "flop house for the ridiculously stuck-up and spoiled" for forty-five minutes. I'd left new piles of chaos everywhere and made an already foul kitchen even worse with stinking garbage. A job well done.

I collected my things and went to the door. I paused and looked at the wall-sized TV, and then took a deep breath, feeling every crack and splinter in my chest. I rolled my tongue across my gnarled tooth, felt my scraped bullet-wound in my shoe, and my bruised and stabbed ass in my pants. I took my brick out of my bag and hurled it into the vast flat-screen TV. It made a very satisfying crash when it went through.

I pulled the door shut and went to my car, calm as a brush salesman, and drove to the nearby pharmacy at a Smith's grocery store.

I didn't know what I would say or how I would react when I saw him at work. I thought I might reach up and grab the murdering psychopath by his silver locks and drag him to my car. I thought I might just tell him to enjoy watching TV tonight and call the cops. I wasn't in my right mind; I was madder than I'd ever been. I had a concussion. I realized I was holding my gun. I put it away before I stormed into the store.

The hospital had given me three prescriptions.

"I'd like to fill these," I said angrily to the clerk behind the glass, a middle-aged woman with thinning brown hair.

"Not a problem," she said. "It'll just take a few minutes."

"Is Rex here?" I said. Well, demanded, really. I wasn't making friends. I could see my intensity was frightening the woman. A male coworker stepped alongside her.

"No, Rex is on vacation," she said.

"The fuck?" I said.

"He's on vacation," she said. "He's out of the country, I think."

With that, she scooted away from the window and back among the shelves of identical white bottles.

"What's your problem?" the man wanted to know.

"I'm looking for Rex," I said.

"Why?"

"So I can pummel the ever-living shit out of him, play marbles with his eyeballs, and piss down his severed neck."

He smiled.

"I'd love to see that. I think all of us would," he said. "But like Mrs. Collin said, Rex took a vacation. He said he was going to win some video game contest in Asia."

"What day is it?" I said to myself. "I should have seen this coming. I'm an idiot!"

"He'll be back in two weeks," the man said. "I hope you catch him."

I bought a box of donuts and a sports drink. I ate dinner in the blood-pressure chair next to the pharmacy counter, chewing on my options and pain pills.

CHAPTER FORTY-ONE

My whole life taught me to go with the flow. I'd floated through life like Huck and Jim, careless and without a purpose greater than freedom, which was actually a pretty great purpose really. But, at that moment, my purpose was my physical and spiritual salvation—another great purpose. The path of least resistance was not a bad pattern to use when playing detective.

My new river pointed me into more trouble. I'd go. I didn't know what would happen, couldn't think of what to do once I was there, but the stream flowed to Thailand, and so to Thailand I would go.

But first, a little nap. The adrenalin I'd ridden in Rex's apartment was long gone and the sugar was fading, about to be lapped by the pain pills that could cause drowsiness when taken as directed—a single pill every six hours, not three at once. Plus, there was that concussion to think about.

Finding a place to sleep in one's car is not as easy as it sounds. If you just pull into a parking lot, you have maybe twenty minutes before somebody knocks on your window to make sure you're "all right," which is Good Samaritan for "not dead." A rest stop off a major freeway is ideal. You could leave a corpse in a parked car undiscovered for months at one of those, but I didn't have the energy or desire to go so far. I needed a garage. I needed a bed. I went home.

Someone had been there. The place had been tossed. No one had thrown a brick through my TV, but the irony wasn't lost on me.

I decided to worry about it later and passed out.

* * *

Mid-afternoon, I woke up to pounding on my door. I lay in bed beneath my covers for fifteen minutes until I heard a throaty truck drive away.

My aching jaw was swollen. My ripped tongue rubbed against my broken tooth, and breathing with cracked ribs was an adventure. Just for a full inventory of injuries, I rolled over until I could feel my stabbed ass, egg-induced bruises, and scabbed gunshot wound against my cotton sheets. Check. All there.

I showered, cleaned up, and packed for a vacation. I found my yellow Fly Away jacket wadded up in the closet. I shook it out once, and it snapped into perfect pressed presentation. It was a miracle of modern fabric engineering.

Then I made a phone call.

* * *

I left my house with as much stealth as I could. I should have let the garage door open completely, but I was in a hurry, and antennas are overrated anyway.

I drove looking through my mirror more than my windshield, my head swiveling like a radar dish tracking potential threats. Nothing jumped out at me, rammed me, or shot at me, and I soon found myself in my old neighborhood in front of Nancy's house.

It was getting easier to think of it as Nancy's house now, and not mine, or used-to-be mine. It was never mine. It was always Nancy's. Every house had always been Nancy's. I was always a passenger in her life, staring out the windows. Along for the ride.

There was an unfamiliar car in the driveway, but I knew the thin mustache that got out of it and marched to Nancy's door. What did McGraw want with her?

I drove by.

Twenty minutes later, McGraw was gone. I parked away from the house, and under the dazzling disguise of a Mariner's baseball cap, I strolled up the neighbor's driveway and into their backyard like before. I hopped the fence with all the grace of a guy with cracked ribs. I glanced up the street in time to see an approaching orange block, which was Randy's school bus.

The key had been moved. The rock wasn't even there. I checked the old mortar slot. It wasn't there either. Sound came from the house. Randy yelled a greeting. I peeked over a windowsill into the kitchen.

"What are you doing, Tony?"

I screamed.

It wasn't a manly, agonized, arterial spray kind of howl, more like a teenage-girl-finding-a-spider-in-her-slipper kind of screech.

She'd walked right up behind me, and I hadn't noticed. Sam Spade spun in his grave, Sherlock Holmes cursed me, and Father Brown shook his head and lit a cigarette in disgust.

"You scared me half to death," I said, slumping against the house.

Nancy stood with her arms akimbo, dirty gardening gloves on her hands. She wore that look on her face that'd etched a thousand lines in mine.

"What happened to you? You look like you got beat up. There was a cop here looking for you. Is this what he meant when he said it would be better if he found you before the other guys?"

"That was nice of him," I said. "What other guys?"

"He mentioned bounty hunters," she said. "Is that who hurt you?"

"Different guys," I said. "I'm still on the case."

"Playing detective? Looks like you're good at it."

"Actually, I am, Nancy. You'd be impressed."

She turned my face to get a better look at my chin.

"Open your mouth," she commanded. I complied. "Your ribs, too?"

I nodded.

"Come in."

I did.

We sat at the kitchen table, and she made me coffee. She'd offered me some "strong wine," but I passed on that.

The kitchen had returned to some of the utility from before Leaf-caller. Gone were some of the Chia-pet planters of herbs and the crystal wind chimes over the sink. It wasn't as I'd known it, but it wasn't as I'd last seen it either.

"Where's Mudge?"

"Leafcaller is teaching," she said. "He'll be back later."

I almost began telling her what I knew about him, but then thought better of it.

"Is he what you want?" I asked.

She sipped her coffee, and I saw a glimmer of the woman I'd married.

"I thought so, but now I don't know. It's okay for a while," she said. "Maybe not forever."

"Really?"

"He's focused and ambitious like you never were. But he might be disposable. I need disposable right now. We were married too long, Tony. We should have made it work properly or tossed it in sooner. We screwed up."

"I don't know. It worked all right. I'm not complaining."

"I think we lost valuable years."

"I'm offended."

"I'm sorry," she said. "You were teaching me a lesson, and I just didn't get it."

"Offended again," I said.

"No, not that kind of lesson. Not a cruel payback or anything. A life lesson. You were always laissez-faire, and I was always rigid and disciplined. I think you were happier."

I dissolved sugar cubes in my coffee with slow circle eights.

"I don't know about happy," I said. "I may have been carefree, but I didn't have a purpose. You've always had one of those. I just barely got one. It's a good thing."

"What's your purpose?"

"I need to find Rose's killer," I said.

"They can't convict you of that. You didn't do it."

There was no reservation in her voice. It was like a weight lifted off me.

"Thanks for saying that," I said.

She touched my cheek and smiled.

I said, "The police won't put in the effort to go past the obvious: me. The people who cared about her, and there are many who loved her, are going to be let down. They believe the cops because, well, they're the cops."

"What was she to you, Tony?" The question was honest and non-judgmental, but I suspected she suspected something.

"She was a young, beautiful girl who wanted to get to know me. She waited until I was available and pounced with indefensible feminine tactics of flattery and interest. She was self-sufficient, and even though she had a string of friends, ex-lovers, and business associates, she was alone."

Nancy watched me and sipped coffee.

"I really don't know much about her, Nance. I would never have lasted. She was a grifter and a thief. She went through men like Kleenex, sold drugs, never paid taxes, and collected nostalgia. I would have liked to have gotten to know her better, but I didn't get the chance."

"And that's why you're doing this? Why you're letting yourself get beaten up? For a girl you didn't know?"

"But I did, Nancy. I knew her because she was a real person, an individual, not a copy. She was me, or some part of me. Maybe the person I want to be, maybe the person I used to be. I don't know. But she mattered."

"The cop said he's added a long list of crimes to your charges. Looks like you're only making things worse."

"You've been talking to my lawyer, haven't you?"

"No," she said indignantly.

"That's what he always says," I said. "Yeah, I've been getting in deeper, but I don't see another way through. It's me, too, don't forget. Not just Rose Griff, but Tony Flaner who has something at stake in figuring this out."

That made more sense to her. To me, I was the lesser motivation, I realized, but she was used to my selfishness and could hang it there. I let her.

"So how long for Mudge?"

"Until it's not good anymore," she said. "Three months, a year maybe."

I had to ask. "Are you giving him money?"

"A little."

I raised an eyebrow.

"He needed a loan. He offered me the title to his car as collateral."

"But you didn't take it," I said.

"No."

"You might want to rethink that," I said.

That did it.

"Tony, your jealousy is tiring. Here I thought we could be friends, and you're digging into my business like it's yours."

"Sorry," I said.

That stare was back, but there was uncertainty behind it. I waited for her to ask me if I knew anything.

"What are you doing here, Dad?" Randy came into the kitchen. "Mom said you weren't allowed here anymore."

I glanced at her.

She shrugged. "Your presence makes things difficult between Leaf-caller and me."

"I understand." I opened my arms to hug Randy. He was a teenager, so he stared at me like I was holding bloody cleavers. I dropped my arms. It was better for my injuries to wave anyway.

"What happened to your face?"

"I got beat up," I said. "All great detectives get beat up at least once every case."

"And this is yours?" he said.

"Actually, this is my second beating. Maybe third. Fourth? The cops did it first, then someone tried to kill me in Vegas, and then that same guy got me beat up on the street. Oh, and in a parking lot after a burrito. This time, I got a concussion and everything. I puked on a nurse's shoes and spit out a piece of my tongue with tooth fragments."

"Cool," said Randy. His mother glared at us.

"That means you're getting close," he said, ignoring his mother. He'd adapted his natural, pubescent ablative shield to Nancy's glare frequency years ago.

"Precisely," I said. "Actually, Randy, I came to see you. You've got the clue I need. Did you find it?"

Nancy swung her lasers back on me. I held up my arm as a shield.

"Sorry, Dad. I don't have much to tell you." He took a box of high-fiber cereal out of a cupboard and sat down with it, popping handfuls into his mouth and chewing. It sounded like a rock tumbler.

"You found nothing? It's all kosher?"

"I think there might be something," he said. "Phil, John, and I watched every replay we could find from RexingBall. We don't know how he's winning. He didn't used to. He doesn't play as well as other players, but now he wins."

"Go on," I said. Nancy poured him a glass of milk after he coughed up a hairball of wheat-germ-hemp, edible-fiber, vitamin-enriched turf.

"There's a calculator in the game. APM—Actions Per Minute," Randy explained. "It's a measurement of how many things you're actually doing in a game. The higher the APM, the more things you're doing. You know, like telling this guy to attack while keeping that guy back, and harvesting that fungus, and building that tower. Well, Rexingball's APM is way low. It's nowhere near the levels of other good players. He's in the nineties, and they're in the two hundreds. He should be getting his ass handed to him."

"So he's just that good?" I asked.

"Can't see that either. There're certain moments in the game that put you behind if you don't do them on time. Like, you have to build a food cache at eight workers so it's ready when you hit ten or you run out of food. Sooner than that, it doesn't pay off. RexingBall ignores them and goes into hunger nearly every game. It's an obvious error, but he's getting away with it."

"So he's cheating?"

"We don't see how. The game is the game. Everyone gets the

same game. There's no room for any kind of hack, particularly at a tournament."

"Because if one player had it, everyone would?"

"Yeah, plus you'd see it. It's televised and recorded. A cheat screen would be a little obvious." He drained his glass. "The hack would have to be built into the program, and only the programmers would know about it, and they're forbidden to participate in tournaments."

The smile hurt my swollen face.

"Randy, you're a genius," I said. "I don't know how I missed it."

"What?" said Nancy, her eyes no longer weapons, but saucers of surprise and interest.

I fished the green napkin out of my pocket and unfolded it on the table before my son. Nancy craned her neck to read it.

"Someone CP at two?" she said.

I ignored her.

"Ignore your mother, son," I said, not for the first time I was ashamed to recall. "What could this mean?"

"S O M one CP at two," he read aloud.

"I've seen it written with an 'at sign' instead of spelled out," I said. "If that helps."

Randy stared at the napkin. His young synapses fired in a way I could only envy. My phone rang. There was a knock on the door. Nancy got up. I hushed the phone to voicemail and turned to look down the hall.

Nancy marched to the door.

"Mrs. Flaner," said a gruff voice. Nancy didn't open the door more than three inches. She had to look up—way up—to see the man she was talking to.

"Yes? What do you want?" she asked.

"We're looking for your ex-husband, Tony Flaner. We were hoping you could help us find him. Do you know where he is?"

She hesitated and closed the door a little. My ribs hurt.

My phone vibrated. I had a message.

"I don't know where he is, and if I did, I doubt I'd tell you."

"Interesting," he said.

Nancy made to close the door. That woman had no sense. Why didn't she just announce that I was in the kitchen?

"He's wanted for murder," the man said. I could see his foot in the house. It was a big foot.

"Dad," whispered Randy.

He pointed to the backyard window. A man was falling over the back fence into a bush. I dropped to the floor and scooted under the window.

"Act normal," I said.

Randy nodded.

"Hey, Mom!" he yelled as loud as he could. "There's a strange man in the backyard!" The windows shook from his volume. The boy had a pair of lungs in him.

"Should I call the police or get the gun and *stand my ground?*" he yelled. I knew the intruder in the backyard could hear him too. That must have been the intention. I loved my boy.

"Both," Nancy yelled and slammed the door. She threw the bolts and hustled back to the kitchen.

She and Randy watched out the window for a minute and then relaxed.

"They're gone," said Nancy.

"No, they're not," I said. "Can you help me get out of here?"

"Where are you going?"

"To hell in a bucket, but first I'm off to Bangkok."

CHAPTER FORTY-TWO

Nancy helped me out of her car trunk in front of airport terminal two. I smelled like a spare tire, and my legs were cramped and crippled from being in a ball for an hour. I stretched and looked around.

"Were you followed?" I asked.

"Yes. A huge brown truck with two guys in it."

"How'd you lose them?"

"City shopping mall parking. Only eight-foot clearance. I came out on State Street. If they followed me in, they'd need a wrecker to get out."

"Good thinking," I said, putting on my yellow jacket.

"Good luck, Tony," she said and carefully planted a kiss on my non-swollen cheek.

Armed with my yellow Fly Away blazer, I walked right around security without as much as a glance, let alone a cancer scan or search from the TSA. I met Mittens at the gate.

He led me through the service door and out on the tarmac. He took my luggage, slapped tags on them, and tossed them onto a conveyer.

He handed me a ticket envelope. "You have a layover in Los Angeles for an hour. Don't get off the plane."

I nodded.

"Don't do anything stupid, okay? You've got no passport, and the Thai have a reputation. Call me when you're coming back. Are you coming back?"

"I'll call you," I said.

I was traveling under the name Jake Hammer. I hadn't as much as a scribble on tissue paper to back up the claim, but I wouldn't need it.

From his coffee-stained luggage desk, Mittens checked me in and printed a boarding pass.

"Did anyone unknown to you pack your bags or put anything it them?"

"Has anyone ever answered 'yes' to that question?"

"No. It's logically impossible to answer 'yes.' If you answer yes, then you know, and the question requires that you don't know."

"Then I don't know," I said.

"Okay. Are you transporting anything dangerous? Chemicals or firearms?"

I pulled my gun out of my pocket and handed it to Mittens.

"Here you go," I said. "You keep this."

"Damn," he said. "I was joking. Sure you won't need it?"

"No, but if you have it, I won't be tempted to add skyjacking to my list of recent naughties."

"Okay," he said and put the gun in his pocket. "You have a room at the Imperial. That's what you wanted, isn't it?"

"Yes. How'd you pull that off? I was sure the place would be booked."

"I cashed in a ton of frequent flyer miles."

"But I don't have frequent flyer miles," I said.

"Yes, you do. Lots and lots." He winked.

* * *

The flight took forever. The Pacific is a big ocean, and the wait in L.A. was actually four hours. The first-class seat made things easier, but even so, I was damn happy to get off that plane; warm nuts and moist towels only go so far.

Bleary-eyed and half-drunk on complimentary martinis, I collected my suitcase in Bangkok and stood in line for a taxi outside.

An eighty-foot, full-color illustrated, mural-quality banner was draped over the road. Amid depictions of deserts and forests, spiders, tanks, eagles, and dragons were the words "Welcome, Colonies Champions!" in a dozen languages.

I was in the right place.

Mittens had invented, transferred, and forged millions of sky miles for Jake Hammer, of 123 Somestreet, Anytown, U.S.A. and upgraded him across the board. Jake, who never needed to show ID, had platinum accounts on every airline that shared miles with Fly Away, which was every airline that flew into Salt Lake City, which was every airline I could think of. He had traded in the miles for a penthouse suite in Bangkok during the biggest convention of the year because "We gotta look out for each other."

The room was larger than my house. I had two fruit baskets, one bakery basket, and six bottles of liquor, all compliments of the hotel, and a dozen air carriers who appreciated my patronage and were happy—no, thrilled—to see me "enjoying the rewards of my travel."

The real coup was the plastic VIP all-access convention pass I found on the bed by flowers and a deluxe collector's copy of Colonies, compliments of Stormfront Games. I couldn't imagine how many thousands of miles that had set Jake back. Checking in, I'd asked the concierge how much a ticket to the tournament would cost and was told it was sold-out. But he knew a guy, who knew a guy in the mob, whose little brother's second aunt's cousin would sell me a half-day, semifinal pass for one-hundred thousand Thai Bot, about thirty-two-hundred U.S. dollars.

I'd lost a day to air travel. It was Saturday night in Bangkok. I strolled my luxurious suite in bare feet and boxers, wondering what my next move should be. Sleeping wasn't out of the question, but I was jet-lagged, not tired. I'd slept plenty on the plane.

The lights of the city were foreign and exotic. It occurred to me that I didn't have to do anything. I could just stay in the suite until I was sick of it or my miles ran out, and then just disappear. Another American expatriate wouldn't be noticed, and I doubted anyone would come looking for me, even if they knew where to look.

I drank chilled champagne out of the bottle. Not a good idea.

The fizz shot up my nose and out. I let it "breathe" in my open mouth before swallowing the second time.

I thought of my detective heroes whose leads I'd followed. I had spent many an hour reading detective fiction. Nancy used to chide me over it. She said that if I wasn't reading something useful, I was wasting my time. Jury's still out on that one, I guess.

What had Marlowe done? What would Poirot do? How much evidence did Easy Rawlins, Mike Hammer, or Haratio Bosch need to close a case? How did they pull it all together? They all had friends on the inside, old cop buddies or rubes like Lestrade. I didn't even have McGraw out here.

I was in too deep to pull out now. One more push and the fingers would touch, and I'd have the solution to the trap or be hopelessly caught.

My phone rang.

"Hello."

"You made it," said Randy.

"I did. What time is it there?"

"Three in the morning. I'm calling on Mom's cell because the rates are better."

Smart boy.

"Dad," he said. Something in his voice made me smile.

"You found something, didn't you?"

"Yes, Dad. I found it."

And he told me. I took notes and repeated it all back to him to make sure I got it. There was pride in his voice, and I hoped he could hear it in mine. After we hung up, I knew I couldn't live in exile; I loved that kid.

My room had come with a full closet of formal wear, separated by size numbers like in a department store. I found a white dinner jacket, silk shirt, tie, and slacks. Feeling like James Bond and looking a little like him, I collected my VIP pass and went downstairs.

The manager saw me getting off the elevator and asked me to wait.

I'd have run like a scared rabbit if I could have thought of anywhere to go. Instead, I stayed and sweated, trying to think up a plausible explanation for the sky miles deception.

He returned accompanied by another guy. They both bowed and the bellman said, "Mr. Hammer, this is to be your man. Compliments of the hotel."

I'd heard about Thai sex tours. I guessed it started here. The five-star hotel went way beyond my expectations. They were providing me with a complimentary male prostitute. They'd assumed I was gay, probably due to the suit. I didn't want to be rude and refuse. I'd never gone that way before, but here was my chance, and when in Bangkok . . .

"Okay," I said. "Do I have to feed him?"

"He's your man. He will guide you," the manager said. That was good since I was a novice at homosexual sex; a guide would be useful.

"Has he been checked for diseases?" I asked. "AIDS and such?"

The manager's smile fell at the edges, then shock dawned in his eyes.

"No," he said. "Not like that. He's your slave."

"Leather and whips?"

"No. A slave man."

"You're giving me a slave man?" I asked. "That's nice. But how can I get him through customs?"

"No, sorry," he stammered. "Not slave. Servant. Butler."

"Oh," I said. I don't know if I was relieved or disappointed.

The hotel manager explained that he came with the suite. My man would be my personal assistant for as long as I needed him. Compliments of the management, he reiterated.

"I'll mention this in my report," I said. I didn't know what else to say, but the reply made him happy, so it was all good.

My butler bowed low and, seeing my VIP pass, offered to show me to the Colonies tournament in the "Coliseum."

The Coliseum made the Rio's pit look like a pit. Whoever designed the space was a genius. The hallway glowed in gold-leafed Thai designs that worked together in a modern interpretation that screamed wealth and history. The hallways smelled of jasmine, cigarettes filtered through air conditioners, roasted nuts, and sandalwood.

The show floor was set up like the Rio had been, with a raised platform at the bottom and surrounding seating. Booths circled those on upper levels and then bleacher seating for the cheap seats above that. The booths all had multiple monitors to watch the action. The floor seats had Internet hookups and folding desks for laptops. Another JumboTron hung above the space and video screens strobed throughout, all reflecting off the gold and jewels in the walls. Even the carpets reflected lights as if silver threads had been sewn into the design. In black light, the carpet changed to a dragon pattern that was invisible in normal light. I wished I'd brought acid.

"Hey, buddy," I said to my chaperone. "How about you go get us a couple of drinks."

"What would you like, sir?"

"Call me Tony," I said. "What's your name?"

"My name?"

I nodded. "Yes, your name. What do I call you?"

"You may call me 'man,'" he said.

I frowned and shook my head.

"Fah," he said. "My name is Fah."

"Okay, Fah. You're my man for as long as I need you. Right?"

"Yes, sir."

I glared.

"Yes, Tony."

"Okay, go get me a drink. I want what you drink. Whatever you like to drink, bring us back six of those, and tell your boss I'll need you the rest of the night."

He left obediently. Frequent flyer miles were a new kind of currency I'd never considered before.

I settled into my private VIP box and turned on the screens to watch the second game of the third quarterfinal match. It featured two Thai players. The style and speed of the game was unlike anything I'd seen in Salt Lake or Las Vegas.

Fah returned with four paper cups filled with thick, sweet alcohol. I forced one into his hand, and we toasted sky miles.

Fah wasn't much of a conversationalist at first, but two drinks in and I knew all about his family and his love of Colonies. He pointed out other VIPs to me in adjoining boxes. Everyone loved Colonies. There were three ministers here and the city mayor. He recognized the CEO of Stormfront, Alex Dorsey, with his entourage spread out over three boxes. Even the chief of police, still in uniform, stood transfixed watching the games.

A man with gravitas and a tuxedo wandered the periphery of the platform and visited boxes.

"I hope you enjoy your stay in our lovely country, Mr. Hammer," he said in upper class British. It unsettled me he knew my alias.

"I will," I said. "Thank you."

He bowed and stepped away. Damn polite people, I thought.

I said, "Fah, who was that guy?"

"That was Prem. He's the Colonies World Tournament organizer."

"Part of Stormfront?"

"No," said Fah thoughtfully. "He's a government man, a state official, part of the Thai Sports Ministry. This is his event."

I watched Mr. Prem perambulate the Coliseum. He was invisible and everywhere. Whenever I looked for him, I'd find him scrutinizing a document or scanning the audience like a Secret Service agent looking for snipers. He shook hands with everyone of note and many who just introduced themselves to him. He was well-known in the arena, the face of the state-sanctioned computer sport.

"Is he an honorable man?" I asked Fah.

"Oh yes, very honorable. All government officials in my country are kept to the very highest ethical standard."

"Really?"

"We execute corrupt officials."

That was motivation I could relate to.

Properly lubricated with another round of fermented fruit, Fah provided me with the names and bios of the best Thai players. He tried to explain the intricacies of resource management and small-scale attacks that made the Asian players so deadly. I glazed over, but I liked his enthusiasm. I let him talk. He commented on the current match and pointed out blunders and brilliancies. I could see most of it through my drunken eyes, but I wasn't an expert, as apparently everyone else in the room was.

Finally Fah mustered the courage to ask what "line of work" I was in. It was midway through his third drink. Even so, I could tell he was worried that he'd overstepped.

"Crime," I said. No need to lie. No need to tell the whole truth either.

My answer satisfied him thoroughly. It must have gone far to explain me.

There was betting everywhere. When I went to the bathroom, or rather staggered there from strong drink, I saw men holding fists of paper money above their heads, calling out odds in a dozen languages for the next match and taking bets on the spot. Police stood by to make sure everything went smoothly and honestly.

Then in the hallway, heading back to our box, I saw them.

I saw the cowboy first. I wasn't sure of the face, but I never forget a concussion-causing belt buckle. Behind him, walking like a prince through peasants, came the silver-haired Rex Merkin. He was on his way to his quarterfinal match. He'd played all day yesterday and was the only American left in the tournament, one of only two westerners who'd made it to the round. The other was a Dane called Ole Svendson who would be facing Rex next.

Rex walked like he had stick up his ass and he looked down his nose. He returned their low bows with tiny, regal head nods. He deigned to sign an autograph for one fan and accepted a wreath of flowers from another, all while never making eye contact with the peons.

Then our eyes met.

Rex's superior air blew away like a fart in a sandstorm. His face contorted in what I hoped was anger and fear, then returned to a fractured replica of its earlier conceit. He kept walking.

"Here, Fah," I said, fumbling in my pocket for a card and pen. "Take this to the white-haired freak over there walking beside that side of beef."

On the back of my card "Tony Flaner, I did not kill Rose Griff," I wrote, "But you did."

Fah took the card and dutifully presented it to Rex. He read it and furrowed his brow. When he looked up, I gestured for him to turn it over. Man, he was dense.

He turned it and read the note. His faced darkened. I liked seeing that. It made me happy.

Rex turned his back and walked away.

Fah and I returned to our booth.

"Fah, are you a betting man?"

"All Thai are," he said proudly.

"Go put all you have on Rex Merkin to win his next match."

"But he's the underdog. Six to one, at best. Ten to one mostly."

"I know," I said. "He shouldn't even be here."

"Right. A real surprise. He hasn't been favored in any match so far. The odds of him winning the tournament were something like a thousand to one."

"Go put money on him," I said. "Bring us back some water."

I pulled my last hundred out of my wallet and gave it to him.

"Bet this for me," I said as encouragement.

He shrugged, then probably remembering my line of work, hustled off to find a bookie.

I sat back and put my feet up on the table. This drew the sidelong glances of nearby box-sitters with better manners than I. I replied with my brightest, warmest, toothiest grin.

I gave a deliberate, slow, respectful nod to the chief of police, who responded in kind. He didn't seem to have a problem with my posture; it mimicked Alex Dorsey's in the Stormfront booth. An American thing.

I tried to catch Dorsey's eye, but he had at least twenty people trying to talk to him at once. He was the man of the hour.

Fah returned and gave me a ticket.

"So, who's Tony Flaner, Mr. Hammer?"

I winked at him as the show began.

Rex made a Rocky Balboa entrance. Gone was the proletariat sponsorship jacket he'd worn in Vegas. Now he was in a flamboyant crimson suit. With his hair coloring, he reminded me of road flare. He looked like a 1970s Bond villain. I didn't know designers or fashions, but his outfit wouldn't have been out of place at the Oscars or a ten-car pile-up diverting traffic.

His opponent wore a shirt advertising Tuborg Beer. It looked like a soccer jersey. He looked his age, young and hip, with a soul patch on his chin. Rex looked older than his age, which was already off the scale among his competitors.

They were introduced. Neither received overwhelming applause, but there was polite clapping and respect. The real heroes were the Thai players, two of which were already in the semifinals.

The players took their seats, donned their headphones, and began the match.

I mirrored Rex's screen on one of my monitors. Whatever he saw, I'd see.

The semis would be the best of five games, the finals seven, but all these earlier matches were the best of three. Rex beat the Dane in two.

"He was lucky," said Fah. "And so are we."

He took our tickets and went to fetch our money.

"Fah. Hold up."

I pulled another card and scribbled a note on the back again.

"Get our money and then take this to Mr. Prem," I said. "Give it only to him."

He took the card, bowed, and left. I knew he'd read it—he'd obviously read the last one—but I was growing attached to my personal man, and if it benefited him, I didn't mind. Inside information doesn't come easy.

CHAPTER FORTY-THREE

The next day, I dispensed with the black tie. I put on my usual casual American attire—shorts, tennis shoes, tie-dye T-shirt. I looked like a five-dollar tourist, so I felt like myself. I wasn't in the mood for any more deception, not even my own.

I put my dead cell phone in the charger. I cringed to think what the bill would look like. Could I pay it in sky miles? Would I have a chance to try?

The hotel manager did a double take before he recognized me, but when he did, he again asked me to wait while he fetched "my man." I waited. I knew he disapproved of my clothes, but he was too well mannered to say anything. Thus, the rude and loud dominate the polite and quiet.

Fah and I found our box. He was happy. He had made a killing on his previous day's bet. He told me I was the best companion he'd ever been assigned to. That made me glad.

"Are we going to make bets on the semis?" he asked, eager to get a wager in before the start of the first match.

"I don't think I better," I said. "But if you want to, you can. You know where to put your money."

Fah left and returned before the match started.

Rex was against a Thai hero who was favored to win the entire tournament. DragonCos was his name, and everyone knew it. His only competition, common wisdom held, was another Thai playing in the other semi, ChimChimmy.

"The bookie thought I was crazy," Fah said. "Said he'd been unable to lay off any bets at all on RexingBall."

Fah spoke proper English, but he knew betting parlance like a Jersey loan shark.

"What odds did you get?"

"Eighty to one," he said. "I think I could have gotten higher, but I took pity on him."

"Keep a low profile when all this is over," I said.

He nodded.

The match began. The stadium fell silent, all headphones and flickering screens. I watched Rex's movements carefully for the first two and a half minutes.

The first battle was met. DragonCos rushed Rex at one minute with workers and a single soldier. Rex was completely surprised and fell back until the two-minute mark. Then his soldier spawned a moment later and met the foe. The one soldier fought back against the workers with perfect surgical precision, driving the spiders back into the jungle.

Fah leaned over to me. "DragonCos should surrender. Against any first-rate player, the game would be over now."

"So why doesn't he?"

"Because he thinks RexingBall just got lucky."

The game went long, much longer than a game starting with such a bloody rush should have. Fah watched the entire match beside me, shaking his head throughout. Rex won a series of very close skirmishes and built a fortified siege line around the spider nest, and DragonCos GG'd.

The crowd was stunned.

Fah shook his head. He was on his way to riches, but his patriotic pride was hurt.

Game two was a surprise, for me at least. Rex had tried to reproduce the rush DragonCos had unleashed on him in the first game. I watched Rex's view carefully. He hit the spider base at one minute fifty-six seconds and was immediately embroiled in a bloody massacre. It was over at two minutes thirty seconds. Rex had stayed on the battle to try to salvage anything. When he flashed back on his command post at three minutes, he clicked it, and GG'd.

The crowd cheered. Reality was returning to the world.

Game three Rex stayed home. He built defenses and drones. The difference between the two players' views was striking. At one minute forty-five, Rex looked only at his command post while DragonCos was building up his actions-per-minute into the hundreds and flashing to every corner of the screen. He monitored scouting spiders and built structures, drones, and soldiers the instant enough resources were available. Rex did nothing whatsoever between one minute fifty-five and two minutes. At exactly two minutes, he made a click on the command post. Two seconds later—an eternity in Colonies time—Rex flashed around to his scouts, buildings, and resources as DragonCos had done, though not as effectively or as quickly, as measured by the APM meter.

I looked to the adjacent box. The Stormfront booth had been emptied of paparazzi and groupies. Dorsey, Stormfront's CEO, was only entertaining dignitaries today. Prem looked up from his monitor and glanced at me. There was real disgust on his face, an expression shared by many in the booth.

"Flaner," came a low voice behind me. I jumped, but Fah was on his feet between the voice and me before my neck had turned.

It was the cowboy, Rex's man, the thug who'd kicked the shit out of me and was now doting on Merkin.

He took a step toward me. Fah put his arm up and caught him on the chest, halting him. Fah was at least a foot shorter than the weight-lifting shit-kicker, and at least eighty pounds lighter, yet the cowboy hesitated.

"What do you want?" I said.

"Mr. Merkin wants to talk to you," he said in his slow drawl. He kept his eyes on Fah.

"That's great," I said. "I want to talk to him, too. This saves Fah a trip and you a fall."

"What?"

"Never mind. When and where?"

"His room, after the match."

"No, I don't think so. I want someplace public; how about Madame Simone's restaurant? I'm sure we can get a table."

"Mr. Merkin wants to meet with you in private," the crusher said, still watching Fah. Fah's arm was as straight and firm as ever.

"He can talk to me in private at a restaurant," I said. "Unless he wants to do something more than talk, that should be fine."

I could see wheels turning in the cowboy's mind. His thoughts weren't on me. Testosterone pooled in the big man's muscles as my little Thai butler kept him at bay with one arm. It hurt his feelings and his pride, and maybe even his chest. Had Fah delivered some kind of ancient secret "five-finger palm strike of discomfort" to the titan's breastbone? Where's Bill?

The cowboy said finally, "Match should be over by noon." He finally took his eyes off my man and set them on me. "He'll meet you there."

"What if he loses?" I said.

He smirked. I didn't like that. Neither did Fah. He did something with his hand that brought the cowboy's gaze back to him.

"Be there, Flaner," he said.

"Grand," was my clever retort.

Rex's thug took a step toward the door, and Fah lowered his arm. Suddenly, the cowboy arched his back and rolled his shoulders, launching a massive overhead roundhouse at Fah. Fah reacted fast as a snake. He ducked to his left as an arm brushed his shoulder. Before the American bully could recover his balance, Fah struck with a deep, straight finger poke under his ribs with his left hand, followed immediately by a folded finger palm into the man's gut.

The man's body folded at ninety degrees and held. Then he teetered forward in slow motion, swiveled a little to the side, and crashed onto the floor like a collapsing brownstone.

He lay there, bent and unmoving, for a long time. He breathed, but his body seemed paralyzed. Fah stepped over him and refilled my water glass from a crystal decanter. I took a sip. It was delicious. Fah sat down next to me, and I poured him a glass. He took it, and we tapped rims before draining them in one gulp as I'd shown him.

The crowd made a collective moan, and we looked up. DragonCos's surrender appeared on the screen over images of a burning spider command post. Rex was up two games to one.

After a while, the bully moaned and wiggled his feet. Then he bent his knee and rolled over. His left arm was working, but his right hung like a garden hose. He stood up on uncertain legs and left the box stumbling.

Game four was one for the ages. Even I knew I was watching something extraordinary. Rex played his same cautious opening, and DragonCos flanked him with a diversionary attack. Rex fell for it and went in. He annihilated the diversionary group, but DragonCos's sudden webs and precise control of his units on two fronts flustered Rex. Most of his units spent their time marching from the battle back to the base and then back to the front, all the while being harassed and picked off by ranged units. Rex fought hard, winning every engagement by a hair, but eventually was drawn so far away from his base that when a raiding party of long-legged spiders flung across the tree tops into his base, he couldn't get back in time to save it.

"Rex should commit," Fah said. "He's retreating. That's totally wrong. If he goes into DragonCos's base, he could still win."

"But he's trying to play it safe," I said.

"Yes. He's a fool."

Rex didn't make it back in time. DragonCos had left enough units to slow the returning army, giving his long-legged spiders enough time to devour the command post before they arrived. Losing the command post was like losing your king in Chess. Game over. Victory DragonCos. GG.

Rex was visibly shaken. The JumboTron zoomed in on his twisted, unhappy face. The crowd cheered. DragonCos stood up and made a bow. It was a brilliant game.

In the fifth game, Rex again started defensively. He repelled an early assault, stayed on his command post at two minutes, and then built tanks and bombers. He stretched out the game, waiting for DragonCos to attack and then driving him back. DragonCos spent his resources on replacements while Rex got reinforcements. In the end, Rex whittled away at DragonCos's army and sent a modest force into his base, which fought its way through webs and trap door spiders to set fire to the spider command post.

DragonCos fought hard and well, but in the end, every close battle went against him. He won only the ones where he outnumbered Rex's soldiers four to one or better.

As his spider hive burned, DragonCos rage-quit. He stood up and threw his headphones to the ground and stormed offstage without a surrender, without a GG, bow, or a handshake. It was a horrific display of poor sportsmanship.

The stunned crowd overcame their own silent rage and reacted to DragonCos's bad manners with catcalls and hisses. I'm not sure an American audience would have even noticed, let alone cared. We're used to prima donna celebrities.

"Such behavior is for barbarians," Fah said, meaning Americans and other non-Thai. "There will be repercussions."

"He was provoked," I said.

"Shouldn't matter. Such behavior is inexcusable."

"Haven't you ever lost your temper? Don't you play video games?"

"Of course I do."

"And you've never lost it?"

"Never."

"Liar," I said.

He blanched and looked scandalized.

"Liar," I repeated.

He blushed. "I've never acted out in public. Alone in my apartment is another thing. DragonCos is a national hero. His behavior should be as great."

"Different stakes," I said.

"Still, he dishonors himself, the sport, and the country. He will be sanctioned."

"Someone will take steps?"

"Steps?"

"Never mind." I stood up and stretched.

Fah said, "Even though he's made me rich, I don't like that American."

"Neither do I," I said. "Time for lunch."

CHAPTER FORTY-FOUR

At Madame Simone's I waited alone in a booth, wondering how I would pay for the meal with sky miles at a restaurant whose menu didn't list prices.

I could hear Rex and his entourage before I could see them. Reporters, fans, and photographers mobbed him as he walked. The reserved Thai demeanor I'd seen so much of in the luxury hotel wasn't on display now. His cowboy had to push away grabbing fans to move them through. Rex humbled himself long enough for photos and an autograph at the door. He wore an air of smugness and superiority like swamp gas. He was naturally taller than the Asians around him, but he'd added an inch since yesterday thanks to a pair of platform shoes.

The restaurant welcomed the famous champion and stripped him from the throng of admirers. He was shown to my table. His Texan chaperone followed two steps behind and limped.

"Tony Flaner," said Rex with a shit-eating smile that would make Mother Theresa ball a fist.

"Rex Merkin," I said. "Sit down. Let's talk."

He sat down.

"And your goon?" I asked. "Do you want him to hear this? How is he feeling, by the way?"

The smugness slipped a little as Rex made uncomfortable calculations.

"Doug," he said. "Go find that little shit who messed with you. Make sure he's not up to something."

Doug, the cowboy goon, wandered away and out of the restaurant. His right arm still hung a little funny. Permanent nerve damage, I hoped.

"I want you to know that I have been on the phone with Dewey, Cox & Leik. They're preparing papers as we speak. I think they're also in contact with the Salt Lake Police Department. Your bail release didn't include transpacific tourism."

"Nope," I said. "I'm on the run."

That made him smile.

"So there's no need to file papers? You're not going back to the U.S.?"

"We'll see."

A petite waitress appeared with two boys. The boys set tea on our table, and the waitress suggested the imported veal.

Rex ordered a fish I couldn't identify and doubted I could eat. I wanted a spicy shrimp curry thing with rice and vegetables. I couldn't pronounce it, but the girl accepted my order with a pointed finger at the menu.

"I'm surprised they let you in here dressed like that," Rex said when they'd gone.

"I know people," I said.

"Yes? That little WOP of yours? He shook Doug up a little. What that was about?"

"I wonder."

Rex was dressed in high-designer fashion like before. It was brown today, trimmed and tailored. With his white hair atop it, he reminded me of a vanilla ice cream cone in heels, which was a shame because I'd been fond of vanilla ice cream cones.

"Is that silk?" I said.

"The shirt is. The coat is satin and cashmere."

"Nice."

"Shall we get to it, Flaner?" Pleasantries were over.

"You killed Rose," I said. "I have all the pieces."

"What do you have?" He laughed, but it wasn't convincing.

"I have motive, means, and opportunity," I said. "Those are the three ingredients for a murder conviction main course."

"Fascinating. Do tell." He leaned back in the classic tell of a bluffing poker player. I leaned back, too—not to bluff, but to relish.

"I noticed you're not wearing the windbreaker," I said. "No sponsorship? You could be making serious bank."

"It was a bit tacky and common, don't you think? Besides, I am making serious bank. There's three million dollars for the winner of this thing, and I'm one match away. Plus, the odds have been kind, and I've done well there, too."

"Yes, so have I," I said. "But you wore the jacket in Vegas and I know why."

"Why?"

"To show that everything was still to plan. Because Justin wasn't dead yet, and he'd be watching."

Rex looked interested, but didn't speak.

"GBM LLC WTF LOL," I recited. "I got the WTF and LOL, and the LLC, of course. The whole thing was an inside joke. Rose, Justin and yourself: Griff, Bertone and Merkin. GBM. The name of a company to sponsor your game play and divide the winnings."

"Justin?" said Rex. "I don't know a Justin."

"Bullshit. Justin Bertone, Chronoboost junior programmer. His job was to copy and paste code into the new Colonies patch. Stupid grunt work, but the kind of thing that doesn't get scrutinized."

Rex sipped his tea. I wanted to break his little finger. Who actually sticks it out that way? I mean really?

"I got a call from Justin after Vegas. You almost had me there, by the way. I totally underestimated you. Of course, I didn't know it was you then, but I still should have been more careful. I was chasing a murderer after all."

"Justin?" he said, bringing me back to topic.

"Yes, Justin. I can prove the connection through Rebecca Taylor, who put the contract together. But I figured it out because you and he both used my alias, Easy Marlowe, which I'd only given to Taylor."

"Thin," he said.

"Thanks. I've been exercising."

He glared at me.

"When Justin didn't meet me for confession," I said, "I found him at Chronoboost. He was very sick; ambulance, stretchers, seizures, a coma—a regular buffet of misery. All very bad. But I found the bottle." I let the statement hang, expecting a reaction, but his smug face held smug. "I talked to the hospital last night in a very expensive phone call. Justin's not receiving visitors. In fact, he's not actually conscious yet, but he will survive. And eventually, he'll wake up, and he'll talk."

Color seeped from Rex's face by steady, tiny degrees, though his bemused, uninterested expression was as firm as ever.

Our food arrived.

I took a bite and rolled sweet curry over my broken tooth with my mangled tongue. I chewed on the other side and ordered an orange juice. Something about citrus and curry always worked for me.

"And all this means I killed Rose? Why would I do that?" The head was still attached to Rex's fish, and it stared blankly at the ceiling as he pulled meat off its ribs with a fork.

"Money. You're in serious debt. Along with photos of Doug the cowboy mugger, I saw your credit card bills in your apartment before I tossed a brick through your big new TV. Your family cut you off because you're a complete bastard screwup. They've probably not forgiven you for raping that girl. I know I haven't."

My orange juice arrived. It was cold, freshly squeezed, and very good. It cooled the curry and soothed my tongue.

"Rose sold pills for you, but then went into real grifting after you two had a falling out. Maybe the rape thing, more likely Simon. Maybe she just wanted something new, I don't know. Rose was like that."

Rex's fish looked like it had gone through a combine, yet I hadn't seen a single piece find its way into his mouth.

"I think it was Justin's plan," I said. "He figured he could put code into the new Colonies patch that did nothing until it was triggered, and then it would beef up your units. The normal behavior would be circumvented with optimum programming. As long as you didn't totally screw up, like you did in game three today, you couldn't lose. The computer was on your side. Of course, Justin couldn't capitalize on it himself. He was barred from competing."

"This is preposterous," Rex said.

"S O M one on CP at two," I said. "I found that written out like a confession at Justin's office. I found the same code written on a napkin in the garbage at your apartment—the garbage I dumped and left rotting on your floor, by the way. I recognized Rose's handwriting."

"You had no right to search my house. That was illegal and inadmissible," he said, and then added, "Even if it were true."

"Yeah, I know. I can't even prove it was the same napkin," I said, letting disappointment show. "But it was. We both know it."

His shoulders loosened, and his smile grew more confident. My confession had cheered him. I have a knack at making people happy. It's a gift.

"I gave the napkin to my son, Randy," I said. "He's fourteen. For his whole life he's had to watch his parents go through a loveless marriage with different goals and lifestyles, only to face the inevitable divorce now, while his father is indicted for murder."

"That's very touching," Rex said. "What does your kid have to do with the napkin?"

"He plays Colonies, and he figured it out. S O M one on CP at two means, 'Shift-Option Mouse-button-one on Command Post at two minutes.' That means at two minutes exactly, you click the mouse button on the command post building, while at the same time holding the shift and the option keys down, like a chord. It triggers the cheat. It has to be done at exactly two minutes or it passes. It can't be accidental."

"And you think I used this cheat?" he said, chuckling.

"I know you did. I watched you use it this morning. When you missed the timing once, you threw a tantrum and quit like the spoiled brat you are."

He put some fish in his mouth. He wasn't excited about it. I'm sure the fish felt the same way.

"You're a greedy, cheating, heartless, murdering motherfucker," I said in calm, soothing tones. "It wasn't enough that you blackmailed your friend and drove him to suicide; you had to kill Rose, who was probably the best thing that ever happened to you, just so you could get a little more money. Fuck you, you fucking fuck."

Rex regarded me coldly.

"What a coward you are."

He chewed.

"You gave her the spiced rum—extra spiced with roofies from your pharmacy, then followed us home," I went on. "Using the key she'd given you in happier times, you stole in and murdered her after the drug took hold."

I gritted my teeth and felt the blood pulse in my temples like drums calling a horde to war.

"You goddamned, psychotic, scum-sucking bastard," I shouted. My cool was officially lost. My hand had left my fork to point between Rex's anemic-blue eyes. It hovered three inches from his face and shook in rage, but he didn't flinch. The other diners stared at us. I didn't care. I longed for the gun I'd left with Mittens.

"I gotta take a walk," I said. "I'll be back. Don't you go away."

I marched off to the bathroom and splashed cold water in my face. Fah appeared like a genie and handed me a towel.

"Are you all right?" he asked. "Do you need help?"

Damn right I did. I'd spent the entire night on the phone, and I was trashed. The future looked bleak. Sweet and her police friends knew I was gone, and they were not happy about it. They were waiting for me with a list of new misdemeanors and charges the second I stepped off a plane and said my real name. Sweet had plumbed law books to find new infractions to pin on me, trying to get brownie points with the higher ups, I figured. McGraw had added a bit of character assassination. Since when is "bad attitude" a crime?

Mollif had read most of the list to me before I'd cut him off.

"So what does it all mean?" I'd said.

"Tony, it's not looking good," he'd said.

"But even all that together has to be better than a murder charge?"

"No, that's still on the list, too."

"Fuck."

But I was in it. The only way out was deeper in. Mollif described to me the coming court battles and motions, and everything else that would be required of his tired body to get me free under the best circumstances. I was in for it. Can't a guy break a few laws to catch a guy breaking a few laws? I guess not. What a world.

I looked at Fah and saw the concern on his face. "Ask me in an hour," I said. I took a deep breath, ran my fingers though my wet hair, and walked back to the table.

"Fall in?" Rex asked when he saw my wet shirt and hair.

"Fuck you."

He smiled. I didn't like that.

"Where was I? Oh, yeah. I figure you took all the bottles from her bathroom in case any had your pharmacy name on them. I'd like to think you took the Flintstone glasses because it was the easiest way to get rid of them, but I think your twisted, fucked-up ego wanted a souvenir. I noticed you still have them, by the way."

"My mother gave me those," he said.

"No, she didn't. Dogs don't drink out of glasses. Where'd she have gotten them?" He didn't understand the insult.

"The cops had an easy suspect in me. You weren't even on the radar. Still aren't," I admitted.

He flaked flesh from the bone. His appetite was better. He seemed interested, but no longer threatened. That bothered me.

"You started killing Justin months ago with mislabeled potassium," I said. "With Rose and Justin gone and the lawyer ignorant, you'd get to keep all three million dollars you'd steal at this fixed tournament."

"I ordered some orange juice while you were gone," Rex said. "It really is very good, isn't it?"

"So do I have it?" I said.

"It's a nice story." He sipped his juice. "But what proof do you have? It's your word against mine?"

"No, not really. There's proof," I said. "I can fit all the pieces together. I have witnesses and documents, videotape, and computer code. Since we know where to look now, the clues I got by being naughty can be replaced by shinier ones."

He smacked his mouth. "Excellent juice," he said. My fist balled up. I felt like Mother Theresa.

"I got you," I said.

"I don't know about that. I'm not confessing to anything, so if you have a wire, stick it up your ass."

"I don't have a wire," I said, popping a shrimp into my mouth. "I have truth."

He laughed. "Do you know how stupid that sounds?"

I did actually, and regretted saying it.

"You're a wanted man, Tony Flaner. They'll arrest you the second you set foot in America. I'll make sure of it."

"Yes, probably. But I bet they'll arrest you too if I get there first."

"Yes, they might," he said slowly. "But I don't really have any reason to go home, do I? I like it here. I'm a hero. I can come in second and still have it made. I don't have to get caught if I don't want to. Living abroad isn't the worst thing. Who wants to go back to Utah, for God's sake? It's a hellhole. Bangkok, Tokyo, Amsterdam, London—all are nicer places than Salt Lake City. I could live like a king here on my gambling winnings alone, and I understand Thai extradition is a real bitch."

I nodded. "I've heard the same thing."

Rex lifted his glass and toasted me. I stared at him, unmoving.

"You should really consider staying, too," he said. "Maybe I could be persuaded to help you out financially. For Rose's sake."

"Her share?"

"If you mean a third of my winnings? That might be acceptable. If I win the tournament."

"You've given me a hard choice," I said. "I don't like hard things. This whole detective thing has been hard. But you know what? The payoff is pretty good. A job well done and seen through to the end is surprisingly satisfying. Who knew?"

"This isn't the end," he said. "This is lunch."

"Yeah, but this is where I get off, in more ways than one."

I cleared my throat.

"Go fuck yourself," I said. "I'm going to sing like Brittany Spears."

"Sing yourself hoarse, you idiot. I won't go back."

"I know," I said.

He drank juice. I stared at him. Something in my expression gave him pause.

"What's that look about, Flaner? This isn't Utah. You're not a cop. You can't touch me."

"Remember a while back when a foreign runner got caught cheating in a Bangkok marathon? He was Canadian. He got twenty years here in Thailand for cheating at a sanctioned sport."

I signaled a table across the restaurant. A group of men stood up and approached us.

"Rex, you know Mr. Prem, the Colonies organizer, Thai Minister of Sports? And of course, Alex Dorsey, CEO of Stormfront games. Say hello, boys. The gentleman with them is the Chief of Police. I don't remember his name. I couldn't pronounce it anyway. Sorry, Chief."

Rex stood up. I joined him. It was only polite.

"They'd like to talk to you about this morning's game and the previous games in the tournament, all of which have been studied by computer wizards in a forensic all-nighter, which is why I'm so tired. There's also video tape."

From the corner of my eye, I saw policemen swarm Doug, the rib-kicker, in the hall. He was all sneak attack and cowardice. Before they said a word to him, he was crying like a scared toddler.

Four more uniformed policemen headed toward us.

Rex bolted.

I wrapped my foot around his ankles and dropped Rex flat on his face.

Thai police lifted Rex to his feet and cuffed him. Blood poured out of his broken nose in torrents. It ran like a river down the front of his expensive, tailored suit.

"Thank you, Mr. Flaner," said Mr. Prem.

"Not a problem." I said, lifting my juice glass and handing it to the Chief of Police. He took it with a raised eyebrow.

"Don't drink it," I said. "It's poisoned."

CHAPTER FORTY-FIVE

It was Regular Night at the Comedy Cellar, which meant that Barry could charge a cover and run a limited open mic. We didn't get a taste of the gate, but it was still a special night. Our names appeared on the marquee, and we knew everyone in the club. It was like a birthday party for narcissists.

Perry was headlining. He'd go on last. The strongest is last. The second strongest is first. I was second. Garret and Critter opened. Dara followed me, and Standard followed her in the palette-cleaning position. His job was to scrub the dildo races out of the audience's collective memory before Perry polished his act on them. Perry had landed a west coast club tour, San Diego to Seattle. He called it the "SanSea tour de Farce." He was on his meds again, which didn't detract from his comedy and made talking to him easier, but less interesting. The van in front of his house had moved, he told me. It was now on the other side of the street.

I leaned back in the booth and stretched my arm in the age-old surprise embrace I'd mastered in tenth grade. Delores smirked as my arm dropped around her. She snuggled in closer and dropped her hand on my thigh. She leaned in real close, nose to nose, and moved her hand a centimeter toward my crotch under the table.

"Chicken?" she asked.

Delores and I hooked up shortly after my final release from jail.

She was still working in the supermarket, but she had been promoted to assistant manager. I'm a sucker for a woman with power.

Mollif was right about how much trouble I was in. Most of the dodgy stuff I did they never found out about, but there were a few things they were sore over.

In the end, the murder charge was dropped. The judge gave me a month for contempt. Leaving the state and the country were specifically forbidden while out on bail for a capital crime. Though I explained how the ankle bracelet had chaffed, the judge was not amused I'd managed to defeat the expensive device so easily. The other charges—and there were many—were dropped, and the light sentence passed down in exchange for me signing a waiver agreeing to forgo any action against the police department and the trigger-happy, ankle-shooting rookie now piloting a records desk, thus averting a costly and ugly PR problem.

Sweet didn't like it, but politics won out, and she dutifully went along with it. Actually, she signed my application for a private detective license herself, and it was approved the same day. She'd earned herself headlines and the respect of her bosses. I'd let her take the public credit for unraveling Rex's web of crime and Rose's murder. She'd made several trips to Bangkok and gained international fame by being associated with the Merkin case.

I had to be grateful to Sweet. She was the person I'd hoped she was. She'd sent Sergeant Barkley to the hospital to watch over me and then let me escape by playing interference with two of Lahkpa's goons, who had come to claim me in the lobby. Whether it was her hunch, some niggling evidentiary proof that weighed on her mind, or my persuasive personality, she'd given me a chance. I'd talked to her from Bangkok before confronting Rex and again after his arrest. She met me at the airport when I returned to Utah. She put me in handcuffs, but not tightly.

"I have to arrest you, Flaner," she'd said.

"Because I broke some laws? I'm a criminal?"

"That's right."

"But not a murderer?" I'd said.

"Doesn't look like it."

I could have kissed her.

I laid it all out for her in the same clockless room as before, careful to weave the most flattering story possible, quick to take the fifth when I needed to. It was like talking to a rock, but she listened and came to life like a Harryhausen golem when I was done. She collected the clues legally that I'd taken shortcuts to get. She proved to be thorough, professional, and cool. Now she was a star in the department and just waited to press charges against Rex.

Rex was still in Thailand. In a trial whose speed was the envy of the civilized world, he was brought up on charges of cheating at a national championship sport and found guilty. They actually have that law. He was sent to a prison whose name translated as "Misery Island." He got thirty-two years: twenty-five for cheating and an additional seven for poisoning my orange juice. Thailand has its own priorities.

Minister Prem, the Chief of Police, Stormfront's CEO, and an army of programmers and forensic computer hacks gave a very clear explanation of the cheat and how it was used and implemented. Chronoboost was destroyed by the scandal. Stormfront went out of their way to save face. In the end, they came out looking as outraged as the Thais, which wasn't easy.

Justin lived. After a month, he came out of his coma. The potassium overdose Rex had given him had scrambled his electrolytes so much he could power a lightbulb. It was touch and go, but thanks to me and the bottle I'd found, they'd isolated the problem in time and brought him back.

Justin didn't know Rex beyond his signature on the forms. Rose had been the middleman putting it all together. The two were never to meet, never to talk, knew nothing of each other. Justin didn't qualify for Chronoboost's medical plan, so Rose had arranged for the pills from Rex. Justin explained that he and Rose had come up with the plan months ago when he'd told her that it could be done. Rose made the connections and arranged for a contract to be drawn up to launder the money, bring it into the country, and divide it up equally among the partners.

Minister Prem sought extradition for Justin to face charges in Bangkok, but it was half-hearted. Justin made a plea deal to wire-fraud and industrial sabotage. He got six years and left the courtroom crying. I felt sorry for him, but reminded myself that he, at least, was still alive.

Sweet and an army of eager federal lawyers returned the favor and nipped at the corners of international law, seeking to bring Rex Merkin back to the United States. Sweet's case had been made publicly across the world, but Rex hadn't actually faced the American charges yet. Thailand was slow to consider extradition, even for murder. The name Rex Merkin had become synonymous with evil in Thai popular culture. Thailand didn't trust the American legal system. They wanted their pound of flesh. Fah kept me updated on the word on the street and told me not to expect Rex Merkin back to the United States for thirty-two years.

Rex's family didn't know what to do. Their lawyers limited themselves to fighting for better conditions. Contrary to the quaint name, Misery Island is a terrible place. But Rex was still better off in Thailand than he'd be in Utah where he would face the needle—not the electric chair. The government made no bones about seeking the death penalty for Rex Merkin and reminded everyone that there is no statute of limitations on murder. American pride of punishment was at stake.

Standard took the stage before a traumatized audience.

"I am so glad you didn't have to follow Dara," Delores said to me.

"What the fuck does that mean?" Dara snapped at my girlfriend.

"It means you savaged the audience," I said. "Stan's up there trying to return humanity to their femininely damaged minds."

Dara had killed of course. She'd taken a big, round lollipop on stage with her, which at first added to her innocent look, but quickly became an obscene accessory. Five minutes and five edible bra jokes later, the audience was either on board or gone. This crowd, being our fans, were on board, but the change of gears from blue comedy to Standard's never-before-heard relationship jokes was a hard left turn at speed.

"I think Dara brings a breath of fresh air to the sexual tension of modern America." It was a good point, but it lost something coming from a puppet. Critter nodded his head slowly in sagacious certainty. Garret ignored him.

"I think she opens the lid on an unflushed toilet," said Delores.

"I'm sitting right here," Dara said.

"But you laughed," I pointed out.

"She was funny," said Delores.

"That's what fucking counts," said Dara.

"Ignorance is the defense of stupid minds," said Standard on stage. The crowd applauded. Utah jokes went over well in Utah. Go figure.

"What time is Randy coming over tomorrow?" said Delores.

"Nancy said she'll drop him off by ten."

"What are we going to do?"

"I don't know. Hang out, I guess."

"Thrilling," said Delores. "I'll be working."

"Then we'll go to Captain Happy's Super Fun Park and Adventure Land. It's free cotton-candy day. You'll be missed. Have fun at work."

"Yuck yuck," said Delores.

Randy and I were getting along better than we had in years. I could still lose him to a video game for days at a time, but in between we could talk about anything.

Nancy dumped Mudge three months ago. He received some handsome parting gifts: a Rolex watch, three gold chains, and season basketball tickets. They were all "gifts," Nancy maintained, but changed the subject as quickly as possible when I pressed.

We are friends, Nancy and I. We have Randy in common and fifteen years of history. So that is good. She's learned to relax a little, somewhat to her financial misfortune.

Mittens still works at Fly Away. There's a rumor about it being bought out again. No one ever caught on about Jake Hammer's sky miles. Such is the magic of electronic currency. Comes and goes at the speed of light without questions or counts.

And me? Well I'd learned to finish something.

I hooked up with Delores. She's nice. She can't have kids and gets along great with Randy. She can even beat him at Tetris but not Colonies. Never Colonies. She may be a keeper. And if not, then not.

I got an invitation to Calvin and Tonya's wedding. Then a retraction of invitation, citing a break up. They sat at their usual table up front by the stage. Calvin had a black eye, and Tonya wouldn't look at him. At least they were together. That's something, I guess.

Morris Mollif is still a public defender. He assures me that he could have saved my bacon, but he was damn happy to be done with me. I tried to talk him into hanging up a real shingle, but his temperament is too well-suited for the depression of public defending.

McGraw comes to see me about every other week. At first he'd come by to intimidate me. He came out looking bad in the Griff murder case. Sweet hadn't done anything to hide the obvious defects of his work—his cousin had, so McGraw was still a detective. He played hard guy for a month and a half with me, and then he'd just come by and shoot the shit. At the end of the fourth month, he came with a case file and asked me to look them over. I pointed out obvious leads he'd missed, and by the sixth month, when he saw the obvious ones himself, mostly, I'd point out the trickier ones. Last week he brought in his first armed robbery suspect, and the case was solid. He gave me a bottle of bourbon for my help. Always the perfect gift.

I've been a gun-packing gumshoe for about eight months now. Lately, I've felt the old wanderlust stirring in my belly. I'm keeping an eye on it, but it's weak this time. I'm content.

I'd had three real cases and a couple of marital stalkings. Marital work sucks. It's like being a porno paparazzi. I charge double time for that kind of thing now, so most people go elsewhere. I much prefer to find where missing kids have gone or who stole a family knick-knack. The knick-knack case was actually pretty good. I got punched once and threatened twice. In the end, I had to arrange a sting on the brother-in-law on an upward-bound ski tram with Perry, Stan, and Dara.

Stan finished his act with a long, hilarious story about hanging out a window of an upward-bound ski tram. The crowd loved it. I hoped he'd forgiven me.

I visited Rose's grave last fall. She had no family. I don't know who paid for the tombstone or the plot. It was a nice stone, granite and chipped, the way it should be. It said only her name and the meaningless dates that said nothing but tragedy when you did the math.

I sat at the grave for a long time. I couldn't see her face in my mind until I lit it with strobes and put it to the Thompson Twins. She'd been beautiful. She'd been alone and alive. She'd been a wanderer like me. I didn't know her, not really, but I loved her and mourned her as I would a friend, a lover—part of myself lay in that grave.

I'd meant to leave the finger trap on the stone, but didn't. Rose wasn't there, and the cemetery garbage pile was no place for such a powerful talisman. I had it mounted like a trophy fish and hung it above my desk.

Everyone asks about it. Sometimes I say it means "it's easier to get into trouble than out." Sometimes I say it means "the way out is further in." I change it up depending on the situation. Randy said it looked like a cocoon. He was studying them in biology and explained how a caterpillar would make one out of spit and plants, crawl inside, mutate, and exit a butterfly. That didn't happen to me. I didn't get wings, just a fresh pair of legs.

ACKNOWLEDGMENTS

I'd like to thank my publisher, Chris Loke, and editors Lauren Grange and TJ da Roza at Jolly Fish Press for their patience and work. Thanks to Kirsten Carleton for early advice and encouragement. Though we have yet to hook up, she gave me the strength to press on.

I'd be remiss if I didn't mention *Day9* and *Husky,* my video tutors and late-night streaming companions for inspiration; the comedians who gave me the idea, Marc Maron and Jim Earl; as well as Raymond Chandler, Elmore Leonard, Mickey Spillane, Agatha Christie, Dashiell Hammett, and the wonderful Tim Dorsey.

Finally, big love to my long-suffering wife, Michelle—well past our fourteen years and going strong; to my kids who actually read this one, and my eternal cheerleader, Diane, whose optimism shines like a hopeful star in a dark and stormy night.

JOHNNY WORTHEN is an award-winning, best-selling author of books and stories. Trained in modern literary criticism and cultural studies, he writes upmarket multigenre fiction, symbolized by his love of tie-dye and good words. "I wear tie-dye for my friends. I write what I like to read," he says. "This guarantees me at least one fan."

Johnny lives in Sandy, Utah, with his wife and sons. Visit him online at www.johnnyworthen.com